MAZEPPA AND THE WILD HORSE ATTACKED BY WOLVES.

# MAZEPPA;
## OR, THE DWARF'S REVENGE.
### A ROMANCE OF THE WILD HORSE OF TARTARY.

MAZEPPA AND ZISKO IN THE ARMOURY.

## CHAPTER I.

### THE PAGE'S SECRET,

THE shade of night had fallen over the Castle of Laurinski. The moon—dim and pale—hung over its lofty turrets, inundating, with a cloud-veiled brilliancy, the outbuildings, the moat, the drawbridge, and the country, which lay still and hushed around. There was scarcely a sign of life in the place. A sentinel paced dreamily to and fro, and a glimmering light showed itself ever and anon at one of the tower windows; this was all that proved there were living beings within, and one to watch without.

You knew the man was a sentinel, by his measured tread and the gleam of the short bayonet of his gun. His form, however, was but indistinctly visible in the muffled light; and but for that tread and that gleam, he would have passed unobserved among the shadows.

He stopped several times in his walk along the drawbridge, and appeared to be listening; and at length, emerging from the darkness into the moonlight, gazed anxiously round.

"Either my head is dizzy to-night, or there is some one creeping round the moat hereabouts. I am certain I heard a noise."

He stood still and listened.

Not a sound.

"Well, well," he said, "it may, after all, be my fancy. I'll take another turn or two, and if all is well, I'll go warm myself awhile at the porter's fire."

The man had grown confident by constant immunity from peril.

Night after night—month after month, he had paced that drawbridge, during the early watches, without seeing even the shadow of an enemy. Poland was at that period in a state of quiescence, far different to its present convulsed condition; and the position of a sentry at the Castle of Laurinski was, after all, but a sinecure.

So, after a turn or two he withdrew, as he had said, into the large hall, and sat down by the blazing fire.

Scarcely had he departed when one of the shadows seemed to take form; a man emerged from behind one of the huge buttresses, and after looking round him, advanced cautiously until he was within a few feet of the window where the uncertain light still flickered. The white tunic, the light pantaloons, the short cloak worn jauntily on the left arm, and the octagonal cap, at once proclaimed him a page.

What could he, the page of the Castellan, want at that midnight hour beneath the window of the Lady Theresa? What could he desire to say to her that he could not tell her in the broad daylight, in the presence of her friends?

He approached still nearer, and then cast upwards a glove, the metal button of which struck lightly on the glass.

"Theresa, dearest!" he cried, "I am here."

The casement opened gently.

"Is that you, Mazeppa?" whispered a voice sweetly.

"Yes—yes, beloved Theresa, it is I," cried Mazeppa, eagerly. "I could not rest this night without once more gazing at your beloved form. Hopeless as our love truly seems, when I sleep, at least, you are my own sweet bride, and ere I close my eyelids I desire to hear again from your lips that you love me—me alone."

"Yes, yes, dearest Mazeppa," exclaimed the young girl, with visible agitation, "you know that I love you; but pray fly hence. Were you discovered here, all would be lost. My father might forgive your love, but a clandestine meeting, never."

"My dearest, my beautiful," he murmured, "it is hard to leave you."

She was, indeed, beautiful, and standing as she did at the half-open casement, she looked like the centre-piece of a picture. She had been sitting up in her chamber, thinking of the cruel fate which separated her from one she loved—of the wide gulf which appeared impassable; and she had not doffed the picturesque costume which she had worn during the day. In her short pelisse of crimson velvet embroided with gold, over a short white dress trimmed and edged with fur, and displaying to advantage her superbly moulded figure, she appeared pre-eminently lovely; and Mazeppa gazed at her, as he prepared to depart, in all the misery of a hopeless passion.

While he yet lingered, the great door creaked on its hinges.

"Adieu!" he cried, "adieu! The sentinel is coming. Adieu, until to-morrow."

The casement was closed noiselessly, and the light extinguished in an instant, but Mazeppa had no time to fly.

The sentinel seized him by the arm.

"Whom have we here?" he cried.

The page laughed.

"It is I, Mazeppa!" he cried.

"What do you here?"

"Nay, tell me, rather, why you were absent from your post, that you did not observe my coming?"

"Tush! we'll let that pass," returned the soldier. "I have ever been your friend, Mazeppa—tell me, why are you here?"

"To watch the stars, and gather the dews of night."

"Methinks the stars you watch, Mazeppa, are closer to you than those of the heavens, and yet as difficult to grasp. I know your secret. You love the Lady Theresa!"

Mazeppa started angrily.

"Zeminski!" he cried, "I like a jest, but this is beyond one."

"Nay, nay," returned Zeminski; "be not afraid to trust me. I know all, and have known it for a long—long time.

Besides, I have that to tell which no one else has thought fit to tell you; for, mark me, my lad, you have made few friends at the castle, save the Castellan, his fair daughter, and your humble servant."

Mazeppa grasped his hand.

"You are a worthy fellow," he said; "a worthy fellow; and perhaps some day I may reward you for your disinterested affection. Disinterested it is, indeed; since what can I, the poor, despised page, give to you in token of my gratitude? So I will even confess you are right, and beg you to tell me your story."

"Come, then, with me," said the man, "and I will tell you. Here we may be observed."

The sentinel led him along the broad stone terrace overlooking the moat, and sat down with him on the parapet.

Above them towered the lofty turrets of the Laurinski Palace, which seemed to pierce the skies—beneath lay the still waters of the moat—beyond, the hamlet and the whispering meadows, where the newly-growing corn nodded towards silver streamlets and shady groves.

"I've watched you some time," said Zeminski; "and I have watched, too, the Lady Theresa. Others must be blind not to see that her eyes brighten when you are near her, and wander restlessly when you are absent—that you tremble in her presence, yet are moody when she is away. You love and are beloved, Mazeppa. These is no doubt of that; but of what avail is it?"

The young man sighed.

"Of what avail, indeed!" he answered.

"I have that to tell you which will chill your young blood," said Zeminski, with some emotion; "yet it must be told. To-morrow comes the envoy of Stanislaus, Count Palatine."

"For what?"

"To demand in marriage the hand of the Lady Theresa."

Mazeppa grasped his arm.

"You are jesting, or, at least, are in error. The Lady Theresa is mine—mine only."

"Mazeppa, you are mad to talk thus. You must meet the evil with a bold front. Theresa is the daughter of a powerful lord—you are her father's page. What can there be in common between you? But come, let me tell my story. The envoy of the Count Palatine will arrive here to-morrow, and I know, beforehand, that the Count's offer will be accepted. He once saved the Castellan's life in battle, and the favour has not been forgotten. There will be a tournament and a grand gala-day when the Count arrives. Your course I leave to you, but be silent and prudent."

Mazeppa answered not.

He was crushed, overwhelmed, with despair. All his dearest hopes were swept away in a moment, and he felt in that hour as if the darkness and gloom of the tomb would have been more welcome than the bright sunshine which would soon flood everything, but which would bring, also, the emissary of his hated rival.

"Come," cried the sentinel, "let us part now. If we were found here it might awaken suspicion. You have many enemies here, Mazeppa; therefore, beware."

The young man grasped his friend's hand, and walked away.

Scarcely had he done so when another shadow seemed to detach itself from the wall behind his retreating figure. The sentinel had turned away towards the drawbridge, and saw nothing.

Fearing no discovery, therefore, the new-comer sprang upon the parapet, and prepared to drop into the moat.

It was a queer figure which stood there in the moonlight—short, broad-shouldered, crooked—a hunchbacked dwarf, with a hugh head and thin bandy legs.

"Ha, ha!" he laughed, as he swung over the stone parapet, and dropped down into the slimy ledge at the bottom, "ha, ha! No friends! no friends!"

By a dexterous leap he sprang across the water, and then, after rubbing from his clothes all signs of his peculiar exit, he presented himself boldly at the drawbridge, as if just arrived from the country beyond.

"Who goes there?" cried Zeminski, in a drowsy voice.

"Zisko, the dwarf," howled the other in discordant tones. "Come, be quick; I'm perished with cold."

"Where have you been?"

"In the village."

"What have you been doing there? Mischief, I'll be bound."

"I have been getting some poison for your favourite dog," hissed the dwarf. "Let me in, or I'll kill him to-morrow."

Zeminski, with ill-suppressed rage, let down the drawbridge, and the dwarf, ere it had quite descended, sprang on to the chains and clambered to the terrace, chattering and mumbling like a monkey.

He tried to avoid the soldier, but the latter seized him by the ear, and detained him.

"I warn you, my young imp," he cried, "that you'd best play no tricks with me or my hound, or I'll wring your twisted neck for you."

The dwarf grinned, though he was writhing with pain.

"Ha, ha!" he chuckled; "capital, capital! I'll tell you a secret if you'll let me go."

Zeminski, having administered a last admonitory twist to the huge, misshapen ear, released him; and the dwarf, with one spring reached the door of the hall.

"Your secret—your secret?" cried, the soldier, laughing.

The dwarf's face assumed an expression of demoniacal glee.

"What will my lord, the Castellan, say to the soldier who allows secret interviews with the Lady Theresa and her servant, eh?" exclaimed he, and he clapped his hands. "Ha! ha! ha! Zeminski, I have you there."

And then, before the soldier had recovered from his surprise, he was gone.

Meanwhile Mazeppa retired, sad and gloomy, to his chamber.

Eighteen years before, the Castellan, when pursuing through the forests a horde of Tartars who had made one of their periodical incursions into that part of Podolia, had seen a child of some two years wandering, naked and disconsolate, amid the trees. Fierce as he was in battle, he did not war against helpless creatures, and directing one of his men to take up the child, he had it brought to the castle, where it was reared and educated.

The child could give not even the faintest clue to his parentage; his appearance, however, and the manner of his discovery, proclaimed him a Tartar.

From his infancy he had been brought into constant connection with the Lady Theresa, the daughter of the Castellan; and as they ripened from childhood into maturity the affection of the children became the strong passion of man and woman.

It was when Theresa was fifteen that Mazeppa had an opportunity of performing a service which raised him high in the estimation of his master, and gave him a position of confidence in the household.

Near the castle ran a stream—a rapid, deep, and turbulent stream—by whose banks, however, were most beautiful meadows and shady retreats, which Theresa loved to frequent.

One day the young girl, accompanied by some of her women and Korstusky, one of the pages, was walking by the stream, which had been swollen by recent rains.

Across its turbid waters ran a bridge—a light fantastic thing, such as one might expect to see over an artificial lake—a structure quite inadequate for the purposes of daily use.

On this bridge Theresa ventured, and leaning over the slender parapet, watched the rapid waters and the wild flowers it carried on its bosom.

Suddenly the whole fabric gave way—the bridge broke at either end, and Theresa was precipitated, head foremost, into the water.

Korstusky hesitated. The water was deep, dark, and dangerous, and he could not swim.

Of what avail was it wilfully to cast away his life?

He glanced at Mazeppa.

Mazeppa, however, had not waited for his glance; he had already divested himself of his tunic, and as Korstusky gazed he plunged headlong into the stream.

He swam strongly and well; but for a long time the swell of the water baffled his skill.

Again and again the turbid waves closed over him, while Theresa floated further, further away towards the rugged cataracts.

At length, however, the strength of youth prevailed, and Theresa lay upon the shore, senseless, but saved.

After a moment's rest, Mazeppa raised her in his arms and bore her to the castle, where he received the congratulations of everyone, and the eager thanks of the Castellan.

From that moment he occupied a confidential position in the household—was allowed to come and go as he pleased; and, though nominally a page, had no duties to perform, and was never treated as a menial.

His superior intelligence, and his rapid progress in every branch of learning, soon won for him the esteem of his master, who, on several occasions, offered him a high position in his body guard.

Although, however, skilled in the art of war, and fond of martial exercises, Mazeppa preferred retaining the position of page, which enabled him to be near the object of his passion.

It was not long before Theresa saw and appreciated the love with which she had inspired the young man; and, one evening, when chance threw them alone together, Mazeppa told his love, and learned, from her blushes and smiles, that he loved not in vain.

From this moment their lives passed in unalloyed happiness.

Mazeppa, hated and envied because of the preference shown for him by his master, forgot the enmity of the world and the distance between him and his beloved; and Theresa, equally young, was equally blind.

And so, mourning over his hopeless love, and thinking of the dreaded morrow which was to see his adored one betrothed to another, Mazeppa lay tossing on his sleepless couch, until the early morning at length found him tired and slumbering the deep sleep of despair.

## CHAPTER II.
### A DWARF'S HEART.

THE castle and the country were glad with morning light.

Places that had shown ugly and distrustful all night long, now wore a smile, and bright sunbeams sparkling on chamber casements, and filtering through blinds and curtains, upon the eyes of sleepers, shed light even into dreams, and chased away the shadows of the night.

Birds in cages, covered up close and dark, knew it was morning, and chirruped in spite of the gloom; the mice crept away beneath the floors; men in dungeons stretched their cold and cramped limbs, and cursed their cells that no bright sky could warm; while on the outside the flowers, the pure chaste flowers, opened their gentle eyes, and blessed the light.

Very early the people of the castle were astir; for the emissary of the Count Palatine was to arrive at mid-day, and preparations were required for the tournament of the morrow.

Almost immediately after the morning meal Mazeppa sought his beloved.

She was alone in a large chamber overlooking the terrace, when he approached along the corridor; but hardly had his footsteps neared the door when Zenitha, her maid, appeared.

Mazeppa paused as he entered.

"I would speak with you, my lady," he said, "and alone."

As he spoke he glanced at Zenitha.

Theresa smiled.

"You may trust Zenitha," she said; "she is true to me and to you. Besides, were we discovered together, it would be better that she were also present."

"True," said Mazeppa. "Have you heard the dreadful news, Theresa?"

"Of my marriage?"

"Yes, yes; this hated union with the Count Palatine."

"I heard of it but this morning," returned Theresa. "My father has kept this secret in his heart a long time. He did not deem it necessary to inform me of it, since he concluded that whoever was his choice would be cheerfully accepted by me as a husband."

"But he is wrong, is he not, dear Theresa?" said Mazeppa, kissing her little hand.

Theresa burst into tears.

"I know not, dear Mazeppa," she cried, wildly; "what am I to do? How can I avoid this marriage? The Count Palatine is lord of Podolia, and you are our page. How can we hope that he would consent to our union. It is madness—madness to think of it."

Mazeppa sighed as he answered sadly,—

"Alas, Theresa! you love me not, or you would not for a moment doubt as to the course to take."

Theresa glanced up in bewilderment.

"I do not understand you," she said.

"Fly with me, dearest Theresa!" cried Mazeppa, falling on his knees before her, and gazing up wildly in her face. "In the Steppes of Tartary we can defy the united armies of your father and your intended husband. There we can live, if not in wealth, at least in happiness."

The girl trembled.

"Tempt me not, Mazeppa," she murmured; "my father is stern even to cruelty, but I cannot risk his curse. He *would* curse me were I to fly from my home with one of a race of enemies. No, no, Mazeppa; it must not—cannot be."

"You love me not," said Mazeppa, coldly, as he rose; "so be it then, Theresa. Yet if you discard me after all your vows of constancy, you shall never be the wife of this man. He shall not be here in the castle one night ere my revenge shall be complete."

Before Theresa could reply Zenitha ran hastily towards them.

"The Castellan is coming, my lady," she cried. "Dry your eyes, lest he suspect something."

The Castellan entered hastily.

He glanced from Mazeppa to Theresa, and seemed astounded to see the page in such a place.

The confusion on his daughter's face he noticed not; but the crimson flush on the page's cheeks would have been evident to all.

"What are you doing here, Mazeppa?" he said, in some surprise.

It was a fortunate thing that at that moment the page was piqued by Theresa's replies to his questions.

Had he felt confident of her love, he would have declared his affection before her father, and destroyed both her and himself.

As it was, his tongue refused its utterance, and he stood before the Castellan confused and abashed. He felt as if accused of some terrible crime, and as if there was no inducement to deny it.

Theresa came to his aid.

Summoning up all her courage, and forcing a smile upon her lips, she exclaimed,—

"I, dear father, can readily explain the presence of Mazeppa here; and I hope that you will not only pardon his haste, but also grant his request."

The Castellan nodded, as if to bid her proceed.

"You know already the devotion of Mazeppa to me and to yourself," continued the young girl.

"I do," returned her father; "I have never forgotten that you owe your life to his bravery. Again and again have I offered him preferment, and again and again has he refused it. He has himself to thank, therefore, if he bears no lasting mark of my esteem."

Mazeppa bowed.

"I am as grateful as if I were a prince of your making," he said.

Theresa continued,—

"He has come to me this morning to ask me a favour—that I would request the Count Palatine, my future husband, to permit my retaining his services as a page."

The Castellan laughed.

"So that is it, eh?" he cried. "Why, you foolish boy, I will never consent to it. You must ask no such favour for him, Theresa. I name him at once officer of my men-at-arms, who are about to proceed to Warsaw to reinforce the royal army. You will start, Mazeppa, the day after to-morrow."

Mazeppa glanced uneasily at Theresa, whose face was averted.

The Castellan was busily talking to Kolzoff, his chamberlain, who had accompanied him, and did not, therefore, perceive the momentary agony of the lovers.

"Well, Mazeppa, what say you to my lord's offer?" said Kolzoff, to whom the very sight of the Tartar was hateful.

Mazeppa bowed lowly.

"I am overwhelmed with gratitude," he cried, "and can find no words to express it. Since my duty lies at Warsaw I can leave the Castle of Laurinski with less regret."

"Well said," returned the Castellan; "and, by the way, Mazeppa, to-morrow we shall give a grand tournament and exhibition of manly exercises. In this, I trust, you will take a prominent part; in fact, I have no doubt you will, since the Lady Theresa will distribute the prizes with her own fair hands."

Mazeppa bowed, and anxious to escape from a place where his pent-up feelings caused his heart almost to burst, he left the room and the castle, and wandered away towards the open country.

He sat down beneath the shade of a thickly-foliaged tree, near the stream where he had saved Theresa's life at the peril of his own, and gave himself up to the most gloomy and despairing thoughts.

While he was still thinking in this solitary spot—a spot so solitary that the sighing of the trees, and the dipping of the reeds, and the hum of insects were all the sounds he heard—he was suddenly aroused by the noise of laughing, and the rushing of feet, and every now and then a sharp cry.

Convinced that some one or something was being ill-treated, Mazeppa rose hastily and looked round him.

Towards the stream, with his hair flying, his eyes distended, and his tongue out of his mouth, came a distorted being, whom the page at once recognised as Zisko, the dwarf.

At his heels was a motley crowd, consisting of peasants and their wives, and a rabble rout of dogs and boys. Some carried pitchforks, some sticks, while others flung huge stones.

Mazeppa rushed forward and stood over the dwarf, who had fallen panting, breathless, almost lifeless, on the margin of the stream.

"What now—what means this?" he shouted.

"The witch—the imp—the distorted villain!" cried a dozen voices, "he has bewitched our cattle."

Mazeppa smiled disdainfully.

"You are mad," he exclaimed; "do you suppose that a poor weak cripple like this—a creature who is afflicted by a terrible visitation—has power over evil spirits? Return to your homes, and let him go in peace."

"No, no!" growled the peasants, "we will have him."

And they advanced forward with menacing gestures.

"The anger of my lord the Castellan will fall heavily upon you," cried Mazeppa, loudly. "Zisko is of his household, and he allows no one to ill-treat them. I warn you that his vengeance will come upon you without delay if you do not retire at once."

There were fifty peasants in all, and the affair was serious. They held a hurried consultation, and at length one advanced as spokesman for the rest.

"These men, fair sir, are determined to bear no longer the machinations of this creature. He destroys our crops, bewitches our children and our cattle, and he must die."

Mazeppa eyed him contemptuously.

"These are not the words a serf should use towards one of his lord's retainers," he cried. "Back, fellow, and let us pass. Rise, Zisko, and follow me."

But the peasants, thoroughly impressed with the idea that Zisko was working enchantments for their ruin, were roused to a condition of fury and independence quite unusual in them.

A loud murmur was raised, and a shower of stones fell upon them. Seizing a heavy stake from the hands of a peasant near him, while the dwarf, emboldened by his presence, did likewise, he rushed at the peasants, striking right and left without distinction of persons.

The unskilful blows of the clownish serfs were parried in almost every instance, while his strokes fell with terrible effect upon their heads, shoulders, and legs. The dwarf, too, did good service, rushing in between the men's legs and throwing them down. Just as the peasants were becoming dispirited, several soldiers came down from the castle to the rescue. This decided the conflict, and the bruised and bleeding serfs fled in every direction.

The dwarf followed close upon the heels of Mazeppa, and when they reached the castle he pulled him by the tunic.

Mazeppa turned round angrily.

" What now ? " he said ; " do not disturb my thoughts."

" Fair sir, do not repulse me," cried the dwarf ; " I have that to tell you which you will be glad to hear. You have done me a service—you have saved my life—you have fought for me, a poor distorted thing, whom everyone despises, and I am grateful ; for I, dwarf as I am, have a heart."

Mazeppa was touched.

" My poor fellow," he said, " you have won no one's good opinion, nor have you deserved it, I fear ; yet I believe in your gratitude and will trust you. What is it you desire ? "

The dwarf glanced round him suspiciously.

" Not here—not here," whispered he ; " come with me, and I will show you a wonderful secret."

## CHAPTER III.

### HIDDEN PATHWAYS.

THE dwarf led the way to a portion of the terrace where a huge buttress cast a shadow upon the ground. Behind this buttress was a gate, apparently disused.

Here Zisko stopped ; and, after a moment's examination, pressed a spring which caused the door to fly open.

" Enter," said he ; " we are here safe from all observation."

Without hesitation, Mazeppa entered, the portal closed behind them, and they found themselves in utter darkness.

The dwarf took the page's hand, and led him cautiously along a corridor, which was plunged in profound obscurity.

" Fear not," he said ; " I have passed this way a hundred times, and know there is no obstacle."

" Lead on," cried Mazeppa ; " I trust you, and fear nothing."

After a few moments he found himself in a large room surrounded by coats of armour.

They stared down upon you everywhere like mailed shadows of departed heroes, from the walls, from the dark corners, from the very ceiling.

" What place is this ? " said Mazeppa.

" It is the old armoury of the castle," answered the dwarf ; " to this room no one comes, except in times of danger. We are safe here, and can talk at our leisure. Come, let us sit down."

They sat down by the old table, and the dwarf continued —

" I know all your story—I know the secret of your heart; you love the Lady Theresa, and your love is returned."

" Alas ! I fear not ; since she so readily acquiesces in her father's schemes of marriage."

" You are mistaken," returned the dwarf ; " she acquiesces because she cannot help herself. She loves you well ; I know it ; and I know everything that happens in the castle."

Zisko chuckled as he spoke. He knew that Theresa loved Mazeppa ; but he placed no holy value on the feelings. He simply regarded the matter as proving his own clearsightedness.

" Well," he said, " this man—this Stanislaus Count Palatine, is my deadly enemy."

" Indeed ! " cried Mazeppa, as a ray of hope illumined his breast ; " well, tell me, what do you propose ? "

" I propose nothing but what your own heart must suggest to you."

" It suggests nothing."

" Meet this man in the tournament, and kill him, if you are able."

" You seem to hate him ? "

" I do."

" And why ? he never could have been your rival."

The dwarf grinned horribly.

" No," he said ; " but he caused me to be scourged from his door. I have never forgotten it, and never shall forgive it. What say you to my plan ? "

" It is not feasible. I, the page Mazeppa, shall never be permitted to joust with one of the rank of the Count Palatine. No, no ; if I am to meet him in a single combat it must be in secret."

" Good," said the dwarf ; " if it be so I still can aid you."

He rose as he spoke.

" See," he said, pointing to a door, " that leads to the Crimson Chamber. In that chamber the Count Palatine will sleep. If you desire to meet him secretly, open that door—it yields to the touch—and walk straight before you. The next door you meet with is that of his room."

Mazeppa grasped his hand.

" How can I ever thank you ? " he said.

The dwarf grinned.

" Oh ! " he said, chuckling, " you have acted honourably ; you have paid me in advance. But listen ; I have more to tell. You still love Theresa ? "

" Madly."

" That second door," proceeded Zisko, " leads you to the private apartments of Theresa. With her you had better arrange your plans. She, at least, will give you courage, and may even obtain for you, if she will, the honourable position I spoke of in the tournament. I leave you to find the means of accomplishing your fortune and your revenge. I have done all I can, and you must do the rest."

For some moments Mazeppa did not speak.

" Zisko," he said, at length, as he grasped the dwarf's hand, " I feel deeply grateful for what you have done. The act of kindness I did to day was but a simple duty—you have repaid me a hundred-fold. With the knowledge you have just given me, either Theresa will be mine, or I shall be able to take a deadly revenge. Some day, may be, I may be in a position to reward you ; not by money, but by some other means more suitable to your good and greatful heart."

The dwarf's eyes glistened, and a tear stole down each cheek.

" Thank you—thank you," he said ; " you have added now another favour to the former ones. I am yours always, remember ; you can trust me. Let us leave this, or our absence may be wondered at."

They then went together from the armoury—slipped unperceived from the old postern, and separated for the day.

In the afternoon the emissary of Count Stanislaus arrived, received a ring from the Castellan in token of the betrothal, and again departed.

The day passed in innumerable preparations, and the morning dawned upon a gay and brilliant scene.

By eleven o'clock at the forenoon all was ready for the reception of the Count Palatine, and by twelve the lengthy procession wound its way into the large castle-yard, where the tournament was to take place.

At one end was a dais covered with crimson and gold,

On this sat Theresa and her father the Castellan—both eagerly awaiting the arrival of the Count : the one in fear, the other in pleasure.

At length Stanislaus came.

He was a tall, somewhat handsome man of forty, with dark hair and beard, slightly tinged with grey—an upright, manly figure and a proud step.

But there was an expression upon his features which repelled the beholder ; and Theresa shuddered as her father presented him to her and he kissed her hand.

" Just heavens ! " murmured Cassimir, as he stood by, " that such man as this should wed a young and lovely maiden ! "

Theresa having received a warm kiss upon her cold and and trembling hand, Stanislaus took his seat by her side on the dais, and the sports of the day began.

There were broadsword combats and tilting at the ring, and the more serious affair of jousting on horseback. It was a bewildering scene, where men and horses, flags and gleaming lances mingled—where stern men with stalwart forms and dense beards stood by the side of merry-faced pages—where joy, and merriment, and bright display among the many served but to add to the bitter grief and hopeless despair of the few.

Again and again was Mazeppa victorious—in every sport and every contest in which he was engaged he bore off the laurels.

Presently he was nowhere to be found.

Every spot was searched in vain—the castle was inundated with scouts to find the victor of the day.

In his place came a tall knight, clad in armour—black mail, with a tall black plume—mounted on a splendid steed, and accompanied by a dwarf dressed in a fantastic costume.

When they entered the lists the dwarf, who was no other than Zisko, was seated behind his new master, but when they had reached the dais he leapt to the ground and blew a long, shrill blast upon a small trumpet.

A loud murmur of applause greeted this, and the Castellan and Stanislaus, who both recognised Mazeppa in the black knight, were not the least forward in the expression of their amazement.

" Who is this young man ? " asked the Count Palatine.

" He was my daughter's page; he is now captain of the men-at-arms who proceed to Warsaw to-morrow."

" Indeed! he has then served you well ? " returned the Count.

The Castellan smiled.

" He has, indeed," he answered; " to him you owe your bride."

" How so ? "

" In early youth he saved her life. We found him in the woods when quite an infant. He had been left behind by the Tartars in an invasion."

" Mazeppa is a Tartar name," said the Count; " how did you know it ? "

" It was marked upon his breast. But listen—his challenge is coming. This is, indeed, a merry jest of his, and is entirely of his own invention."

The dwarf now, in a shrill voice, gave forth the challenge, which, though under the guise of jest, had evidently a more serious intention veiled beneath it.

No one responded.

The appearance of Mazeppa in his black armour, the evident reality of the challenge, and the new rank of the page, moreover, deterred all; and in a loud voice the dwarf repeated the summons.

" This man is an officer now," cried the Count Palatine; " in your behalf, fair lady, I will break a lance."

Theresa turned deadly pale. She felt that this was all that Mazeppa had hoped for.

" Pray do not go, Count Stanislaus," she cried; " you are unused to such sports as these."

Mazeppa heard her words, and his eyes burned fiercely beneath his vizor.

" She wishes to save him," he muttered, in the blindness of his hate; " he must die."

Poor Theresa !

How he misunderstood her !

She only desired—loving Mazeppa deeply, earnestly as she did—to save him from the consequences of his mad and uncompromising thirst for revenge.

The Castellan, too, was somewhat troubled—why, he knew not. " He was but a page yesterday, my Lord Count," he said; " you cannot break a lance with him."

Stanislaus smiled as he rose.

" He is a soldier to-day," returned he; " and as these sports are in my honour, I must even give this brave fellow a chance of jousting and defeating one who has given him so much trouble, and who was once one of the best tilters in Poland."

In another moment, one of the squires of the Count Palatine

had answered the summons, and Stanislaus advanced into the lists. A second murmur of gratification was heard from the retainers and the neighbours who had been admitted to the tourney, but among the former it was but feigned. The general feeling among them was one of envy—a spiteful sentiment of disgust that the page of yesterday should be the acknowledged favourite of to-day.

The combat began.

Mazeppa parried well his adversary's brilliant passes, until at length both antagonists retired to the extreme end of the lists for a last encounter.

Their lances were placed in rest, and all held their breath.

Everyone expected something serious to happen.

Theresa grasped her father's arm.

" Stop this conflict," she cried.

The Castellan glanced at her in great surprise.

" Why so, dear child ? "

" It alarms me."

" Nonsense; it is but jest."

" No, no ; it is not jest ! " she cried ; " they seem too much in earnest. I fear some accident will happen."

" Fear not," returned the Castellan; " they are both skilful horsemen, and understand the use of the lance."

As he spoke the trumpets sounded, and the combatants rushed towards each other. The lance of Mazeppa struck the Count Palatine full in the chest, and horse and rider rolled in rolled in the dust.

Mazeppa remained firm and steady on his steed.

The Castellan sprang from the dais.

" What means this ? " he cried ; " methinks this was a foul stroke."

" Nay, nay ; " exclaimed the Count as he rose somewhat painfully; " this finale was arranged between us. I acknowledge myself conquered, for this young man has an eagle's eye and a lion's arm."

He was, evidently, severely shaken, and with some difficulty mounted the steps of the dais.

" You are hurt, Count Stanislaus," said Theresa, with some anxiety.

The Count Palatine smiled.

" A little, my fair bride," he said; " a little. Yonder page of yours is young, and has a powerful arm. He deserves to be the victor."

At eleven that night Count Stanislaus retired to rest.

Long before that hour Mazeppa and the dwarf had entered the castle by the secret door.

The chamber in which the count was to sleep was a large and lofty one, furnished in a style which at that period, and in that country, was considered gorgeous, but which now would be regarded as gloomy and sepulchral.

The bed occupied the centre of one of the walls, and a high carved canopy overhung it.

On the walls were suspended varieties of weapons, swords, arquebuses, battle-axes, shields ; while in each corner stood a coat of mail, upright and connected, as if filled by its original occupant.

The casement overlooked the terrace and the moat, and, of course, commanded an uninterrupted view of miles of country.

At this window Stanislaus stood for some time musing—thinking of the scene before him—of the beauty of the young maiden who was so soon to become his bride—of the events of day, and the dangerous prowess of Mazeppa.

" By St. Peter ! " he cried, as he sat down by the table and prepared to undress for the night; " one might almost have imagined that he fought in earnest. His eye burned like a coal, and his voice was hoarse and angry."

As the Count spoke his eye fell on one of the corners of the room.

He started, and laid his hand upon his sword.

Well he might, for one of the old coats of mail was advancing towards him steadily, noiselessly as a phantom.

MAZEPPA SURROUNDED BY THE CASTELLAN AND HIS RETAINERS.

## CHAPTER IV.

### THE BLACK KNIGHT.

It was no error.

One of the coats of mail which had been standing motionless in the deep shadow of the ancient chamber, was advancing towards him.

The Count Palatine was not a superstitious man.

His station, and the education it had brought him, relieved him from those petty fears which would have agitated the breasts of the peasantry.

Yet the hour and the place were not calculated to increase his confidence.

The night was still as death. All the inhabitants of the castle seemed to have retired to rest, and the lamps burned dimly.

And the noiseless form still advanced.

The Count rose and drew his sword.

"Who are you," he cried, "who thus dares to invade my privacy?"

The intruder laughed mockingly at the Count's haughty tone.

"I am one who dares do anything which is not dishonourable," he answered boldly. "You have come hither to bear away from the castle one whom I love. You are my rival. I seek this method of destroying you, since the opportunity will not come again."

"Would you then assassinate me?" exclaimed the Count.

"Assassinate! Oh, no! I mean no murder. I come to give you fair battle."

"Here!"

No. 2.

"Yes, here, where we shall not be disturbed. Come; time presses; on your guard!"

The Count kept the point of his sword lowered.

"I refuse," he said.

"What!" exclaimed the stranger, in derision; "are you then a coward?"

"No; I am no coward; but I cannot fight with one I know not. Who knows what you are? you may be some serf—some servant."

"I am neither," cried the unknown, raising his visor so as to disclose the face of Mazeppa. "You fought me to-day in jest; you must do so now in earnest. Be not afraid that I shall take advantage of you. I donned this coat of mail for concealment only, and will doff it again if you wish it."

The Count eyed him sternly.

"Young man," he said, "you are sadly presumptuous. How can you, the page of the Castellan, be my rival?"

"Because I love Theresa."

"Mad youth!"

"No, not mad; she loves me in return. I warn you of this, my lord, so that if you force her to this hateful marriage you will know that her heart is buried with him whom you must first kill."

The face of Stanislaus grew livid with rage.

"Begone slave!" he cried, "ere I am forced to call the domestics to chastise you. I will not soil my sword with servile blood like yours."

The words were rash.

Another moment and he repented them.

With one bound Mazeppa was upon him, and left him no time to think of anything but self-defence.

Stanislaus Count Palatine had been trained from early youth to the use of arms; and he had no fear, therefore, as to the issue of the conflict.

He was too confident.

Mazeppa was young, active, vigorous, and fierce, too, with passion and despair.

The Count was twice his age—wearied by the constant battle-field and the mental toil of a conqueror—and was fighting at a disadvantage. If he won the battle, it was no credit—if he lost it it was a disgrace.

At last, maddened by the ill-success of his attempts, he made a desperate lunge.

It was parried; and in another moment the hot steel of Mazeppa's sword had penetrated its adversary's chest.

At the moment he fell there was a commotion without.

Loud voices were heard, and the Palatine, who had not the fierce uncompromising daring of his antagonist, cried,—

" Help, help ! "

Finding that he was helpless, and could not open the door, the domestics, headed by the Castellan, broke it open.

" Great Heavens ! what has happened ? " cried the latter, rushing forward.

The Count Palatine was half-kneeling, and leaning for support upon his sword; while along the corridor rushed a dim figure.

The blood on the floor, and the disorder of the room, sufficiently testified to the combat which had just taken place within it.

" Your page, Mazeppa," murmured the Palatine, faintly.

" What of him ? "

" He has been here disguised as a knight, and, attacking me, forced me to a conflict. I fear he has succeeded in compassing my death."

The Castellan raised him and helped him to a couch.

" Talk not thus, my lord," he said; " all will be well. You will yet be the happy husband of my daughter, and this dastard shall be punished. Nothing but an ignominious death can repay such an outrage as this, for which there is no reason."

The Count Palatine smiled bitterly.

" You are wrong," he said; " there is great reason."

" What can it be ? "

" He loves your daughter, and regards me as his rival; and what is far worse, he states she loves him in return."

The Castellan's face grew livid with anger.

" He has dared to say this ? " he shouted; " then let him be pursued at once. No punishment, no torture is too great for such infamy as this."

The retainers of the Castellan spread themselves everywhere.

With the exception of the old passage leading through the disused chambers to the terrace over the moat, there seemed no outlet.

Certainly there was the door leading to Theresa's apartments; but as this resisted their efforts, they withdrew from it at once, never believing that Mazeppa could possess a secret key.

Meanwhile, Mazeppa, when he saw his enemy falling before him, and heard the sound of angry voices without, had thought it prudent to make his escape as hastily as possible.

Passing, therefore, through the corridor, he reached the door of the passage pointed out to him by the dwarf as leading to Theresa's rooms, and, hasily entering, closed and bolted it after him.

He hurried on without thinking who might be before him—without dreaming once of the danger which might be awaiting him—without even staying to doff the black armour and the sombre plume or to sheathe his sword, dyed in the blood of his rival.

Theresa shrieked with terror when she saw the Black Knight enter her room by a door of whose existence she had hitherto been ignorant.

" Hush ! " cried her lover, as Zenitha was about to open the other door and call for help. " Hush ! for Heaven's sake hush ! It is I, Mazeppa."

" And what does this mean—this reeking sword—your haggard looks—your wild words ? " cried the young girl, as she clung to him. " What has happened ? "

A gloomy smile crossed the face of the young man.

" I have met my rival," he said; " we have fought, and I have left him for dead. Your father is even now pursuing me to destroy me."

Theresa was so agitated that she could not speak.

Zenitha spoke for her.

" Oh ! fly at once ! " she cried, " fly. I hear the voices of your pursuers."

He folded his arms.

" No," he said calmly. " Since your mistress has decreed my death, let her see them drag me to it."

Theresa grasped his hand, and looked imploringly in his face.

" Oh ! Mazeppa," she cried, " do not speak to me so cruelly; you know how I love you—why, then, do you wish to break my heart ? "

Mazeppa gazed upon her for a moment sternly, and then her beauty, and her mild eyes filled with tears, moved him.

He clasped her to his breast.

" Oh ! dearest Theresa," he cried, " at this moment, oh think again of my dismal fate; fly now, fly with me. Without you I cannot go. I will rather remain where I am, and let your father's vengeance burst upon me."

Theresa's form trembled violently.

She looked imploringly at Mazeppa, and from him to Zenitha.

Her maid's face only expressed extreme pity.

" Oh ! decide, my dear mistress," she cried, " pray decide at once. Footsteps approach this door; they will be here in a moment, and your lover will be destroyed before your eyes."

A violent struggle seemed taking place in the young girl's breast.

She pressed her hand against her bosom, as if to still the wild beatings of her heart. She gazed upon her lover, and then closed her eyes as if conjuring up some terrible vision.

Then suddenly she seemed to regain courage.

" Mazeppa," she said firmly, " I will go with you."

" My own, my dearest Theresa ! " he cried, as he raised her in his arms, and bore her towards the secret door.

As he did so, a loud knocking was heard at the other entrance.

" Who is there ? " cried Zenitha, in as firm a voice as she could assume.

" It is I, the Castellan."

" The Lady Theresa has retired."

" I *must* enter," cried the father, sternly. " She must be awakened, and informed that I am here."

" It shall be done, my lord," cried the girl : " I will go and awaken my mistress."

" Now my dear lady," she whispered; " go at once, or it will be too late."

Mazeppa heard her words, but Theresa did not. She had fainted from the violence of her emotions, and lay senseless in his arms.

Zenitha followed, and after passing along the secret corridor they arrived in the armoury, which the castle retainer had but just abandoned after a diligent search.

Crossing this, they were soon in the second corridor, and passed into the open air without meeting a soul.

On the parapet of the terrace was a figure, crouching in the bright moonbeams.

It was Zisko.

Immediately he saw them he darted off towards the drawbridge, which Zeminski at once lowered.

Then page and mistress, with Zenitha, the dwarf, and the sentinel, fled from the castle and sought refuge in the dense forest by the river.

---

## CHAPTER V.

### THE WITCH OF THE GLEN.

NEAR the river side, in a little wide-encircled glen, stood a small cottage, or rather hut, built of rough timber.

It was so ricketty, so unprotected, so unlike anything

human, that it seemed impossible that anything pertaining to mankind could exist in it. It was more like the habitations of the ourang-outangs of Borneo than the dwelling of one of our race.

Yet so it was; and its inmate was a woman.

She was one whose age it would have been useless to guess.

She was short, thin, and wrinkled, though her figure was so bent that she might once have been tall.

No one knew when first she came to the glen, but most people believed that it was at some date anterior to the birth of any one of the inhabitants.

Her hut, which sprung up in a single night, contained two rooms.

The front room contained the ordinary necessaries of an apartment which was made to serve the double purpose of sitting-room and bed-room. The second chamber was fitted up in a fashion of the most sepulchral and gloomy kind.

Round the walls hung a drapery of black, and when the visitor entered without a light, crosses and a variety of images appeared around him.

A large table stood in the centre, on which were various chemical instruments. Behind was a high glass cupboard, inside of which was a furnace, with a fire which was never quite extinguished. Here and there in the chamber were stands, with strange birds and animals of various countries and appearances.

A large sturgeon's skeleton was suspended from the ceiling, while the skeleton of a man stood in a corner, apparently supported by its own joints, but in reality so joined by machinery that it could be moved in any direction.

People said it was the skeleton of her husband.

This room the witch—old Neida, as they called her—rarely entered, except when some one came to consult her. Now and then she went into it for the purpose of concocting a new supply of drugs; but that was all.

On the evening we introduce her to the reader—the evening of the tournament at the Castle of Laurinski—Neida was seated, or rather squatting, by a huge fire, which roared and crackled in fantastic forms up the broad chimney.

On the hearth at her feet sat a large dog, of a wiry build.

His hair was black as night, and stood all over his body, as if he had had a terrible fright, and had never recovered from it. His eyes, too, were black, and only distinguishable from the rest of his head by their brightness.

Over them, on a black beam which crossed and supported the ceiling, were perched a raven and an owl.

The old woman had not lit her lamp, and the bright moonbeams filtering through the murky window, cast a sepulchral halo over the strange group.

Presently a step was heard without, crackling along the path.

The old dog listened.

"Ah! Polinski," she said, patting his head—she had named the animal after her husband——"ah! Polinski, there's some one coming. It is well, since there is scarcely a crust in the cupboard."

A shrill voice was now heard without.

"What, in the name of Satan, have you extinguished your light for?" cried the new comer. "Are you trying to drown your friends?"

The old woman chuckled to herself, probably thinking of the pleasant sight of one of her enemies—all mankind were her enemies—struggling with grim death in the dark waters.

Then she rose and opened the door.

The stranger was Zisko.

"Well, well, mother Neida," he cried, as he deposited his distorted body on a chair by the fire; "you are becoming careful—you are positively stingy. I nearly fell into the river."

The old woman chuckled.

"What a loss *that* would have been," she said, "to lose you, who are such a beauty! How sad all the villagers would have been; there's not one who would have failed to put on mourning."

he dwarf grinned angrily.

"I didn't come here to listen to your satire," he said; "I came to ask some questions. You know the page, Mazeppa?"

"I do."

"Who is he?"

The old crone shook her head.

"You ask strange questions," she said. "You wish me to say who he is, when you have just told me. He is the page of the Castellan of Laurinski—what more?"

The dwarf stamped with impatience.

"Do you wish me to tell you all that story again?" he cried; "how he was found in the wood, naked and hungry, where he had been left by the Tartars in their flight—how there was no means of discovering who he was, except a star and his name tattooed on his chest—how he was adopted by the Castellan, and from the position of a page has risen to that of officer of men-at-arms."

The old woman listened attentively.

When he had finished, she said, as she rose—

"I am old, and my memory is not so good as it was. Come with me into the back room—into my laboratory—and I will read the stars."

The dwarf rose to follow her.

In those days every one believed in astrology, and Zisko was no exception to the rule.

The room was unillumined by any lamp, but the walls were covered by mysterious signs and crosses.

A faint glimmer proceeded from the furnace, and the witch, entering the glass cupboard, roused the embers, and a bright flame shot up towards the ceiling.

Then she returned to the room, and drawing a heavy rope, caused a portion of the roof to move aside, so as to disclose a patch of star-spangled sky.

"Is that your teacher?" asked the dwarf.

"Yes, that is my book," replied the old woman. "It is a better instructor than man, and never fails to answer."

The furnace fire now shot up a clear flame, and the witch again entered the laboratory.

Here she cast some dust of a yellowish tint, upon the flames, and immediately a dense vapour encircled her and issued forth into the room obscuring nearly every object—rushing out into the cold night air, and almost suffocating the dwarf by its pungent smell.

The old woman left the laboratory, and, seating herself by the table, waited patiently until the fumes disappeared, and then within the glass cupboard appeared the dim figure of a man.

"Slave of the stars," cried Neida, in a solemn voice; "read to me this book."

She opened a large volume, and there was a deep silence for many minutes.

Then the figure vanished suddenly, and Neida spoke.

"The slave of the stars has read to me the book," she said; "but his fate is scarcely written. A great, a terrible danger threatens him. If he escapes he will be rich and powerful, but the peril is of unheard-of horror, and there is little chance of safety."

The dwarf listened eagerly.

"Is that all you know?" he said.

"Yes—all."

"Do not the stars tell you who are his ancestors, and to what inheritance he is born?"

"They tell no more."

"'Tis well," said the dwarf. "I must, then, be content. But now, good Neida, come again with me into the front room, for I have a favour to ask."

The old witch rose, lowered the fire, closed again the aperture in the roof, and led the way into the front room.

"What now can I do for you?" she said.

"I want money."

"Money! oh, ye Heavens!" cried Neida, raising her hands; "to come to me for money! What folly!"

"Come, come, good Neida," said the dwarf, in a wheedling voice; "I know you have a rich store somewhere—you once told me so. Living as you do, frugally, and even cheating yourself into the belief you are poor, you cannot have spent it."

The old woman rocked herself to and fro for a few minutes in silence.

At length she turned round sharply.

"How much do you require?" she asked.

"Fifty gold pieces," he answered.

The old woman laughed.

"You think me rich, then?" she said.

"I think nothing," returned the dwarf, somewhat testily. "I only know that I want the money for Mazeppa, and that the time is passing rapidly. Say, will you let me have it?"

"Yes, I will lend it to you," said the old woman, and she rose and opened a large box which stood on the sideboard.

The lamp had now been lit, and the dwarf's eager eyes saw the glistening of the gold pieces.

He sat quietly, however, and took the fifty pieces with thanks.

Then he said farewell and went out into the night.

He walked rapidly for a few yards, until he reached a little clearing near the river side.

Here he stopped and glanced around, to see if Neida was watching him. Seeing that the door of the hut was closed, and only a dim light flickered in the window, he uttered an exclamation of delight, and flung himself down on the ground.

Here he twisted and writhed about in the moonbeams, muttering to himself the while a variety of expressions of delight.

"Ah, ah!" he cried, glancing up at the sky, and winking at the moon, as if he were taking her into his confidence; "ah, ah! she has a goodly store, and Mazeppa shall be rich yet."

He rolled over and over, and contorted his body again for a time, until he desired a little variety, and then he darted off along the river's side, and chased an imaginary foe.

About ten o'clock he crept stealthily back, and, stealing noiselessly up to the hut, peeped in.

All was still.

"Ah!" he said; "the old witch is asleep. The stars don't tell her that I am here to rob her of her gold."

He took from his pocket a small instrument, which he inserted in the lock, and the old rickety door gave way immediately, and creaked back on its hinges.

The old woman was fast asleep, and the dog was slumbering, too, for he had eaten a piece of meat from Zisko's hand, and he slept the sleep of death.

The dwarf crept in and partially closed the door after him, so as to exclude the bright light of the night goddess.

He was not long in reaching the spot where stood the box he coveted.

He tried to lift it. It was heavy, and as he staggered he touched a cup, which fell on the floor with a crash.

Neida started up.

"Ah! robber!" she cried; "would you ruin me?"

She had not recognised the dwarf.

He sprang towards her.

"Silence," he cried; "or this hour shall be your last."

She saw him then, and knew his voice.

"Oh! treacherous villain!" she exclaimed; "treacherous, base villain, I will destroy you!"

"I will kill you if you are not quiet," he muttered hoarsely. "Your screams will attract the man at the ferry. Silence, I say—silence!"

The old woman still struggled, and shrieked for help.

He grasped her throat with his long, bony fingers.

"Miserable woman!" he cried; "if you cease not your cries I will be your death"

After a moment he relaxed his hold.

Neida was quiet.

"She has fainted," he murmured. "Now is my time."

He lifted the box in his arms with a demoniacal grin, and staggered with it out into the night.

He carried it with him away into the little clearing, and laid it down. Then, after he had rested, he recommenced his gambolings, and danced round it in a perfect ecstasy of delight.

After performing these little eccentricities, he took the box in his arms and walked rapidly to the edge of the wood, where three horses were waiting, held by a serf whom Zisko had bribed.

"Here is the box," cried the dwarf, as he approached "It is very heavy, and I am glad to be rid of it."

The serf relieved him of his burden.

"It is heavy, my master," he said. "Where, shall I place it?"

"On one of the horses," returned Zisko. "Place it on the gray mare—that is the one I am to ride. I am the lightest of the party."

The serf did as he was bid, and Zisko walked away towards the castle. When he arrived at the drawbridge, Zeminski stopped him.

"Is all ready?" he said.

"Yes—all."

"I am coming also," continued the sentinel. "If I remain here, nothing but death awaits me."

"But we have no horse for you," said the dwarf, petulantly, "How can you come?"

"I can obtain a horse," returned Zeminski: "before all is ready. Go and wait near the secret door. It is nearly the hour when we are to expect Mazeppa.

The dwarf did as he was bid, and seated himself on the parapet of the terrace in the moonbeams.

Zeminski, after casting a scrutinising glance around him, left his post, and dived down into the dark country.

In about a quarter of an hour he returned, drew up the drawbridge, resumed his walk along the terrace, and approached the dwarf.

"I have my horse ready," he said; "and have tied him to a tree at the beginning of the wood yonder."

He pointed over the moat to a spot where the trees jutted down into the road.

"That is where I left Strogonoff, the Russian, with our horses," said Zisko. "Did you see him?"

"No."

"That is strange. I left him but a moment ago."

"He may have heard me coming, and drawn into the forest to avoid me," said the sentinel. "No matter; we shall find him easily enough. Keep good watch, and when I see you coming I will let down the drawbridge."

## CHAPTER VI.

### THE CASTELLAN'S REVENGE.

THE time which elapsed between the discovery of the wounded Count and the loud knocking at Theresa's door, was passed by the Castellan at the bedside of Stanislaus.

Roderigo, an Italian, who was a confidential servant of the Castellan, and who had studied medicine, was at once summoned; and it was with a grave face that he assumed the responsibility forced upon him.

"These wounds are serious, my lord," he said, "very serious; it will be weeks before the Count Stanislaus can be moved."

A smile passed over the face of the Count Palatine.

"Thanks, my friend," he said; "you speak of removal in a few weeks. You, therefore, give me hope of life?"

The Italian bowed in acquiescence.

"Oh, certainly, my lord," he answered; "these wounds, I trust, will not prove mortal. But their treatment by me can only end successfully if your mind is easy and free from all agitation whatever."

The count smiled.

"There is no fear of my being agitated," he said, "not the slightest, if you tell me that I shall not die. I could not bear to think that I died by the hand of that base slave."

"Fear not, then," said the Italian doctor, "you shall be saved."

At this moment the retainers, who had been spread through the castle, returned to the room and proclaimed their failure.

"He can be found nowhere, say you?" cried the Castellan, fiercely; "some of you must then be in his secret."

The steward advanced, and bowed humbly.

" I trust there are no traitors here, my lord," he said. " If you will allow me to suggest something, I might be able to discover this man for you."

The Castellan knew that Kolzoff hated Mazeppa, and did not, therefore, doubt that he was sincere.

" Speak freely," he said, " this is no time for ceremony."

" If my lord desires to find the page Mazeppa, he must seek for him in the chamber of the Lady Theresa; for there, I doubt not, he has taken refuge."

The Castellan of Laurinski glanced uneasily at the Count Palatine, and then turned fiercely towards the steward.

" What reason have you for this statement?" he said. " It is no light thing to say that the Lady Theresa has sheltered the assassin of her future husband."

" There are but three doors in the armoury," replied the steward. " The one leads to the terrace, the second to this room, the third to the apartments of the Lady Theresa.

" Well, and what does this prove?"

" The first and second we have explored. Zeminski, the sentry, whom we know to be a faithful servant, declares that no one has passed along the terrace to-night; Mazeppa, therefore, must have escaped by the third door into the chamber of your daughter."

" Lead on, then," said the Castellan. " I will learn the worst."

We have already narrated the reply which Zenitha gave to the first summons of the Castellan.

For a few moments the enraged father stayed his wrath; but finding that no reply was given to a second, third, and fourth summons, he directed the door to be broken open.

The first sight was enough.

The open door—the still, empty room—at once testified to the flight.

The Castellan pressed his hand to his brow.

" Just Heavens!" he murmured; " for what am I being punished?"

Poor man! In his ignorance he imagined that his own cruelty was justice, and Mazeppa's justice cruelty.

Then—his grief gone—rage succeeded.

" Come," he said, " let us scour the country. They cannot be far distant. Let every armed man in the castle follow me."

Then drawing his sword, he rushed towards the door which Mazeppa had left open in his flight, and followed along the old disused corridor as far as the terrace.

The deserted appearance of the terrace, the drawbridge, which lay across the moat, and the absence of the sentinel, proved at once that Mazeppa had friends to aid him.

" There has been treachery here," cried the Castellan, as he dashed over the drawbridge, followed by the steward. " Zeminski has betrayed us. Woe to him if he come within the reach of my revenge."

About twenty armed men followed the enraged Castellan, as he dashed down towards the wood.

He never once dreamed of a preconcerted plan, and, therefore, did not take the precaution to institute the search on horseback.

Two hours passed thus.

They scoured the sides of the river and the wood, and at length entered the cottage of old Neida, the door of which was open.

" Here, perhaps, they may be concealing themselves," said the steward. " Zisko, the dwarf, has disappeared—he, no doubt, is with them—and I know him to be a great friend of the witch."

They lit the lamp which stood on the rude sideboard.

All was very still.

The dog was lying on the hearth, the old woman was lying on the bed.

They seemed asleep, and it was not until they touched them that they found both were cold and dead.

" There has been murder done here to-night," said the steward, as he pointed to the dark circle round the old woman's throat. " Who can have done this?"

" Mazeppa," suggested a voice.

The Castellan turned quickly.

" You know him not," he said. " If he kills, he kills with a purpose, and not for the sake of paltry plunder or mean revenge."

Then, as if he had already said too much, he quitted the cottage, and prepared to resume his search.

His mind was strangely distracted.

From youth upwards, Mazeppa had been his favourite; he had trusted him in every way, and his confidence had always been rewarded.

He knew Mazeppa to be of a noble mind; he knew that had he been a powerful and wealthy man he would have been proud to have possessed him as a son-in-law; but fortune had made him a page, and it was the Castellan's duty to punish him.

At length, just as he was beginning to despair, and when he had just enjoined silence upon his men, that he might think and ponder upon his difficulty, he detected the sound of whispering ahead.

He beckoned to his steward.

" They are before us now," he said; " let the men surround them."

Then, like Indians, noiselessly, slowly, stealthily, the retainers of the Laurinski Castle spread themselves through the wood, while he advanced towards the spot where he imagined the fugitives to have concealed themselves.

Meanwhile Mazeppa, Theresa, and their two followers had passed down from the drawbridge of the castle and made for the wood.

When they arrived there the silence was so deathlike that a chill insensibly crept into their hearts.

Not a soul could be seen, not a vestige of life, either animal or human.

" Strogonoff, Strogonoff!" shouted the dwarf, in a tone of agony, " where are you?—where are you?"

There was no reply.

" Seek him not," said Mazeppa, bitterly, " he has betrayed us. Let us rather press forward, and avoid pursuit."

The dwarf was frantic with rage and grief.

He stamped and writhed upon the ground.

" The box! the box!" he cried, " where is that?"

" What box?"

" A box I confided to Strogonoff," shrieked the dwarf; " it contains gold in heaps—it was so heavy I could scarcely bear it. It was Mazeppa's marriage portion that I bestowed upon him, and Strogonoff has betrayed me and stolen it."

It was too true. The Russian serf had seized both the horses and the treasure and turned his face towards the country of the Czar.

Finding all search for the thief useless, and fearing immediate pursuit, they plunged into the wood and made for the wooded glen at its further extremity.

Here they were ensconced when they heard the sound of approaching footsteps.

" We are pursued," cried Mazeppa; " we had better remain here."

But all attempt at concealment was useless. The quick ear of the Castellan detected the slightest sound, and in a moment after he had given the order to his steward, and the fugitives were surrounded.

" Yield!" cried the Castellan, as he darted into the centre of the group; " resistance is useless."

Mazeppa rose, sword in hand.

" My lord," he cried, " I love your daughter. I have won her in fair battle, which you have chosen to term a murder. I heard you brand me as an assassin. I now give you the lie, and refuse to yield to one who does not deserve the name of master."

The Castellan flushed crimson.

" Slave," he cried, as he advanced impetuously, " I would not soil my sword with your blood. And as for you, degraded girl, were it not that I wish to save my fair name, I would destroy you upon the spot."

Theresa had sat, trembling and downcast, and scarcely dared to raise her eyes.

She now sprang up.

"Kill me then, father," she said; "it would be a blessing I should dearly covet. Kill me, but spare Mazeppa."

The Castellan, with eyes inflamed by anger, raised his arm, as if about to comply with her terrible wish, but reason soon came to his aid.

He flung down his sword.

"Kolzoff," he cried to his steward, who now stood beside him, while the retainers surrounded the dell on all sides, "arrest these men, and bring my daughter home."

Resistance was useless.

To combat such numbers would have been detrimental to his own interests as well as to those of Theresa; and Mazeppa therefore yielded up his sword, and, with Zeminski, suffered himself to be led back to the castle.

These only went, for the dwarf Zisko had escaped.

On arriving at the Castle of Laurinski, Theresa was placed in her own room under a strong guard; while Mazeppa was immured in one of the lowest dungeons.

Zisko was found coiled up in his usual corner in the huge kitchen, and no one suspected him.

And all this time Strogonoff, the Russian serf, who had caused all this mischief, was dashing along towards the Russian frontier, with four horses and ten thousand Russian roubles in gold, silver, and bank notes.

The morning dawned.

A sad morning for all.

Count Palatine had enjoyed a good night's rest, and Roderigo, the Italian doctor, gave every hope of his recovery.

Mazeppa remained still in his dungeon, no one visiting him except the man who brought him his food.

Theresa kept in her room, refusing to see anyone—even her father.

The Castellan was morose and gloomy, as if something terrible was weighing on his mind, or as if he dared not trust himself to form a plan of punishment.

There was a terrible responsibility in his position.

In those days he would certainly have been regarded with suspicion by all who heard of this midnight outrage in his castle.

And yet Mazeppa had been his favourite page.

What was he to do?

Evening waned, the sun set in a crimson glory, and the Castellan sat at his window, gazing out upon the quiet country.

He was a man of quick passions, excited to a terrible pitch of anger by sudden occurrences; but when a lapse of time had passed since the event, he was ever prone to forgive.

He was just meditating upon a plan for sending Mazeppa away, and foregoing the fierce scheme of revenge he had at first determined upon, when Kolzoff, the steward, burst into the room without waiting to knock and announce his coming.

His face was deadly pale, and his agitation was so great that for a few moments he could not speak.

The Castellan expected at once the announcement of a terrible calamity.

"Speak, man!" he said, "speak! What is the matter?"

"Oh, my lord—my lord!" gasped the man.

"Well, well—what is it?"

"The Count Palatine is dead!"

The Castellan recoiled as if shot.

"Dead!" he cried, "dead! What mean you?"

The man pointed down the corridor.

"He lies dead upon his couch," he cried. "I found him dying there when I went in to give him his medicine. I ran to the Italian and brought him to the bed side, but it was too late—the Count was dead."

"How did he die—of what?"

"Of poison, my lord."

"Of poison, and in my house!" cried the Castellan, as he moved hastily towards the chamber of death; "who could have done this terrible deed?"

"The Count's last words were—'That villain, Mazeppa, has destroyed me.' That is all I know."

After gaining the room, and gazing for a few moments in silence at the dead body of his friend, the Castellan turned hastily to Kolzoff.

"How can I punish this audacious assassin?" he cried. "What fearful vengeance can I take?"

The steward's eyes glistened. Now was the moment to gratify his thirst for revenge.

"You have still in your stables the untamed Tartar steed," cried he. "Tie this murderer upon his back, and send him back to his native wilds."

The Castellan's face expressed a terrible fury.

"Yes, yes!" he cried. "Bring out the wild Tartar horse. Let every retainer in the castle issue forth into the courtyard, that they may see what a fearful revenge I take on those who abuse my benevolence and cast a slur upon my ancient name. Go, Kolzoff, and lead the prisoner forth, while I see that the Tartar steed is brought into the courtyard."

---

## CHAPTER VII.

"Bring forth the horse."—The horse was brought.
    In truth he was a noble steed,
    A Tartar of the Ukraine breed,
Who looked as if the speed of thought
Were in his limbs; but he was wild,
    Wild as the wild deer, and untamed—
With spur and bridle undefiled.
                BYRON'S "MAZEPPA."

ALONG the terrace of the castle burned a hundred torches—lighting up its ancient gables, its rugged walls, its time-worn turrets, the still moat. and the country beyond.

In the courtyard, also, blazed innumerable lights; and there was not a living being in the Castle of Laurinski, who did not crowd to one spot or to the other, to witness the execution of the Castellan's terrible edict.

The Castellan himself, stern and implacable, stood on the summit of the steps leading to the courtyard, with his arms folded, scarcely deigning a glance towards the spot where Mazeppa stood, stripped of all his clothes, and with only a pair of short drawers around his loins.

The page, held firmly in the grasp of several menials, who gloried in this chance of exhibiting their animosity, was calm and undismayed.

His eyes burned with a fierce fire—his chest heaved with his rapid breath, but his brow was serene, and his head uplifted in conscious innocence.

Stanislaus Count Palatine, had been murdered—poisoned by some treacherous hand, no doubt—but his was not that hand.

At the foot of the steps, trembling in every limb, and weeping bitterly, was the dwarf, Zisko.

Was he the poisoner?

If so, why did he weep? Was it because he had sought to aid his benefactor, but had failed?

At any rate, there he crouched, watching Mazeppa with eager eyes, and ever and anon glancing up at the fierce and passionate countenance of the Castellan.

At length the horse was brought.

He was a Tartar steed, fresh from the Ukraine, and had been caught but a few days before. He was completely wild, therefore, and required the strength of several men to hold him.

He came prancing and snorting into the courtyard, the foam all over his sides and his limbs, his eyes starting wildly, his whole frame in a tremour of agitation.

He was at once a sight of terror and beauty.

"Bind the traitor on his back," shouted the Castellan: "let there be no delay."

The menials had just seized Mazeppa, and were about to raise him on the back of the wild steed, when a piercing shriek rent the air, and Theresa rushed to her father's side.

Here she flung herself upon her knees, and clasped his.

"Oh! spare him this terrible trial, my lord," she cried. "Oh! if you must kill him, kill him, but do not torture him thus."

Her father eyed her sternly.

"Go girl," he cried "go hence. This is no scene for you."

" I will remain here till you have promised his release," said Theresa firmly. " His sentence is unjust—I will never remain calmly by, and see him sacrificed to your blind anger."

The Castellan called one of his attendants.

" Conduct the Lady Theresa to her apartments," said her father with suppressed fury, " and see that she does not issue thence to-night."

The Lady Theresa stood up proudly before the man.

" Back, fellow," she cried; " lay no hand upon me."

As she spoke she drew a glittering poignard from her bosom. The man drew back.

" Since my words will not avail," she continued, " and since my feeble strength will not suffice to rescue him from the hands of those hateful menials, I will remain here to see this terrible sentence fulfilled, that, when I think of Mazeppa, I may curse my father."

She then advanced as near her lover as the throng of men permitted her.

" Adieu, Mazeppa," she cried, in a voice almost suffocated by sobs, " adieu, my loved one! Even through this terrible trial you may come with safety if you have only trust in Providence. Think of me in your wild flight, and remember that I am yours for ever."

" Farewell, beloved one—farewell!" cried the captive page.

He had time to say no more; for, seizing her by direction of the Castellan in an unguarded moment, the domestics bore Theresa away to her room.

Then the last scene in the terrible drama was enacted.

Mazeppa, helpless in the hands of so many, was raised upon the back of the wild steed. His legs, arms, and body were tightly lashed round the animal, and then the Tartar horse, neighing and trembling with fury, was led towards the drawbridge.

Here he was released.

He stood for a moment irresolute, glanced round as if to be certain he was free, and then, with a fierce neigh, he plunged forward, and was soon lost amid the darkness of the forest.

And into the forest we must follow, leaving, for a moment, the fortress, with its throng of shouting menials, and the one heart which, in its depths, was mourning the loved and lost.

Oh, what a ride was that!

On, on, on! through a wild plain, bounded by black forests, without a town or village on the track; without a trace, indeed, of human life, but now and then the distant battlement of some stronghold built of old against the Tartars.

But a year before a Turkish army had ridden over that plain, and the verdure had rotted with the blood of thousands.

And so over the rugged, dusky plain, under a dull and leaden sky, the Tartar steed rode on, his mane bristling, his form trembling with terror at his unwonted burden, flying aside at every sound; while Mazeppa, perspiring at every pore, gazed round him.

After passing the edge of the plain they neared a forest, so wide that there seemed no bounds to it.

It was studded with old sturdy trees—trees so strong that not even the wildest breeze which swept across the Siberian waste could have made them tremble.

Here and there were young trees nestling by the old ones, and wild underwood, threatening every moment to overturn the wild courser in his terrible career.

The summer was nearly over, and already the autumnal red was discolouring the leaves, which stood stiffened upon the trees or fell into heaps like the gore-stained mounds of a battle-field.

On, on they rushed, rustling through the leaves like wind, leaving shrubs, trees, and wolves behind them.

But it was not always so.

The helpless victim, bound upon the back of the steed, which seemed never to tire, could hear the wild animals on the track, steadily pursuing them with their long gallop, which can bear up against the fleetest hunter.

By night they followed closely; by day they left him not, but pranced along by his side.

So two nights and one day passed, and the burning sun of the third day came down upon his blistered limbs, scorching him, blinding him, overwhelming him with its fierce light.

His brain reeled, the skies seemed to whirl round like a huge wheel; the trees and the ground itself appeared to dance and rise and mingle with the clouds.

Just as he was losing his senses he heard a noise as of the galloping of thousands of horsemen. The earth trembled beneath the on-rushing steeds. Clouds of dust obscured the sun.

Nearer and nearer came the sounds, and at length he saw the reason of the tumult.

Far and wide over the plain was a horde of wild horses, galloping to and fro, careering from side to side, neighing, snorting, prancing, with their long manes and tails streaming in the wind; but all following their guide, a tall horse with a jet black coat, without one spot of white upon him.

The wild horse stopped a moment, gazed round at his friends, and then, as if determined not to be deterred from his purpose, plunged onwards once more.

The wild horses saw their fellow-courser, and rushed after him, dashing against him ever and anon, and bruising the limbs of the unfortunate Mazeppa, who had not the slightest covering to protect him.

The wild animals snorted and started away as they gazed upon the strange burden which their brother carried, and at length, as if afraid of man even in his helpless state, they turned round and rushed away to the forest.

Then the evening came again, and the dim twilight, and the dark night, and the wolves were once more baying on their track.

Onwards they came with their quick gallop, lolling their blood-red tongues fresh from some scene of slaughter.

Onwards, onwards—while the wild horse, beginning to tire, slackened *his* pace, while they quickened theirs.

Onwards, onwards—while the man closed his eyes and prayed, and the horse neighed and snorted with terror.

Onwards, onwards—under a starlit sky, with the trees whirling past like black phantoms, the yelping crew behind, the unbounded waste before.

Suddenly a distant murmur fell upon the ear of the rider.

The horse paused an instant, sniffed the air, which now blew freshly and more cool, and then, as if some wild hope had lightened his heart, bounded forward more rapidly than before.

The yelping pack were for a moment distanced, and evinced their anger by a long chorus of yells.

Then there was a leap, and a plunge, and a gurgle.

They were saved—they had reached a river!

Bravely the wild horse stemmed the stream, the cool water giving fresh strength to his limbs, and restoring life and sense to his nearly fainting burden.

Refreshed and restored by his bath, the Tartar steed sped onwards again, never pausing a moment to take food.

The pangs of hunger were now beginning to torture Mazeppa.

The terror of the plains and the forests had been great always, but while life was yet strong within him, and while the natural energy of his frame was still unimpaired, they had not presented themselves to his mind in their full horror. But now, when he was faint with hunger, when his head was reeling and his brain rapidly becoming delirious, morbid fancies arose before him.

Around him seemed to be floating the forms of those he loved and hated. Theresa bent over him, and followed him in his flight; Zisko sat upon his chest; and the Castellan, with Stanislaus, were close beside him, threatening him on either side.

The horse now began sensibly to slacken his pace.

His frame was pouring with sweat—the foam dropped in thick masses from his mouth; and every new and then he staggered as if about to fall.

Mazeppa felt that the wild ride was nearly over.

He uttered a fervent prayer for safety, for he felt that soon his senses would be gone, and that his power to pray would leave him.

PUNISHMENT OF MAZEPPA.

"Oh! dearest Theresa," he cried, "my life will soon be sped—my sufferings will be over, and with my last breath I will bless you."

Scarcely had he spoken when the horse gave a loud neigh—staggered forward, and fell upon its knees.

It uttered a distressing neigh, and endeavoured to arise; and then, with a tremor and a groan, rolled over.

Presently Mazeppa felt a tremor pass through the animal's form, and then it gradually became stiff and cold.

The Tartar steed was dead.

Mazeppa himself had been rapidly becoming delirious before, and the terrible situation in which he now found himself completed the unsettling of his senses.

He raved to the winds, calling fondly upon Theresa, wildly cursing her father for his terrible revenge, and appealing to Heaven for aid.

Terrible forms were around him.

In the latter part of his wild ride he had seen a vulture hovering in the air, and now, in his disordered mind, he saw a bird of huge size perched upon the horse's head, pecking at its eyes, and flapping its wings with an ominous sound.

He dreamed in this delirium that he freed his right hand, and fought this immense bird, which tried to tear his flesh, and had just succeeded in killing it, when the yelping of wolves was heard afar, and presently a pack of hungry and red-mouthed animals were around him—above him—fighting for his wild steed, and gazing at him with ravenous eyes.

Then these in their turn vanished, and a gentle form leaned over him—a bright-eyed maiden, with long, waving hair, falling over her neck and bosom, and habited in the garb of a Tartar shepherdess.

Was this a vision, or reality?

He knew not, for now his senses indeed left him; the earth and sky became blank, and he fainted away.

## CHAPTER VIII.

### THE FOUR CONSPIRATORS.

On the edge of a broad plain, bounded by rocky eminences —the last of the chain which separates Tartary from Poland — were grouped an infinity of rude Tartar huts and tents.

Above, stretched rocky pathways, where rough bridges of trees stemmed fierce torrents below; along green pastures, grazed horses and cattle.

Here a shepherdess, clad in the picturesque and wild garb of country, reclined under a tree and watched her flocks; here a Tartar horseman rode hither and thither, and kept a careful eye upon the war-steeds and the cows and oxen, lest they should wander too far along the boundless steppes. But the greater part of the men were lazily reclining at the doors of their dwellings, or beneath the shade of overhanging rocks; while the women were preparing the morning meal.

Grouped at a short distance from the rest were four men, three of whom, reclining in the shade of a huge tree, seemed to listen with great respect to the words of the fourth.

MAZEPPA'S RESCUE.

"Comrades," he said, "the time has come for action. I am tired of this lethargy."

"And I."

"And I."

"And I."

The responses were loud and earnest

The first speaker glanced around him with apparent uneasiness.

"Nay, my friends," he said, "speak not so loudly. There are traitors everywhere, and here may be no exception."

"You are right, good Hussein," said one of his audience—a rough, savage-looking fellow, of about thirty years. "There are traitors here, I think; for when we have been conferring I have seen shadows flitting hither and thither around our tent. But come—what is it you propose, good Hussein?"

"I will trust you," returned he, "for I know you three—Ali, Hassan, and Suliman—are faithful friends. I am, as you are aware, the brother of your king."

"We know it."

"He is old and decrepid—I am still young. I was the child of my father's age by a young wife; so that I am but the half-brother of Abder Khan."

"You, then, are the heir to the throne?"

Hussein smiled.

"Precisely so, my friends," he said; but listen. A deadly hatred has ever existed between myself and my brother. Why, I know not. I was always willing to be on terms of kindness and affection with him; but he has invariably repelled me. I suppose he regards me as the rival of his dead son."

No. 3.

"Ah!" said Hassan, "where is that son? Is he indeed dead, as you say?"

A smile of contempt passed over the lips of the chief.

"He is dead," he said. "Twenty years have passed since this child was lost, and for twenty years have our people lived the life of shepherds."

"A degraded life," murmured the three conspirators.

"You are right, my brothers; we do live a degraded life. At the time of our last incursion into Poland, I was but fifteen. Listen, while I tell you something in a whisper. I was but fifteen, but I knew that the son of Abder Khan was the one great stumbling block in my path; I knew that if he were once removed, I should be the heir to the throne. I was too young, however, to think of murder, and so, while all were engaged in the fierce combat which ended in our defeat, I drew the child, then but two years old, away from the fight, and told him to remain behind a tree. The frightened child readily acquiesced, and there he was left."

"A capital scheme," exclaimed Ali.

"And one that answered well," put in Hassan; "for the boy has never returned."

"Nor will he ever," Hussein continued. "No doubt he was devoured by wolves. Well, as I have said, since that day we have had no incursions—our king has adopted the style and life of a prophet, rather than of a warrior. Our people are degenerated—they begin to see their own degeneration—they talk of it in the tents by night, and brood over it by day. They want a soldier-king, and here is one for them."

The three conspirators would have raised an enthusiastic cheer, had he not restrained them.

"Hush!" he cried, "you will betray us. Oh, here comes our worthy king. See how he leans upon his staff—see how restlessly his glance wanders over the hills, as if every moment he saw his boy returning. Bah! we want no sentiment—we want a warrior who scents the battle afar off, and lead his troops to victory."

Down a steep pathway from a rocky eminence, the aged king was approaching with two trusty followers.

He was a tall, finely-built man, though age somewhat bent his form and dimmed his eyes.

Hussein's words were false.

He was *not* decrepid.

Sorrow had saddened his brow and given a listlessness to his movements—had imparted, in fact, a kind of apathy to his whole manner. But there was still a latent fire in his dimming eyes, which ever and anon shot forth; while the eloquence of his tongue was equalled by none.

Upon a rocky eminence, overlooking the huts of his people, the old king dwelt alone.

His hut was composed partly of wood and partly of rock.

It was formed into two compartments—the one in front being his dwelling-place, and that behind being a study, where he sat for hours engaged in meditation, or in the perusal of old books.

From the rock in front of his hut could be commanded a view of the superb country—on the one hand tiers of purple hills; on the other, boundless plains.

Here and there he would sometimes recline—now glancing at the far-spreading steppes, now at the lofty mountains.

On either side of the hut were two others, inhabited by two followers and their families.

These men, faithful adherents of the sorrowful king, kept watch over his declining years, but scarcely ever intruded on his privacy.

What he did in that back room—a dark, dreary place, at the best—was scarcely known at all; but he spoke of visions seen, of voices which spoke to him in dreams, and ever and anon predicted events with unerring exactness.

Thus, from being honoured as a king, he became reverenced as a prophet.

To the generality of his people this was but a new cause for love—to the conspirator, Hussein, it was a point of ridicule and sarcasm.

Hussein's story was a false one.

Abder Khan II., the reigning king of Tartary, was the elder son of Abder Khan I.

His mother, a beautiful and accomplished woman, lived to see him fifteen years old, and then died suddenly.

At the period of her death the country was in a state of wild confusion.

War was the order of the day.

Not an hour passed without bloodshed, and great as was the king's grief, he had no time left him for investigation.

Everyone, however, suspected that she had died of poison, and that the murderess was her own sister, a young creature of sixteen.

This sister was a girl of most exquisite beauty.

In those climes women are ripened more quickly than in ours, and Oneida was a woman of mature and developed beauty at fifteen.

If, however, she thought that by the death of her sister, she would become at once queen of Tartary, she was mistaken.

Though ravished by her beauty, which far exceed that of the murdered queen, Abder Khan the First remained for ten years faithful to his first love.

During those ten years Oneida remained single, and paid attentions to the king, which, in kindness and tenderness, could scarcely have been exceeded by the deceased queen.

At length she triumphed.

Abder Khan, weary of his lonely life, espoused the still beautiful Oneida, and after five years of marriage (that is to say, when Abder Khan the Second was thirty), Hussein was born.

At the time of our story, therefore, Abder Khan was sixty-five, and Hussein thirty-five.

The future king naturally regarded the offspring of this suspicious union with anything but affection.

The result proved the correctness of his dislike: the son of the murderess became a deadly snake in his path.

So the old king on that morning came down from the mountains and went among his people.

Round him gathered several of the chiefs—some of those well-disposed towards him, and some of those who had secretly espoused the cause of Hussein.

"Chieftains," cried the old king, in a deep and sonorous voice, "Heaven has sent me a vision."

"A prophecy—a prophecy!" cried some.

"Some more drivelling," sneered Hussein, and a significant murmur ran through the ranks of the disaffected.

The king observed this not.

"It is no prophecy," he said; "it is simply a warning. I saw in my sleep a gentle dove, pursued by a hawk. The dove took refuge in my bosom, and the hawk fled back. I pursued it and destroyed it, and lo! great honour and great glory fell upon the Tartar race. So, men of Tartary, be prepared. Brighten up the arms which for twenty years have been idle by your sides—instil into the minds of your sons the glories of the past, that they may emulate them in the future. War is coming, my friends, and it must find us prepared."

A loud shout of joy rent the air.

Hussein and his fellow-conspirators stood aghast.

"What does this mean, good Hussein?" asked Ali, under his breath.

"It means," said Hussein, "that the king, in his old age, is recovering his martial taste, and that if we are to strike we must strike soon."

"Say the word," cried Suliman, "and we will rush upon him and destroy him."

"No—no," said Hussein, "that would be madness. It would enrage the people, and they would all side with him. No—no, Abder Khan must die as his mother died—in secret."

He said no more.

He advanced towards the king.

"Most noble brother," he said, in a voice of deep respect, but with a manner and with words calculated to cast ridicule upon the royal personage, "you speak of war—I rejoice to hear it—so do your people."

The chiefs again shouted in joy.

"They do rejoice," said Abder Khan, "and I too, since Heaven calls upon us to fight."

"You have named no cause."

"I know it not myself as yet—that will be made known to us in good time."

A smile of bitter irony passed over the lips of Hussein as the king spoke.

"My brother is vague in his intelligence," he said with mock respect.

"Heaven does not always vouchsafe me the exact knowledge of things," returned Abder Khan, with calm dignity. "I pretend to no gift of prophecy. I am a man, like the rest of you; if I were not, I should be unfit to be your king, because I should not understand your wants. Now and then I am enabled to foresee events, because constant study gives me the power—but that is all."

He then bowed to the assembled throng, and took his way back to the hut,

Hussein and his three friends pushed their way through the people, and entered the tent of the former.

---

## CHAPTER IX.

### ZULISKA, THE CIRCASSIAN.

THE old king passed that day alone, wrapt in deep meditation.

Evening still found him in profound thought in his study.

This study was, as I have said, at the rear of the hut, and was formed out of the solid rock.

It was protected on all sides, and the coldest night rarely produced within it the slightest chill air.

Its furniture was but scanty—a large table occupied the centre of the room, some rude shelves round the walls were heavy with old volumes, and two divans completed its adornment.

It was here that at nine o'clock, when the shades of night had covered the landscape, and when from the summit of the rock nothing could be seen but the twinkling fires of the Tartars, that Abder Khan was sitting reading by the light of a lamp, when a gentle tap was heard at the outer door.

It was *so* gentle that at first the king heard it not.

It was repeated.

Abder Khan started.

"Who can it be," he murmured, "who thus disturbs me at this hour?"

A sudden thought struck him.

It might be Hussein!

He knew well the character of his brother; he was well aware of his plotting heart, his thorough want of scruple, his eager desire to be King of Tartary.

He had noticed, too on that morning, the angry flash upon Hussein's face when he heard his warlike speech and the bitter irony of his brother's voice, too, when he spoke of prophecy.

What if it should be he?

What, if maddened by the prospect of for ever losing his chance of the throne by the increased popularity of the king, he should perpetrate some terrible crime?

Hussein knew well that if Abder Khan could so induce the people, he would never allow him to become King of Tartary.

Might not this, then, be some plan of destruction?

The knock was heard again—this time a louder knock than before.

The king rose, approached a corner, and drew thence a long and heavy sword, which he unsheathed

"My trusty friend," ha said, as he surveyed the bright and shining blade, "long have you remained unused. This night, perhaps you may once more save your master's life."

Again a knock.

"They are impatient," he muttered, with a bitter smile, as he approached the front door.

"Who knocks?" he cried aloud.

"It is I, Zuliska," answered a gentle voice; "I thought your majesty was ill, since I heard no sound."

The old king smiled.

"Is it she, then, poor child," he murmured, "who has thus frightened me for nothing?"

He laid aside his sword and unlocked the door.

A young girl entered, and then, rebolting the entrance, he led her into his study.

She was scarcely sixteen, with a beauty far above any to be found among the Tartars.

Tall and finely proportioned, she possessed a soft grace and refined loveliness, rarely met with among these wild and rugged tribes.

Her face was oval, her eyes were large, almond-shaped and languishing—her mouth, full and red-lipped, was like a budding-rose, and her walk, graceful and light, was like that of the women of Andalusia, who of all women in the world know best how to walk.

Zuliska was but half-Tartar.

Her father, one of the highest in rank among the chiefs, had rescued her mother—a lovely Circassian—from the hands of some Turks who were bearing her off to Constantinople.

Sold to these men by her own friends, the beautiful girl preferred trusting herself to the rude Tartars then to her own kindred, and after a time became the wife of Cassim, her preserver.

The fruit of this union was a daughter, who was a reproduction of her mother, and seemed as if she had no trace of Tartar blood in her veins.

So she was called Zuliska the Circassian.

"Well, my child," said the old king, "what brings you here?"

"Treachery."

The king started.

"Treachery! what mean you Zuliska?"

The girl looked around her as if to see whether they were alone.

"Are we quite safe from observation here?" she asked timidly.

"Yes—yes, my child, fear not," said Abder Khan; "no one can overhear us; speak freely."

"I overheard to-night," returned Zuliska, "a plot against your life and throne."

The king sighed.

"And my brother was the chief conspirator," he said, sadly.

The girl gazed at him in surprise.

"How know you that?" she asked.

"Oh! I have long known it;" he said, "but tell me, what is this new scheme?"

"A terrible—a treacherous scheme," cried Zuliska. "You announced to-day to your people, that war was coming."

"I did."

"This war is to be the signal for your death."

"How so?—the people are joyful at the tidings?"

"Yes—yes, that is true," returned Zuliska, "so also will Hussein and his followers pretend to be. They will be among the most eager—the most joyous, and will gladly accompany you to the battle-field. There a treacherous shot will destroy you, and none will know the hand which speeds it."

The king smiled, and patted her fair head.

"Dear child," he said "you have saved your king, and he will reward you. Your father—when I have destroyed the traitor Hussein—shall become king."

The girl's eyes sparkled for a moment, and her bosom heaved beneath its gauzy covering.

Then a dark shade crossed her brow.

"You are anticipating your death, my king," she said.

"Not so. I shall soon give up the sceptre, and see my people happy under another ruler ere I die. Have you more to tell?"

"Yes," said the girl, eagerly, "I have much more to tell. Hussein, your brother, has the blood of your son upon his hand."

The old king leaped up—his eyes flashing, and his whole frame convulsed by emotion.

"Ah! villain, traitor!" he cried, "to-morrow shall see his destruction."

The girl seized the old king by the arm, and drew him gently down upon the divan.

"Hush!" she cried, "we shall be discovered. You have no proofs of Hussein's treachery, and if you kill him without them your people will be wroth. No—no, watch and be careful; but be patient."

The king smiled grimly.

"You are right," he said, "I must not be too precipitate. But tell me, how did this man destroy my child!"

"Nay, then, I have been too hasty," exclaimed Zuliska, "I should have said, if your son be dead, Hussein is his murderer. Is he dead?"

"Alas! I know not. Twenty long weary years have I mourned for him—I have searched for him everywhere, but in vain. I fear that it is too true he is no more."

"Where did you lose him?"

"In a forest in Podolia, during one of our incursions."

"Why did you not seek for him there?"

"We did, but in vain. No doubt the wild beasts or some blood-thirsty Polish peasant destroyed him."

"Heaven grant it may not be so! Hussein, then fifteen years of age, took the child, in the height of the battle, and hid it behind a tree. This he did with the avowed object of becoming king himself."

"Fool!" muttered the king, "when I have the power of disposing of the succession. My dear child," he said, "I am most grateful to you for your kindness. Have you any further news to tell?"

"None as to Hussein," said the girl; "but this night, as I came hither, I saw a terrible vision."

"A vision of what?"

"Of the Phantom Horseman who haunts the mountains."

The king smiled.

"That is a shepherd's legend," he said, "an idle tale, told by men to frighten women. It must have been the result of your disordered brain."

The girl shook her head.

"No—no," she cried, "it was no fancy. I saw the steed—a large and beautiful steed, covered with foam—dash across the hills and plunge into the darkness close by the well. On his back there was a horseman—not riding as other men ride, but lying full length on his back."

"If you indeed saw it," said the king, "it is some human being. Depend upon it, Zuliska, these spectral beings exist not. Go now in peace, and fear nothing. If my son—my long-lost son—returns not soon, your father, Cassim, shall be King of Tartary."

He rose, kissed her brow, and, leading her to the door, accompanied her to the edge of the rock.

Above them towered the lofty mountains, with the crescent moon between their rugged summits.

Below spread the immeasurable steppes, with here and there the twinkling fires of the Tartars.

"Adieu, my child," said the king. "Is not this a lonely road for one so young?"

"Who is there to harm me?"

"True—true. Farewell, Zuliska. A king and a father thanks you."

Abder Khan then returned to his hut, closed the door, and was soon buried in profound slumber.

Meanwhile Zuliska, fearing nothing, and not dreaming of molestation, proceeded down the rugged mountain path towards the Tartar encampment, or, we may call it, village, since, during those twenty years of inactivity, most of the tents had been abandoned for wooden huts.

Just as she reached a bend of the road, where it led over a torrent, a man's form suddenly appeared before her.

She trembled and started back.

"Who is it?" she cried, in a voice of fear, "who is it who thus molests me?"

The new-comer laughed.

"The night must be dark, indeed, and the moon must be false," he cried, "if Zuliska does not recognise Abdallah."

The girl blushed and smiled as she gave her hand to the new-comer.

"Oh, Abdallah," she said, "I knew you not. I have been talking of terrible things, and I fear every shadow."

She stood still as she spoke, leaning against the side of the little wooden bridge.

"Will you not come home?" said Abdallah; "I will willingly see you in safety."

The girl looked down into the deep ravine, as if reading there her fate.

"No," she said; "what you have to say, say here."

"Why so?"

"I wish to go down to the huts alone."

"Why, again?"

"I *have* reasons. I have had a dream, and I wish to await its fulfilment ere I am spoken of as the betrothed of any man."

Abdallah laughed.

"Zuliska," he said, toying with her tiny jewelled hand, "you are a little dreamer—I ever knew that; but dreams scarcely ever tell us to be false."

"No; but be patient and wait."

"For what?"

"I know not."

"You are speaking in riddles."

"Am I?"

The young Tartar chieftain looked sadly on the ground for a moment, and then glanced up into her face.

"Zuliska," he said, tenderly, "you know I love you well, and you have promised to be mine. Our parents have agreed to smile upon our union. Why, then, is this sudden coldness?"

"I mean not to be unkind, dear Abdallah," returned Zuliska.

"What then?"

She pressed her hand to her brow, and glanced up at him with an expression of pain.

Her whole form was agitated: her eyes swam with tears, her lips were parted, her bosom was tremulous with emotion.

Abdallah caught her to his heart, and imprinted a passionate kiss upon her lips.

"Dear one, you are suffering. Tell me what ails you?"

She was in tears now.

"Nothing, nothing, Abdallah," she murmured, as she gently disengaged herself from his embrace.

"Why, then, these tears?"

She smiled.

"I scarcely know myself," she answered. "Question me not, Abdallah; another time, and I will tell you all. Let me go home now."

She suffered him to imprint another kiss upon her lips, and then hastened down the path.

She darted along so swiftly that she saw not that at the very bottom of the rugged road a man was standing, and as she tripped lightly on she fell almost into his arms.

She started back with a wild cry, but the man had seized her by the wrist.

It was Hussein.

"Ah, traitress, I have you at last!" he cried, in savage accents.

Zuliska's courage, even at this trying moment, did not desert her.

She stood erect, defiant, before him, looking steadfastly in his eyes.

"I understand you not," she answered.

The man laughed brutally.

"I will explain, then," he said. "Where have you been spending your evening?"

"I am not bound to render any account to you," returned the Circassian maiden.

"I will tell you, then," said Hussein. "At eight o'clock I and some trusty followers had a meeting in my tent."

"You did."

"At that conference we discussed the necessity of finding a successor to our present dotard king. They spoke of me, of his hatred for me, and suggested means for ridding the people of his follies."

"In other words, of murdering him!" returned the undaunted girl.

"You defy me! Well, well; your time of punishment is at hand. After listening to our conferences, you have been to the hut of the Prophet King, and betrayed to him our schemes."

"I have. I have told him all—I have warned him against your treachery; but how knew you this?"

Hussein smiled.

"You are not the only spy," he said.

"Who has betrayed me?"

"Ali."

"Ali!"

"Yes, Ali—the man whose love you despised, foolish maiden—he who will be one day my highest chief. He suspected you, and watched your movements. He saw you leave your father's tent, creep towards mine, and conceal yourself behind the canvas, in the shadow of a lofty tree, and listen to all we said."

"Why did he not stop me?"

"Interrupt me not. The conference over, he saw you steal away, and disappear along the mountain path. He followed you noiselessly, and beheld you enter the king's hut."

"Well, and what then? What if I confess all this is true?"

"You seal your own doom."

"My doom! You dare not harm me. Remember I am within call of a thousand warriors, who would fly to my assistance at the first cry."

"When it was too late," sneered Hussein. "Fear not—I

THE DWARF DISCOVERS THE ADVANCE OF MAZEPPA.

am no fool, and would not soil my hands with your blood in a spot where I should be found out. But remember one more betrayal and your doom is sealed."

The girl gazed at him in contempt.

"I fear you not," she repeated. "Ere many suns have risen and set your race of treachery and folly will be over. Now release me, or I will cry for help."

Hussein still detained her.

"There is one chance yet left you of safety," he said.

She made no answer.

"You have rejected Ali," he said, "and you have rejected me. Become my wife and you are safe; not only safe, but queen of Tartary."

The girl shuddered.

"Release me," she murmured.

"I have loved you long," resumed Hussein. "Among the women of our tribe there is not one so beautiful as you. You are the star of our plains, and should be the queen of all. I love you too well to see you the bride of another."

Zuliska made no reply, but struggled to release herself.

"Consent or die!" muttered the man, in a hoarse voice.

"Help! help!" cried Zuliska, as she saw the glitter of his dagger, which he had just unsheathed.

As he spoke a dark form sprang from a rock, the dagger flew from his hand, and Zuliska was rescued from his grasp.

It was Abdallah, who had heard and understood all.

He laid the half-fainting girl gently upon the rocks, and turned to take vengeance upon Hussein.

It was useless—he had disappeared.

## CHAPTER X.

### AT MORNING BY THE WELL.

It was early on the morning following her adventure on the mountain path with Hussein, that Zuliska, the Circassian, left her home, soon after the rising of the sun, and proceeded to the well, near which, on the evening before, she had seen the Spectre Horseman of the Mountains.

She came down towards the well, pensive and lonely.

Her thoughts were occupied with her lover, and the imminent danger in which he and the king stood, from the inveterate enmity of Hussein—a danger in which she also shared.

She sat down on the edge of the well to think, but scarcely had she done so when a groan attracted her attention.

She glanced up, but could see nothing.

She listened.

Again the sound.

"Some one must be concealed near this spot," she said, rising, and gazing round her.

Near the well was a thicket—a dense thicket of olive trees—and from this thicket it seemed that the sound proceeded.

She approached it.

What made her start back, and utter a cry of horror?

On the ground lay a horse, stiff and dead, and upon its back a man was bound—naked, bleeding, helpless.

"He is dead!" she murmured, as she knelt down by his side.

A handsome fellow was this Mazeppa, with noble features, and a well-built frame; and Zuliska gazed at him—first in admiration, then in pity.

She placed her hand over his heart.

There was a faint throbbing.

" He lives ! " she cried, as she began to unloose his bonds.

When she had relieved his limbs from the thick leather bonds which confined them, she ran to the well and fetched some water.

With this she bathed the temples and moistened the parched lips of the stranger, and then she darted up the mountain path towards the dwelling-place of the prophet king.

She knocked eagerly.

Abder Khan appeared.

He gazed at her in surprise.

" You here ! " he cried, " at so early an hour ? "

The girl looked around her.

" Are we alone ? " she said.

" Yes, quite alone."

" Then for a moment I will enter."

She entered and closed the door.

" I have great news," she said.

As she spoke, she took his hand, and gazed up kindly into his face.

" What is it you have to tell ? "

" I bring joy, triumph, honour to your house," she answered. " What was the name of the son—lost many years ago—the son so deeply mourned—so earnestly looked for ? "

The old king trembled.

" Why remind me of him ? " he said.

" Because it is of him I have to speak. Say, what was his name ? "

" Mazeppa."

" Then come with me—he that was lost is found. Down by the well he lies—bleeding, and lost to all around him, but living still—living to become king of Tartary, and the avenger of his terrible wrongs."

The old king passed his hand to his forehead.

" My brain reels," he murmured ; " what is this you are telling me ? Last night you spoke of treachery and villany—this morning you speak of the brightest hope of my life."

The young girl took his hand.

" Come," she said, " one glance will suffice."

" One glance at what ? " asked the bewildered king.

" A young man, as I have said, lies by the well—naked, wounded, bleeding. On his breast is a star, and the name of ' Mazeppa.' He is your son—the heir to your throne."

The old man stood for a moment like one amazed.

Then he advanced to the door.

" Go," he said, " I will follow."

The well was soon reached, and the king knelt down by the side of the wounded man.

" Yes, yes ! " he said, as he kissed the pale brow of the youth ; " he *is*, indeed, my son ! Come, let us bear him to my hut. If Hussein and his followers find him here, he will die."

The old king took the head and shoulders of his son, while Zuliska took his feet, and they slowly ascended the mountain path towards the cavern.

Not a soul met them on their way—not an eye glanced at them from the cottages which were on either side of the mountain's brow.

They entered the hut, therefore, without being perceived by any one.

The old king laid his son on his own bed.

" Let him remain here," he said, " and let no one know he is here, except your father and mother. Until he is well, and able to defend himself, it will not be safe to make his presence known. With so many enemies around me, who knows what danger might not threaten him ? "

The girl was gazing on the face of the young man as Abder Khan spoke.

Her mind was busy with strange and unknown feelings.

For a time, at any rate, Abdallah was forgotten ; and she thought only of the handsome stranger, who must have undergone so many wild and unknown perils.

Abdallah was the first man with whom she had been brought in intimate connection ; and, as her parents approved of the young man's suit, they had been much in each other's company—more, indeed, than is usual in Tartar tribes.

Yet, now Mazeppa had appeared—though he had scarcely opened his eyes—though he had not uttered a word—he had assumed a place in her mind which seemed almost incredible.

She forgot Abdallah—forgot all the sweet dreams her passion had raised in her mind ; and her only wish seemed to be to remain near Mazeppa, and tend him until he was well.

" I will go at once," she said, with downcast eyes, as if the old king could read her thoughts ; " I will go at once and tell my father that your son has returned."

" Yes, do so. Ask him to come and see me directly."

" Yes, and I will then request his permission to remain here, and help you to nurse the prince."

Without waiting for a reply the young girl then darted away, and directed her steps eagerly towards the tent of her parents.

After casting one more glance at his son—who, with eyes fixed, and flushed face, lay in the first moments of delirium—Abder Khan proceeded to a little cupboard, and brought thence a square box made of cedar wood.

Opening this, he took out three little bottles, and then, lighting a lamp, held over it a vessel, which in shape somewhat resembled a large spoon.

When this was red hot, he poured from one of the bottles some powder of a whitish colour. Then, when this was calcined, he dropped some liquid from each of the other bottles on the white ash—one of a rich ruby colour, the other a dull opal.

An aroma of an intense and pungent description filled the apartment, and the old king, pouring the steaming liquid into a fourth bottle, waited patiently till it was cooled.

Then he presented to the young man—who was now shrieking and shouting in the agony of delirious madness—a horn containing three drops of the medicine diluted in half-a-pint of spring water.

The sufferer, whose lips were parched and cracking with thirst, swallowed the draught eagerly, and by degrees his ravings became less loud and more indistinct.

" The wolves ! the wolves ! " he murmured. " Oh ! save me. Just Heaven ! This is horrible—horrible ! Coward ! to choose such a revenge as this ! Oh ! that precipice—all is over now. Welcome death ! "

And thus he raved on, though every moment his words became less articulate, and at length died away in whispers. After half an hour sleep came over him—a quiet refreshing sleep, and the old king smiled, saying,—

" He is saved ! "

It was just after Mazeppa fell into this slumber that Zuliska returned, bringing with her her father, Cassim.

Ambition plays strange tricks with men's characters, and it was with a sensation of alarm and anger too that he had listened to the news brought to him by his daughter.

He made no observation to her, however, expressive in any way of the thoughts which crowded into his mind, but came immediately to his interview with the old king.

When he entered the hut he advance immediately to the bedside of the young prince.

Here he stood for some moments in contemplation, after drawing aside the sheepskins which Abder Khan had thrown over the sleeper.

" This is no Tartar," he said at length, as he turned towards the king.

The king started.

Was this man becoming his enemy also ?

" What mean you ? " he asked with an air of sternness and displeasure.

" This youth," returned Cassim, " is, I repeat, no Tartar. Look at the smoothness and fairness of his skin—look at the effeminate beauty of his face. He is some Pole, passed off upon you by an impostor."

Abder Khan shook his head.

" No, no," he said ; " I have undeniable proofs that he is my son. Look at his breast, and see the word ' Mazeppa,' fashioned there by my own hand—see, too, the star I placed there, and the royal vulture soaring above."

The chief leaned down over the sleeper, and examined the marks on his chest.

"Bah!" he said, "these are easily to be accounted for, even on the breast of a stranger."

"How?"

"The boy you lost may have died, and the mark have been copied on the chest of this fair Polish youth by some impostor. Such a slender proof as this should never be allowed to sway your choice of an heir to the Tartar crown."

Abder Khan eyed him severely.

"Cassim," he said, "I have ever regarded you as a brave, noble, generous chief. But ambition has robbed you of your heart. It is not now according to your heart you speak, but according to your pride. This *is* my son, and shall be my heir, though a thousand chiefs opposed him."

Cassim drew himself up to his full height.

"Abder Khan," he said, "the respect due to you as my king precludes me from expressing myself as strongly as I could wish; but I can say this much, you have ever led me to suppose that I was to be the king of Tartary; the chiefs regard me as their future sovereign. And then to descend from this position and cast aside all my hopes of sovereignty because a boy comes hither in an assumed delirium, and foists himself upon you as your son——No, sire! Great as is my respect for your majesty, I will now, once for all, state that I shall be the first to oppose such an imposition."

The old king smiled grimly.

"Alas, Cassim!" he said, "ambition has deprived me of your friendship. Nevertheless, I can make some excuses for you. It is a great thing to be monarch of these wilds—lawless, but brave and warlike and powerful tribes; and I can understand that you relinquish with pain your hopes of sovereignty. But I must now and for ever destroy these false expectations. There are marks here on this young man's chest which no man could have imitated, because they are nature's marks. See here upon his left side three moles forming a triangle, and in their centre a star! This *is* my son, and he is king of Tartary!"

Cassim paced the room in silence for a few moments.

His mind was in a strangely perturbed state.

He reverenced the king, his relative—he had once loved him.

But then the throne?

Was he not about to lose it?

Was it not, too, by this king's instrumentality?

At length he stopped.

"Abder Khan," he said, "I will say no more at present. We will wait till this youth is recovered. From his own lips we will then learn his story. If he prove the true heir, I must bow my head to the decrees of heaven; if not, he is an impostor, and must die. Farewell. Zuliska, follow me."

The young girl stood irresolute.

"The king is old," she said; "he has need of some one to aid him in tending his son. May I not remain?"

Cassim regarded her with a scowl.

Pretending friendship towards Abder Khan as he did, he could not well refuse his daughter's request, and so with a bad grace he consented.

Abder Khan saw him to the door of the hut, and then said,—

"Cassim, you were my friend."

"I am."

The king shook his head.

"No, no," he said, "you are not now."

"Why do you think so?"

"Because jealousy has invaded your heart. However, I have one thing to ask in the name of our former friendship."

"And that is?"

"That you will hold my secret sacred."

"What secret?"

"The secret of this youth's appearance and his residence here. There are those among my tribe who would destroy my son while he is helpless, and I will not deliver him helpless into their hands. When he has his strength restored to him I will declare his presence, and proclaim him king of Tartary."

The old king, in his enthusiastic joy, forgot whom he was addressing.

"I will preserve your secret," said Cassim, as he strode away.

"Will he?" asked Abder Khan, turning to Zuliska.

The young girl sighed.

"Alas!" she answered, "I know not. The brilliant dream of empire has turned his brain and affected his heart also. He has lived upon the hope of being king of Tartary, and it is hard to abandon that hope in an instant."

The old king took her hand and led her back into the other room to the bedside of his son.

Then he lifted Mazeppa's feverish hand and placed it in that of Zuliska.

"There," he said, "is the hand of my son. Your father cannot object to relinquish the throne that his daughter may be queen of Tartary."

At this moment the image of Abdallah presented itself to Zuliska, and falling on her knees by the bedside of the prince, she shed bitter tears.

Had she known the heart of Mazeppa she might have spared herself illimitable sorrow.

---

## CHAPTER XI.

### THE CAVERN OF THE WINDS.

ABOUT a mile from the spot where the old king's hut stood was situated a cavern, formed by nature, in the side of a wild precipice.

It was called the Cavern of the Winds.

It was a large, dark place, where the light of day had scarcely ever penetrated.

Its walls were dank and noisome, reeking with the damp of ages; its floor was full of pools and weeds, and through its slime crept vermin and reptiles.

It could scarcely, indeed, be termed a cavern; it was, strictly speaking, a tunnel, and led from one ledge of rock to another.

Here, on the night following the arrival of Mazeppa, there were assembled about ten men.

A bright fire burned in a large recess, and around this th warriors were crouched, though they required it more for th sake of the light than the heat it diffused.

Foremost of these conspirators—for they were conspirators—was Hussein.

With them were Ali and Suliman, his two friends; the others were seven chiefs, who had been chosen from among the others because of their known dissatisfaction.

"Friends," cried Hussein, rising, "I have important news for you. I told you at our last conference that the Prophet King was dying, and that it behoved you to choose another."

"We have chosen," cried Ali.

"Yes—yes; we have chosen," repeated the others, as if with one voice.

"He has spoken of approaching war," proceeded Hussein; "and cannot tell when it is coming. He tells of great deeds of prowess and courage which will be demanded of us, and talks of leading us to battle; but if we do battle, for what is it? For what but to keep an old and imbecile man on the throne?"

"Yes—yes; he is too old to reign."

"He is; but let me proceed. Danger threatens us. This morning, as Ali was proceeding to the well, he saw a strange and unusual sight. By the well lay a horse dead and bleeding; and on his back was bound a young man, naked, and apparently lifeless."

"The Spectre Horseman of the mountains!" echoed all present.

At the same time a shudder ran through the assembly.

"No, no, my brothers; no, no, it was not the Spectre Horseman of the mountains. The horse was a human steed, and its rider was a being of flesh and blood like ourselves. The question remains, who was he?

"The young girl, Zuliska, the daughter of Cassim the presumptive heir to the throne, was at this moment beheld descending the rocky path leading to the well. Ali remained concealed, curious to see what would follow. Zuliska approached, glanced at the young man in astonishment, and then, loosening his bonds, brought him some water to wet his parched lips.

"After this the young girl ran up the mountain path, brought down the old king, and together they bore the wounded stranger to the royal hut.

"Meanwhile, Ali had made a strange discovery.

"On the young man's breast were divers strange signs and marks, and the name of Mazeppa."

"Our young prince! Long live our young prince," cried the chiefs.

Hussein glanced angrily round.

"Are you mad?" he exclaimed. "Mazeppa, our prince, is dead."

"Who, then, is this?"

"A Polish youth."

"And the marks and the name graven on his breast—what then?" asked an aged chieftain.

"They are the work of an impostor," returned Hussein. "Listen, and I will explain all. This beardless youth, whom some one has foisted off upon our Prophet King is the page of a Polish nobleman. His father, knowing the story of young Mazeppa, who was lost when *I* was a boy in the forests of Podolia, has graven on his body these signs and tokens of sovereignty, that he may come hither and wrest from us our kingdom for Poland. It is a scheme in which many Polish nobles have joined in order to subvert our power."

"But the old king knows his son—knows his own writing, and cannot be deceived," said one of the chiefs; "he will detect the imposture."

Hussein shook his head.

"No," he said, "unfortunately he does not detect it. He is thoroughly deceived."

"How know you that?"

The chief smiled.

"The Prophet King imagines," he said, "that his cavern is entirely free from observation. It is not so. It is cut, truly, out of the very bowels of the earth as it were; but it, nevertheless, has an inward outlet. Beyond this cavern, as you know, there is a broad ledge of rock. If you keep straight along this ledge of rock you come to a narrow opening. Entering this, you are, after some time, stopped by the solid rock, or a slab of rock, which appears solid; but which, in reality, is cloven in twain, from its summit to its base. Through this fissure you can see all that passes in the old king's cavern.

"Well," continued Hussein, "through this fissure I have beheld the impostor. As soon as the King and Zuliska began the task of carrying the stranger up to the hut, Ali came and informed me, and we stole together to the post of observation. Scarcely had we reached the spot, when we saw enter the room Cassim. The young man lay upon the bed, and his well-assumed delirium had been allayed by a sleeping draught administered by the old king."

What ensued between Cassim and Abder-Khan was now minutely detailed to the chiefs by Hussein, who proceeded:—

"Cassim, therefore, may, I am assured, be won over to our cause; and if I have your consent I will go this very night and broach to him the subject."

The adhesion of so powerful a chief as Cassim was of course desirable in a conspiracy of the kind now in progress, and the offer of Hussein, therefore was welcomed with acclamations.

"Remain here, then," he said; "I will go at once and inform him of our plans. If he is not with us he will not be against us, for his mind is too noble to allow him to betray us."

He was about to leave the cavern when Ali detained him.

"What now, my friend?" he asked.

Ali put his finger to his lip, to intimate that he wished a private interview.

They stepped out upon the ledge of rock in the bright moonlight, before the mouth of the cave where the faint glimmerings of the fire were just visible, and spoke in low accents.

"You forget one thing, my brother," said Ali.

"What is that?"

"You desire to become king; so does Cassim. How will you identify your interests?"

Hussein smiled.

"Do you imagine," he said, "that I, who am plotting for a kingdom, forget such small links in my chain. Cassim may have the kingdom if he will, but I will soon succeed him. The better way will be to propose an election. I am content to abide by the chance of such an election, among the chiefs, who are nearly all my way of thinking."

"Good Hussein," returned Ali, "since you are provided against the emergency, which certainly seemed to me alarming, I will go in and await your return."

He then re-entered the cavern, and Hussein descended towards the tents.

At the door of Cassim's hut he found him whom he sought. Cassim eyed him with surprise.

They rarely spoke, for they were recognised rivals in the country—rivals in courage—rivals in the field—rivals in their pretensions to the throne.

"Good evening—peace be with you," cried Hussein, as he bowed and advanced.

"What strange change have we here," thought Cassim, who at all times viewed Hussein with suspicion, and who, after his morning's interview with the king, was far from being in the humour to be friendly; "but, no matter what the change is, I must, I suppose, pretend to be his friend, for he is a dangerous foe."

"Good evening, my friend," he said extending his hand; "what brings you to my tent, to-night?"

"A danger which threatens us both," he answered. "Can I enter, or will you rather come to my tent?"

"Let us leave this spot altogether," he said; "let us walk up the mountain's side, where we shall not be overheard. Here, as everywhere else, there are traitors."

They walked up the rugged path, where Cassim's attention was soon attracted to the glimmering light which issued from the Cavern of the Winds.

"What is that?" he asked.

"It is the light of our conference fire," said Hussein; "where we have been discussing this danger."

"What is it?"

"The arrival of an impostor, who claims to be the heir to the throne of Tartary."

Cassim smiled.

"Abder Khan imagines that he has kept this arrival of his son a secret from everyone. How, then, have you learned it?"

Hussein smiled in his turn.

"That," he said, "is *my* secret—one, however, which you shall learn after we have arranged our plans."

"What can there be in common between us?" returned Cassim. "We may confess here where no one can listen, that we are rivals in our pretensions to the throne. How can we, then, act in concert?"

"Easily," said Hussein; "to crush this impostor I am willing to relinquish all my claims."

"Who is to trust you?"

"I will do so publicly in a conference of the chiefs," replied Hussein, "if you refuse to give me credence."

Cassim pressed his hand.

"This is generous—most generous," he said; "but I will not consent to it. We will let them elect their own king, and then, no matter whom that choice may fall upon, we will attack the common enemy. Kill him, but spare the king."

"Agreed," returned Hussein; "we will leave the choice to the chiefs. As for the old king, his time on earth cannot, in ordinary circumstances, be very long. Leave him, therefore, his life; but take his throne. We will call upon him formally to abdicate."

"And when and how do you propose to act against this impostor?"

"That must be decided in the meeting of the chiefs."

"Good."

THE DWARF SUSPECTS MAZEPPA'S CONSTANCY.

"Are you ready to see them now?"

"Quite."

"Then follow me."

Hussein then led the way to the cavern, at the door of which Cassim stopped him.

"Tell me one thing," he said.

"What is that?"

"We can act better if we understand one another thoroughly," he returned. "Do you believe this young man to be an impostor or not?"

"No," said Hussein; "I believe him to be Prince of Tartary!"

---

## CHAPTER XII.

### TWELVE TRAITORS.

THE entrance of Cassim and Hussein was greeted by the chiefs with loud acclamations.

"Welcome, my friends," said the former, who knew himself to be popular, "welcome! In this time of common danger you see I am not long absent from among you."

This *apropos* speech was greeted with another burst of applause which struck to Hussein's heart. He feared to see his rival too popular. He was, however, certain in his own mind of the result of the election if it took place at once; and his alarm, therefore, had no reference to the present.

The conference lasted far into the night.

Hussein proposed instant action.

"Let us go at once into the king's hut," he said, "destroy this usurper, and call upon the imbecile prophet to abdicate his throne at once."

This met no one's approval. In the midst of all, traitors though they might be, there was yet remaining a kind of respect for their king, which forbade the idea of forcibly entering his home and tearing from him what many considered to be his idolised son.

Hussein mistook his audience.

Cassim knew them well, and treated them far differently.

"My brother," he said, "has spoken from his heart, no doubt, and has spoken, too, with wisdom. But let me suggest that the plan he proposes is rash."

"It is, I fear," said Ali.

"It *is*, indeed, my friend," pursued Cassim. "This young man may, after all, be the real son of Abder Khan—he may, in truth, be the long-lost Mazeppa, Prince of Tartary."

Hussein trembled.

"My brother," he said, "is saying dangerous things."

"Not so," returned Cassim, "not so. If he be Mazeppa, what then? Has he not lived away from us twenty years—has he not been bred and educated in Poland? Is he not a Pole in heart if he be a Tartar by blood? Do we want some one on our throne who is the friend of our deadliest foe? Do we wish to see as king of Tartary some one who will deliver us over to slavery? No. Whether this stranger who has come among us shrouded in so much mystery be Mazeppa or not, he must be destroyed for the good of the country. But let us wait."

A burst of applause, in which Hussein joined, followed this speech.

"And now, my brother," said the latter, as he rose when Cassim had completed his speech, "and now there is one thing to be still arranged. Abder Khan will be called to vacate the throne; therefore, we may consider the throne of Tartary vacant. On us, the twelve highest chiefs, devolves the duty of appointing his successor. Let us perform this duty to-night."

A thrill shot through the assembly.

All felt that the next few moments would decide an important question.

"How is this to be decided?" asked Ali.

"The urn—the urn must decide," returned several of the chiefs.

They wished to vote secretly.

Evidently their views had changed.

It was the custom in the Tartar councils to use an urn made of porcelain, with a round hole at the summit. The chiefs were supplied with a flat stone and a round one. The latter denoted assent, the former dissent.

The urn was now produced.

All waited eagerly the names of the candidates.

Ali rose.

"We have here among us," he said, "the two men whose claims to the throne are the greatest of all. Between them we are called upon to choose; their names are Cassim and Hussein. The flat stone shall represent Cassim, the round Hussein—let us proceed to vote."

The assembly was as still as the grave while Ali went round with the urn.

When all had voted Ali took a round stone and placed it in the urn saying,—

"Hussein has been my friend for many years, and, in my own mind, I have ever regarded him as my king. I have no reason to disguise my vote; I give it to Hussein."

The urn was then opened.

There were ten stones in the urn—nine flat, one round.

So, with the exception of Ali, all had voted for Cassim.

A deadly pallor overspread the features of the baffled traitor.

He was too prudent, however, to allow his anger to be seen.

"I congratulate you," he said, grasping Cassim's hands, "you are by unanimous consent King of Tartary. The greatest boon I crave is to be your right hand in peace and war. And now let me ask how long you propose to wait, and what plan you have in view?"

"I propose," said Cassim, "to wait until this young man is recovered from his illness. Let him then show himself and prove his claims. If not, the voice of the people will be against him and the old man upon whom he has imposed. Let this conference be ended for to-night."

The chiefs rose.

They had chosen their king, and they obeyed him.

In a few minutes they had all bade him a respectful adieu, and he stood alone with Hussein.

Ali had descended with the rest.

"Well, my brother," said Hussein, "you have triumphed— a strange triumph, indeed, when it is remembered that I gathered the conference together. I have ripened this plan— I have always been spoken of and treated by those men as their future king. No matter, the victory is yours, and, as I said before, I am willing to accept you."

"That is well and kindly spoken, friend," returned Cassim, who, in reality, saw through the rascal's words and manner completely; "we will work together, and it will be hard indeed, if, between us, we do not crush this foolish boy, whose father must be truly mad, if he imagines that Tartary will accept him for its king. Adieu—to-morrow in my tent, I shall be glad to see you."

He then withdrew and passed down the mountain path with a firm and haughty step.

"Fool!" muttered Hussein, "can he dream that I shall tamely submit to be his tool? Fool, too, that I am, to have brought him to the council, instead of hurling him over the rocks as we walked to it together."

He stood in the moonlight, gazing with bitter hate at the retreating form of his rival.

Then suddenly a deadly design entered his mind.

If Cassim were dead, he alone would be the person to take the reins of sovereignty.

If, moreover, he died at this period suddenly it would raise the question, and enable him to proclaim to the people the presence of Mazeppa in the king's tent.

So, with this deadly purpose in his heart, he descended the rocks and entered amid the rude village of the Tartars.

Moonlight slept amid the tents, and on the dusky slopes of the mountains. It filtered in patches on the floor through the trees; it lay boldly and broadly on the plain; it crept stealthily into the nooks and crannies of the rocks, and danced amid the foam of the torrents. It nestled amid the wild flowers, and sparkled from the spear-heads of sentinel warriors—it cast a holy light over all things, yet it softened not the man of crime as he stalked on towards his sin.

He advanced almost as noiselessly as the moonbeams, keeping watch on all sides, lest any man might see his face, and tell of it on the morrow.

His heart beat wildly—not because he was thinking of his intended crime, but of the glory it would bring on him, and the chance, after all, of being hindered in its execution.

He hoped to reach the tent before Cassim arrived, and stab him in the back as he entered.

But he was foiled.

Cassim had hastened home far more rapidly than was his wont, and had already thrown himself upon his bed.

All was still, and Hussein peered into the darkness like a spirit of evil.

Cassim slept.

Like a true soldier, he had the power, as it were, of commanding sleep, and could fall into a slumber at a moment's notice.

Hussein crept in.

"He sleeps," he murmured, as he drew his dagger—"he has lived his last."

The tent of the royal chief—for so we may truly term Cassim—was divided into two compartments.

The front compartment was inhabited by Cassim, the back compartment being occupied by his wife and daughter.

The husband thus kept guard over those he loved.

The beautiful Circassian, whom time had dealt leniently with, and who really appeared more like the sister than the mother of Zuliska, was lying on her bed with her head reclining on her hand, which tapered gracefully from her exquisitely-rounded and alabaster arm.

Hair black as night fell in luxuriant curls around her exquisitely-formed shoulders.

Her eyes, large, languishing, and bright still with unimpaired brilliance, were fixed with a pensive glance upon her daughter, who, crouched upon a divan by the side of the bed, was also wrapt in thought.

Suddenly the Circassian spoke.

"Zuliska, my dear child," she said, "can you tell me what ails your father?"

Zuliska sighed heavily.

"Alas!" she said, "I know too well."

"Does danger threaten him?"

"Yes—and no, I may answer, dear mother."

"You speak in enigmas, dear child. Can you not trust me?"

Zuliska smiled.

"You are my mother," she said, "and I should trust you even if I did not wish to do so; but in this case I hold another's secret. Has my father told you aught of a young stranger who has come among our tents?"

"Yes, he told me a story; but how far it is right I cannot say, for he has reserved much, I am certain, from his manner."

Zuliska, having thus an excuse, began her story, and told it to the end.

The mother listened with a smile.

The young girl did not express in words her sudden and growing love for the Prince of Tartary and the decline of her affection for Abdallah; but the glowing tones in which she spoke of the stranger sufficiently proved the fact.

When she had completed her narrative her mother patted her head.

"This stranger has fascinated you, I fear," she said.

"Oh, no, mother."

But as she spoke she blushed deeply.

The Circassian laughed.

"Well—well, Zuliska," she said, "we will not discuss that question, but will leave it to time and Abdallah to discover. Your father has always disliked Abdallah, and would doubtless smile on this stranger."

Zuliska's eyes filled with tears.

"Alas! no," she said, "my father already hates Mazeppa, and is plotting his destruction. He told the Prophet King this morning, that he disbelieved in the identity of this stranger, and to-night I saw him with Hussein, in friendly converse."

The Circassian trembled.

"What mean you?" she said; "you surely cannot intend me to understand that your father would aid in murdering this stranger, in order to obtain the throne."

"I do," returned Zuliska, firmly, "ambition has changed his character."

There was a moment's silence.

Then both started

The silence was so intense that they could hear the regular breathing of Cassim.

Then came a scraping noise, and the canvas of the tent shook.

A dread presentiment seized on Zuliska's mind, and she started up and rushed to the door.

On opening this she paused not an instant, but darted in.

Then her mother heard a sharp cry, a muttered curse, and Zuliska's voice calling for help.

---

## CHAPTER XIII.

### THE DOOM OF A TRAITOR.

THE cry and the noise of the fall aroused Cassim.

He rose instantly, for he slept the light sleep of the soldier; and gazed for a moment in utter bewilderment at the scene before him.

Hussein was standing, dagger in hand, near his couch, or rather half leaning forward; while Zuliska, still grasping his wrist, was lying upon the floor, with one hand pressed over her breast, as if still feeling the pain of a blow.

Her mother was crossing rapidly from the inner room.

"Villain! what means this outrage?" cried Cassim, as he seized Hussein's wrist, while the Circassian raised her half-fainting daughter from the ground.

Hussein smiled as he placed his poignard in its sheath.

"You are hasty, my brother," he said; "hard words are easily said, but not so easily recalled."

"They need no recall," exclaimed Cassim, fiercely. "With my own eyes I have seen your villany and cowardice. I have seen my daughter lying at your feet, struck down by a treacherous blow. This night must see either my blood or your blood flow."

Hussein trembled.

Not with the the fear of death.

No—villain as he was, he did not dread the contest; his heart was no prey to cowardice. He remembered only that a feud between himself and Cassim might be the ruin of all his plans.

"Of what am I accused?" he asked, with proud disdain; "and by whom? You cannot accuse me yourself, for you were buried in sleep when I entered."

"Why are you here—can you explain that?"

"I can."

"Do so then at once; for I am impatient."

"You know the result of the conference?"

"I do."

"You are aware of my last words?"

"I am," returned Cassim, who saw that he was striving to delay, that he might invent some tale.

"I came, then," continued Hussein, "to tell you something which neutralised the whole affair."

"And this was?"

"I refuse to tell."

"It is false," cried Cassim; "why did you steal into my tent? Why was my daughter lying at your feet? Why was your dagger in your hand?"

"Let him not answer—do not believe him," cried Zuliska, starting forward. "I can tell all. He crept into our tent by night, that he might destroy you—I saw him leaning over you in your sleep—I saw the gleam of his dagger—and I rushed forward in time to stay his hand. He is a traitor—a murderer—a perjured wretch, who would lead you to destruction."

Cassim waited to hear no more.

His sword was already unsheathed, and calling upon his adversary to keep on his guard, he went with him outside the tent.

In those days, and in those localities, people waited not for seconds to watch the result of a combat; and in the bright moon-light, therefore, the swords were drawn and the fight commenced.

The clang of steel soon attracted a circle of warriors.

The combatants were silent.

Not so the spectators.

Various were the surmises ventured as to the cause of the conflict.

Among some, and these the most numerous, it was regarded as the vent of a private and sudden quarrel; by a few who had assisted at the secret conference in the Cavern of the Winds it was looked upon as the result, on Hussein's part, of disappointed ambition.

No one interfered.

In those times justice was distributed in a curious manner.

The cause of the victor, whoever he might be, was the cause of justice.

The combatants fought well.

They were both skilled in the arts of war—both were tried chieftains—both had given unnumbered proofs of tact and courage.

The contest did not, however, last as long as might have been expected.

Hussein's courage and skill were great, but they were not a match for the coolness and determination of Cassim, who fought for revenge as well as for honour.

A rash thrust was the signal for a skilful parry, and in a moment after the sword of Cassim gleamed through the moon-light and passed through the body of his adversary.

With a bitter curse upon his lips, Hussein fell to the earth.

A few indistinct words and a gurgling noise then escaped his lips, and in a few moments all was over.

In a few words Cassim explained to the Tartars around him the cause of the quarrel, and in less than half an hour the body of Hussein had been conveyed to his tent, and the place had resumed its ordinary appearance of quietude.

On the following morning Zuliska took her way as usual towards the home of the Prophet King.

Abder Khan welcomed her with a smile of gladness.

"You seemed pleased, my lord, this morning," she cried, as he kissed her brow; "is the prince better?"

"He is, indeed—his delirium is gone—a few days will see him in possession of perfect strength."

"I, too, have good news," returned Zuliska; "Hussein is dead."

Abder Khan glanced at her in incredulous astonishment.

"Dead!" he said; "it was but yesterday he was plotting against my life."

"True; but since yesterday strange events have happened."

She then narrated to him the treachery of Hussein, and the punishment he had received at her father's hands.

"Heaven is just," cried Abder Khan, when she had finished her story. "It has before protected my son from the anger of tyrants and the fierceness of wild beasts, and it has now protected him from the treachery of enemies. Mazeppa is now sleeping; come, and I will tell you his story, which is almost fabulous in its wildness and its horror."

Zuliska sat with eager eyes and open mouth while Abder Khan told the wonderful story of Mazeppa's wild ride from the Polish castle to the steppes of the Ukraine.

Her bosom heaved with terrible emotion when he spoke of Theresa and the deep love for her which had been Mazeppa's ruin.

Young as the prince was, she had imagined that his heart would be free; and her soul sank within her as she heard that his fearful ordeal had been the result of his deep passion for another.

When the king had finished his recital, she sat with clasped hands, and in deep silence.

Abder Khan attributed her agitation to the terror inspired by his narrative.

"I wonder not at your emotion, my child," he said; "the tale, is, indeed, a fearful one. But we will have a deadly revenge."

"Upon the Castellan?"

"Yes," cried Abder Khan; "upon him and his perfidious daughter."

"Do you, then, believe that she betrayed you son?"

"No; not absolutely betrayed him; but I believe her to have been the cause of his ordeal."

"And how so? What makes you think so?"

"Because I think it was she who poisoned the Count Palatine."

Zuliska thought a moment.

Her woman's breast was at war with itself. By favouring this idea she might secure Mazeppa to herself; but she had formed in her own mind a far different opinion, and justice would not permit her to do other than proclaim it.

"I fear, my lord," she said, "that your anger has carried you away."

The king smiled.

Who would not have smiled, too, if he had seen that aged man, with long white locks, listening to his youthful and beautiful counsellor?

"My dear child," he said, "perhaps my anger has done so. Tell me, what is your reason for saying so?"

"I believe the Lady Theresa innocent."

"Who, then, is guilty?"

"Zisko."

"Zisko!"

"Yes; this dwarf, whose friendship for your son was of so sudden a nature."

"And why think of him as the poisoner?"

"Because he is evidently, from what your son has told you, one of those impulsive, reckless, unscrupulous characters who would do anything for the person whose cause had been espoused in consequence of some great service. Mazeppa saved the dwarf's life; the dwarf previously had ever borne the character of a mischievous, ill-natured, evil-disposed being; he acts, therefore, according to his character, and recklessly removes all obstacles from your son's path."

The old king pondered for a moment.

"You are right," he said, "the Lady Theresa is doubtless innocent; yet I should scarcely wish to see my son the husband of a Polish maiden."

"The Poles are our natural enemies," said Zuliska. "After all the terrible dangers he has passed through he will scarcely wish to be her husband. Such a fearful trial as he has endured is enough to cool the most ardent love."

She scarcely reckoned Mazeppa's love by her own.

Would she have been induced by any trial, however terrible, to give up her heart's idol?

Besides, was not Mazeppa's love the growth of years, and was not hers but the growth of days?

"You are wrong Zuliska," said Abder Khan; his "trials and privations seem only to have increased his love for this girl. I cannot gainsay anything which is wished by the son whom Heaven has so mysteriously restored to me. If, therefore, he desires to marry this woman, he shall do so, although I have wished to see him wedded to you."

The girl trembled, but did not reply.

"You, perhaps, will not be sorry," proceeded Abder Khan; "nor will Abdallah, I am certain."

He then rose, and led the young Circassian into the room where Mazeppa was still sleeping.

The slight noise made by the creaking of the door roused him, and he half rose and glanced round him.

His eyes remained fixed for a moment upon Zuliska.

Then a faint smile stole over his lips.

"Who is this angel?" he said; "methinks I have seen her before."

"You have, my son," returned Abder Khan. "It is to her you owe your life and your kingdom; for she it was who found you, and helped to bring you hither."

"I owe my life, then, to a maiden of exquisite loveliness," he returned. "Were Theresa here, I fear me she would be likely to be jealous."

Zuliska smiled sadly, but the proud blood of her race found for her her answer.

"The Lady Theresa would have no reason to be jealous of me," she said, "since I am the betrothed of another. Mazeppa may be my beloved brother, but that is all."

Mazeppa smiled too, but it was scarcely from the same cause as that which induced her.

"Your lover shall be my greatest friend," he said. "To you I owe my life, and he, whoever he may be, is entitled to my friendship and esteem."

## CHAPTER XIV.

### THE ABDICATION.

FOUR days after the visit of Zuliska to the Prophet King described above, Mazeppa was sufficiently recovered to be presented to the people.

The report had spread that the king's son had returned, and was ill in his tent; and it was not, therefore, matter of great surprise when one morning Abder Khan called together a council of chiefs for the purpose of presenting Mazeppa to them.

The young prince entered the council chamber dressed in the full costume of a Tartar chief.

His face was still pale, but he looked strikingly handsome, nevertheless, and a burst of admiration broke from every side as he entered.

The old king leaned on his arm.

"This, chieftains," said he, "is my son—the heir to the throne of Tartary. I am glad you thus welcome him. Listen while I unfold to you his story."

The chiefs listened in wonder and anger to the king's recital.

The council consisted of a hundred of the noblest Tartars, and included but few of those who had formed the treacherous meeting to which Cassim had been introduced by Hussein.

When Abder Khan had finished a thrill of indignation ran through the assembly, and one of the chiefs rose.

"Abder Khan," he cried, "you see surrounding you the faithful chiefs of your race. The Polish Castellan, by his insult to Prince Mazeppa, has insulted us and you, and we are ready to march against him and destroy him."

The old king smiled.

"Good," he said; "it rejoices my heart to hear you thus address me. I have spoken of a war that was coming soon upon us, though I could not say from whence. It is coming now. With our armies we will descend upon this castle and destroy it, and wash out in blood the insult laid upon our country."

"We will!" cried the savage chiefs, as they clanged together their weapons.

"But I," continued the old king, "am too aged to lead you into battle. I am weary of the trials and fatigues of government, and here, before this solemn conclave, I abdicate my crown in favour of my dearly beloved son Mazeppa."

So saying, he took the crown from his head, and placed it on that of Mazeppa,

A shout of enthusiasm burst from every lip, and Mazeppa, when silence was once more restored, rose and spoke.

"Chieftains," he cried, "what my feelings are I cannot

MAZEPPA ASSERTS HIS TRUTHFULNESS TO THERESA.

describe. Brought hither among you by a wonderful inter-position of Providence to a father and a throne, when I only expected death, I can scarcely understand my own position. But I have learned from your words and your enthusiasm that you are as eager as I am to avenge this insult to our country. We will march upon our common foe and destroy him. Not a stone in his castle shall stand upon another; we will raze it to the ground, and grass shall grow upon his hearth.''

Loud murmurs of applause followed this speech, and after arranging the details of the campaign the conference sepa-rated.

It was a week after this that the plains presented a strange and bewildering spectacle.

Early in the morning the warriors had left their tents, and joined together in a variety of groups.

Here and there over the plains lofty poles had been stuck in the earth, and from their summits waved flags of various colours, denoting the starting point of the different leaders.

Ere the sun was high in the heavens masses of armed men were moving about over the plains.

As each body received all its members it passed over the hills and remained on the opposite side.

This continued during the whole day, and in the evening, just as the sun was setting, a vast and glittering array passed across the Dnieper, and took its way towards the forests of Podolia.

It was a magnificent sight to see those thousands of men, clad in bright dresses, with glittering lances and axes, and mounted on superb and wildly prancing steeds.

Long did the Tartar wives and mothers linger and gaze after them. Not till the last horseman had disappeared in the shadowy horizon did they return to their tents—some to weep, some to pray.

In the van rode Mazeppa, side by side with his father, whose youth seemed, indeed, to have returned to him, as he sat proudly on his splendid horse, clad in his brilliant dress.

Just as the shades of night had fallen over the country, and the Tartars were still pressing eagerly forward, Cassim approached with another horseman.

"My lord," he said, addressing himself to Mazeppa, "can I have speech with you for a moment?"

"Yes, certainly, Cassim," cried the young king. "Can I be of service to you in any way?"

"Yes, my lord," answered the chief. "I have to recom-mend to your notice a young warrior, now with me, who is most anxious to be near your person."

Mazeppa gazed curiously at the young Tartar.

As far as he could distinguish in the moonlight, the aspirant was very youthful and handsome. He did not, however, scrutinise him much. Had he done so he would have per-ceived, from the roundness of the limbs and the swell of the bosom, that it was a woman.

A woman whose mad passion had induced her to brave the horrors of a rude campaign—to enter the ranks amid thou-sands of rough and untutored warriors.

Need we say it was Zuliska?

"Well, young man," said Mazeppa, in a voice expressive of some curiosity, "may I ask the reason of your great desire to be near me?"

The girl blushed.

"I have dreamed," she said, in a soft and melodious voice, "I have dreamed a strange and wonderful dream."

"And what was it?"

"I have dreamed that I was your favourite officer, and that I twice saved your life."

"And you believe this dream?"

"As to the first, that is a matter of the future; as to the second, I do believe it."

"Well, what is your name?"

"Selim."

"Good. Then, Selim, you shall be with me as you wish. Recommended by Cassim, how could it be otherwise? Remain, therefore, always near me; and rest assured that if you are made the instrument of heaven in saving my life, my gratitude will be unbounded; you shall ask your own reward."

"My lord, you are most gracious," murmured the girl. "You raise in my mind great hopes for the future."

"The realisation of which is in your own hands," added Mazeppa.

"Would it were so," murmured Zuliska, as she took her place just behind the young king.

"When do you expect to reach the castle, my lord?" asked Cassim.

"I scarcely know," returned Mazeppa; "I have no means of calculating. My first journey was so wild and rapid, that I could form no idea of time or distance. I suppose we may reckon on arriving there in about five or six days."

Cassim mused a moment.

"Proceeding as we are now proceeding," he said at length, "and halting the necessary time to rest the horses, it will take us ten or twelve days, I should think, at least."

"So long!" cried Mazeppa, in amazement.

"Yes, indeed. Your horse bore you on unceasingly until he fell dead from exhaustion, never stopping to take food or rest. We—who have to fight a great battle at our journey's end—cannot waste the strength of our animals or of ourselves, but must arrive before the castle fresh and ready for action."

"True—true," said the young prince, smiling; "I had forgotten that we ever rested. My impatience even now is so great that, were it not from fear we should arrive at our journey's end too fatigued, I should be inclined to press forward, and never once stop to rest. But it would be imprudent, and I must restrain my eagerness."

"Say but the word, my lord, and every man will be as anxious as yourself to push onwards unceasingly. But if you will take my advice we will proceed slowly, keeping in the forests by day when we near the castle, in order to conceal ourselves from the peasantry, who might otherwise carry news to the Castellan of our approach."

"Cassim is right, and counsels prudently," said Abder Khan, who had drawn near them during the latter part of this colloquy. "Our steps must be stealthy at first, though we may burst like a thunderclap upon them in the end."

To describe the march would be tedious and useless.

It was the same thing every day and night, until they reached the huge forests of Podolia.

Then, following Cassim's advice, Mazeppa concealed his army during the day, and advanced only under cover of the darkness.

It was on the eleventh night that they crept up to the very walls of the Castle of Laurinski.

Their movements had been so noiseless that they had certainly the right to believe that their approach had been unsuspected.

But it was not so.

Lights gleamed in every window of the castle.

The flash of steel appeared along the terrace and the battlements. The moat had been widened, and filled afresh with water; the drawbridge had been removed entirely, and a heavy barricade was in its place.

Mazeppa gazed with anger at these preparations for defence.

"What can this mean?" he said, turning to Cassim; "have we a traitor in the camp?"

"I trust not, my lord," returned Cassim, with a troubled countenance: "I hope there lives not a Tartar who would betray his race to the Poles."

Somehow or another Mazeppa suspected Cassim.

Yet without cause.

Since the death of Hussein the band of conspirators had been broken up, and Cassim had entirely discarded his original plan of action.

The desire of his life had been to be recognised as one of the royal families of Tartary; but now that the young heir to the throne had returned, and the people had shown themselves enthusiastic in his favour, his mind cast aside at once all thoughts of empire, and settled itself to the carrying out of a far more feasible plot.

This plot had for its object the union of Mazeppa and Zuliska.

It was with unfeigned pleasure, therefore, that he learned how far the young prince had already made way in the affections of his daughter. He at once encouraged her to cast off Abdallah, who so long and so patiently had loved her; and the young girl, under his influence, once more gave herself up to her passion for Mazeppa, and indulged again in the hope of winning him to herself, in spite of the fact that he was even then preparing to march against the Castle of Laurinski, to wrest his bride from the hands of her friends and his enemies.

It was with the most unbounded delight that Zuliska received the intelligence that her father desired her to accompany the expedition in the disguise of a young warrior.

It was a plan which, among her many wild dreams, had suggested itself to her; and but for the many difficulties in the way of its accomplishment she would have carried it out without her father's concurrence, had he refused.

For she knew no fear.

Love never does.

Cassim, then, was no traitor; and Mazeppa, in his own mind, accused him unjustly. But he had heard several hints from the old king—slight hints, indeed, but still sufficient to produce an unpleasant feeling in his brain.

When he spoke of a traitor in the camp, therefore, he almost felt inclined to name Cassim in the first moment of his fierce indignation. But a short reflection proved to him how suicidal it would be to procure his settled enmity, even were he truly a traitor; and he determined, for a time, at least, therefore, to dissemble his sentiments.

---

## CHAPTER XV.

### THERESA IN PRISON.

As soon as Mazeppa had fairly been launched from the castle, on the wild horse, the Castellan had directed his attention to the safe custody of his daughter, and the disposal of the Count Palatine's body.

Two days after the death of Stanislaus, Zeminski, the faithful friend of Mazeppa, was shot, and on the same morning the body of the poisoned man was carried in solemn state to the castle of his ancestors, where it was received by his brother.

The fiery and enraged Pole at first seemed inclined to vent his anger on the Castellan; but on learning the terrible vengeance he had wreaked upon the supposed murderer, his passion turned to grief.

He, however, was less unreasonable than the Castellan.

He was anxious to have the murderer punished, but he desired the real and not the supposed one to receive chastisement.

"You say," he said, "that this page was in a prison—in a dungeon—when my brother was poisoned?"

"Yes—he was."

"How, then, could he have done this horrid deed?"

"He, of course, did not commit it with his own hands. He employed another."

"That other, then, remains to be found?"

"The one I suspect is already dead."

"Who was he?"

"Zeminski, who for years had been my trusted servant,

and who betrayed me. He was shot in my courtyard this morning."

On his way home the Castellan occupied himself with the future of his daughter.

Not in his wildest dream did he imagine that Mazeppa could escape from the wild horse. But he regarded Theresa as the author of the evil which had befallen him, and he resolved, while punishing her, to prevent the possibility of her ever again losing her heart, or, as he expressed it, " bestowing it on a low-born menial."

As soon as he arrived at the castle, he went to his daughter's room.

When he entered he found her seated on a divan, in a paroxysm of grief.

Her hair was dishevelled, and hanging in wild masses over her shoulders; her eyes were red with weeping; her bosom was heaving with emotion, and her hands were wildly clasped together.

Zenitha, who had been pardoned by the Castellan in some unaccountable fit of leniency, had just been speaking to her of Mazeppa, and the mention of his name, and his terrible fate, had renewed all her grief.

" What ails you, Theresa?" asked the Castellan, sternly. " Are you mourning for the great crime which has cast a slur upon our house?"

" Yes, my lord—I am."

" You then regret the death of Stanislaus?"

Theresa looked up in stern sorrow.

" No, my lord," she said; " I think not of him, but of Mazeppa, and the crime committed by you in sending him forth from your house, naked and helpless, to become the prey of wild beasts, and be a lasting disgrace to your name."

The Castellan was so confounded by this bold speech, that for a few moments he could not speak.

At length his fury burst forth.

" What, proud, ungrateful girl!" he cried, " do you dare to accuse me of a crime?"

" I do, my father," she said; " before heaven you are guilty. Why should I say you are innocent!"

" You shall rue this boldness, minion," cried the Castellan fiercely; " here in close confinement you shall remain until your proud spirit is broken, or at any rate until I find some noble who will take you off my hands, and who will be ready to tame you."

" Fear not, my lord," said Theresa, quietly, " I shall soon be tamed. Death will come to me—a welcome refuge from your tyranny and my own sorrow. Day and night a phantom haunts me—the phantom of a young, brave, and noble youth, who fell a victim to your cruelty, and the base treachery of others. Do you not think, then, that seeing this, day and night, I pray day and night for release? Place me in durance if you will; but think not it is a punishment. Were it not so I would refuse to see the faces of men and women who had tacitly helped you in your malice and your crime."

The Castellan paced the room in wild and almost ungovernable passion.

" By Heavens!" he cried " I warn you not to provoke me too far."

Theresa smiled.

" Any provocation of mine," she said, " could but obtain for me death at your hands—a death that would indeed be welcome. Therefore I fear nothing; so do not attempt to frighten me into submission. I will remain here till the day of my death, if you wish it, more gladly, because I can mourn my lost love without being insulted by the notice of others."

The Castellan said no more; but hastily quitted the room.

From this time Theresa was a prisoner—but a prisoner quite willing to remain.

Her doors were closely bolted and barred upon her; but she never once attempted to pass through them. She remained in her bedroom sorrowing always—wasting each day, each hour—becoming but the shadow and the remembrance of what she once had been.

Yet there was a strange fatality in her love.

Something or another seemed to tell her she would one day see Mazeppa again, and this hope—wild—absurd—unsupported by probability as it was—served to sustain her existence.

In this hope she was kept also by Zisko the dwarf, who roamed through the castle unsuspected, and at length obtained the post he had long coveted—that of attendant upon the Lady Theresa.

It was Zisko, then, who brought to her her meals, and Zisko who beguiled many a tedious hour by relating tales of wonderful escapes and supporting her by wild and improbable surmises.

Zisko was a strange being—a mixture of good and evil seldom to be met with.

He had been brought up in misery, and nurtured in ridicule—had been the butt for all the vicious propensities of every rascal in the village—had been kicked and cuffed from the door of the Count Palatine, and had been received into the Castellan's household as a stray dog might have been received.

While there he had been true and faithful, but had received no reward—no thanks.

And his faithfulness was like that of an animal—he was given no education; his mind was quite obtuse—his feelings were blunted—he scarcely knew good from evil.

He had half-throttled Neida, without meaning to kill her; but his mind was in no degree horrified when he learned she was dead.

He had poisoned Stanislaus Count Palatine, because he thought he was serving Mazeppa.

Mazeppa, having once done him a service—a service rendered as from one man to another—had enrolled thereby among his friends one who was totally unscrupulous, be it said, but one, nevertheless, who would never desert him.

The words of Neida, vague and indistinct as they had been, had left an impression on the dwarf's mind that Mazeppa was destined to live and be one day a great man.

Though he had seen him, therefore, bound naked upon the back of the wild steed—though he had seen the untamed and desperate animal plunge away with him into the dark forest—he would not believe in his death.

He was speaking of him on one occasion to Theresa.

She took his rough uncouth hand in her's.

" Zisko," she said, " why this wild hope?"

" Because I have faith in his destiny."

" You almost make me hope."

Zisko smiled.

" I hope so," he said; " but stay, I will tell you more."

" What—what can you tell that will give me real hope?"

" If the wild horse had been dashed to pieces, his mangled body would have been found."

" True; but the wild beasts."

The dwarf smiled again.

" Wolves don't eat bones," he said; " there would at least be two skeletons left to tell the tale."

Theresa shuddered at the dreadful picture; but the dwarf continued,—

" For two days I have followed in their track. There was a line of wildly prancing hoofs; but no stoppage. Out along the broad plains I glanced. What was there to cause his death out in those boundless solitudes? No—no. The horse has rushed onwards to his home amid the wild steppes of Tartary, and will die of exhaustion. Then Mazeppa can break his bonds and be free."

Theresa trembled.

" But he is naked—with no food to eat—no weapon to defend him."

" He is a Tartar—he will meet with those who will feed and clothe him."

" Alas! yes," thought Theresa, in the selfishness of love, " and forget me."

It was not a month after the departure of Mazeppa that Zisko appeared one evening on the threshold with disordered looks as if he had run a long distance, and with a finger on his lip, as if enjoining caution.

He came in and closed the door noiselessly behind him.

Theresa's heart bounded, and with brightened eyes and heaving bosom she sprang towards him.

" What have you to tell?" she cried.

" Hush," he said, " be calm. Let not the walls hear. Nerve yourself to hear great news."

Theresa trembled the more.

" I know what you have to tell," she exclaimed; " Mazeppa lives."

" He does," whispered the dwarf; " but be calm, betray him not."

" You are not deceiving me? Tell me, how have you learned this?"

" To-day I went to my usual post of observation. Along the plains moved a huge and undulating mass of horses and men with bright banners and glittering spears. They marched on steadily, silently, over the plains, and in the van rode three men."

" And among them?"

" Mazeppa."

Theresa clasped her hands wildly together, and looked upwards.

" Oh, heavens, I thank thee!" she murmured.

Then, turning to Zisko, she added—" You are certain that you are not in error?"

" No, no. I saw him; I knew his face well, although he was dressed in bright and warlike array. He is evidently the leader of the hostile forces, for all seem to regard him as such."

" Why did you not speak with him?"

" Because I hastened to you with the glad tidings. This night, however, I will meet him, and give him news of you."

Theresa was silent for a few moments; then she said—

" Give him this cross;—tell him that upon this cross I have pledged my love to him. Tell him I have mourned him long and hopelessly, thinking I should never meet him but in heaven. Now, however, my heart is gladdened by the welcome tidings of his return, and my heart pants to see him. Let him rescue me from my confinement, and I will fly with him to any point upon the earth."

She extended to him, as she spoke, a small diamond cross, which Zisko took; and, after pressing it to his lips, darted from the room.

It was about eleven that night that Mazeppa was taking a nap in his tent, preparatory to the grand attack on the castle, which was to be made with the first glimmerings of the dawn.

At his side stood a young warrior, leaning on his lance.

This was Zuliska.

Faithful to her promise to guard over him, she would allow none to watch over him while he slept.

The moon shone brightly over the forest, and here and there illumined the clearings, and filtered in patches through the trees.

Towards the tent a form came creeping, through the darkness, through the moonlight—while the prince was still and sleeping, in the first watches of the night.

He was close to the young guard ere she was aware of his presence.

She seized his arm.

" Who is this?" she cried.

" Zisko."

" You cannot enter here," she answered.

She knew the name, and feared some message from Theresa.

The sound awakened Mazeppa, who sprang up from his couch.

" Ah, Zisko!" he cried, " they have, then, spared you? How is Theresa—is she well—does she still love me?"

Zuliska pressed her hand in agony over her heart, while the dwarf, advancing with his grim smile, presented to the Tartar prince the diamond cross.

## CHAPTER XVI.

### LOVE'S PENALTIES.

WITH an expression of amazement Zuliska beheld the prince receive the diamond cross, and as he fervently pressed it to his lips a shadow of indescribable agony crossed her face, which instantly attracted the attention of the dwarf, and aroused in his mind a suspicion of the sex of the mailed form attending Mazeppa.

A malicious twinkle lit up Zisko's eyes, as, with an apparent carelessness he watched Zuliska retire from Mazeppa, and turn her face from the unwelcome intruder.

" Sent she no message?" asked Mazeppa with eagerness, of the bearer of the diamond cross, who still stood with eyes fixed upon the movements of Zuliska. " Does she love me still, Zisko?"

The tone and import of this question made Zuliska look anxiously round, while Zisko, ere he answered, turned his eyes sharply towards her, and read in one look the secret of her sex; shrewdly guessing the feelings she entertained towards his benefactor and friend. Quick as lightning the thought flashed across his mind that Mazeppa knew it all; and in his new love for this disguised companion he had grown careless of the affection of Theresa.

Mazeppa saw a flush of indignation darken Zisko's brow, and as he still remain silent, the prince's heart sank within him; a doubt of Theresa's faithlessness weighed upon his mind, and a sadness of feeling came over him which paralysed his tongue and racked his brain with torturing fears.

Thus stood the three actors in this extraordinary scene, each a problem to the other. Mazeppa doubted Theresa.

The dwarf believed in the prince's perfidy.

Zuliska feared the one she so madly idolised, and loathed the ill-proportioned being who, in a few moments, had brought a dark cloud over her brightest hopes, and turned her certain bliss into a chaos of fear and doubt.

In her soul she cursed, with her bitterest curse, the wretch who had dashed the cup from her lips, and left her a prey to despair.

What is love without hope?

Oh! what an awful feeling is that, when the young aspiring soul, teeming with overflowing love, delirious with hope, and mad with the wild joys of inspired imagination, dreaming the sweet visions of life's sojourn with its worshipped idol, finds that idol a mockery; or, more bitter still, that the idol is real, but another's!

Death seems a welcome visitor, and to that fever of the troubled heart and brain there seems but one envied sleep—the long, quiet rest of the tomb.

Zuliska's feelings lent an unusual lustre to her beautiful eyes; but there was a look of the most abject misery engraven in unchangeable intensity on her features, as she gazed in a half-dreamy state at the silent dwarf, awaiting his dreaded response, which she feared to hear, yet anxiously listened for.

Zisko at last broke silence.

He turned towards Mazeppa, who still held the cross before him with his eyes riveted on it, while memory led his willing thoughts through scenes long past.

" Theresa bade me tell you," said the dwarf, " that the diamond cross would be to you a sign—" And here he paused, as again his searching eye caught the fixed expression of Mazeppa's attendant.

" A sign of what?" asked Mazeppa, impatiently. " Come, tell me quickly why Theresa sent this token—for token it must be—either of love, or,"— he stopped.

" Or what?" said Zisko.

" Or memory," replied the prince, slowly, and with a sigh which brought Zuliska again near him, for neither dress nor position could prevent the workings of her jealous nature.

Again Zisko watched her countenance.

Again he felt convinced it was a woman, and that the prince knew well his attendant was an accepted rival of the fair Theresa.

" I think a token of love," quietly said the messenger; but with such emphasis, that he sent each word like a barbed arrow into the core of Zuliska's heart. And then, as if with a sudden determination to put Mazeppa to a test, and draw from him a confession of his faithlessness, he said—

" Theresa charged me to tell you that which I cannot tell you here; we must be alone; it were not prudent I should tell you now. The night is lovely. If you will accompany me a short distance—as I must now return—I will tell you all."

THE UNEXPECTED SENTINEL.

"I will willingly do so," said the prince, rising and throwing around him a large fur which enveloped his whole frame; "but you need not fear to tell me here."

Zisko led the way, and Mazeppa followed him out into the wood. Zuliska watched him go, begging she might accompany him, in case of danger.

"No" was the only reply she received; and in that one word there was a world of mystery.

Willingly would she have risked her life—anything but Mazeppa's displeasure—to have followed and heard that message which to him seemed the wish of his life; but to her, dreaded as a message of death.

Brightly shone the clear, pale moon, silvering the trees, and casting on the sward the shadows of the noble figure of the prince and his short, grotesque-looking companion.

For some moments they walked in silence.

Theresa's ambassador doubted still if he should serve his mistress by truth or deception; he scarcely knew whether it were better he should deliver her burning words of love and devotion, or forge a tale to give her time to prove the being whom she so wildly worshipped, but whom Zisko half-doubted still.

"Come," said Mazeppa, "I am eager to know what my beloved Theresa bade you deliver with this welcome emblem. Does she love me still, Zisko? Come, tell me that, and I will listen then with patience."

"Do you still love Theresa?" asked the dwarf, evasively.

"I do, with all my soul! More dearly now than ever," was the impulsive reply. "Give me but the same answer with as much truth, and I shall be happy. You, Zisko, know well if Theresa still is mine. That I must know, and at once."

The dwarf looked up in Mazeppa's face, and as the moon's bright beams fell upon his handsome features, Zisko turned round to him, and seizing his hand, was about to speak, when suddenly a dark shadow fell across their path, and they both started simultaneously, but looking round, could not see any living thing; not a sound could be heard save the sighing wind moaning through the upper boughs of the tall trees.

Each looked at the other inquiringly in the face, and Mazeppa was about to speak, when a sudden and rapid rustling was heard among a large heap of leaves and underwood about fifty yards from where they stood.

They moved to the side of a stout old tree, which entirely hid them from the moon, and prevented their shadows being seen; then carefully taking a survey, and looking in vain, the prince stepped forward and was again about to speak to Zisko, when the loud ring of fire-arms rang through their ears, and Mazeppa fell to the ground with a suppressed groan.

"Good heavens!" cried his companion, "what enemies can we have here?"

A loud roar shook the very trees, as an echo to another report of a musket, when a huge bear darted by with a bound that startled the fear-stricken companions, and quickly after the monster came one of Mazeppa's followers.

"Help!" shouted the dwarf, running towards the new-comer.

The step was a rash one, for the pursuer again levelled his musket at the sudden challenger, saying,—

No. 5.

"Who are you, and why are you here at this hour? Speak, or in one moment I will shoot you too."

"Help for Mazeppa!" shrieked Zisko, half-mad with fear. The word was magic.

"Mazeppa!" said Cassim, with surprise; "what help for him? Where is he?"

"Come quickly—follow me. The prince is shot in the shoulder by your first fire, and lies bleeding under yonder tree," stammered out the dwarf, as he led the way.

Cassim hastily followed, anxious for the prince's safety, and terrified at the result of his pursuit of a large bear he had been tracking for some hours.

"Heaven save the prince!" murmured Cassim, kneeling down and binding up the wound of the insensible Mazeppa.

Mazeppa was not long before he began to recover from the effects of the pain and fright. Seeing Cassim and Zisko near him, he inquired the cause.

Cassim explained how he had been following the bear, and that the prince and his companion being behind the tree, they had escaped his observation, and just stepping out as he fired the unfortunate prince had thus been grazed.

The wound was slight, the suddenness of the accident having affected him more than the pain.

He rose, and leaning on Cassim's shoulder, walked towards his tent, when Zisko exclaimed, "I must return, and I will see you again before to-morrow night. Adieu!"

"Stay," said Mazeppa, as the departure of Zisko carried the prince's thoughts again to Theresa, "stay, and answer me that one question now. I will not move until I know it. Was it a pledge of love?"

"Yes," was the brief answer, as Zisko waved his hand, muttering something to himself, and darted swiftly off, leaving the wounded prince to be taken to his tent by his friend, whom Zisko only knew as Cassim.

---

## CHAPTER XVII.

### THE ATTACK.

A COLD wind whistled through the turrets of the castle of the Castellan as the grey mists of morning chased each other over plain and wood—a flitting symbol of the fleeting armies, soon to rout each other in the omnipotence of martial powers.

Sleep fled before the blushing light of the awakened morn, as the camp alarm called to life and warfare the slumbering followers of Mazeppa.

The prince started at the sound, but awoke from ideal visions of Theresa to the realisation of a feverish restlessness and acute pains from his recent wound.

On his return to the tent the previous night Mazeppa had been met by Zuliska, whose tremor and grief at the condition of her master were so unsoldier-like, that to anyone less occupied than the prince all would have been revealed at a glance.

He saw it not.

Through the long night Zuliska kept her sleepless vigil, doubting and hoping; dreaming of visions too happy to have faith in, followed by misgivings and wonderings too saddening to encourage.

She longed for the morning.

One of her noblest characteristics was a daring spirit.

Hers was no timid love. She would willingly have sacrificed her life for the wounded slumberer, and the thoughts of coming warfare, with the dread mission for which she had perilled life and honour, never caused a fear.

Many a time during her watch over Mazeppa, in the dead silence of that long night, she breathed a soft and holy prayer that victory might smile upon the noble prince.

She earnestly prayed that he might win his conquest, never dreaming that her prayer craved destruction to her own happiness.

How often do we blame Heaven for not answering our impulsive requests, which, if granted, might prove a veritable curse!

At the sound of the alarm, as Mazeppa rose with a low murmur of pain, Zuliska stealthily left the tent.

The tramping of the armed men, and clattering of weapons, soon brought their leader in the midst of his followers.

Mazeppa told them of his accident, and assured them he was nearly recovered.

A shout rang through the woods, as he bade them still rely upon his presence and guidance as their champion.

"It was but a scratch on my left shoulder," said Mazeppa; "my right arm is good, and the accursed Castellan shall soon have cause to dread it."

Another shout of triumph rang through the wood.

"Prepare to march," was the order given, and horses and men were in an instant on the alert; and, ere the sun had broken through morning mists, Mazeppa and his followers were on the road to the Castle of Laurinski.

Long before they reached the open plain from which they could discern the turrets of the castle, dark clouds had gathered over the heavens, and veiled the sun.

An oppressive atmosphere made the journey very fatiguing, and so affected the spirits of the stern warriors that the cavalcade went on in the deepest silence.

At length they broke from the wood, and the beautiful palace of the Castellan burst upon their sight.

At a signal from Mazeppa, they halted.

Cassim, Abder Khan, and his son, at length agreed that the whole troop should proceed to hide behind a cover of trees, some short distance to the left hand, from whence a good view of the castle could be kept.

Mazeppa, alone, wrapped in a large fur, strolled towards the castle.

It was a magnificent building—large, massive, and well proportioned—surrounded on the north and east by hills, thickly studded with wood, and looking from the south over miles of verdant, open country.

On the northern terrace, near the postern, walked a sullen sentinel, with heavy and measured tread; while, sitting on a stone buttress, some fifty yards away, was the restless dwarf.

For hours a storm had been gathering over the face of the heavens.

Suddenly a vivid flash of lightning lit up the whole scene, startling Zisko, and chaining the sentinel to the ground.

Flash after flash leapt forth in wrathful fury, dancing round the turret towers, and like serpents of fire, darting along from terrace to terrace.

The thunder echoed among the distant hills, until it became one unbroken roll, each minute coming nearer and nearer to the castle.

The castle was covered by one of those dark and dreadful clouds, which obscure everything, and seem almost as " palpable to feeling as to sight."

A mighty wind swept through the forest, and the Storm King rode over wood and plain in dread magnificence.

It was a fearful scene.

One deathly dart, more vividly intense than any previous one, at length struck the centre of the northern parapet, and instantly a loud crash of thunder, like the discharge of a park of artillery, burst into a tremendous roar, shaking stone after stone to the ground with fearful rapidity. One huge mass struck the affrighted sentinel, who fell to the ground a mangled corpse.

Mazeppa, in spite of the awful grandeur of the heavens, still walked on, for the wild war of the elements and the sublime music of the storm seemed to accord with the emotions then swaying him, and with a majestic air he still kept his path towards the castle.

A shriek, almost unearthly, struck his ear, and turning sharply round, he saw the dwarf, with a face livid and distorted, running frantically about.

"Merciful Heavens! save me, save me!" shrieked the dwarf, as Mazeppa strode up to him, and, seizing him, said, "Zisko."

At this sound the dwarf ventured to look up, and at once gratefully recognised the prince.

"What is the matter?" asked Mazeppa.

" There, there ! " replied Zisko, pointing towards the corpse of the ill-fated sentry.

Mazeppa hastened to the spot, and removed some of the heavy, blood-stained stones from off the body, while Zisko described how he sat watching the sentinel before he was killed, and brought to Mazeppa's memory the night when that sentinel, like Zeminski, allowed the prince to hold converse with his beloved Theresa.

" I know him well," said the prince, with a heavy sigh. " When did it fall ? " asked he.

" But now," replied Zisko, moving away the last piece of stone, which had forced in the chest of the poor sufferer.

" Look at that blue line down, his face ! What can it be ? " inquired Mazeppa.

" The lightning," answered Zisko.

" He was a good servant and an honourable man," said the prince, turning away, and silently musing as he walked towards the eastern gates of the castle, closely followed by the half-terrified imp.

The leader knew well every entrance to the palace.

Having arrived at the drawbridge he crossed it, and was about to enter when Zisko called to him in a low tone.

" What now ? " said the prince moodily.

" You will not walk into the jaws of death—will you ? " whispered the dwarf.

" I fear nothing," was the only reply.

" Stay ! " cried Zisko, in a louder tone, and with increased energy. " If he comes ! "

" Who ? " asked Mazeppa.

" The Castellan ! Death would then be instantaneous. His hatred would know no bounds if he saw you here again ; so be warned in time," answered the dwarf, with an impassioned fervour which arrested the attention of Mazeppa.

" Does Theresa love me still ? " asked he.

" She does, deeply—far too deeply for you to hold your life so lightly," was the welcome answer.

" Zisko, I must see her ! " exclaimed the prince.

" Mazeppa, you cannot."

" By Heavens, I will ! " said the prince in a lordly tone.

" You shall not now," Zisko shouted, in a fury of passion, which had been gathering during the conversation, and which now burst forth beyond his control.

Mazeppa turned full round upon the dwarf, and, hurling his heavy fur into the gateway, would have strangled the ugly attendant, but, as the prince rushed to grasp the miscreant's throat, a loud, clear note from a trumpet rang through the castle-yard, and Zisko darted through the postern and was lost ere the echo died away.

Mazeppa, impelled by feelings which he could not analyse, threw his fur again around him, and walked on into the castle.

Instinctively he wended his way towards Theresa's chamber ; and just as he reached the entrance to the corridor leading to her room, a tall, handsome man, dressed as a page, came abruptly from an adjoining corridor.

They both started.

Each stood speechless, until the Castellan's servant sufficiently recovered himself enough to ask the name of the stranger.

" Mazeppa," replied the prince.

" Mazeppa ! " re-echoed the man, with amazement ; then, quick as thought, shouted, " help ! help ! "

" Cease," said the prince, with one blow striking the surprised menial to the ground.

Scarcely had Mazeppa done so, before a number of pages from every corridor came rushing to the spot, in bewilderment at the cause.

The prince was seized, while a dozen asked his name, and, as the Castellan arrived with Theresa, the serf on the ground shouted out " *Mazeppa !* "

---

## CHAPTER XVIII.

At the sound of Mazeppa's name the Castellan stood petrified, while Theresa trembled for a moment, then rushed into the midst of her servants and faced the noble form of the prince, who stood in a defiant attitude, with his eyes fixed on the approaching lord of the castle.

The pages fell to the right and left as their master came forward towards the cause of the uproar.

Mazeppa never moved one muscle of his stern face ; his eye was like a blazing coal, his brow was knit, his mouth firmly set, and never did painter or sculptor create so grand a model of daring and defiance, as Mazeppa presented at that moment. It was an attitude and expression worthy of the genius of Michael Angelo.

Gradually the intense fire of his look melted into winning softness as his eyes turned from the father and fell upon his lovely daughter.

Theresa had stood awed by the grandeur of her lover's attitude and animated expression. She was speechless, and with mouth half-open, was unconsciously riveted to the spot until Mazeppa's eyes alighted upon her.

Like an electric shock, the blood shot from her heart, and illumined her face with crimson blushes.

Hers eyes fell instantly they met Mazeppa's gaze.

A deathlike paleness superseded the crimsoned confusion which had lent such transient charms to her lovely features.

The Castellan looked from Mazeppa to Theresa again and again until his face glowed purple with rage, and his fury increased almost beyond control, as he watched the magic influence of the prince's gaze upon his entranced lady.

" Bear him away to the armoury," at length roared the Castellan, in curbless anger, " bind him in chains, bar the door, show no leniency, on your lives—away at once ! "

" Touch me not, minions ! " said the haughty prince, with one long lingering look at Theresa, and a scornful curl of the lip as the pages came towards him. " Stand back, I tell you ; lead the way, I will follow ; but if you lay one finger on me I will make you all as helpless as your brother menials."

There was a danger in his look which made the servants of the castle quail.

Two braver than the rest led the way, while Mazeppa, waving an adieu to Theresa, and with an expression of hope to her, turned and followed, with a majestic and fearless air.

The armoury was soon reached, into which the prince walked, and sat on a rudely-carved table, bidding his guides depart quickly ; the door was shut and bolted outside with two massive bolts.

Two guards were ordered to watch, and sleep not, on pain of death.

Suddenly a loud crash of fire-arms was heard without.

The fearful storm had not half spent its rage, ere Abder Khan became anxious for the safety of his son, and after a long conversation with a number of his followers, agreed to march down upon the castle.

They felt sure that Mazeppa would be found somewhere near the castle, and would assume the command of his troops.

They searched in vain.

Several trustworthy men were sent round the outskirts of the castle to find their leader.

North, south, east, and west, the hills, and the outskirts of of the wood were searched over and over again, and a strong band had actually neared the castle's northern entrance, while the events narrated in our last chapter were occurring.

The lightning still flashed, and the thunder still rolled, reverberating its hollow boom over the hills, and shaking the very earth.

At length Cassim, with a band of daring friends of Mazeppa, resolved to enter the castle.

Foremost among them was Zuliska.

So well was she disguised, her father could scarcely have known her.

Crash went their muskets against the doorway on the northern terrace.

A myriad of amazed retainers and straggling soldiers came out upon the terrace.

At a small window over the gateway peered the head of Zisko. Cassim saw him in an instant and asked admission.

" The door is open and the sentinel killed," replied the dwarf.

All through the eventful scenes in which Mazeppa had been playing the hero, Zisko had watched, from a secret casement, the action and its issue. He was only too glad to see deliverance for Mazeppa so near at hand.

Cassim and Zuliska entered, closely followed by their faithful band.

With a heavy, solemn tread, they marched down the principal avenue, until they met a number of the Castellan's retainers and a few of his military marauders, who were so amazed that they were perfectly helpless.

Terror seized the menials and paralysed their energies.

"Where is Mazeppa?" asked Cassim.

"In the dungeon," answered a soldier of the castle.

"In bonds?" asked Cassim, surprised.

"Yes, chained in the armoury," was the reply.

A shout of defiance rang through the corridor.

Cassim looked at Zuliska, and traced the dark shadows of a secret pang flit over her features; then seizing a page by the throat, said,—

"Lead us to the armoury, or breathe your last."

"Mercy!" shrieked the page

"The armoury or death," re-echoed a score of Cassim's followers.

The page directed the road and led the way.

Clash went the arms—tramp, tramp, tramp, sounded the march of the troops, as they rushed eagerly to rescue their beloved leader.

Like fire the news spread through the castle; right and left came servants and soldiers; and ere Cassim, with his faithful band, had traced through two corridors, a shout of the Castellan arrested their progress, and they stood face to face with the fiery lord of the castle.

"What means this?" demanded the infuriated Castellan.

"Death and revenge!" was the answer from Cassim.

The Castellan turned from a flushed red to a deadly pale hue, as Mazeppa's followers one and all re-echoed their chief, and cried out, "Revenge!"

"Who are you?" demanded the Castellan.

"Where is Mazeppa?" was the answer.

"Whence come you?"

"Where is Mazeppa?" again shouted the men, with impatience.

"Give us Mazeppa or die, tyrant," said one of the foremost in Cassim's rank, and as he said so, he aimed a blow at the Castellan's head, which would have proved fatal had not another sword parried the blow, and spared the old man.

That saving sword was Zuliska's.

"Thanks, my young warrior," said the grateful Castellan; "you, and you alone, shall be safe while beneath my roof."

At that instant a large reinforcement of the soldiers of the castle arrived—tenfold the number of Cassim's band.

"Bear those invaders to the eastern tower," was the Castellan's infuriated order.

Cassim waved his hand to his small troop, who, at the signal, yielded to the command.

They were seized and led away.

"Grant me a favour," said Zuliska, as the Castellan released her from the grasp of a soldier and bade her remain with him.

"I will—what is it?" answered the owner of the castle.

"One word with my father," said Zuliska, as she stepped towards Cassim.

"Let them speak together," was the signal for the retainers of the Castellan, who had charge of Cassim, to release him.

"Cassim," said Zuliska, loudly; then gradually lowering her voice, until she scarcely whispered, she said, "trust me to deliver you all—yes, all—you, my dear father, and the noble Mazeppa. Rest quietly for a short time. I will be your deliverer—will you trust me?"

"Yes, Zuliska."

"You will take no other steps, then?"

"No."

"I will be faithful and speedy," said the daughter, as she returned to the Castellan, and anxiously watched the troop of her faithful friends led away to captivity.

"Come with me," said the Castellan.

Zuliska hesitated for an instant, watching the movements of her new master.

He repeated the request in a tone so full of kindness that the disguised warrior could not but consent, and was taken by the Castellan to his own private and secret chamber.

"What is your name, my noble youth?"

Zuliska did not deign an answer. She was busily occupied in gazing upon the magnificent adornments of the gorgeous chamber in which she stood.

It was a master-piece of Oriental art. The dazzling hues of the rainbow glittered around her.

Sculpture of the most costly kind graced every corner of this chief room of the palace.

Zuliska was bewildered.

She heard not the reiterated question.

The Castellan was struck with the beauty of form and graceful bearing of this youthful champion.

"How long have you studied war, my gallant defender?" said the Castellan, laying his hand upon an arm as soft as down.

Zuliska started, and looking the questioner full in the face replied,—

"Just long enough, sire, to be of use to those whom I wish to defend."

"What is your name, my youth?"

"Selim," answered Zuliska.

Such was the name by which Cassim, her father, had introduced her to Mazeppa, and as Selim had the prince hitherto addressed her.

The prince's tongue had made the name sacred to its fair owner, and she loved it better than her own.

"Well, Selim," said the Castellan, "will you tell me why these troops have come to invade my peaceful domain?"

"For their prince, Mazeppa."

"What think you of this Mazeppa, Selim? Come, speak boldly."

"I love," was the unguarded and impulsive reply, "the very name," added Zuliska, after a pause.

"Why?"

"He is noble and brave."

"But he must die," muttered the Castellan, as with haughty step he paced to and fro.

"May I see him first?" begged Zuliska.

"Yes, I will not deny you that; only once, mind, and now."

The Castellan and Zuliska in a few moments stood face to face with Mazeppa.

---

## CHAPTER XIX.

MAZEPPA, once fast in the dungeon and left in solitude, began to reflect on the recklessness of his conduct, and to meditate the probable result.

Still one thought ever came uppermost in his mind, keeping all other ideas subservient to it, just as the splendour of the sun hides all meaner light and holds our vision by its absorbing brilliancy.

Love, the master passion, held sway over the young hero's soul.

Danger might threaten—would love give way? Never.

Confinement might restrict his movements, ruin his health, and prostrate his energies—but could love be chained and imprisoned?

No!

Illness might threaten his life, and despair of revenge rack his brain until death haunted his fancy, and the tomb became a perpetual dream.

But would love die?

No! not while reason kept its throne, and the tongue could utter a prayer for Theresa.

Theresa was the one thought that made captivity light.

He longed to see her.

He knew there was a door in the armoury where he was confined which led to her chamber.

But his chains were heavy.

He had not strength—for his recent wound was yet painful.

He tried many times, in the dark and dismal chamber, to feel his way round the wall, and find the door leading to his heart's idol.

His chains rattled, and the guard without was instantly on the alert.

At length, overcome by the weight of his fetters, exhausted by repeated attempts, and sick at heart from repeated failures, Mazeppa threw himself upon a rude ottoman in one corner of the armoury, and gave himself up to deep despondency.

There was not one ray of hope.

Nature's sweet Sabbath, sleep, was for a time stealing all the cares and trials of his unhappy life away, when the name of Mazeppa was heard in a whisper so sweet that an angel might have breathed it.

The prisoner opened his eyes in fear and wonder.

" Mazeppa," again repeated the syren sound, almost like the shadow of an echo—but so sweet, it sounded almost supernatural.

" Good heavens ! " breathed the aroused slumberer, " what can this mean ? "

It was no angel, but Theresa.

A gentle creaking of a door, a flash of light, and Mazeppa arose in a tremor of fear, which in an instant changed to a transport of joy.

Oh, the bliss of that moment !

Sorrow, suffering, adversity, and affliction—all the frail sons of humanity are tutored to endure ; but sudden joy or fortune —how few are brave enough to be true and noble when such dowers are sent to them.

Theresa stood before Mazeppa,

With her delicate finger raised to enjoin silence, she entered the armoury.

Her footsteps fell like velvet.

The light of a small lamp she held in her right hand made her beauty look unusually brilliant.

Like a gleam of sunshine, she seemed to illume that dreary dungeon ; Mazeppa rushed frantically towards her, covering with kisses the jewelled hand she put forth to greet him.

Clash ! went the huge bolts on the exterior of the armoury door.

Swift as thought, Theresa darted back through the secret passage by which she had entered.

Mazeppa dashed the lamp to the ground just as the guard, who had been aroused by the noise of Mazeppa's chains when he flew to Theresa, entered, and demanded the cause of the noise.

" I am restless," was the indignant reply ; " take off these fetters, and I will rest."

" I dare not, or I would," said the sympathetic guard.

There was something about Mazeppa's noble appearance and fearless spirit which had won the admiration of his keeper.

" How long am I to endure this ? " asked the impatient prince.

" You will be taken before the Castellan's council to-morrow at noon."

At that moment Mazeppa's quick ear caught the sound of a gentle pressure at the secret door, against which he had placed himself when the guard had entered.

" Adieu ! let me rest, my friend," said Mazeppa aloud ; " do not disturb me before morning."

" Adieu ! " said the guard, and clash, clash, went the bolts once more, and a silence like death seemed to reign within and without for a moment.

Mazeppa cautiously opened the door leading to Theresa's chamber, and she glided into his cell like a fairy spirit, bringing to him comfort and joy.

She placed another lamp, which she had brought, in a niche in the wall, and sat by the side of her beloved Mazeppa.

She bent her head down and turned it aside, as if to hide the tears of joy which were welling up from her overflowing heart.

She was too happy.

How often do we find joy the herald of sorrow !

How sad it seems that the gorgeous effulgence of the setting sun, flooding the earth with a paradise of beauty, should be but an unerring presage of that reckless storm which shall soon throw a pall of darkness over all creation, and with a lightning-tipped finger write ruin over many a lovely scene !

Theresa was too happy for a few moments, then came the shadowy doubts casting a gloom over the transient dream of joy.

" You did love me once, Mazeppa, I know."

" Never more than now, sweet love."

" Would I could think so," said Theresa, slowly, finishing with a sigh so deep that it startled and alarmed Mazeppa.

Zisko had in conversation, by hints more than assertions, led Theresa to imagine the existence of a rival.

Zisko believed in one, but would not, for Theresa's sake, let her know all.

Theresa had tried many times to draw from the torturing dwarf a secret which defied all her skill.

Conjuration and threatening were equally unavailable.

" Do you love me still ? " asked Mazeppa, anxiously.

" Such as you were, I loved you—loved you more than life ; but if love yet lingers in my soul, I fear I must learn to conquer it."

Mazeppa was amazed.

A pang of anguish crossed his brow as he looked in Theresa's swimming eyes, and clearly read the sincerity of her words.

She looked at him for some moments with a pale face, till a bright, earnest look gathered upon it ; her searching eyes gazed into the depths of his, and as he deigned no reply, the tears dried upon her cheeks, and no fresh tears fell. She thought she read truth in his noble face.

Woman hopes where hope is vain ; she strives where strife seems useless. If she loves, amidst a darkness that to man would seem impenetrable, woman will approach the shrine man would fail to find, and kindle the sacred fire which his less sure touch would extinguish.

Hope lit up Theresa's face, and sun-like in its radiant beauty did her countenance become, as there she sat looking into Mazeppa's eyes, letting secret hope re-light the torch of love within her heart.

" You know my soul is yours dearest Theresa," were the welcome words which broke the long silence.

" I thought so," faintly murmured the trembling girl.

" Well, do not misjudge me now, then," said Mazeppa, with an air of dignity which attracted Theresa's gaze, and made her brow flush with admiration for the noble being at whose side she sat, and whom she so longed to call her own. " Do you love me the same, Theresa ? Tell me that."

" I do. If it is not "—she paused.

## CHAPTER XX.

### THE SECRET MEETING.

There was a dead silence for a few moments between Mazeppa and Theresa.

At length Theresa, after thinking for some moments about the hints which the invidious dwarf had thrown out, and brooding over the demon thoughts of jealousy which seemed on a sudden to take immediate and entire possession of her soul, turned abruptly towards her wondering companion.

She looked at him full in the face, with a stern and steady gaze.

" Mazeppa, are you sure I have not had a rival in your love since I last saw you ? " said the trembling girl, almost afraid to hear the answer, yet burning for it.

Mazeppa was amazed.

A flash of indignation lit up his whole face.

A searching glare seemed to come from his eyes, which were fixed on his questioner.

The lamp flickered with a very uncertain light.

The prince tried to read the thoughts of doubt and love as their shadows fluttered over the fair features of his soul's idol.

" What can you mean ? " asked he.

" Oh, Mazeppa, I dare not think of it, but surmises will

creep into my thoughts, that in your home, among my father's enemies, you may have found another more worthy of your noble love, and with whom you could be more happy than with the daughter of your persecutor."

Mazeppa rose; his noble form seemed to dilate with scorn, his proud look and haughty mien made him imperial in his attitude, and the deep emotions of his soul lent a brilliancy to his expression and a pathos to his voice which awed the crouching dove who had nestled at his feet.

" Shame on you, Theresa ? " burst forth the resentful lover, " shame on you ! Is it for this I have dared the dangers of the wild woods? When sent forth by the heartless tyrant who owns the castle and calls you daughter, I heard your own assurance that you were mine. The words were engraven on my very soul; they were my heart's life. I saw them written in letters of light, day after day, and night after night, as I rode the hard race for life or death. Noonday and midnight, still one figure haunted my every thought; sunlight made it glorious, and the moonbeams made it holy. The sun seemed to show me the glowing glories of a brilliant and happy life of love with thee; while the moon's silent, soft, and silvery glimmering foreshadowed the chastening influence of trials and sufferings.

" Still it was for thee.

" Oh ! glorious thought !

" When that wild horse bore its unwelcome burden on its reckless track, the hidden paths of the secret forest, I thought but of thee.

" When the howling and hungry wolves followed in the trail with their wild yelps for my fevered blood, and Death, with grinning mockery, seemed to hover in the air with a malicious smile, pointing at them as his ministers, what one ray kept the reeling brain together and forbade reason to abdicate her throne?

" The one ray of hope which still was reflected from thy image.

" And from those lips I still heard, far above the angry winds and the hollow-voiced bays of the parched wolves, the sweet music of that life promise, ' You are mine.' "

" Forgive me, Mazeppa," implored the almost bewildered girl, as she gazed at her erect and eloquent lover, whom the thought of the past seemed to have inspired, and spoke with an earnestness that shook the very soul of his timid and loving listener.

" Shame on you ! " again resumed Mazeppa, growing more emphatic and vehement as the flood-gates of memory were opened and the tide of thought came swelling upon his soul.

" In my father's tribes are many lovely girls, whose lives were laid at Mazeppa's feet, willing serfs to his will and pleasure; but the brightest image paled before thy picture.

" Think you I came to war with you? No! it was your imperious and heartless father, the enemy of our race. And when my father (whom I have now found, thank Heaven !) proclaimed me king, and our faithful band marched forth to take revenge for my ignominy, what was the first sweet thought which won my soul for victory? Why, you, Theresa.

" Shame be on the mind that can think as yours has ; shame be on the tongue that can speak as yours has. Let your own heart pass its sentence upon you ! "

Theresa's tears burst forth in an uncontrollable flood.

Her beautiful bosom heaved like a snowy wave.

Her sighs seemed to rend her very heart.

Her tongue was charmed with fear.

Mazeppa's eloquence had charmed her, though she was terrified by its earnestness.

Her only answer was woman's most efficacious one—tears.

How often do we find that we are stoical, almost severe, with the woman we love, when she is smiling or satirical—and they are nearly always one or the other. But be we never so cross, in a fever of rage or torrent of passion, if they but let one tear come silently down the velvet cheek, our very hearts are thawed in an instant, our stern features relax, and our hearts open spontaneously, while our arms seem sympathetically to be inflicted with the same weakness.

Had Theresa rose in anger, as would many of her sex, and

with scornful sneer, or taunting retort, giving anger for anger, and added fuel to fire, then Mazeppa's spirit would have been aroused like a lion.

But Theresa's tears were too powerful; they came like a flood, and bore down everything before them.

" You did not mean it, then," said Mazeppa, in a softened tone; " say that you did not mean what you said, Theresa."

" No, no, Mazeppa," answered the weeping syren, made more happy by Mazeppa's affectionate tone than she was convinced by his rhetoric.

" I love you alone, dear," said he.

" My own dear Mazeppa" was the only audible response, save a sweet liquid accompaniment that seemed to draw their faces nearer to each other, and kept them so for a long time.

Kiss after kiss until they grew too fervent.

Mazeppa, in his joy, forgot his chains, and throwing himself at his idol's feet, would have sworn eternal fidelity, had not his chains made so much noise that his sentinel was awakened, and the dreaded bolts in an instant were heard slipping back.

Quick as thought Theresa snatched the lamp with one hand, and gently placing the other over Mazeppa's mouth to enjoin silence, she led the way through the secret passage, and closed it quietly behind them.

They listened.

Creak went the door on its heavy hinges.

" What's the matter ? " asked the half-sleepy sentry.

No response.

" Are you awake ? " again asked the voice more clearly.

Still no response.

The guard by this time began to get awake, and, obtaining a light, walked round and round the armoury, getting more bewildered each time.

" Where can he be ? " said the trembling sentinel to himself,

" I know where you are, my fine fellow; so come out, and spare my calling for aid," said he, loudly.

Still no echo, save the ringing of his own sound through the dusky vault.

Terror seized him. Again and again he searched every nook and corner of the place.

Each suit of mail he shook, and shook in vain.

Behind each old piece of tapestry—beneath the rude couches, and behind the muster of old and unused arms—everywhere he could possibly think of he sought, without success.

Awakened by the fright and fear of his master's displeasure, he went out, and walking down the corridor to the northern terrace, he called the night-guard to accompany him.

" What means this ? " said the terrace sentinel.

" Mazeppa has escaped," answered the trembling criminal.

" Nonsense ! "

" He has, I tell you."

" How ? "

" I know not."

" You have been to sleep on your watch !"

" No, indeed not," muttered the now thoroughly awakened culprit.

" He could not escape."

" I can assure you he has."

" Was your door bolted on the outside ? "

" Yes."

" Quite securely ? "

" Yes, quite."

" Then we will find him, I warrant, and quickly, too."

The conversation, while walking down the corridor, had brought them right to the door of the armoury.

They procured another light, and entered.

All was still as the grave.

The silence was almost palpable.

They kept closely together, as if Mazeppa was about to start from the wall and frighten them.

Still they searched, and in vain, until with blank looks they stood face to face in wonder and fear.

" Shall I give the alarm ? " asked the faithless watcher.

" Yes, at once."

Boom, boom, boom! sounded the great gong in the corridor.

Crack went a musket on the terrace.

Loud and long rung the brazen sound of alarm from the trumpet in the castle-yard.

The castle was one scene of confusion.

Soldiers and servants came gathering down the corridors.

Foremost among them was Zisko.

Zisko, half guessing the cause of this unusual night brawl, learned from the guard of Mazeppa's escape.

Zisko, on the instant, rushed into the armoury, and disappeared.

Zisko was not seen nor heard of any more that night.

Several pages and soldiers entered into the armoury, not getting any reasonable answer from the affrighted sentinel.

"Make room! make room!" was the cry, as the crowd suddenly fell back; and the Castellan, in a fume of rage, demanded the cause of this confusion.

"*Mazeppa has escaped!*"

The Castellan stamped with fury.

"Follow me, one and all!" said he, as, snatching a light from a menial, he rushed into the armoury, with a numerous body of retainers.

They all fell back with amazement when they found, right facing them, a huge door wide open.

It was at the mouth of a long, dreary passage.

The Castellan entered.

---

## CHAPTER XXI.

### THE WARRIORS IN WAITING.

ABDER KHAN, who had remained behind with the troops, began to get impatient at the delay. He had noticed the progress of his warriors in search of Mazeppa, and seen them go towards the castle.

As to his son, he knew not whither he had gone, nor could he guess the cause of his sudden disappearance.

A murmur of discontent went through the tents.

Conferences were held by many of the suspicious followers, who almost feared the dangers of war.

They suspected that Mazeppa had led them into the hands of the enemy.

The storm raged on.

The blue fire still leapt over the hills, and brought into relief the tents of the troops.

The thunder still shook the forest, making gigantic trees tremble like reeds.

The untied winds still played havoc with the smaller bushes and trees, and howled their dismal dirge over hill and plain.

The tents of the chiefs seemed at the mercy of the elements.

Searchers were sent out to hunt for the missing ones, but no tidings could be gained, and they returned.

Abder Khan ordered an alarm to be sounded through the camp.

Loud and long rang the brazen summoner.

Troops of chiefs assembled round their noble leader.

Rank after rank of eager-eyed and fiery soldiers came marching up in irregular lines.

"My worthy friends," began Abder Khan, "will you accept me as your leader until we again discover my son and your king—Mazeppa?"

"Yes!" shouted the whole band.

"Will you obey my orders, one and all?"

"Yes!" reiterated the troops.

"Will you help me to make an attack upon the castle at once?"

"We will."

"Now——"

A loud peal of thunder rent the air, and shook every inch of ground around the council of war.

"Decide at once!" said Abder Khan, whose voice had been stopped by the loud artillery of heaven, while the echo reverberated over the distant hills.

A few moments silent conversation took place between the immediate friends of the newly elected champion.

Silence reigned over the whole scene.

It was a council of life or death.

Several minutes passed ere the leader had arranged his plans.

The troops were at last arranged, all the tents were struck, and preparations made for departure.

"Advance!" cried the leader.

In an instant all were ready for the attack.

With steady, stern, and warlike steps, they marched on to victory or death.

Death looked them in the face.

Destruction hung in the very air.

They were about to walk into the very mouth of their enemy's quarters.

They believed in their leader—they knew he was brave and fearless.

They looked at his noble bearing, and were confident of success.

The long cavalcade moved along until they got within sight of the castle.

At the word of command they halted.

They were impatient for action, and longed to see their beloved Mazeppa.

They made every preparation, and as their champion mounted his magnificent charger and rode forward to the castle, with an almost endless line of followers, a loud shout rang through the air.

That shout was "Victory!"

---

## CHAPTER XXII.

### MET BUT TO PART.

IT was Zisko who opened the door which (as we stated at the end of Chapter XVIII.) the Castellan and his troops found yawning before him.

This done, he disappeared into the secret passage.

The passage was, as I have said, buried in profound darkness, and he could see nothing.

He stopped short.

Where had they gone?

Had they rashly hurried onwards into the very jaws of danger, or were they still buried in the shadows?

He listened.

The irregular breathing of the young girl first attracted his attention.

"Hist!" he whispered, "hist! Theresa; are you there?"

There was no answer.

"Theresa!" he cried; "it is I—Zisko. Fear nothing."

It was Mazeppa's voice which answered.

"Zisko," he said, "have you a light?"

"No; but let us advance—we are in danger here."

"But whither can we go?"

"To Theresa's chamber."

"No, no. The danger is worse there. I have already found that the Castellan has there too easy access."

The dwarf uttered a low, chuckling laugh.

"You know little of this place," he cried. "I, who have been a wanderer in this mansion since my youth, understand the secret outlets of the castle. Let us advance into the room. There, at least for a time, we can conceal ourselves."

Guided by the dwarf, who seemed to advance as well in the darkness as in the light, they proceeded along the corridor and entered the room.

They had scarcely entered and closed the door behind them, when a slight rustling noise was heard, and a female form entered.

It was Zenitha.

In her hand she held a lamp.

"Thank God," cried Zisko, "we are saved!"

Mazeppa smiled.

"Saved!" he cried; "how saved?"

"Now," he said, "I can find the secret door."

He took the lamp from her hand, and advanced towards a panel in the wall, which at his touch slid aside.

"Come," he said, "my friends—here is safety."

They followed him in silence, and the door closed behind them.

Shall we tell the story of this secret door?

The father of the Castellan, who was named Stanislaus in honour of the Count Palatine, was a man of strong and ungovernable passions.

In the village just below the castle lived a girl whose name was Mathilda.

Her parents were poor, but they enjoyed the privilege of freedom.

They were not serfs.

Mathilda was eighteen when the Castellan cast his eyes upon her, and as she had learned a variety of accomplishments, he easily persuaded his wife to take her into her establishment.

The girl rejected his offer with scorn.

The money he offered her, the distinctions he guaranteed to shower upon her family, she laughed at; and the consequence was that the Castellan, exasperated by her refusals, determined on her destruction.

He employed some workmen in his castle, and desired them to form in the wall near the chamber now occupied by Theresa a smaller room, which should communicate with no other.

Among the workmen employed, however, there was one who had a liking for Mathilda—who, indeed, had hopes of being her accepted lover.

He had heard the Castellan's secret vow—he had overheard a conversation between him and Mathilda, and he constructed on his own account a passage which led from this inner chamber to the moat.

Mathilda was immured in this chamber, and left for dead; but the hope of life was strong within her, and she escaped.

Into this room Zisko led his friends.

But what was their chance of escape when the passage was full of water?

From Theresa's chamber a spiral staircase led to the subterranean passage through which Zisko and his friends hoped to reach the open country.

Of course, however, as the castle was entirely surrounded by the moat, this passage passed beneath it; and it was fashioned, too, near a part of the moat which was broader by far than elsewhere.

Immediately upon the receipt of the information as to the approach of the Tartar army, headed by Mazeppa, the Castellan had, it will be remembered, given orders for the strengthening of the defences and the widening of the moat.

Neither he nor any of the other occupants of the castle were aware of the existence of the subterranean passage, and in their work the labourers displaced one of the stones with which it was rudely arched over.

When, therefore, the water was turned into the moat, it rushed through the aperture and completely filled the passage.

Zisko saw at once what had happened.

"Mazeppa," he said, "we are baffled."

"How so?" cried the prince, who knowing nothing of this secret passage, understood not the danger.

Zisko pointed to the still waters which lay, black and dismal, at their feet, save where here and there the light of their lamps fell on it in bright patches.

"The passage is filled with water," he cried; "we must return."

Theresa clung to Mazeppa in mingled terror and despair.

"Oh, no," she cried, "we cannot return—it would be death for both."

The dwarf smiled grimly.

"No so," he said, "death only for Mazeppa; captivity for you."

"Which is death," murmured Theresa. "Oh no, we cannot return."

"Can you suggest nothing?" cried the prince.

Zisko glanced musingly at the fair girl, who, with streaming eyes and panting bosom, leaned against her unfortunate lover; while Zenitha, her maid, crouched in abject terror at her feet.

"I could suggest something," he said, "were I sure that you loved each other sufficiently to be patient."

Mazeppa stamped his foot impatiently.

"Speak not in riddles," he cried; "every moment now is precious. If the Castellan discovers Theresa's absence, it will be impossible for us to return."

"Well then," said Zisko, "if the Lady Theresa will consent to return, and be patient once more for a time, I undertake to save Mazeppa."

Theresa was the first to speak.

"Oh yes!" she cried, seizing the dwarf's hand eagerly; "yes; save Mazeppa, and I will remain and be patient."

"Good, then," said the dwarf; "my plan is simple. Theresa and Zenitha must return to their chamber—Mazeppa must remain in the secret room, where the Castellan will never discover him. I will procure, during the next few hours, a dress and a complete disguise for the prince, and will undertake to see him safely beyond the precincts of the castle. Come, let us not delay; as you have said, each moment is now precious."

With hearts full of mournful feelings, they retraced their steps, and at the entrance of the secret chamber Mazeppa took a sad leave of his mistress.

Scarcely had the two young girls re-entered the room, before a loud and angry knocking was heard at the door.

It was the Castellan and his retainers, who demanded admittance.

"Open immediately," he cried, in a voice hoarse with passion.

Theresa herself went to the door and undid the fastenings.

"Let my father enter alone," she cried; "let him not insult my sorrow by suffering these menials to molest me."

In spite of his anger, the Castellan was touched by the aspect of his daughter.

Again disappointed in her most cherished hopes, she appeared, indeed, crushed with grief.

Her eyes were red with weeping—her cheeks wan with lack of repose—her lips pale and quivering, while her panting breast would scarcely permit her to speak in audible accents.

"Remain here," cried the Castellan, after hesitating a moment; "I will enter alone."

He then strode into the room, and the door closed behind him.

Had he known the danger in which he stood at that moment, he would certainly have pardoned both Mazeppa and Theresa.

If his daughter had not, in spite of all his tyranny, been imbued with a deep feeling of respect and love for her father, he would have been made a prisoner.

They had simply to open the secret door, release Mazeppa, and by their united efforts force the Castellan into the place of concealment.

They could have then made his life and liberty dependent on the safety of Mazeppa and the delivery of the castle to the Tartar forces.

But the idea of such treachery never for a moment entered the mind of Theresa.

"My father," she said, meekly, as she sank upon an ottoman, "what is it you seek here?"

The Castellan eyed her sternly.

"You do not deceive me," he said, "by this show of simplicity. I seek the lover whom you have here concealed."

"Search," answered the young girl, "search; you will then see how you wrong me."

"You say search," returned the Castellan; "can I singly search two rooms? Kolzoff, my steward, must enter with me."

He strode to the door and admitted the man, who, with a grim smile, eyed the group, consisting of Theresa, Zenitha, and the dwarf.

"What does that mis-shapen being here?" cried he.

Theresa glanced at him with angry contempt.

"He is here because I wish him to be here," she said. "My father, your master, sent for you to aid him in a search —not to remark on my attendants."

The Castellan turned hastily round.

"The Lady Theresa is right," he said, haughtily; "if Zisko is misplaced here, I am the one to speak, not you."

THE EXPLOSION IN THE COURTYARD.

The steward looked abashed.

This was the first time that he had been thus spoken to by the Castellan; and in his own heart he treasured up the insult as due to the Lady Theresa.

His hate was bitter before—it was terrible now.

The hate of no man is so much to be feared as the hate of him who finds himself losing, through another, a long-enjoyed influence.

The Castellan and his steward now proceeded to prosecute their search.

Need we say it was useless?

They searched everywhere; but not a trace of the fugitive could be discovered.

The Castellan's rage knew no bounds.

He foamed at the mouth with rage.

"He has not left the castle—of that I am convinced," he cried. "Let not a nook be left unsearched. When I capture him, woe be to him and to his friends! A terrible, a horrible vengeance shall be mine."

Kolzoff smiled.

"They are melting lead below in the castle vaults," he said, in a low tone.

"I understand you," returned the Castellan. "To you I will leave their punishment."

They then left the room.

Theresa had heard these words, and was half-dead with terror.

When they had departed she fell upon her knees.

"Oh! heaven preserve him!" she cried, clasping her hands and looking upwards with her tearful eyes; "oh, heaven preserve him from my father's anger."

Zisko raised her.

"Rise," he said, firmly but kindly; "this is not the hour for repining. We want all the strength and courage that is possible. To you I resign the task of comforting Mazeppa; in four hours he shall be free."

He kissed her cold hand and left the room.

It was now midnight.

All was still in the castle.

Nothing was to be heard but the sighing of the wind amid the huge trees of the neighbouring forest and the tall turrets of the castle, and occasionally the footsteps of the pages, as they passed from one part of the building to the other, with news of the movements of the enemy.

As soon as Zisko had departed, the doors were secured and Mazeppa was admitted.

He had heard the conversation between Kolzoff and the Castellan, but upon him it had not taken the same effect as upon them.

He believed in Zisko.

The dwarf had already carried him through so many dangers, that he could well trust him again.

The lovers spoke little.

Theresa lay in Mazeppa's arms, listening to his unfrequent words, and whispering ever and anon the hope and comfort of a loving heart.

But, as we have said, their love-making and their caresses were carried on mostly in silence, for in the midst of all, their ears were waiting eagerly for the sound of the approaching footsteps which were to be the signal of freedom and safety.

At length, about half-past two, a light step was heard hurrying along the passage.

Then came three taps at the door.

This was a preconcerted signal.

Theresa rushed to the door and opened it, while Mazeppa, for fear of treachery, concealed himself behind the heavy hangings of the windows.

It was Zisko who entered.

In his arms was a large bundle.

"Here," he cried, as he approached Mazeppa with a triumphant smile, "here is your disguise. Hasten, for at this moment, if you follow my directions, escape is certain."

Mazeppa and the dwarf at once entered the inner room, and in a few moments the young prince appeared as one of the Castellan's body guard.

Over his smooth face was now a heavy beard and moustache, and the disguise was so complete, that had not Theresa expected his entrance, she herself would have been deceived.

"Adieu, dearest love," cried Mazeppa, as he strained his mistress to his breast, "adieu—though but for a few hours. Ere a week has passed, not a stone of this castle shall rest one upon the other."

"Listen," said Zisko, "ere you leave this room let me give you instructions. Take this letter—it is a note from the Castellan to the sentry who watches near the drawbridge. If any one questions you, show the letter and bid him not delay you at his peril."

The young prince then took the letter, grasped the dwarf warmly by the hand, and quitted the apartment.

He needed no further directions, for every corridor in the castle was familiar to him.

## CHAPTER XXIII.

### ZULISKA.

WHEN Mazeppa had proceeded down the first corridor, and was preparing to enter the long, dark passage which led to the terrace, he saw approaching him a form he well knew.

It was Zuliska.

She was hurrying towards Theresa's chamber to inquire after Mazeppa, the news of whose escape resounded from one end of the castle to the other.

Disguised as Mazeppa was, she did not recognise him; and when he grasped her arm, she cried roughly—

"Unhand me, menial."

Mazeppa laughed.

"What! do you not recognise me, friend Selim?" he cried.

Zuliska started.

"That voice—that voice! Yet no, it is impossible," she murmured.

"It is not impossible, Selim," he answered, quickly; "it is I, Mazeppa; I am escaping. In a few minutes I shall be far beyond their reach. Tell me how I can release our friends."

Zuliska glanced round her hurriedly, and drawing Mazeppa into the shadow, said—

"Cassim and his men are now imprisoned in the topmost turret of the eastern tower. They are watched over by four sentinels; two outside the inner door, and two outside the outer door, which leads on to the battlements. The inner door it would be in vain to attempt to destroy. It is immensely thick, and by the time it was demolished the staircases would be one mass of soldiery. During the night a large reinforcement has arrived from the Castle of Spolovsky, and it would be madness to attempt any rescue which was not secret."

"Then how, in Heaven's name, can we reach the prisoners?"

"From the outside."

Mazeppa smiled.

"You are a young warrior, and may therefore be forgiven," he said; "but you are talking of impossibilities."

"Not so," cried Zuliska; "listen to me patiently, and you will see it is not so. Do not interrupt me, because at any moment a page may come by and betray us. On the summit of the tower I have fastened to a cannon a long knotted rope, measuring a hundred and twenty feet. To this rope you must, when let down by me, secure a ladder."

"Which you will draw up."

"No; I cannot. Even the casting over the rope involves danger. Some brave and reckless spirit must climb the rope, and draw up the ladder after him. I shall with difficulty emerge on the battlements even for a moment."

"Well, this done?"

"The sentries must be gagged. Then you will silently break down the door of the cell, and let out the prisoners."

"Who will descend in the same manner as we ascend."

"Exactly."

"And will you contrive to be there?"

"I will; and we will assist you from within."

Mazeppa mused a moment.

"What ails you, my lord," said Zuliska, "do you disapprove of my project?"

"No, no. The escape seems feasible enough, I must say."

"What, then, is the difficulty?"

"If we mount the turret to release Cassim and his companions, could we not, in like manner, capture the castle?"

Zuliska started.

"No, no," she cried; "the eastern tower is isolated. Take it, and you are in the same position as before."

"Well, we will think of that," said Mazeppa. "Many thanks, my brave young warrior. I shall leave all to you, and when victory crowns our efforts, you shall be the first thought of."

"Alas, no!" sighed Zuliska.

She added aloud—

"To-morrow, at midnight, be beneath the eastern tower, and a heavy stone shall fall into the moat. To this stone will be attached the rope. Farewell till then."

Mazeppa grasped the tiny hand extended to him, and hurried away.

At the extremity of the long passage a guard stopped him.

"The watchword?" he cried.

"I know it not," said Mazeppa, haughtily.

"You cannot pass, then," returned the guard; "stand back."

"It is you who must stand back," replied Mazeppa, catching at an idea; "or, by our master of Spolovski, I will send a bullet through your skull. I am the bearer of a letter from the Castellan to the sentinel of the drawbridge. Delay me at your peril."

## CHAPTER XXIV.

### CONFIDENCES.

THE ruse was successful.

The voice of the prince was unfamiliar to the guard; but yet, supposing him to be one of the newly-arrived reinforcements, he said,—

"Be not angry, my friend. My instructions are as precise as yours. You will show me the letter, of course?"

Mazeppa did so.

"Right, my friend," said the soldier, drawing back. "Good-night."

Without deigning a reply the Tartar prince once more advanced, and in a few moments his brow was fanned by the welcome breezes of night.

But his difficulties were not yet over.

What if, when the soldier had received the letter, he should not allow him to pass further?

He trusted, however, to chance to befriend him, and desiring no further delay, walked hastily along the terrace, and approached the sentinel.

"Who goes there?" cried the latter.

"I bring a message from the Castellan," said Mazeppa.

"Good. What is it?"

"It is a written message. See, here it is."

The man made a wry face, took the note, and approaching

the lamp which swung over the drawbridge, turned it over and over curiously.

Mazeppa guessed his dilemma.

"I am to ask you to be quick," he said, impatiently; "open it; it is most important."

The man glanced at him.

"My friend," he said, "the Castellan has made a mistake. I can't read."

The young prince laughed.

"Well, brother," he said, "that is soon got over. I can read it for you—they teach us better at Spolovski."

The man hesitated.

"If he knew I allowed you to read a private letter," he said, "I should be shot."

"Oh! no fear!" returned Mazeppa; "I shall not tell him. It is ten chances to one if I live to come back here again."

"Where are you going, then?" asked the man, in surprise.

"You will see by the letter. Come, time presses—it will soon be morning, and my mission must be performed while it is yet dark."

The man doubted yet.

"Well, then," said the prince impatiently, "I shall return to the Castellan, and inform him you refuse to perform his bidding."

He turned to go.

"Nay, friend," said the sentinel, detaining him, "that must not be—you are too hasty. Here is the letter; read it."

The Castellan's letter, in reality, ran as follows:—

"A plot is being formed to release the prisoners. On your life keep good guard. They have been removed to the eastern tower—watch it well."

"Ah!" thought Mazeppa, "Selim must have let fall some indiscreet word, or he must have been seen casting over the rope. Never mind, this man must be deceived."

"Your master writes no very clear hand," he cried aloud; "but, nevertheless, by the aid of what he himself has told me, I can decipher the note."

He then pretended to read thus:—

"The bearer of this note, one of my new guards from Spolovski, is commissioned by me to reconnoitre the enemy's position, and to keep watch over the western tower from without. Let down the drawbridge as quietly as you may and allow him to descend. Be ready to re-admit him at any moment. I will send other sentinels to guard the terrace—do you, therefore, keep watch by the moat."

There was nothing suspicious in this. All seemed straightforward, and the man, without a moment's hesitation let down the drawbridge.

He was assisted eagerly by Mazeppa.

In a few moments the road was clear.

"Come to the other end of the bridge with me, my friend," said the Tartar prince; "there I can show the spot where I am about to lie in wait, that you may know from which direction I shall come when I return."

The man did so.

In an instant they stood on the ground beyond the moat.

"You see the tents of the Tartar army yonder?" asked the prince.

"I do."

"Tell the Castellan, then, that the bearer of his note fled to those tents—tell him Mazeppa has escaped!"

Then, before the man had recovered from his astonishment, he had disappeared amid the shadows of the night.

The man hastily returned to his post.

He looked eagerly round.

No one was within sight.

"Good!" he said; "I will fix the drawbridge again—I will destroy the note, and no one shall know how the Tartar devil has tricked me."

He did so.

He was not alone, however.

Out from the shadows came a weird-like frame.

It was Zisko.

A low, chuckling laugh proclaimed his presence to the sentinel.

"Ah! misshapen wretch," he cried, "have you been watching?"

He raised his gun, as if about to strike him with the butt-end.

The dwarf skipped lightly on to the battlements, and laughed at him.

"Ah!" he cried, "so Mazeppa has beaten you—eh? What will the Castellan do to you? Why, he'll have you boiled alive."

The man muttered an oath.

"The Castellan will never know it," he said musingly.

The dwarf chuckled again.

"The Castellan will know it," he cried, "for I will tell him."

"No, good Zisko; do not tell him," said the man; "I entreat you, no."

"Ho, ho! your tone is changed, is it?" returned the dwarf. "But a moment since now I was a misshapen wretch—now it is good Zisko. Kick away, my man—insult me—I am but a dog; but a dog sometimes bites."

The man cursed his own rashness, as he answered—

"Nay, then I repent me of my evil words; do not tell my lord of my folly; I have done thee no harm; I repent me, indeed I do."

"A fig for your repentance!" exclaimed the dwarf, scornfully. "Spit upon me one moment, and caress me the next, and ask me favours. No, no; if I do not tell the Castellan, it is because I have a use for you. Mark my words well."

"I do, my good Zisko."

"Are you the sentinel here to-morrow night?"

"No."

"Where are you posted?"

"On the summit of the eastern tower."

The dwarf grinned.

"I thought as much. Well, to-morrow, at eight, you are told off?"

"Yes."

"Contrive to change suits with another."

"Not with you," said the man; "you would never pass for me."

"A truce to your jests," cried Zisko, angrily. "Before you are told off for duty, you must give me your suit of armour, and a friend of mine will take your place on the parade."

"Well?"

"That is all—you understand me well?"

"Perfectly."

"Good—see that you are faithful."

The dwarf moved off.

"I will see that the Castellan knows all," muttered the man, as he paced up and down once more.

The words were fatal to him.

Zisko, who had concealed himself once more in his favourite hiding-place, heard him, and as he turned his back he sprang upon him.

Into his defenceless shoulder rushed the cold steel, and out upon the terrace rushed the hot life-blood.

A shrill cry escaped his lips.

Then all was still.

He was dead!

Zisko's project had failed, but his secret, at least, was safe. There was no time for thought, for the sound of approaching footsteps already struck his ear.

Rushing, therefore, into the passage leading to the armoury, he mixed among the advancing guards, and entered Theresa's chamber.

"Has he escaped?" asked Theresa and Zuliska, in one breath.

"He has," said Zisko; "and one who would have betrayed him is dead."

"Thank heaven!" murmured the two girls together, though not in the same words. "Thank heaven!" said Theresa. "Allah be praised!" murmured Zuliska.

Theresa glanced at Zuliska meaningly.

"I know your secret," she said.

Zuliska trembled and changed colour.

"What secret?" she cried.

"You are a woman, and love Mazeppa," answered Theresa.

Zuliska sank on her knees.

"Yes, yes," she exclaimed, "I am a woman, and I *do* love Mazeppa, but he knows it not. He does not dream that I am with the army. He looks upon me merely as Selim—a young warrior—a friend of my father. I am no rival to you, dear lady, except in thought. He will never know how I love him, or what I have sacrificed for him. He loves you well. It would be unjust to you and to me to let him learn my devotion."

Theresa took her hand—her soft, trembling hand—and raised her up.

"Rise, my sister," she said; "your secret is safe with me. I love Mazeppa—mine is a prior claim, because he loved me long ere he saw you. I cannot relinquish for anyone the dear hope of one day being his; but, if you will accept me for a friend, I am ready to be a sincere one."

Zuliska pressed the hand that raised her.

"I blame you not, dear lady," she said. "When I came hither it was with feelings of bitter hate and aversion. These have long since left my breast. I love Mazeppa—I shall never love another. But I know that he loves you well—I have been witness of your many troubles. My only wish now is that Allah may permit me to die in his defence, and save him for a long life of happiness."

There was a long pause.

Both felt a keen sense of sorrow.

Zisko broke the silence.

"I have endeavoured to aid your scheme, Selim," he said, still addressing the young girl by her masculine name, "by obtaining a suit of armour for you, and persuading one of the men to absent himself from the parade to-morrow evening. I have failed. The man promised to befriend me; I found him about to betray me, and I killed him."

Theresa shuddered.

"When—when will this bloodshed cease?" she murmured.

"Never," answered Zisko, "until the Castellan is dead, or is a prisoner in the hands of his foes. His blood-thirsty heart knows no mercy."

## CHAPTER XXV.

### BY NIGHT ON THE EASTERN TOWER.

MAZEPPA, when he fled from the sentinel, made straight for the Tartar tents.

The outposts saw a man running towards them, and imagining him to be a spy or a deserter, they at once surrounded him.

Tearing off his false beard, the young prince was at once recognised, and borne in triumph to the tent, where Abder Khan and several of the chiefs were meditating over the attack proposed for the morning.

The assault, which had been proposed and begun after the fiery speech of the old king, had been abandoned in consequence of a message from Zisko, describing the imminent danger of Mazeppa, and counselling the old Tartar king to wait and trust in him.

On seeing his son enter, the king rose, and with a cry of joy flung himself upon his breast, while the chiefs testified their delight by loud acclamations.

Far and wide through the Tartar hosts the news spread, and tremendous were the cries which rent the heavens.

In his castle the Castellan heard these cries, and knew too well their meaning.

The young prince lost no time in explaining to his friends his plan of action for the ensuing night.

The first thing to be prepared was the rope ladder, a hundred and thirty feet in length, and this a large number of men were at once commanded to begin.

The next day passed quietly.

Scarcely a shot was fired.

It was the lull before the storm.

At length the night came.

The night was dark, gusty, and tempestuous.

The moon had fallen some two hours, and left a cold grey sky, which soon was robed in clouds that came driving up from the north-west with singular rapidity.

It was a night for an act of desperation, such as that which they were about to attempt.

At half-past eleven a chosen band of twenty warriors, headed by Mazeppa, crept along the dark ground and approached the eastern tower.

There was nothing to discover their presence to the inmates of the castle.

Under the moonless heavens they were undistinguishable from the ground, and they arrived unheeded beneath the walls of the grim old tower, which stood out boldly against the cloudy sky.

"At midnight a stone shall fall into the moat," Zuliska had said.

The gong of the castle struck the hour of twelve.

Then there was a dull splash.

Mazeppa stretched out his hand and grasped a massive rope. He pulled it vigorously—it was taut above.

"Now," said Mazeppa, to the chief of his band, "you see this rope?"

"Yes"—

"Well," continued the Tartar prince, in a low but firm, clear voice, "I shall ascend by this. It will safely bear but one man. Once up, I will haul up the rope ladder. That will support ten at least. Let parties of five ascend at a time. I will descend again to let you know all is well."

"No—no; not for the world; remain there; it will be time saved and the risk is unnecessary."

"But how shall I know you understand me?"

"At half-past twelve the first man shall place his foot on the first rope" returned the Tartar; "but even now, my prince, let me beg of you to desist from this enterprise. Let one of the men—let me, whose life is not so valuable as yours —ascend first."

"No, no, my friend," said Mazeppa; "I alone know the place."

"You can explain all to me."

Mazeppa made no reply.

He had thirty minutes to do his work in, and his time was precious.

While several below held the cord tight, Mazeppa, his sword between his teeth, his gun on his back, began his ascent; shaken by the fierce wind, stunned by the thunder which now boomed fearfully over the country, and seeing, as he mounted, the terrace, the ramparts, and the far-off forests.

It would have been imagined that no man not inured to the sea, and who had not, during a hurricane, gone aloft to furl top-gallant sails, or who had not sat out at the leeward end of a yard plunging almost at every moment into the waves, could have got up in safety.

But he did.

He looked upwards on one side, but never once down.

His thoughts, moreover, were so bent upon his enterprise that he had no time for dizziness to seize him, and in ten minutes he had reached the summit.

He was about to climb over, and had raised one leg, when he saw a man seated on a stone bench exactly opposite the spot where he must reach *terra firma*.

Mazeppa felt his head swim.

His daring attempt in favour of his friend's liberty was about to fail before an unforeseen accident.

No one could have foreseen that the sentry would have planted himself exactly opposite that spot by accident, when his duty was to be ever on the move.

In twenty minutes, however, the companions of the young prince would be climbing up, perhaps, a half-fastened ladder.

Inside the port-hole, which was large, lay a heavy cannon, the carriage of which was mending.

On this depended the whole success of his enterprize.

He ensconced himself as well as he could outside, on the stone projection which served as a gutter, holding on inside the port-hole.

Then he unfastened the rope, and passed one end round the cannon.

To this, watching the sentry the whole time (the man seemed to sleep), he attached a heavy piece of iron, prepared for the purpose, which he then began lowering, by this means aiding himself in slowly drawing up the rope ladder.

The quarter struck, and the sleeper slightly moved.

Mazeppa went on deliberately with his work, as if the man had not been there, and soon found the end of the rope ladder in his hand.

At this moment the man moved again and rose.

Mazeppa had laid down his gun, but he clutched a dagger and a heavy pistol.

He had never taken life deliberately; but he now was resolved to spare not this man if he stood in the way of his success.

The sentry went to the side facing the open country, looked over, saw nothing suspicious, and returned to his seat.

In another minute he was again asleep.

"It is a mercy," murmured Mazeppa, "there are not two here to night."

Zuliska had been misinformed.

One sentinel only guarded that part of the battlements.

The Castellan believed them to be impregnable from without.

The young prince now passed his body through the loophole—crossed the battlements, and in another moment was on the top of the tower, crouching in the deep shadow of the wall.

"Who goes there?" said a deep commanding voice, that made Mazeppa shudder.

He lay still, and made no reply.

His hands clutched his pistol and his dagger, for he was resolved that no man made by God's hand should cause his enterprise to fail.

The man looked sleepily about, muttered to himself that he saw shadows everywhere, and again fell asleep.

He thus most certainly saved his own life.

At this instant Mazeppa heard distinctly the first stroke of the half-hour.

His heart sank within him.

The ladder was not safely fastened on one side.

On he went, however, with cool and steady hand, knotting and tying, until he heard the deep-mouthed bell cease to vibrate.

He had not finished yet, and his companions were ascending.

But still he pursued his task, and in a few minutes the work was completed.

The ladder seemed as firm as a rock.

Then he rose up boldly and walked slowly up and down the platform of the tower.

Meanwhile those below waited in eager impatience.

They looked like a dense black mass, so anxiously did they huddle together to watch the ascending prince.

At first they could see him well enough, but presently they lost sight of him, his figure mingling w th the darkness, except when a flash of lightning revealed his presence.

Still the vibration of the rope told he was ascending, for several below were holding it.

Suddenly this ceased.

Then an anxious moment of silence followed, all eyes being cast upwards toward the summit of the tower.

"It ascends," said the chief in a low whisper that went round the whole body like an electric shock.

Up it went, quickly at first, then slowly, and at last with so slow a motion as to alarm the daring youths.

"Mazeppa finds it too much for him, I fear," said the chief, with a shudder? "two should have ascended."

"It goes up again," exclaimed one, with an exclamation of delight.

From that moment its ascending motion never ceased.

But when about twenty yards remained uncoiled, a man exclaimed, in a startled whisper—

"He is letting something down."

All drew their breath.

Their suspense was not of long duration; they soon saw the piece of iron—Mazeppa's ingenious device for lessening his labour.

The chief lost not a moment.

He cast loose the piece of iron as soon as he could lay his hands on it and set the rope adrift.

It went up again with extreme rapidity.

Then an anxious pause ensued, and the clock struck half-past twelve.

All pressed forward.

But the chief was wise and thoughtful.

"Give him one minute's grace," he said; "he may not be quite ready."

That minute decided the fate of the entire enterprise.

Had Mazeppa not had that minute, the ladder would have fallen directly.

As it was, it was but ill-fastened.

The chief—Abdulaman—having seen that his signal, however, was safe, put his foot on the ladder and bade four follow him.

They began the ascent.

They were all brave and resolute youths—young men only had been chosen for the enterprise.

But the peril was so extreme—the undertaking so hazardous—a chafed rope might cast all headlong to the earth or on the heads of their companions—a sentry might give the alarm—that not one but felt his heart beat quicker than it had ever done before.

The ladder, to the first company, was comparatively easy.

To the last it would be terrible.

Then it would hang loosely, and shake at the will of the wind.

This wind, too, was unusually fierce.

It roared terribly amid the turrets of the castle, and among the trees of the stately forest.

Overhead boomed the low thunder.

Above, below, on every side, the vivid lightning seemed to flash, illumining the face of nature with a lurid glare and striking terror into the hearts of the boldest.

On they went, these five men, with their guns on their backs, their swords between their teeth, their daggers ready at hand.

Every man vowed a pilgrimage to Mecca, if ever he lived to enter a mosque again.

They climbed with steady and measured steps—a proceeding of considerable inconvenience when they were half-way up, for, as the thirteen left feet descended on thirteen ratlins on the left side the ladder swung fearfully to and fro.

"Stop," cried Abdulaman, suddenly, to the man next to him.

Then, as the word passed down, he bade them step, one on one side and one on the other.

They found that this remedied, in a great measure, the evil complained of.

"Allah be praised! what terrible mishap is this?" cried Abdulaman, suddenly, in a frantic tone, as he felt the ladder give way, and already saw himself, with his unfortunate companions, cast upon the heads of his friends below.

At the same instant a terrific jerk, sufficiently proclaiming that for a moment the danger was over, nearly cast them from their holding.

Then the rope remained steady.

All breathed again.

There was not a face at that moment, could their faces have been seen, but was blanched with terror.

Their hearts had almost ceased to beat.

Their wrists were wrenched.

Their hands, though clutching the thick rope, convulsively seemed about to refuse their office.

What could it mean?

Was it safe to take another step?

Or would that other step be the signal for their death?

"Shall we proceed?" whispered the man next to the leader.

Abdulaman was praying.

"We had better wait awhile," he said, "until the prince gives us notice."

But they waited in vain.

Nothing was to be heard but the roaring of the wind among the trees, and the booming of the thunder.

"Allah preserve us!" muttered the chief, "we must ascend

and take our chances of safety. We cannot now be far from the top—that once reached, we can make the ladder secure for those who follow. Upon us depend, not only our own lives, but those of others; let us be bold, then, my friends, and advance."

"We will," murmured the men.

They felt the force of his words—yet not one was there whose voice did not tremble as he answered.

Some had wives waiting for them in Tartary.

Some had beautiful girls anxiously watching their return.

They did not fear death in battle.

Battle was their legitimate sphere of action, and it presented no horror to their minds.

But death, such as was now threatened, was cold, deadly, unmanly.

Yet once more on the swaying, straining ropes they advanced, expecting every moment to be hurled, at one plunge, a hundred feet below.

----

## CHAPTER XXVI.

### IN THE TOWER.

THE first five adventurers at length reached the summit of the tower with the feelings of men snatched from sudden death.

Their first act was to examine the fastening of the ladder.

A hastily tied knot had become unfastened, and the loosened cord had given the ladder two feet of additional length.

Nothing had saved them from destruction but that the top rattlin of the ladder caught in two projecting stones of sufficient strength to bear them.

They took care now to make the whole so firm that those below had nothing to fear.

When those who were anxiously awaiting their turn felt the ladder fall for one second loose in their hands, and become two feet longer, their first impulse was flight, and some dashed away to save themselves from destruction.

Two, however, held on, and the panic, which lasted little more than a second, being over, the whole again congregated fearfully at the foot of the tower in whispered conference.

There were several brave men and true, who afterwards were not ashamed to confess that but for very terror of the others they would have retreated.

All understood that the ladder had partially given way, and even now it was possible every minute that the whole might come down about their ears.

They listened then with deep anxiety, and kept their eyes fixed upwards.

Then came the sound of a horn.

It was now one general rush towards the ladder, and the inferior chiefs had some difficulty in preventing the whole from ascending at once.

As it was positive that those above would now see to their safety, ten ventured to ascend.

At half-past one all were safely up—having performed one of the most daring feats on record, and in a cause far more justifiable than was usual in those days of wild deeds, when men judged an action less by its object than by the manner of its accomplishment.

The first instalment of the Tartar battalion had seized and made captive the sentinel, who feared instant death if he resisted.

When all were up Mazeppa advanced to the door of the cell, and knocked three times.

He was answered from within.

Then with their weapons and the tools they had brought with them, they commenced the destruction of the door.

They worked as silently as possible, and amid the roaring of the gale the sounds of their labour were heard by none.

The door was massive, and the tools used by the Tartars very unequal to the task.

Two hours consequently elapsed before the huge portal yielded to their efforts.

But it did yield, and at half-past three Cassim and his followers saw Mazeppa enter with his brave troops.

Zuliska rushed to the prince and grasped his hand.

"Welcome, brave prince," she cried, "welcome!—thou who art not only our king, but our friend and saviour."

"But what means this?" exclaimed Mazeppa; "you are in chains, Cassim."

It was too true.

Each prisoner was chained to the wall.

The irons were heavy.

"This defeats our purpose," said Mazeppa; "we have no weapons with which to undo these fetters."

Zuliska approached him.

"Below," she whispered, "is the gaoler. In his keeping are the keys which unlock these massive padlocks. Close the door, extinguish the light, and I will bring him hither; once in the room, we will make him captive, and force him to release them."

"Good, my friend," said Mazeppa, "you are a bold and sagacious youth. Do as you propose, at once."

Zuliska extinguished the lamp.

Then she tapped at the door.

The sleepy sentinel was some time in answering.

A harder blow from Mazeppa's hand on the portal roused him.

"What ho, there!' he cried.

"It is I, Selim."

"Well; what then?"

"I desire to descend."

The man grumbled.

But the orders of the Castellan were peremptory.

Selim was to be allowed to come and go as he pleased.

He opened the door, therefore, and Zuliska, stepping out, hurried down the dark staircase.

The gaoler was asleep in bed.

He was so fast locked in slumber, that her loud summons at the door failed to wake him, though it brought out his assistant.

"I must see Stroveski, the gaoler, at once," cried Zuliska.

The young man looked frightened.

"I cannot wake him now," he said.

"Why not?"

"I dare not; he will strangle me if I disturb his rest. You know as well as I his fierce and ungovernable temper.

Zuliska stamped her foot impatiently.

"You must wake him," she cried; "it is a matter of life and death."

The young man was obstinate.

"No," he said, "unless by order of the Castellan, I will not wake him."

Here was a dilemma.

What could she do?

Was she to allow an enterprise to fail, in which Mazeppa had risked his life already, because this youth refused to obey her?

"If you will not wake him," she cried, "let me pass. I will risk his anger."

The youth stood in her way.

"No, no," he said, "that would be worse than all. Depart, I say, for I will not disturb or have him disturbed for anyone, except the lord of the castle."

"I tell you he *must* be roused," exclaimed Zuliska, passionately.

"And I," cried the youth, "tell you that he must not, and that if you do not leave this room I will pitch you out into the corridor."

This was enough.

Zuliska measured with her eye the stature of her opponent.

He was rather below the middle height, yet built vigorously.

Would her soft and yielding form, her pliant limbs unused to exertion of any kind, have any chance against his manly frame?

She resolved to risk the chance.

To fail was to expose Cassim and Mazeppa to a cruel death.

She put on a most persuasive tone.

"Will you not let me in?" she asked.

The youth replied roughly.

"No!" he said, "I have already answered you. Leave the place at once."

"Take, then, the consequences of your brutality," cried the Tartar maiden, as she sprang at his throat.

The attack was so sudden and so unexpected, that he was borne to the earth before he was aware of what had occurred.

He had no time to resist.

Before he could place his hand upon his short sword, Zuliska's dagger was at his throat.

"Struggle," she cried, as she knelt on his chest, " and I will kill you."

She first took the precaution of disarming him.

Then, with her belt, she bound his hands, and with his own belt his feet.

After this she stuffed a piece of his coat, which she tore off, into his mouth, and proceeded, with her dagger in her hand, along the corridor leading to the gaoler's chamber.

Her first idea was to awaken him, and induce him to mount the stairs, on pretence of the dangerous illness of one of the prisoners.

But his heavy slumber gave rise to a far different scheme.

Would it not be better to creep into his room, steal the keys, and hurry back with them herself?

Full of eagerness for the success of this plot, she advanced rapidly.

Confident in the integrity and sagacity of his assistant, Stroveski had not locked his door, and it yielded at once to Zuliska's hand.

She entered the chamber noiselessly—stealthily.

A lamp burned brightly by the couch of the sleeping gaoler.

She glanced anxiously round her in vain.

The keys were not to be seen.

She traversed the room with step as light as that of a fairy, examining each nook and corner.

But what she sought was nowhere to be found.

What was she to do?

Was she to give up the search, wake the gaoler, and risk his anger?

Even if she did not exasperate him, would not the sight of the bound assistant in the passage prove that she had come with no friendly intent?

At length an idea struck her.

Would not the most natural spot for the safe custody of the keys be beneath the gaoler's head?

She approached the bed, and, kneeling down, felt beneath the pillow.

A thrill of joy rushed through her frame.

The keys were there!

Slowly, without any show of an impatience which would have been fatal to her enterprise, she withdrew them; and, passing across the chamber, entered the corridor in safety.

Then she turned and locked the door of the room she had left.

A low groan attracted her attention as she was preparing to ascend the stairs.

It proceeded from the captive assistant.

Zuliska, actuated by a feeling of pity, stopped and spoke.

"You will soon be released," she cried. "Fear not—I will protect your life."

She then, with a light step and a lighter heart, rushed upwards towards the summit of the tower.

When she reached the door of the chamber in which Cassim and his followers were immured, and where Mazeppa and his men were beginning to be alarmed at her absence, she was at once admitted.

"Ah!" she cried to the sentry, "the lamp is extinguished —pray enter and light it."

The man obeyed.

No sooner had he entered with his light than she closed the door.

He lit the lamp.

Scarcely had he done so when he saw how matters stood, and that he had been betrayed.

He at once understood his situation, and the best method of meeting it.

He dropped his keys and slid into a seat.

"It is useless to resist," he said ; " do as you will."

"You say well, my friend," returned Mazeppa ; "it is useless to resist. Remain quiet, and no harm shall reach you."

Then, with the assistance of Zuliska, he undid the bonds which held Cassim and his followers powerless.

In five minutes they were free.

Thirty armed men held possession of the eastern tower.

Silently, with hearts full of emotion, Cassim and Mazeppa grasped each other's hands.

It was some moments before they spoke.

"My prince," cried Cassim, "to you I owe my life, my honour—everything."

Mazeppa smiled.

"And I," he said, " owe everything to the young warrior to whom you introduced me."

He turned towards Zuliska.

The young girl blushed.

"I have done but my duty," she said—" nothing more."

"And now," said Mazeppa, "the question is—what are we to do next? Have you any idea, Selim, of the number of men in the tower?"

"Seventy."

"And we are but twenty."

"Surely, my prince," cried Zuliska, in alarm, " you do not dream of holding the tower?"

The prince smiled.

"Indeed, yes," he said; "we must have reinforcements."

"But how?"

"I must descend the rope, and call up a fresh body of men."

Cassim stepped forward.

"No, my prince," he said, " this shall not be. If you thus endanger your life again, I swear I will raise an outcry which will have for its effect my capture and death."

"But what else can be done?"

"Some one else, lighter than you, must descend."

The prince looked around him.

His company were all stalwart men, though but youths in age.

He smiled.

"It seems to me," he cried, " that I am the lightest in the room."

Zuliska rushed forward.

"My prince," she exclaimed, "you are wrong. I am the lightest."

Mazeppa glanced pityingly over the soft girlish form.

Yet even then, when for the first time his eyes wandered over its rounded outlines, he suspected not her sex.

"My boy," he said, " would you trust yourself to such peril? The ladder is unfastened below, and the wind may sweep you away."

"I fear not," returned Zuliska; "I will descend at once. In one hour the turret shall be garrisoned by a thousand men."

She turned towards the door.

Mazeppa still hesitated.

"Come," she cried, "come; time is precious. An hour yet, the sun will rise, and your enterprise will fail."

Mazeppa and Cassim followed her mechanically.

So, also, did several of the band.

They admired the undaunted courage of the active young warrior, to whose presence of mind, indeed, they all owed their lives.

She led the way to the battlements.

Fortunately the wind had sunk.

Yet still the ladder flapped idly in the breeze.

Mazeppa's heart sank within him.

---

## CHAPTER XXVII.

### THE SECRET DISCOVERED.

"See, Selim," he cried, "the ladder is a hundred and twenty feet in length. Have you strength—have you courage to hold out so long?"

Zuliska stood undaunted.

"Yes," she said, quietly; "fear not. I am equal to the task. Hold the ladder firmly above, and in one hour your men shall be with you."

"Go, then, and Allah preserve you!" rejoined the young prince, as he embraced her; go, and take with you our blessings. Come, let me aid your descent."

He led the young girl to the battlements, helped her over the fearful brink, and then, with Cassim, held the ladder.

The young girl gazed with unmitigated terror at the dreary waste of space above—around—below her.

But she must not fail.

Her heart must be strong—unyielding—courageous.

Everything depended on her—the honour, the success, the life of Mazeppa.

Meanwhile the young prince leaned over the battlements, and watched the girl as she descended.

"A cloud obscures my mind," he said; "I cannot well understand my own feelings. Selim has for a long time been an enigma to me; and yet a moment ago the enigma seemed solved. The form that embraced me but now was that, I am convinced, of a woman. Yet who can it be? It is not Theresa."

He mused a moment.

"A woman it was, I am certain," he repeated; "for as I pressed the form to my heart, I felt the fullness of her bosom against my breast, and the roundness of her figure, too, in my arms. Who can it be, since it is not Theresa? Can she be a traitress?"

This idea, however, he cast from him in scorn.

"A traitress and brave such dangers! No—it is impossible. I am sadly unjust. It may be some girl to whom I may have unwittingly made myself welcome; yet I know of none but Zuliska."

The idea once formed in his mind, he turned to Cassim.

"Cassim," he said, "I have a strange notion."

"What is that?"

"About that young warrior."

"Indeed!"

"Yes; I believe it to be a woman."

Cassim started.

"Why think you so?" he asked.

"The form—the carriage—the manners, all bespeak the female sex. When but a moment ago I clasped the young warrior to my heart, I felt that my arms enclosed a woman's body. Who is it Cassim? Can you not tell me, since it is to you I owe my introduction?"

Cassim felt confused; yet he answered calmly,—

"I cannot tell."

"You said you knew him."

"Yes, as the offspring of a well-known chieftain of our tribe."

"Who is he?"

"Abdulaman."

Mazeppa mused.

"Are you sure it is not Zuliska?"

Cassim flushed.

"Why should she be here?" he asked.

A smile answered him.

"Why, I say?" he repeated.

"That is not for *me* to tell," said Mazeppa, calmly and proudly.

Cassim's answer came angrily—threateningly.

For a moment he forgot to whom he owed his life and freedom.

"Why should you suppose that my daughter is here in your body-guard?" he asked. "Do you imagine, because you are Prince of Tartary, that the women of our tribe could so far forget themselves as to become your satellites? No, Mazeppa"—

Mazeppa caught his arm.

"Hold, Cassim!" he cried, "let us not quarrel at this time of danger."

Cassim hung his head.

"True," he said, "to you I owe my life."

Mazeppa made a gesture of impatience.

"I meant not," he said, "to remind you of that; but it would be sad to quarrel over what, in my mind was but a surmise. Your daughter might be here against your will. Women are wilful. I speak not of myself, because I can safely assure you that I never, by word or deed, tampered with your child's affections. But in the army there may be some warrior whom she adores and for whose sake she has thrown off the fears, as she has done the clothing of her sex."

Cassim's heart sank.

Mazeppa's words too truly proved his complete indifference.

"My schemes are useless," he muttered; "Zuliska has no charms for him while Theresa lives."

And then the devil tempter whispered in his ear,—

"What if Theresa were dead? What if a traitor destroyed her?"

But his heart, in truth good and noble, rejected the vile suggestion.

"No," he thought, "better to die—better lose for ever all chance of inheriting the crown of Tartary, than to have the guilt of innocent blood on my head."

It was a long time to wait.

A time, too, of awful suspense.

Mazeppa and Cassim walked to and fro with excited strides.

Of one thing, however, they were satisfied.

Zuliska was safe.

Even at that height they would have heard her cry of anguish, had she fallen from the ladder.

The twilight which precedes the dawn had already begun to spread itself over the castle, before a warning shake of the ropes announced that some one was about to ascend.

The ladder was now held tight above and below, and in ten minutes after the first warning was given, ten men stepped upon the ramparts.

Among them was Zuliska.

Mazeppa hurried to her.

"Brave girl!" he cried, "I have penetrated your disguise. Who and what are you?"

Zuliska was so taken by surprise that she almost fell.

He caught her in his arms.

"Tell me," he said; "confide in me. Tell me which of my warriors it is who has won your priceless love, and he shall be made my chief for your sake."

Zuliska recoiled.

He had said, "I have penetrated your disguise."

Naturally, therefore, she imagined that he knew her to be Cassim's daughter.

"And do you suppose, proud prince," she cried, "that the daughter of Cassim would condescend to wed a mere soldier—the daughter of Cassim, who, until your coming, was looked upon as future king of Tartary?"

Mazeppa gazed at her in surprise.

He took her hand.

"Brave girl," he said, "be not offended with me. To you I owe all, as I have said—honour—liberty—life itself. I would destroy the man who dared insult you. Believe, then, that all I say is said in kindness and respect. Tell me who it is whom you love, and if it be in my power to order it so, your desires shall be gratified."

The men were still crowding on the battlements.

The attention of all was directed towards the rope ladder.

None noticed the prince and the young warrior, who now gradually withdrew from the throng to a spot where the shadow of the inner tower concealed them.

Zuliska, was a wild, untutored girl.

Her whole hope in life was to obtain Mazeppa for a husband.

Not as her father wished it.

He wished him as a son-in-law, because the union would bring into his family power, and wealth, and distinction.

For these she cared not.

All that she coveted was his smiles—his kind words—his love.

And now, as he bent over her, as her arm rested on his, as his face was turned towards her, and his eyes seemed to beam with a more kindly light—all her resolutions gave way.

ZISCO INFORMS MAZEPPA OF THERESA'S PRESENCE AT THEIR FRIEND'S CASTLE.

She forgot what she had said to Theresa—forgot everything but that the one she loved was by her side; and knowing not that it was not her place to speak, waited but an opportunity to pour forth the love of her aching, breaking, heart.

"Tell me," said Mazeppa, kindly, "tell me—who is it you love?"

Zuliska sank upon the stone parapet, sitting carelessly, fearlessly there, though beneath her—a hundred and twenty feet beneath her—was the hard plain, and one false movement would have been her destruction.

At that moment love absorbed all other feelings.

"Oh, Mazeppa!" she cried, with deep emotion, "can you ask me!"

He sat down in alarm by her side, and took her hand.

For a moment neither spoke.

She awaited in fear his reply.

He feared to give it. A bewildered feeling was in his mind. Could this girl love him?

Yet why?

He had never encouraged such a feeling.

Still, had she not tended him in illness? had she not twice saved his life? had she not begged to be attached to his person?

"Dear Zuliska," he said; "tell me—is it I whom you love?"

She threw herself into his arms.

"Yes, yes, Mazeppa," she cried frantically, "it is you—you alone whom I love."

He kissed her pale and throbbing brow, and pressed her weary form to his.

No. 7.

What could he do?

What could he say?

Nothing in this world is there so difficult for a man as to reject the love of a beautiful and innocent woman.

The Genius of Sorrow himself could scarcely invent a situation more trying, more heart-rending than that of Mazeppa at this moment.

And yet for her he could feel no love.

When he kissed her—when he pressed her to his heart—it was as a brother might a sister—nothing more.

"Dearest Zuliska," he said, "will you listen to me patiently?"

She answered "Yes."

Yet her heart sank.

She felt the import of his coming words.

"You know, Zuliska," he proceeded, "you know well—I love another."

"Alas! yes."

"You know, also, that I am beloved—betrothed, and that, for the sake of this beloved one this army has besieged this castle."

"I do."

"Forgive me, then, if I say that you must tear my image from your heart; forget me—I am unworthy of your innocent devotion. Allah himself knows that you have proved yourself worthy of any man's love. Forgive me if I am ungrateful. You are a good, brave girl—I esteem you, I honour you—next to Theresa, I love you."

"Thank you, even for that," said the sorrowing girl.

At this moment Abdulaman's horn sounded shrilly.

Mazeppa and Zuliska started up.

" One favour I crave," she cried.

" What is that ? "

" Let my secret remain as before, even to my father."

Mazeppa pressed her hand.

" It shall be so," he said; " but your father surely knows you are here ? "

" Yes."

A cloud crossed the brow of the youthful prince at this reply.

What, after all, if she loved him but for his power ?

Zuliska saw his frown.

Her woman's heart guessed its reason at once.

" Ah," she murmured, " you deem me unworthy, I perceive."

" How so ? "

" You believe that my presence with the army is but part of a conspiracy to keep the succession to the Tartar throne in our family, I swear it is not so. My father would welcome our union, that it might bring him power and distinction. I should have welcomed it as the union of two fond hearts. Now I should greet with pleasure a death which would free me from a world where my heart is cast away on one who loves me not, and where my dearest hopes are misinterpreted and abused."

Before he could detain her she had passed away, and was lost amid the throng.

----

## CHAPTER XXVIII.

### THE FALL OF THE TOWER.

THE horn blown by Abdulaman, announced that the first body of men had arrived on the ramparts.

There were now in the tower one hundred men, and as the dawn was fast breaking, it was deemed prudent to delay no longer taking final possession of the place.

Mazeppa accordingly, with eighty men, proceeded down the stairs towards the courtyard.

Abdulaman and the rest remained above to superintend the ascending of the troops, who still kept pouring in in bodies of tens.

In the whole tower there were but twenty men, and in a few moments these were all prisoners.

The youthful assistant of the gaoler, to whom Zuliska had promised safety, was then sent by Mazeppa to announce to the Castellan the capture of the eastern tower.

He was also commissioned to demand a capitulation, or at least a conference.

At first the Castellan, dismayed, and foaming with rage at hearing of the capture of the fortress under his very eyes, refused all idea of conferring with one whom he denominated as an impostor—a traitor, a low-born menial.

At length his better sense prevailed.

" This man," thought he, " is more powerful than I. A little longer and I shall be his prisoner, if the king sends me not reinforcements. Perhaps, after all, I had better see him."

He mused a moment.

" Yes," he said to the youth, " tell him that in a quarter of an hour I will meet him alone in the courtyard."

The youth shook his head.

" I fear he will not consent."

" Why not ? "

" You know these Tartar dogs," resumed the youth; " he will suspect treachery."

" True," said the Castellan, " we will meet alone; but in the presence of our soldiers, who will keep at a respectful distance. Go, now, and give him my message."

The youth did so.

Mazeppa joyfully acceded.

He hoped for this as an opportunity for humbling his enemy.

He drew up his soldiers near the entrance of the Eastern Tower, and waited.

The time soon passed.

The door of the courtyard opened, and the Castellan appeared, heading a hundred soldiers.

The latter remained near the portal, and the Castellan advanced.

The lord and his former page met in the centre of the pavement.

The Castellan was the first to speak.

" Well, haughty Tartar," he cried " who have by stratagem robbed me of a part of my fortress, what is it you now demand ? "

" Can you ask such a question ? " retorted Mazeppa, coldly.

The Castellan made no reply.

" I demand," cried the young prince, " the unconditional surrender of this fortress."

" Well, and that granted."

" I demand it to be delivered up to me in four-and-twenty hours—the men to march out unarmed, and the castle to be utterly destroyed by my army. I have sworn that not one stone shall stand upon another. I shall keep my vow."

The Castellan could scarcely contain his wrath.

But he did, and said—

" Well, and then ? "

" I demand the hand of your daughter."

" And then ? "

" Your public recantation of the injurious epithets you have applied to me, and a public apology for the disgraceful injury you inflicted on me by fastening me naked to a wild steed."

" Vile menial ! shameless impostor ! " shouted the Castellan, in a fit of ungovernable fury, " never will I allow thee to dictate terms to me."

" Have a care, proud man."

" Of what ? "

" Of my vengeance ! It will be terrible," said Mazeppa, with stern coldness.

" I scorn it ! Do you suppose I am brought down so low as to receive terms from you—to see my soldiers disgraced—to wed my daughter to a discarded page—to apologise for treating you as one does faithless serfs ? No—no; if your army conquers it will find but a heap of ruins, and I will destroy my daughter ere I myself die."

The words were uttered in such a tone of cruel rage that Mazeppa doubted not for one moment that he meant all he threatened.

His heart sank; and as that moment it was with the utmost difficulty he restrained an impulse to destroy the tyrant on the spot.

But prudence and his respect for good faith restrained him.

He prepared to go.

" Return, cruel and insatiable tyrant," he cried, " to whom age has not brought wisdom or respect for justice. Return to your castle and your grave."

He then turned on his heel without vouchsafing to await a reply.

" By Heavens ! " cried the Castellan, as he re-entered his stronghold and the heavy door closed behind him, " by heavens ! that haughty boy shall rue his insolence. Go, Kolzoff, and see my orders are obeyed. I myself will give the signal."

Meanwhile among the opposite party there was a council of war.

Along the edge of the courtyard on one side ran the battlements encircling the tower, and on the other side ran a passage which communicated with the basements.

This, however, owing to its peculiar formation, favoured the besieged rather than the besiegers; and Mazeppa at once resolved to destroy it.

He divided his men accordingly into two parts.

One, headed by Cassim, was to destroy the stone passage.

The second, headed by himself, was to attempt an entrance by the door through which the Castellan had passed.

The first was an enterprise of no very great danger, though it involved considerable difficulty.

It was exposed to none of the cannon of the fortress, and to none, moreover, of the small windows from which the soldiery could fire their muskets.

Mazeppa and his companions were far more exposed to peril.

Above and around the portal through which the Castellan had entered, there were barred casements, or rather loop-holes, at every one of which could be distinguished the mailed forms of Polish warriors. But Mazeppa little knew that these armed figures were there not to fire upon their enemies as they advanced—not to ward off an attack upon the castle; but to be the spectators of a fearful scene.

Beneath the court-yard were vast vaults, which had been used from time immemorial as the repositories of grain and other necessaries of life.

Since the beginning of the siege, however, they had been put into requisition by the soldiery as store-houses for their guns and ammunition.

They were, indeed, well adapted for this purpose, as it was next to an impossibility for any of the missiles of the Tartars to reach them.

The precaution, however, could scarcely be considered necessary.

The Tartars were entirely unaccustomed to the operation of a regular siege, such as that of the Castle of Laurinski.

Their experience lay in warfare widely different from this.

They were used to wild maurauding expeditions—the laying waste of corn fields, the destruction of villages—the burning of forests.

It was against their courage, but more against their wily stratagems, that the Poles had to take precautions.

Their sole weapons were their muskets.

In the Tartar army there was not one single cannon.

Mazeppa was the guiding spirit of the whole expedition.

Without him, the army would have been a body without a soul.

Against him, therefore, the Castellan was urged by prudence and by the special hate he bore him, to direct his first attack.

A train of gunpowder accordingly had been laid during the conference between Mazeppa and the Castellan; and as Mazeppa and his men advanced from the eastern tower, the Castellan gave orders to fire the mine.

The vault containing the powder was near the basement of the eastern tower, and it could, therefore, be safely concluded that the western tower would be uninjured.

The followers of the young prince had scarcely passed more than four or five yards across the immense courtyard, before the explosion took place.

The floor of the courtyard swelled up at the edges, as if under the influence of an earthquake, while the centre burst forth like a volcano, vomiting smoke and flame.

For a moment the smoke was so dense as entirely to conceal the devastation caused by this terrible ruse of the Castellan.

When this cleared away a fearful scene presented itself.

Dead bodies were strewn here, there, and everywhere, each one deprived of some limb.

Amid the horrid confusion, three persons at length rose and assisted in helping out of the debris several others.

These there were Mazeppa, Cassim, and Zuliska.

Their escape was miraculous.

Cassim was in the act of climbing up a ladder held by Zuliska, and Mazeppa was issuing a last order to his men near the gate of the eastern tower.

The explosion did not, therefore, reach them sufficiently to do them any material injury; but only to shake them from their feet.

" Come," cried Mazeppa, when all who had escaped rose to their feet; " the vengeance of the Castellan will fall upon himself. Come quickly—follow me."

He seized the ladder and rushed towards the battlements.

All followed.

This was no time for explanation or parley.

They reached the wall, clambered over it, and were soon on the terrace.

Here they would have halted had they been in greater numbers.

As it was there were but ten left, and at any moment the Castellan could sweep them before him.

Hastily letting down the drawbridge, before the eyes of the affrighted sentinel, they left the castle, and dashed round towards the basement of the eastern tower.

" Hold !" cried Mazeppa; " do not approach too near."

" Why ? " said Cassim.

" Because in another moment the tower will give way at the base, and fall upon our enemies."

" But our friends at the base ? " asked Zuliska.

" They must perish," said Mazeppa, gloomily; " we cannot help them."

This was enough.

Without another word, Zuliska darted towards the base of the tower.

Her speed and her disordered looks alarmed the men.

She was reckless of danger.

" Fly—fly !" she cried ; " fly, in the the name of Heaven ! "

They asked nothing further.

All had heard the explosion—had wondered at its cause, and had no need of her words to make them connected with her fears.

There were but fifty there.

Some were already in the tower—some on the summit— some still climbing up the ropes.

None of these could be saved.

Five minutes passed in awe-stricken silence.

They all watched in deadly fear the doomed building.

They were quickly joined by numbers of men from the camp, amongst the foremost, Abder Khan, who silently pressed the hand of Cassim.

" My son," he said, seeing Mazeppa's frantic looks, " what ails you ? "

" In another moment the tower will fall," he cried, " and bury in its ruins five hundred of our bravest warriors."

As he spoke a body of five men came rushing towards them.

They were those on the ladder who had seen the panic and descended.

And now, clambering over the battlements—running over the terrace, and leaping into the moat, came scores of others who had guessed the imminence of their danger.

They were met on the terrace by a body of the Castellan's troops.

Ill-fated men !

They were the victims of an insatiable and ungovernable rage.

The Castellan, however, had not ruthlessly placed them in danger.

He had never calculated the peril which would accrue to him and to his men by the adoption of his cruel scheme to destroy his foes.

At length the crash came.

The tower tottered—a roar as of artillery was heard—the walls were split in every direction; and the fabric which for a hundred years had braved wind and tempest, fell in a crumbling mass.

A cloud of dust obscured the face of the heavens.

Shrieks and groans, and cries for mercy were mingled horribly—mingled, too, the voices of friend and foes.

From his window the Castellan saw the fall, and trembled.

In her still chamber Theresa heard the sound and wept.

From their posts the soldiers beheld the fearful scene, and began to murmur against their leader.

A superstitious awe seized them.

It seemed as if Heaven itself were warring against them, and punishing the Castellan for his reckless waste of human life.

Out on the plain it was different.

The whole Tartar army knelt and prayed for the souls of their slaughtered brothers; while Mazeppa in his heart registered a vow of vengeance.

## CHAPTER XXIX.

### THE CONFLAGRATION.

A GLOOM was over the entire Tartar army.

There was not a heart there, however, which was not impressed with a deep sorrow at the loss of so many brave companions.

And yet with this gloom mingled a stern spirit of revenge.

During the day the whole body of men remained quiescent.

Here and there a gun was fired by some outlying picket, hidden behind the fallen masonry, at some stray sentinel or scout.

But this was all.

There was a lull over everything.

They seemed to be awaiting a fitting opportunity for revenge.

Night came on, and with it a movement took place in the Tartar army.

This movement was made independently of the chiefs, for they were engaged in deep consultation in the tent of the young king, and knew nothing of all that occurred.

The tents furthest removed from his, however, were soon emptied of their inmates, who, with various weapons of offence and defence, and unlighted torches, took their way through the silent wood.

What could be their errand?

Evidently it could not be one of mercy, for their brows were knit, their lips compressed, and they walked with the determined air of men resolved to dare all in a desperate revenge.

Meanwhile Mazeppa was unfolding to his chiefs a detailed plan of siege—a plan which would enable them to meet the Castellan on more even terms.

Amid the ruins of the eastern tower were several cannon,

These he proposed to extricate from the piles of fallen masonry, and place, some in front of the drawbridge, others so as to command the entrance opening into the courtyard.

To defend the gunners while at their work—work novel to them—he proposed to raise heavy works, using the masonry of the destroyed tower to form them.

His plan was received with loud acclamations.

His father especially was enthusiastic in favour of it.

He, more than any there, saw in the young prince the genius of a great monarch.

We need scarcely say that his scheme was at once decided on, and it was proposed to commence operations that very night.

It was just at this moment that a messenger came rushing in.

"The village is on fire," he cried.

All looked aghast.

"Whose work is this?" said Mazeppa, sternly.

"The work of those who love their brothers, and have revenged their murder," replied the messenger,

Mazeppa and the king, followed by all the chiefs, rushed out with one accord and glanced towards the blazing village.

It was but a glimpse, but it showed them the crowd gathering and clustering round one house in particular.

Some of the armed men were pressing to the front to break down the doors and windows.

Some were bringing brands from the nearest fire.

Some were with lifted faces following their course upon the roof, and pointing them out to their companions; all raging and roaring like the flames they lighted up.

They saw some men thirsting for the treasures of strong liquor which they knew were stored within.

They saw others who had been wounded, sinking down into the opposite doorways, and dying, solitary wretches, in the midst of all the vast assemblage.

Here a frightened woman trying to escape; and there a lost child.

There was a drunken ruffian, unconscious of the death-wound on his head, raving and fighting to the last.

All these things, and even such trivial incidents as a man with his hat off, or turning round, or stooping down, or shaking hands with another—they marked distinctly, yet in a glance so brief that in the act of stepping back, they lost the whole, and saw but the pale faces of each other, and the red sky above them.

Mazeppa gazed at his father for a moment.

"This is very sad," cried Abder Khan.

"It is sad—it is madness—sheer madness and cruelty!" exclaimed Mazeppa. "Why should these innocent men and women and children suffer for the wrongs done by the lord of yonder castle? why should they be punished for him?"

Then he turned suddenly to Cassim.

"Order out my body guard," he said; "we must try and stay this riot."

Abder Khan drew him aside, as Cassim departed on his errand.

"My son," he said, "be not rash."

Mazeppa gazed at him in surprise.

"Rash," he cried, "I am not rash; I only seek to put a stop to unseemly violence."

Abder Khan shook his head.

"It is one of the terrors of war," he said; "one which you cannot hope to prevent. The principle of war is that the innocent must suffer for the guilty. Be careful not to irritate your people by repressing their natural impulses."

"I will take your advice," said Mazeppa, "in so far as this goes,—that I will use persuasion, not force. See, here come my men—let us advance."

About a hundred men, headed by Cassim now came up.

Then hastily they hurried through the wood, and made their way towards the burning village.

When they reached it, the conflagration was at its height; the human demons of fire were yelling and shouting with triumph, unheeding the ruin they were heaping upon innocent heads.

The spirit house, with half-a-dozen others near at hand, was one great, glowing blaze.

No one had essayed to quench the flames or stop their progress; but now a body of soldiers actively engaged themselves in pulling down two old wooden houses which were every moment in danger of taking fire, and which could scarcely fail, if they were left to burn, to extend the conflagration immensely.

The tumbling down of nodding walls and heavy blocks of wood, the hooting and execration of the crowd, the distant firing of other military detachments, the distracted looks and cries of those whose habitations were in danger, the hurrying to and fro of frightened people with their goods—the reflection in every quarter of the sky, of deep red, soaring flames, as though the last day had come, and the whole universe were burning—the dust, and smoke, and drift of fiery particles, scorching and kindling all they fell upon—the hot unwholesome vapour, the blight on everything—the stars, and moon and very sky obliterated,—made up such a sum of dreariness and ruin, that it seemed as if the face of heaven were blotted out, and night, in its rest and quiet and softened light, never could look upon the earth again.

The Castellan saw the terrible scene from his window, and trembled.

And Theresa trembled too.

Among those wild men, one was there who loved her.

Only one knew her.

What, then, might be her fate if, in revenge for her father's mad obstinacy, they were to sack the castle, unheedful of the orders of their king?

She was not alone in this thought.

This it was which made the proud lord of the castle tremble.

This it was which made the soldiers stand listless on their posts.

This it was that filled the castle with groups of anxious whisperers, and almost produced a spirit of disaffection among the soldiery.

The conflagration raged until long past midnight.

Then, when all had been saved that was possible to be saved, Mazeppa drew a picked body of men towards the ruins of the eastern tower, and began the work which they had that night decided on.

The night was dark.

The smouldering village now lit up the sky with but a feeble gleam of redness.

But fearing nothing, and desirous of having as much light as possible for their work, the Tartars lit their torches.

These stuck here and there in the masses of fallen masonry cast a lurid glare over everything.

It was a fantastic scene.

Here an untenanted chamber but half destroyed—here a mound of earth, cast up by the explosion of the mine—here a mass of stonework already assuming definite proportions beneath the exertions of a number of Tartars.

From the castle poured an incessant volley of musketry.

They heeded it not.

Amid the hail of bullets stood Mazeppa, conspicuous by his splendid dress.

Yet he remained untouched.

He seemed to bear a charmed life.

In the glare of the torches his very features could be distinguished by the soldiers of the castle.

Yet none seemed able to harm him.

The Tartars worked with enthusiasm.

The presence among them of their young leader, sharing their danger, and even courting especial danger for himself, animated them with the utmost zeal.

Before morning a row of fortifications had risen, and in them were placed the cannon extricated from the ruins,

The Castellan had observed these movements without being able to take any measures to prevent them.

He found himself, therefore, on that morning, opposed no longer to a barbarous horde, but to a regular besieging army.

With the gray of the morning the Tartars opened fire upon the western tower.

They were answered but feebly.

On the side of the castle facing the ruins of the eastern tower, there were, as we have said, no cannon, and the muskets of the besieged were almost useless against the Tartars, ensconced as they were behind their solid fortifications.

Before the evening waned, the fire of the Tartars had effected almost a breach in the wall of the castle, and it was decided by Mazeppa that, after a night spent in rest, the Tartar force should attack the stronghold in the morning, and carry it at the point of the sword.

The night passed.

The soldiers, strengthened by long hours of repose, formed themselves in line almost ere the red flush of the dawn had crimsoned the eastern hills.

The trumpet sounded.

The soldiers advanced, with Mazeppa at their head.

There was no opposition.

They approached the door.

It yielded to their touch.

"Halt!" cried Mazeppa, "there is treachery here!"

---

## CHAPTER XXX.

### A NEW DIFFICULTY.

EAGER as they were to meet their hated enemy, the Tartars, had they been left to their own guidance, would have entered in spite of the suspicious aspect of affairs.

But the history of the eastern tower was fresh in Mazeppa's memory.

He knew full well that the campaign in which they were engaged was, after all, but a personal matter of his own.

They were fighting, not because the Tartar nation had been insulted—not because they were eager to punish the Poles for some victorious foray—but because he himself had been maltreated, and desired to wrest from the hands of the tyrant who had oppressed him the one object of his love.

"Soldiers," cried Mazeppa, "be careful; let us not perish as our brothers did through the treachery of our foe, beneath the ruins of the eastern tower. Let me enter first and see what this silence means."

Zuliska approached him.

"Nay, noble chieftain," she cried, "this must not be. You are our king; upon you depend the hopes of Tartary. You have already risked your life for your people—it must not be again permitted. I will enter alone—the Castellan will not harm me."

So saying, without awaiting his reply, she advanced and entered the corridor.

The silence of death reigned throughout the castle.

She proceeded onwards, but met no one.

The place was evidently abandoned.

After threading a few of the deserted corridors, she returned to the spot where Mazeppa and his followers were anxiously awaiting her.

"The Castellan has quitted the castle," she cried; "the fortress is entirely abandoned."

Mazeppa started.

"Great heavens!" he cried, "whither can they have fled?"

There was a moment's pause.

"I have it," cried Zuliska. "They have fled to the Castle of Spolovski."

"You are right," cried Mazeppa. "We will destroy this place, and we will march thither before eventide. Let us enter now and search for the magazine."

He then led the way into the castle.

It was soon discovered that the Castellan must have taken his measures for some time beforehand.

Not a single musket was to be found; and the magazine was nearly exhausted.

Mazeppa's arrangements were soon made.

A train was made connecting the outworks of the Tartars with the vaults containing the powder, which was so disposed that the explosion would destroy the whole of one of the principal walls.

When everything was arranged, Mazeppa gave the order for his troops to retreat; and when he imagined them to be quite beyond the reach of danger, he fired the train, and ran hastily towards the tents.

In a moment the mine exploded.

As in the case of the eastern tower, the building tottered, the walls split in every direction, and then the whole mass fell, sending up a cloud of dust towards the heavens.

Then a second vault exploded, and the remaining wall fell.

In a few moments was thus destroyed the labour of years, which had withstood the storms of ages.

No time was to be lost.

In order to gain upon the fugitives, and attack the castle ere it was prepared, it was necessary to start at once; and without explaining his motives to any but Abder Khan and the principal chiefs, he gave the order to march.

Across the country marched the vast host, with their banners flying and trumpets sounding.

Before them the country smiled beneath the glory of the setting sun.

Behind them still arose the smoke of the smouldering village, and wherever they passed they trampled down the cornfields and destroyed hamlets, disregarding alike the injunctions of their leader and the cries of the sufferers.

It was midnight ere, guided by one of the peasants whom they had made captive, they reached the Castle of Spolovski.

It was of a construction far different to that of the Castle of Laurinski.

Instead of having lofty towers at either extremity, and a long row of buildings between them, it was low and very extensive, spreading over a length of high ground, approached on every side by slopes.

There was no forest in its vicinity—no place where a hostile army could encamp without at once being perceived.

But, on the other hand, it was capable of being surrounded on every side by a besieging army, and there was no point from which a messenger could be despatched without his departure being patent to the whole of the enemy's forces.

During the darkness the Tartar army was deployed by Mazeppa, so as to encircle the castle.

The earthworks were thrown up, and the host awaited impatiently the dawning of the day.

In the grey light of morning the sentinels on the battlements saw the vast host around them, and, with pallid cheeks, rushed to inform their master of the arrival of the foe.

Spolovski, the castellan of this second stronghold, was a wiley man, one who was not addicted to give way to fierce, ungovernable passions, as did the father of Theresa.

He endeavoured, therefore, to settle the question by a ruse.

A flag of truce was hoisted over the grand gate.

Then in a few moments after an ambassador was sent out.

He advanced with some caution and evident alarm.

The wild hordes before him impressed him in anything but a favourable manner, and he apparently imagined it to be a matter of no impossibility that the Tartars might seize upon him, not to retain him as an hostage, but to immolate him as a sacrifice to their baffled anger.

It was not so. They awaited him calmly.

"I seek the king," he said, as he approached the spot where a knot of chiefs were assembled.

"I am the king," said Mazeppa, advancing.

The envoy looked in some surprise at the youthful prince, and said—

"I come to learn the purport of these strange proceedings."

"What proceedings?" asked Mazeppa, haughtily.

"The assemblage of the troops around our castle."

"We come to demand possession of certain fugitives to whom you have given shelter, or we shall level the place with the ground, as we have done the Castle of Laurinski."

The envoy pretended great surprise.

"Fugitives!" he said; "I do not understand you."

Mazeppa stamped his foot in anger.

"Return, then, to the castle," he cried; "and let me not see your face again. I am not to be deceived by hollow ruses. The Castellan of Laurinski, his daughter, and their retainers are now within your walls; and if they are not delivered up to me within one hour, I shall commence the attack. We have destroyed utterly his home—not one stone remains upon another as it originally stood—the bird will build its nest amid his armouries, and grass will grow upon his hearth. And so, if you defy me, it will be with you and your stronghold."

The envoy turned pale.

"I will deliver your message," said he, bowing and retiring. He did.

"The Tartar king," he said, "is not to be deceived. He feels assured the fugitives are here; and if they be not delivered up in an hour, he threatens to destroy the place."

Spoloviski smiled contemptuously.

"The barbarian," he said, "shall rue his insolence. Let the cannon on the walls be unmasked, and let us take our enemies unawares."

In less than ten minutes after a deadly shower of missiles poured from every side of the castle into the Tartar camp.

Mazeppa saw at once that the foe he had now to contend with was far more powerful than the one he had just conquered and driven into ignominious flight.

The walls were lower—the cannon swept the encampment.

The moat had been widened and deepened on the first intimation of the approach of the Tartar army towards the Castle of Laurinski, and it presented a formidable obstacle.

For some reason or another the Castellan had left it dry.

This reason will soon be evident.

Before engaging in the regular operations of the siege, Mazeppa addressed his chiefs, and bade them transmit his words to the soldiers.

"Friends," he said, "there is before us an arduous and a perilous enterprise. Before we engage in it I have one thing to say to you. You have left your homes, your wives, your children at my bidding. Do any murmur? If so, let them return at once. I fear no good will accrue to you through this campaign, except the triumph of defeating your hereditary enemy. Yet, if for me you are willing to proceed, your king will be your grateful friend. Within yonder walls is the being I hold dearest on earth; within them also is the man who has insulted you, and destroyed with treachery your brethren. Are you willing, then, to advance still?"

There was but one cry—

"Yes!"

Abder Khan had tears in his eyes as Mazeppa proceeded—

"Remember, comrades, I claim nothing from you in this enterprise. If you think I am pursuing a selfish course I will order the retreat at once; but I shall not accompany you. Here, before the walls which keep me from my beloved, my bones shall whiten, and you must choose another king."

"No, no," cried the chiefs; "let us advance and conquer."

"Transmit my speech to the soldiers, nevertheless," said Mazeppa; "they must be consulted also."

"It is unnecessary," said Abder Khan; "they will give but the same answer."

Mazeppa took his father's hand.

"My dear father," he said; "and you, my friends, speak thus because you know me. These men, to whom I am, as it were, a stranger, may think far differently. I do not wish to found my power on the forced service of any soldier and the curses of their families."

The speech of the young prince was accordingly transmitted to their men by the various chiefs.

As might be expected, it produced the utmost enthusiasm.

The men shouted and vowed vengeance in no measured terms.

The reply to Mazeppa's address was given in the shape of a brisk cannonade.

Mazeppa had taken the precaution to bring with him the whole of the cannon of the Laurinski Castle; and to the surprise of Spolovski, a fierce discharge of artillery burst from behind the temporary earthworks.

It would be tedious to write and tedious to read, were we to describe the progress of the attack.

It was but a succession of fierce cannonades—deaths, wounds, yells of rage, of agony, of triumph.

And the night fell upon a drawn battle.

---

## CHAPTER XXXI.

### THE LIGHT IN THE TURRET WINDOW.

ALTHOUGH probability pointed out the Castle of Spolovski as the place to which the Castellan of Laurinski had fled with his daughter and retainers, yet Mazeppa's mind—distracted as it was with the constant changes of the campaign—was full of doubt.

What if, after all, they were not in the castle?

What if they had fled to Warsaw and sought the protection of the king of Poland?

What if, while he was attacking that place, and attacking, as it were, a phantom, the Castellan were to remove Theresa far beyond his reach, or, at any rate, to some part of the country where he could claim the protection of the king?

He was so distracted by this thought that he was unable to sleep. When, therefore, the rest of the army had retired to their tents, he left his and wandered round the encampment.

As he did so his eyes naturally directed themselves towards the battlements, which, on the next day, his troops hoped to scale.

The castle was, as we have said, formed of one continuous line of fortification; but at either corner there was a low turret, which overtopped the rest of the battlements by a few feet.

As he cast a glance around him his attention was arrested by a light which appeared to be moving to and fro in the upper chamber.

He watched it instinctively.

Why he did so he could not explain to himself.

Yet he stood still in the bright moonlight, where he could have been shot down by any sentinel, and gazed upwards, as though he expected Theresa to appear.

Then something occurred which made his heart leap for joy.

The window was opened.

A woman appeared, gazed around anxiously, and then beckoned to some one within.

Then at the casement he saw a form which could belong to none other than Zisko.

A rope, evidently composed of bed-linen, was let down, and the dwarf, swinging himself out as he had been accustomed to do at Laurinski, dropped to the ground close to the edge of the moat.

He did not, however, drop the rope; but, balancing himself, he struck his feet against the wall and sprang forward, so as to land himself on *terra firma*.

Regardless of the danger which he incurred by exposing himself to the observation of the sentinels, Mazeppa rushed forward, and was at Zisko's side at the moment he landed and let go the rope.

For a moment the dwarf was taken aback.

He glanced up fearfully, but was reassured by the first words of Mazeppa.

"Ah, Zisko!" cried the young prince, "you are here, then. Allah be praised that you are not a prisoner!"

Zisko took the hand of the young prince and led him in silence towards the earthworks.

It was not until they were in the shadow of the fortifications that Zisko ventured to speak.

"You have congratulated me, my prince," he said, "upon not being a prisoner. You are wrong. I am a prisoner."

"What mean you?" cried Mazeppa. "You are apparently free to come and go."

"This is no time for jest," replied the dwarf. "I am here at the peril of my life, for it is death to be found here; and one must risk death who at night ventures to leave the battlements in secret. The Castellan and his daughter are in yonder fortress. Immediately upon discovering that you had found means to plant artillery against his walls, the Castellan took measures to vacate his stronghold. The only place to which he could fly was this castle. Spolovski has ever been a friend, and had, as you are aware, already supplied him with soldiers to defend his castle. Here, then, he is concealed."

"Is Theresa with him?" interrupted Mazeppa.

"Yes, yes," returned Zisko. "It is from her chamber I have now come. Through that accursed Kolzoff I have been a prisoner during my short sojourn here. He entreated his master to permit him to be answerable for my safe custody, and, having obtained the Castellan's authority, he placed me in confinement."

"How, then, have you obtained access to Theresa's chamber?"

"Through the lady, herself. She obtained permission to retain me as her attendant; and my place of durance, therefore, has been in a room communicating with her suite of apartments."

"Is the place strong?" asked Mazeppa, moodily.

"Alas! yes. It is doubly as well fortified as Laurinski."

"And the soldiers—are they also numerous?"

"They are, and well disciplined. The fortress, too, is fully provisioned, and can hold out for months."

"By my faith," cried Mazeppa, "everything seems to war against me; fate appears to have enlisted itself on the side of my very foes."

"Do not despair," said Zisko. "Fortune favours you even now. In spite of your foes, you can see the one you love, and, it may be, carry her off before their very eyes."

Mazeppa's face brightened with pleasure.

"Ah!" he said, "I can ascend as you descended. Let us go at once."

He moved as if to go.

Zisko detained him.

"Stay," he cried. "Do not destroy your hopes by your rashness. You must wait in patience to-night."

"And why?" exclaimed Mazeppa, with impatience.

"Because to-night everyone is on the alert. You would be seen, allowed to enter, and then destroyed."

"When, then, can I enter? When can I again behold my beloved one?"

"To-morrow night."

"How am I to understand the time when I may come?"

"I will place a lamp in my window at nine to-morrow night. If this remains, come not; if at twelve it is removed, watch Theresa's window during the next half-hour, and you will see the rope descend. Then rush hastily across the open space and ascend."

"Fear not," said Mazeppa; "I shall be there at the moment."

"Adieu, then," said the dwarf.

And with these words he darted away and fled across the broad open space which separated the earthworks from the castle.

In the morning, ere the sun had fairly risen, a fierce attack was made at a point where the Castellan of Spolovski least anticipated it.

The first work of the soldiers had been to bring, by Mazeppa's directions, the greater portion of the artillery to one point, so as to concentrate its fire upon the gate and the wall immediately next to it.

The half-slumbering sentinels rushed to warn the gunners.

The Castellan leaped from his couch, with an oath.

"These devils of Tartars," cried he, "leave me no time for sleep."

As yet, however, there was no cause for fear on his part.

Unused to the formidable weapons they were now employing, the Tartars fired but wildly; and it was not until the young prince himself took charge of the firing that any impression was made upon the fortress.

Cassim had opened fire, by his instructions, while the prince slept; but by eight in the morning the latter had rested sufficiently, and came up to the guns.

Many a time had Mazeppa fired the cannons at the Castle of Laurinski.

Once, during a revolt of the serfs, when he was but eighteen, he had kept in check a detachment of peasantry by his well-directed fire alone.

As soon, therefore, as he took charge of the guns himself the aspect of affairs changed.

The Castellan of Laurinski at once recognised his hand in the shots which dashed into the timbers of the massive gate.

"You have no trifling foe to contend with now," said he. "Every shot he fires will tell. That gate will not long hold out. The only thing to be done is to construct behind it a strong barricade of stone."

Spolovski turned pale.

"If that be the only alternative," cried he, "we are lost. The men will not work behind a gate through which cannon-balls are continually rushing."

"Oh yes," said the Castellan, smiling; "they would face death in person, I think, rather than those accursed savages."

He was right.

The soldiers obeyed willingly.

When they heard that unless the work was performed the Tartars would inundate the castle, they rushed at once to the spot and commenced their labours.

The cannon-balls crashed through, but on they went steadily.

Mazeppa's shots never failed to tell, and by even-tide the gate was demolished.

"This is the fortress which Zisko said was impregnable," cried Mazeppa, with a smile; and he ordered an advance.

But this movement was a fatal one.

An advance of a few yards showed them the huge mass of stone, sand, and earth which their enemies had raised; and in reply to their yell of rage and disappointment a terrific fire was poured in upon them by the triumphant soldiery.

For the first time, the Tartars fled in disorder.

Dead bodies strewed the ground in every direction. The dying were carried off by their friends.

Mazeppa ground his teeth with rage.

It was the first time that he had seen his troops fly before the enemy.

"Soldiers," he said, "you have disgraced me and yourselves. Rather would I have perished before yonder gate than have allowed our cowardly foes to triumph in my flight. Allah be praised," he added, fervently, "that I did not lead you to the assault!"

The soldiers hung their heads, abashed.

An old soldier with whitened hair approached him, saying—

"Praise not Allah for that, my prince. If you had led us to the assault we should not have fled."

"I then will lead the next attack," said Mazeppa. "There will then be no excuse for cowardice."

During that day, however, it was not considered prudent to hazard a second assault.

The night came, therefore, without any event of moment happening.

At nine o'clock Mazeppa was eagerly on the look-out.

The dwarf was not a moment behind his time.

The great gong at the castle gate had scarcely warned the inhabitants of the hour before the light appeared in Zisko's window.

There it steadily burned till midnight.

As the clock struck twelve the light disappeared.

Mazeppa did not hesitate a moment.

He dashed hastily across the open space, and reaching the moat unperceived in the darkness, crouched down upon its edge beneath the window.

At half-past twelve the rope was thrown down, and he began to ascend.

## CHAPTER XXXII.

### THE STAR OF LAURINSKI.

IN the village which, as we have said, nestled beneath the Castle of Laurinski, and which had been partially destroyed by the conflagration, had lived a peasant named Lobeski, with his wife and only daughter.

The couple themselves were far from young.

They had loved one another when very poor, and had prudently waited until fortune had smiled upon them.

So Lobeski was over thirty and his mistress thirty when they were married.

Of this union there came one daughter, Paulinska.

Paulinska was a beautiful girl—dark-haired, dark eyes, full-bosomed, with a bright, sunny face, rosy cheeks, and a figure which, though inclining to *embonpoint*, was still graceful.

She was the belle of the hamlet.

The young men of all grades sought her hand.

But the Polish youth had apparently little chance.

The Star of Laurinski, as they called her, was destined, as it seemed, to brighten the hearth of a foreigner.

There resided in the house next to the spirit-house, a jeweller,—a Frenchman,—who had settled early in life in the hamlet, and who united to his more fanciful trade those of scribe and tailor.

This man had a son.

Pierre Lefort was a handsome youth, with clear, bold features, but an expression which scarcely tended to improve his beauty.

It was at once cynical, shrewd, cunning; and indicated that its owner would stoop to any deceit to accomplish an object.

But Paulinska did not regard him in this light.

To her he seemed everything that was good and noble, and she would indignantly have resented any idea to the contrary.

Old Pierre, his father, encouraged this attachment.

He himself had doubts as to his son's stability of character, and feeling his health failing, he desired, if possible, to see his child settled, that he might assist his mother in her old age.

Pierre had run riot through the hamlet.

From his extremest infancy he had been the veriest imp imaginable, and when he grew up he carried out his mischievous propensities by making love to every girl in the village.

His handsome face accordingly procured him the favour of being liked by all the women and hated by all the men.

Gradually, however, in spite of himself, he found himself drawn towards Paulinska.

The melody of her voice would have attracted him alone.

The beauty of her form filled him with delight.

Her manners and her evident admiration for him completed the conquest.

For a time he fought against the idea.

His father said to him one day—

" Ah, Pierre, you rogue, you're caught at last ! "

Pierre flushed.

" Indeed, father, I do not understand you," he answered.

" Not understand me ?  Well then, I'll easily explain.  The bright eyes of the fair Paulinska have made you captive."

" You are wrong," returned Pierre.  " There is no girl in Laurinski who has made any impression on me."

The old man shook his head.

" Ah, well," he said, " we shall see."

And what they did see a fortnight after this was Paulinska sitting by their fireside, with her rosy cheeks rosier than ever from the effects of Pierre's words, and Pierre himself absolutely sheepish with happiness.

So things went on.

The girls in Laurinski were disgusted.

They had " always thought Paulinska a forward minx ;" they had prophesied that " she would come to no good ;" and now that she had forced herself into Pierre's good graces, he might marry her, but he " would think none the better of her for her forwardness."

The young men congratulated Pierre on his good luck to his face, and cursed him behind his back.

There was among the retainers at the Castle of Laurinski a young man of the name of Efflosk.

He, too, was a handsome, manly fellow—far more handsome and far more manly than Pierre Lefort.

He, also, was a favourite with the girls of Laurinski ; but he had never toyed with or talked to any of them in a strain of love.

His eyes had been drawn in one direction.

He loved Paulinska.

She knew in which way his heart was directed, but she refused to notice him.

This was in spite of her friends.

Her father and mother liked him.

They and their relations also preferred him to Pierre Lefort.

There was more stability in his character—more steadiness and earnestness of purpose.

His heart was in the right place, and many were the acts of kindness which had procured him the name of " Benevolence " in the hamlet.

He had told the story of his love simply, unaffectedly, to Paulinska, and she had regarded him as weak and effeminate.

Pierre had raved about the moon and stars and bright heavens, and so forth, and she thought he was necessarily strong in his devotion.

The one was the quiet stream rippling on steadily for ever.

The other was the avalanche fiercely rushing to its inevitable fall.

But so it is.

The flash and glitter of such love—or, rather, passion—as this is preferred to the quiet, sterling affection of good men.

Nevertheless, in Efflosk's mind there was a deeper, stronger, more intense feeling than even love itself.

This was hope.

Hoping against hope it truly seemed to him and to all.

Yet still he did hope.

Hope that one day, when Pierre Lefort forsook her for another (which he felt assured *would* take place), he might yet have a chance of again urging his love—a love strengthened and chastened by long trial.

It was one evening that, having obtained leave from the steward to quit the precincts of the castle, Efflosk wandered down to the village, and took his way along a winding path which led from the hamlet to a spot near the wood which from time immemorial seemed to have been the selected rendezvous of lovers.

The evening was a gloomy one.

The day had been cloudy and tempestuous.

Over the castle and the forest and the still country hung a leaden sky.

Scarcely an object was visible when he first ventured forth ; and, as if by instinct, he wended his way towards the wooded knoll whither he had often strolled with Paulinska.

As he approached it the moon seemed to burst suddenly from behind a dense canopy of clouds, and to sail undimmed through an azure sky.

Down upon the tree-tops—down upon the hamlet—down upon the wanderer fell the bright beams.

Down, too, on the wooded knoll they fell, and revealed two figures.

Efflosk started in amazement.

THE DWARF CAUTIONS THE TWO LOVERS.

One was Pierre Lefort.

The other at first he could not distinguish plainly.

But it was not Paulinska.

Of that he was certain.

He crept nearer.

They moved not.

They were too intent on themselves.

He was sitting with her on the trunk of a fallen tree, his arm round her waist, her head resting on his breast.

"Dearest Spolevska," he murmured, "I love you alone."

"But Paulinska, I say again," answered the girl, "what of her?"

"She is nothing to me," replied the faithless lover; "I have long since ceased to love her."

Efflosk listened eagerly, creeping up behind the brushwood stealthily, until he was close to the speakers.

His heart beat eagerly.

Two emotions were predominant.

Hatred for the man who was deceiving Paulinska.

Hope that this man's deceit might be the means of restoring her love to him.

Again Pierre Lefort spoke.

"Dearest Spolevska," he said, "when will you be mine?"

The girl blushed, and her answer was almost inaudible.

These words, however, Efflosk's eager ears caught.

"Soon—oh, soon."

"Say when, dearest—tell me the day."

"Why do you press me?"

No. 8.

"Because I must speak to Paulinska, and break the news to her."

The girl answered not, and the faithless lover, straining her in his arms, pressed ardent kisses on her lips.

Of one thing Efflosk was convinced.

Pierre did *not* intend to make this girl his wife.

His manner towards her proved it.

He was but deceiving her, but in deceiving her he was also deceiving Paulinska.

What he waited for now was to discover the date of their next appointment.

This he soon learned, and, waiting to hear no more, he crept away, and hurried to the house of the father of Paulinska.

The girl was seated alone in the front room of the cottage when the soldier entered.

She glanced upwards, eagerly fancying it to be Pierre.

The look she cast upon Efflosk sufficiently proved how disappointed she was that it was he.

"Good evening, Efflosk," she said, coldly, and continuing her knitting.

"Good evening, Paulinska," he answered, in a trembling voice, "pray listen to me carefully for a moment, for I have much to tell you. This night I have had proofs of Pierre's faithlessness to you."

The girl looked up, flushed and eager, and angry too,

"This is some idle talk of yours," she cried, "to do him an injury. I will not listen to it."

The voice in which the young soldier replied was solemn

"I intreat you, Paulinska," he said, "to hear me. Your happiness is at stake. I love you so greatly that I will not see you sacrificed. If you will not hear me, let me tell your father, that he may see his falseness, and explain all to you."

"No, no!" cried the girl, "speak to me—not to him—not to him. Speak quickly, for Pierre will soon be here."

Then Efflosk told his story.

The young girl bent over her work, and listened eagerly.

She made no interruptions, but her hard breathing, and the heaving of her bosom, proved how intensely she was excited,

When he had finished—

"When?" asked she quickly, "when do they meet again?"

"To-morrow night."

"And will you take me to the spot?"

"Yes—at seven I will meet you beyond the church yonder. It will be best not to meet here. One thing let me beg of you—do not let Pierre suspect you know anything."

"I will not."

She held out her hand.

"Good bye, Efflosk," she said, kindly; "if this be true, you will save me from much trouble."

He seized the hand extended to him, pressed it passionately to his lips, and departed.

Scarcely had he gone when Pierre Lefort entered.

A cloud was on his brow.

"I saw that fellow Efflosk emerge from the house, Paulinska," he said, "what does he here? I thought you had ceased to permit his visits long since."

"He came in friendship merely," returned Paulinska, in a somewhat constrained voice. "Do you never pay visits in friendship to old favourites?"

"You know I do not, dearest," said the faithless one, as he sat down by her side; "you know that all beauty for me—all love for me—all friendship for me is concentrated in you."

"Oh! can this man be a hypocrite?" thought Paulinska.

On the following evening at seven Efflosk and Paulinska were punctual to their appointment.

They grasped one another by the hand, but spoke not.

Both felt that a crisis in their existence had arrived.

As they approached the dell they heard voices.

"The lovers are there before us, you see," whispered Efflosk.

He felt the arm that leaned upon his tremble violently.

But she answered not.

They approached nearer,

Again the warm loving words, again the ardent kisses, this night more ardent, again the depreciation of Paulinska.

A few moments of this were sufficient for Paulinska.

"Let us go away," she murmured.

They passed away quietly until they reached a secluded spot.

"Let us rest here awhile," said Paulinska, as she sat down upon a fallen tree. "I am very, very faint and weary. Oh, I am so unhappy—so miserable! I have none to love me now. How I repent my bitter, bitter folly!"

The arm of the young soldier stole round her waist.

There was no resistance.

"Let me comfort you," he said softly; "let me renew my protestations of love. You have never found me false—you have never seen me with others. Even though you were devoted to another, your image has still filled my heart—my love for you has never once swerved. Let me again dream of happiness, dearest—let me ask you still to be mine."

Paulinska placed her hand in his and looked up into his face.

"To accept your love at such a moment as this, Efflosk," she said, "would be to appear in your eyes unworthy. It would seem that in losing one lover I am only anxious to obtain another. One thing, however, I can say, that I do sincerely repent having cast your constant love aside for the sake of this man. To-night's scene has been a lesson to me."

Efflosk pressed her more closely to him, and then, as if by a sudden impulse, stooped down and kissed her tremulous lips.

"No matter in what manner it is given, I accept your love," he said, "if you can but bestow it on me. Say, may I again hope?"

"Yes."

We need not describe this scene further.

Suffice it to say that the reconciled lovers walked home in happiness together, and that when Pierre came he found instead of his mistress the following note :—

"I have been to the forest this evening, and heard all—let us meet no more."

His astonishment was great, yet he could not resist attributing his fall to his rival Efflosk, and went away swearing to be terribly revenged.

It was on this night that the Tartars descended upon the village and set fire to it.

Being next door to the spirit-house, the cottage of Lobeski, built entirely of wood, was immediately enveloped in fierce flames, and it was found impossible to save it.

Paulinska had sat thinking of her newly-formed plans in life, and, when she retired to rest, fell into a heavy slumber, from which the roaring of the flames and the outcry of the people failed to wake her.

On the eve, then, of happiness—on the very verge of becoming the husband of the woman he loved, Efflosk found himself on the following morning deprived of hope and love for ever.

Paulinska had fallen a victim to the flames, though her father and mother had been saved. A fate—a cruel fate, seemed to have declared itself against Efflosk and his mistress.

For this reason, almost driven out of his senses by his sorrow, the young soldier was devoured by a maddening hate for Mazeppa, whom he regarded as the author of his misfortunes.

It was this man alone, of all the retainers, who saw Mazeppa ascending towards Theresa's chamber.

He saw, and rushed into the castle in eager haste.

---

## CHAPTER XXXIII.
### LOVE'S PLEADINGS.

In a few minutes Mazeppa found himself within Theresa's chamber.

Again united, again locked in a fervent embrace, their feelings can be better imagined than we can describe them.

Theresa gazed with deep love, pride, and gratitude at the handsome features of the lover who had braved so many dangers for her.

Mazeppa, whose mind had been so often racked by sorrows—whom evil fortune had almost turned into a believer in fate—who had begun to doubt whether he should ever again behold his mistress—tired not of gazing at her sweet features, her exquisite form, and the white bosom beneath which trembled the heart which was all his own.

"Dearest Theresa," he said, at length, "I can bear this suspense no longer. Become mine—let one of our elders unite you to me in the solemn bonds of marriage, and I shall then feel that no earthly power can part us."

From one loving him as did the Lady Theresa but one reply was to be expected.

With a blush she answered—

"Yes."

Then, as her head nestled more closely to his breast, she added—

"But how is it possible? how can one of your elders unite us?"

"He can ascend as I did," returned Mazeppa. "What one man can do another can."

"And what a man who loves can do a woman also can do," replied Theresa. "Can I not descend as Zisko has done before me?"

Mazeppa gazed at her in admiration and surprise.

"Brave girl!" he cried, "would you risk that perilous descent?"

"Why should you doubt it?"

She rose.

Approaching the window, she leaned out, and looked down.

"It is nothing," she said, "I will at once descend."

Mazeppa restrained her.

"Stay!" he cried; "do not venture upon this, unprepared."

"Delay may be fatal."

"No—no. No one will guess at such an enterprise. Zisko must assist us. He must remain below while I am above."

As he spoke the inner door creaked slightly.

They turned in alarm.

It was Zisko.

His finger was on his lip.

"Hist!" he cried, as he advanced cautiously; "have you withdrawn the rope?"

"I have," said Mazeppa; "why do you ask?"

"There is some suspicion that you have access to Theresa's chamber. I fear, after all, these meetings must cease, or you will be discovered. This time the Castellan's anger would consign you to immediate death. Ah! the window is open. Close it or you will be perceived."

He rushed across the room and closed it himself.

Mazeppa smiled.

"This is my last visit here," he said, gazing at the blushing Theresa.

The dwarf looked from one to the other in surprise.

"What mean you?" he asked. Are you then so confident, that you hope to take the castle to-morrow?"

"No; but to-morrow night, aided by you and me, Theresa will leave this room; and being conveyed to my tent, will become my wife."

The dwarf's eyes sparkled.

"Good—good!" he cried; "this will be the best revenge you can take upon the Castellan. But we will discuss this more at our leisure—when you leave this, I will accompany you. And now, while you take leave of one another, I will enter the adjoining chamber and keep watch, for I fear interruption; and safety demands your quick departure."

He then left the room.

For a moment there was a silence.

"Mazeppa," said Theresa, in a tremulous voice, as Mazeppa led her back to the ottoman, and pressed her silently to his heart in a last embrace, "Mazeppa, I have one favour to ask of you."

"I will grant it."

"I am about to give you the greatest possible proof a woman can give of my love and trust—am I not?"

"Yes, dearest."

"I am about to leave all—to brave the fierce anger of my father and become your wife—to become your bride amid the terrible tumult of war—to be the only woman among thousands of wild horsemen of the desert."

"I appreciate all your devotion, dearest," said the prince. "What, then, is it you ask in return?"

"I ask you to spare my father."

Mazeppa's brow clouded.

"Theresa," he said, "this is impossible."

"Impossible!" she cried; "nothing of such a kind as that I ask of you is impossible."

"It is impossible," pursued the prince. "I have sworn that, for the deadly wrong he did me I will be avenged. I have sworn that I, coming back as it were from the realms of death, will punish him for the murder he hoped to have committed. From this oath I cannot swerve. If you make the safety of your father the price of your hand, I must still refuse to give you this promise."

Theresa was silent.

The prince proceeded—

"Filial love is good—nothing is better or more holy, except it be the love of man for woman, or woman for man. But in this case it would be folly of the extremest kind to pretend that you can feel respect or love for your father. As far as his will went, he was my murderer. He is a tyrant of the worst kind—he oppresses you as if you were his slave—his character is despicable—villanous. Can you ask me to spare him? Besides, he loves you not. You were not the child of love. Your mother was a Circassian, bought secretly by your father in the slave market of Constantinople, where he saw and

admired her form. This man, whom you ask me to spare, hates you because you will not be his slave and do his bidding—because you have thwarted him in his ambitious plans. No, no, Theresa, this cannot be. The man who tried to compass my death must make atonement. And now, dearest, adieu! Time flies, and I might be discovered. Zisko, who will accompany me, will bring you back word as to the arrangements I have made. Farewell, beloved, until to-morrow."

With a fervent embrace they parted.

Zisko, who entered upon hearing Mazeppa pronounce his name aloud, threw open the casement, and descended first, followed in a moment by Mazeppa.

Theresa, as she leaned from the window, saw their two forms pass away across the open space.

Then she sat down and thought.

Her mind was strangely perturbed.

Her father she knew to be cruel—despotic—unnatural in his hatred.

Yet she could not calmly contemplate the idea of becoming the happy bride of the man who was hunting her father to death.

Then, again, if she refused to comply with Mazeppa's request?

What awaited her?

On one side, a long life of regret and repining over her lost love; and on the other, perhaps a forced marriage with one she hated and loathed.

What delicacy of mind could be possessed by the man who threatened to wed her to a horseboy?

What leniency could she expect from one who had deliberately consigned a fellow-man to the bitter, cruel agonies of that wild ride?

These and many other questions forced themselves into her mind; and when at length she fell asleep, she had determined to abandon her father and trust herself to the tried devotion of her heart's choice.

So sweet and balmy was the sleep induced by these thoughts, that she awoke not when Zisko, on returning from the camp, entered the room, closed the window, and crept away towards his chamber.

The conference between Zisko and Mazeppa had been a long one.

"My principal reason for wishing to accompany you," said the dwarf, "was to warn you of an impending danger."

"Is the Castellan planning any new treachery?" asked the prince; "are we to have any more explosions of mines beneath our feet?"

"No, not exactly that," said Zisko; "this land is so sandy that to form a mine would be a matter of endless difficulty. The plan proposed to be acted upon is of a far different nature. A number of guns have been concentrated near the great gate which you destroyed, but to find a solid barrier beyond. This barrier, as you are aware, faces your tent."

"It does."

"Well, at early dawn a terrific cannonade will be opened upon your tents; and then you will see, as if rising from the earth, hundreds of armed men. These will rush upon your tent and those of your chiefs."

"And from what place will these warriors come, who rush to certain death?"

"They will rise from the moat, to which an underground passage has been formed."

"And what is the purpose of the sortie?"

"To destroy you and your father, with the rest of the chiefs, if possible, and thus discourage the army."

"There will be no means of returning?"

"Yes; that is provided for. These men will, as I have said, rise from the moat and rush across the open space. When they have succeeded or failed, they will return in the same way as they came, covered by the fierce fire of the castle artillery."

Mazeppa thought a moment.

"The men who do this must be brave indeed," he said; "it is a pity they are not employed in a better cause. Did they volunteer?"

"No—they drew lots—they all expect death."

"They expect with truth," returned Mazeppa; "innocent though they be in themselves, they will suffer for their master's crime."

"That is the law of war," returned Zisko, "pray be upon the watch; let them not take you unawares."

Mazeppa smiled.

"Fear not," he said, "I will take measures to set at nought the machinations of my would-be destroyer. More than this my men shall enter the castle by the way they make their exit."

"I fear that will be scarcely safe," replied Zisko.

"Why not?"

"Because the entrance admits but one, and leads into passages where your men would be lost, without being able to attempt anything."

"One or two could enter, however, and open to us the castle gates."

"Yes—if during the first part of the melee they dressed themselves in the costume of the dead, and flying with them stood the chance of being slain."

"It shall be done," cried Mazeypa; "fear not; there are brave spirits among my army who would dare anything."

Zisko now departed, and Mazeppa having called his father and his principal chiefs to a conference, explained to them the nature of the danger which would threaten them on the morrow.

He then posted behind the tents a body of men.

These were destined to receive the attack of the sallying party.

Here were placed also the cannon, hidden behind the tent-cloths, ready to answer the fire of the castle artillery.

Having made these preparations, Mazeppa retired to his couch to snatch a brief repose and to dream of the happiness which awaited him on the night following.

## CHAPTER XXXIV.

### THE FORLORN HOPE.

THE rosy-fingered dawn crimsoned the eastern hills.

The mist which had gathered over the plains and forests rolled away, and the grey twilight which precedes the rising of the sun began to dispel itself into a warmer light.

Just as the castle gong struck the hour of four, a roar of artillery woke the encamped hosts.

But the people of the castle were disappointed.

During the night, and unbidden by Mazeppa, the troops had constructed huge works of earth and sand, which completely screened the tents of the chiefs, and in which the cannon-balls buried themselves with a loud "thud."

Mazeppa, awakened by the loud roar of artillery, rushed to the opening of the tent to join his men.

He started in astonishment when he saw the huge earthwork.

"Who has done this?" he cried to the young warrior who guarded the entrance of his frail domicile.

It was Zuliska.

She smiled.

"Your men," she answered.

"By whose orders?"

"By mine."

Mazeppa pressed her hand.

"Dear, devoted girl," he cried, "ever on the watch to save me from my own imprudence! Now, as you have done me one service, do me another."

"Yes—what is it?"

"Retire out of reach of the guns. This is no place for you."

Zuliska smiled.

"You forget," she said, "I am your special attendant—where you go, in peace or war, I must be with you."

There was no time for further parley.

Moving to the side of the huge pile of sand, into which the balls of the disappointed defenders of the castle continued to bury themselves, Mazeppa could see a mass of soldiers start from beneath the ramparts.

They were allowed to come half across the open space.

Then the cannon belched forth a terrific volley, and the Tartars darted out from every side, and enclosed the forlorn hope.

Desperately, hand to hand, the brave men fought.

Then, when time had been given for Mazeppa's ruse to be prepared, the Tartars opened on the side nearest to the castle.

The Poles, thoroughly dispirited, broke and fled, glad to escape safe to the fortress.

Into the moat they tumbled headlong, scrambling over one another, and fancying that their fierce enemies were following them; although the Tartars, in reality, only pursued them half-way.

At the bottom of the moat they rested awhile to recover their scattered senses, and to see what havoc the deadly missiles of the enemy had effected.

Of the two hundred, but eighty appeared to be left.

Of these, two were Tartars.

At length the foremost man led the way along the moat, rugged with cannon balls and pieces of fallen masonry, until he reached a round hole in the wall.

He placed his hand through this and moved something.

Then a portion of the wall gave way, as it were, and the relic of the forlorn hope returned among their companions.

The Tartars were bewildered, as Zisko had prophesied.

When told to proceed to their respective quarters, they knew not which way to turn; and the captain of the guard at once suspected treachery.

"Why do you not go to your quarters?" he cried.

Neither answered for a moment, but at length one of them, turning to his companion, said, in tolerable Polish,—

"Come, my comrade, let us go in."

He led the way down the first passage he saw.

Fortunately, as he imagined, it led them to the battlements; and to their surprise, they saw before them the only remaining gate of the fortress.

They had no sooner emerged into the light of day, however, than they heard behind them the tramp of soldiers.

"We have fallen into the lion's den," cried one of them, "let us endeavour to conceal ourselves."

Behind one of the buttresses was the beginning of a narrow coping which led to the other side of a turret, and overhung the moat, a depth of some forty or fifty feet.

With death behind them, and safety and honour before them, they did not fear, however, and passed on, seen only by the Tartar army, who, guessing who they were, forbore to fire.

While the company sent by the captain of the guard searched for them in vain, they reached Theresa's open window.

At this window stood Theresa and Zisko the dwarf.

Seeing the costume of the Spolovski retainers, Zisko drew back.

"Treachery!" he cried, "stand back ye villains."

He was about to close the casement, when one of them said in broken Polish,—

"We are Tartars—friends of Mazeppa—escaping from the soldiers."

"Good!" cried the dwarf, "enter."

They immediately entered the room of the wondering girl, to whom, in a few words, Zisko explained the condition of affairs.

Zisko understoood well the language of the Tartars, which Theresa knew but imperfectly, and learned from the lips of the strangers the story of their entrance into the castle and their recent danger.

"Ah!" cried Zisko, "Mazeppa is a brave man, but he is no general. This place is too full of defenders, to be taken by stratagem. Nothing can be effected except by patience, or an assault."

"How many men have you in the castle?"

"Five hundred."

The eyes of the Tartars glistened with a fierce joy.

"We are three thousand," said one of them; "if we have a general assault, our numbers must overcome them."

"I trust so," said Zisko.

As he spoke, there was a movement in the inner room.

"Fly!" cried Zisko, pointing to the rope which was hanging inside the casement.

The men needed no second intimation.

Convinced of the thorough hopelessness of their mission, they were glad to escape from such a centre of danger, and in less than five minutes were rushing away towards the tents.

They had scarcely left the chamber, when the Castellan entered.

Through the open door could be seen the glistening arms of the soldiers who accompanied him.

"Base slave!" he cried to Zisko, "long have I wondered who it was that betrayed me—long have I wondered how it happened that the enemy knew so well my movements. Now I have discovered all; you are the traitor, and terrible shall be the punishment for your treachery. Bear him away," he added to the soldiers who followed him, "bear him away to the court-yard, and await my coming."

Then he approached Theresa.

"Unworthy girl!" he exclaimed, "you have disgraced my name, and brought ruin upon me. No more, however, shall you receive here the visits of your lover as you have done. Nay, deny it not—yonder rope tells its own tale."

He approached the window and leaned out.

A cruel smile broke over his lips.

"Yet stay," he said, "I will prepare for you a worthy punishment. To-night your window shall remain open—you, chained to your seat, shall see him enter—by the window shall wait six soldiers, and when he comes in, he shall be dispatched before your eyes."

Stroveski here entered quickly.

Stroveski, it will be remembered, was the gaoler at the Castle of Laurinski.

"Take six soldiers," said the Castellan, "and guard this window. As soon as the sun sets throw out yonder rope. Leave the casement open, and keep yourself concealed; whoever enters let him be destroyed; meanwhile bind her to her couch, and let her not approach the window on any pretext."

He then turned again to Theresa.

"Wretched girl!" he cried, "to-night shall you witness the death of your treacherous lover—to-morrow I will prepare for you a fate worse than death."

He then walked to the door and left the room.

During the whole of this scene Theresa uttered not a word.

Tears filled her eyes—her bosom heaved wildly with emotion; but she could find no words to express her grief.

The threats of her father had conjured up before her mind a terrible vision; and she could discover no means of thwarting him in his vengeance.

Stroveski, who, having been outwitted before by Zuliska at the eastern tower, was resolved not to be so outwitted again, lost no time in obeying the orders of his master.

He bound the Lady Theresa firmly to her couch, so that she could move neither hand nor foot, and then drawing the heavy curtains of the windows more forward than they were usually, he placed his men in waiting.

The day, however, was not expected to bring forth any occurrences of moment, and they waited eagerly for nightfall.

The soldiers were as anxious as their master to destroy the young king of Tartary.

This useless war was beginning to sicken them.

Meanwhile Zisko had been taken to the courtyard, as directed by the Castellan.

Here the soldiers held him until their chief arrived, and many and bitter were the gibes which were levelled at him.

One reviled him for his treachery, another for his distorted form.

Then there was a sudden hush.

The Castellan approached.

On his brow was a cloud of sullen hate.

Everyone expected his vengeance to be a terrible one.

In a few moments a huge fire blazed in the courtyard.

Over this the Castellan directed an immense caldron to be suspended.

Into this caldron, when it began to be heated, the soldiers poured pailfuls of the molten lead which below they were forming into cannon-balls.

And Zisko looked on and trembled.

He knew full well what was to be his fate.

He was to be cast alive into the molten lead!

As soon as the caldron was nearly full the Castellan cried in a loud voice,—

"Strip him."

The soldiers in whose arms he was held seized him, and were about to carry out this order, when a loud roar of artillery shook the air, and the wall above them, struck by the balls, fell into the yard.

Crash went the masses of stone upon the pavement.

Crash upon the heads of the soldiery.

Splash into the molten lead, casting fiery streams over the courtyard and over the men.

Shrieking, yelling with the pain, they let their prisoner go, and he, taking instant advantage of his liberty, sprang on to the fragments of masonry, and darted up the broken wall to the top of the battlements.

Once there, he ran along the narrow coping which had saved the lives of the two Tartars, and reached Theresa's chamber.

He knew it would be certain death to make his appearance at the window; so there, crouched up, he sat, clinging to the wall until sunset, hidden from those on the battlements by the buttress, and from those in the chamber by the projecting edge of the casement.

At nightfall he expected to be able to creep back to the battlements, and manage an escape.

His distorted figure stood him in good stead on this day.

None but one of his small and twisted form could have kept up such a watch.

He, however, crouching down into the corner of the coping, held on with the desperation of a dying man.

Cramped and stiffened from remaining so long in one position, it was with the greatest joy that he saw the last crimson gleaming of the setting sun.

Just as he was prepared to return by the way he had come, he saw one of the soldiers lean out of the window, and throw down the rope.

This was a mode of escape which he had not hoped would be offered to him.

He waited until the trooper had withdrawn his head, and then, creeping gently forward, he grasped the cord, and swung himself down gently into the moat.

The men within the chamber saw the trembling of the rope, and Stroveski rushed to the window.

"A man is escaping from the castle!" he cried; "fire upon him!"

The men obeyed.

But the night was dark, and their shots were delivered at random.

"Who is it that has escaped?" asked Theresa, anxiously.

"Zisko, the dwarf," returned Stroveski, sullenly.

She clasped her hands.

"Oh! thank heaven, he has escaped!" she murmured; "yet, would that I had been able to say one word to him, to warn Mazeppa."

A scowl passed over the bronzed face of the gaoler.

He remembered how one of the Tartar soldiers had bound his assistant and outwitted him, and he chuckled at the prospect of revenge.

"Mazeppa will be here to-night," he said, with a sardonic grin, "and this night will see the last of his treachery. To-night will end this horrid, useless conflict, and bring peace of mind to many of us."

Theresa did not answer.

"You must excuse me, my lady," he continued, "if I say that your infatuation for this impostor has been the cause of many hundred deaths. It has widowed many a woman and rendered many a couple childless. This man's death will be the best thing that can happen to you. It will restore you to your father's love, and restore also peace to Poland and Tartary."

Theresa eyed him contemptuously.

"Man," she cried, "you are incapable of judging between right and wrong—justice and injustice. Presume not to talk to me."

Stroveski laughed coarsely, and concealed himself behind the curtains.

Night drew on apace.

Theresa had been bound but carelessly. They did not deem it necessary to bind with much severity a tender creature such as she.

Gradually, therefore, when no one was looking, she untied her bonds, which only confined her waist to the couch, and when the clock struck nine she was free.

As the last stroke of the gong died away, the rope vibrated. She trembled.

Every nerve in her body quivered.

Was she about to witness a murder?

## CHAPTER XXXV.

### WATCHING.

WHEN Zisko fled across the clearing towards the Tartar tents, his first thought was to find Mazeppa, and inform him of the disaster which had occurred.

But in the tents not a soul knew where the prince was to be found.

He had gone from his couch some time before, and even Zuliska was unaware of his intentions.

"Can it be possible," thought Zisko, "that he has told her of his approaching marriage?"

"Selim," he said, "or rather, Zuliska, are you aware that he is to-night to be married to Theresa?"

"I am."

"From whom did you learn it?"

"From himself."

Zisko started in surprise.

"When did he tell you this?" he asked.

"To-day; soon after the fierce cannonade which, you say, saved your life—this afternoon."

"Then doubtless he has gone to the castle already," cried the dwarf. "I will go and reconnoitre."

So saying, he left Mazeppa's tent, and once more took his way towards the moat.

It was a dark autumnal night—the wind was strong and very fierce, sweeping along over fields and downs, tearing the branches and the withering leaves from the trees, and screaming along the rocks and tall precipitous hills.

There was no moon in the sky, but from time to time the sudden glance and disappearance of a star showed how rapidly the dull grey clouds were hurried over the face of the heavens.

The moaning of the trees and shrubs, added to the wild whistling of the gale, showed how it vexed the still, reposing, rooted things of creation in its harsh fury, as it swept through them.

On the summit of one of the most elevated points there was a little indentation, extending from the highest point of the downs to the edge of the moat, where it was somewhat lower than in other places.

This little hollow was sheltered from most of the winds which blew, except when a gale came due west, and swept round the castle walls.

In consequence of this protection, some low scrubby shrubs had gathered themselves together, as in a place of refuge, never venturing to raise their heads above the neighbouring slopes; but spreading out broad and tolerably strong in the lower part of the dell.

From them there was a footpath extending on either side.

One led to the top of the slope and wound away towards the tents, and the other along the edge of the moat.

The path had been little frequented, and the short grass encroaching upon it, here and there, almost obliterated the track.

By the side of one of the large rocks which here and there appeared, and guarded it from the direct course of the blast, were seated three men.

One of them was a young man, not long emerged into manhood.

His companions were verging on what is called middle age.

The first was Mazeppa—his companions were Cassim and Abdulaman.

Mazeppa was eagerly awaiting the moment which would bring him to the arms of his beloved bride—his friends were endeavouring to dissuade him from attempting the hazardous enterprise.

Mazeppa, however, was resolved.

"Long have I waited," he said "far too long. I will wait no longer."

"But you have no friend there now to aid you," said Cassim, "no one there in the castle who can instruct you as to the movements of the enemy. You may fall into some ambuscade."

Mazeppa smiled.

"So be it," he said, "let me fall; if Theresa is not to be mine—if the fates are against me, I hope not to live."

Cassim was eager to prevent his running this terrible risk.

He wished by delay to enable the Castellan to escape with his daughter, in order that Zuliska might become the wife of Mazeppa, and Queen of Tartary.

"Have patience, my prince," he said, "patience alone will obtain for you possession of the girl. The castle will in time be infallibly ours—wait then, and hope."

Theresa was that night to be his.

Happiness was, as it were, already in his grasp.

Was he to lose it?

"No, no," he cried, impetuously, "I will not wait. This night I will carry her off."

"This night, then, there will be a catastrophe," said Cassim.

Mazeppa smiled derisively.

"If you are afraid," returned he, "do not accompany me."

Cassim looked at him with a reproachful glance.

"Prince," he said, "you do me injustice. Where you go I will go, and indeed in this enterprise I will insist that I go first."

Mazeppa grasped his hand.

"Forgive me," he said; "I wounded you unintentionally. I do not think for one moment that you are wanting in courage, but it irritates me to think even of delay. I must carry out my design to-night, even if I risk my life in the attempt. Hush! what is that?"

A rustling sound attracted their attention.

Then suddenly a dark form appeared on the edge of the glen.

"Who is there?" cried the Tartar prince.

"I—Zisko."

"What do you here?"

"I have left the castle, never to return."

"Why so?"

"Let me come down there among you first. I will then explain all."

He then crept down among the shrubs and took his seat by the prince.

He related in detail the terrible events of the day.

Mazeppa listened in alarm.

"But Theresa," he cried; "what of her?"

"I know not; I was hurried away."

"Did the Castellan remain with her afterwards?"

"Yes; for some time."

The prince thought awhile.

"Has he discovered, think you," he asked at length, "whether I have visited her or not?"

"That I cannot tell? but I fear he saw the rope. The two Tartars who escaped this morning used the rope to effect their escape, and he must have noticed it."

Cassim and Abdulaman glanced at one another.

Mazeppa noticed them.

"Ah! my friends," he said, smiling, "I see you are thinking of another obstacle. You are wrong—see, yonder is the rope."

The white rope could clearly be distinguished against the dark wall.

The gong of the castle at this moment struck nine.

"Come," cried the prince, rising, "come, my friends; it is time to commence our enterprise."

Cassim laid his hand upon his arm.

"Stay, my prince," he said; "remember, I go only on one condition."

"And that is—"

"That I ascend first."

Mazeppa smiled.

"On this occasion I do not object," he said, "for I do not believe in the existence of danger. You may ascend first because you will meet only Theresa."

They approached the spot where the rope dangled over the moat.

Little did Mazeppa imagine the danger into which he was hurrying his friend.

Cassim stepped forward.

"Now, Mazeppa," said he, in a low whisper, "when you hear me pronounce the word 'Come,' begin the ascent."

He then seized the knotted cord and hastened upwards.

Meanwhile Theresa, who had, as we have said, released herself from her bonds, waited anxiously for the stroke of nine.

What horrible thoughts were hers!

That night, which was to have been her wedding night, seemed likely to witness the destruction of all her hopes in life.

In her mind's eye she could even then see the mangled form of her lover stretched at her feet.

She knew her father had no mercy.

From her maid Zenitha she had learned the horrible fate prepared for Zisko, and it was with feelings of delight she had heard of his escape.

These feelings had been succeeded by those of deadly fear.

Might not the Castellan—supposing Mazeppa only to be maimed—prepare for him a fate as deadly?

So the shades of night deepened, and she sat in fear upon her couch.

Afar off she could hear the murmur of the beleaguring host, and the waving of the trees under the rushing wind.

As the time approached, her blood seemed to curdle.

"I am cold," she cried to Stroveski; "close the window."

The man shook his head and answered with a kind of surly politeness.

"I am afraid, my lady, I cannot comply with your request—my orders are very precise."

"My father did not order that I was to perish with cold," she said petulantly.

The man smiled.

"I don't think he would break his heart if you did," he muttered to himself.

Then he added aloud—

"No, my lady, but he commanded me to keep the window open, and watch for the coming of the Tartar prince."

"Come hither," she said, "come nearer, and sit down by me. I wish to speak to you alone."

The gaoler approached.

"Stroveski," she whispered, "have you a human heart?"

The man smiled again.

"Well, my lady," he said, "I trust I have, too."

"How, then, can you promise to commit unrelentingly the terrible crime ordered by my father? Can you not see that it *is* a crime?"

"No, my lady," returned the man bluntly; "I am obeying orders—I am following the commands of my lord. The burden of the crime is on him, not on me."

Theresa lowered her voice again.

"Mazeppa is wealthy," she said; "he will reward you handsomely. Save him—enable me to fly with him; and riches shall be yours."

The man hesitated a moment.

Theresa pursued what she deemed to be an advantage.

"Oh, indeed—indeed, we will be grateful," she murmured, "and you yourself will run no risk. We can descend now, and from the hands of the Tartars I defy the Poles to wrest you."

Stroveski stroked his huge beard restlessly, as he answered—

"All this may appear very easy to you, my lady, but it is simply impossible."

"Why so?"

"There are in this room six soldiers."

"Well?"

"Every one of these understands the orders of the Castellan."

"What then?"

"Think you they would all join me in such an enterprise as that you speak of, even were I willing to attempt it?"

"I cannot see why they should not—indeed, indeed, I cannot."

"They all hate Mazeppa—they look upon him, rightly enough, I must say, as the author of this war, and the calamities which have befallen them in consequence; and there is scarcely one among them, I believe, who would not gladly be his destroyer."

Theresa shuddered.

"What injustice this is," she said; "when my father's cruelty is the real cause of all these evils!"

"Yes, yes; but in the first place, my lady, Mazeppa poisoned the Count Palatine."

"'Tis false!" cried Theresa. "He did not poison him."

"Who then?"

Her eyes fell.

"That," she said, "I cannot say."

"If *he* did not, that rascally dwarf did. But, hist! the rope moves."

He approached the window and glanced out.

Then he hastily withdrew his head.

"They come, my men," he murmured; "be on the alert."

Theresa pressed her hand tightly over her palpitating bosom.

"Oh, heaven!" she cried in the depth of her great agony, "Oh, heaven! grant that I may save him from this terrible fate."

Then, regardless of the fact that her freedom of action might be seen, she moved slightly forward.

---

## CHAPTER XXXVI.

### THE END OF A CAMPAIGN.

Even had Stroveski, the gaoler, been willing to aid the Lady Theresa in escaping with her lover, there was one in the room who would have thwarted all their efforts.

This one was Efflosk.

He waited in eagerness.

His heart bounded with joy at the anticipation of the approaching hour of revenge.

If he could have destroyed the whole Tartar army, he would have done so; but as this was impossible, he resolved to destroy Mazeppa as the representative of his foes.

Presently a head appeared above the window-ledge.

Theresa screamed and rushed forward.

"Back—back," she cried, "there is danger here!"

She was too late.

The Tartar warrior entered.

In the dim glimmer of the lamp he could see nothing, and the swords of his assailants rang upon his steel armour.

In a moment he comprehended his situation.

Planting his back against the wall, he parried their blows as well as he could.

"Back, ye dogs!" he cried, "back, I say, or your breasts shall feel the Tartar steel. What—ho!" he shouted, as he neared the window, "Mazeppa, to the rescue!"

It was Cassim.

"Thank Heaven!" murmured Theresa, in the selfishness of love, "thank Heaven, it is not Mazeppa."

Again Cassim cried out—

"Mazeppa, to the rescue!"

But no response came.

"What can keep him?" murmured Cassim; "he must surely know I am in danger, for the clang of steel and my shouts must have been heard in the Tartar camp, where is Mazeppa is beneath the very walls."

He was not kept long in suspense.

In another minute a a dark figure appeared at the casement; then another and another, until the room was full of Tartar soldiery.

The Castellan was caught in his own trap.

He had hoped to ensnare an enemy, and the enemy had, instead of being ensnared, invaded the very heart of his citadel.

The six soldiers and the gaoler fought manfully, as men will do when they fight for life.

But it was of no avail.

The wild sons of the Steppes poured in one after another until the room would hold no more; for instead of the rope, there now depended from the window a strong ladder of ropes.

When the last of the Castellan's retainers had succumbed, Mazeppa looked around him for Theresa, who, he imagined, had retired into an inner room while the fierce conflict had been raging.

But she was nowhere to be found.

He searched in vain through the rooms on either side, but there was no vestige of his mistress anywhere.

This is easily accounted for.

Efflosk, who early in the combat had seen which way the fight would turn, had seized Theresa in his arms and borne her from the room.

Mazeppa was distracted.

"Oh! I shall go mad!" he cried, "I shall go mad! Where can my Theresa be? Whither can they have borne her?"

Cassim, though faint with many wounds, essayed to console him.

"My friend," said Cassim, "blame yourself. Why did you delay? Did you not hear my cry for help?"

"Yes, truly; but what could I effect against so many? I hurried to the camp, and claimed the assistance of some of my choicest warriors. I have saved your life; that is one consolation to me in my sorrow."

He paused awhile.

Cassim took his hand.

"Mazeppa," he said, kindly, "remember that to act is our only chance now. Let us break down these doors and force our way along the corridors. Before morning the castle will be ours."

The Tartar prince started up.

"True—true, my friend," he cried, "my grief has obscured my intellect. Come, my men, let us force these doors and destroy this place as we did the Castle of Laurinski before it."

A ringing cheer responded to this speech.

"Cassim," said Mazeppa, "station yourself at this window. As my men pour into the interior of the castle let others ascend. The castle shall be ours, if every man in the Tartar army has to enter it and risk his life. If they perish, I shall perish in their midst."

The inner doors were not made for the rough usage they now received, and soon yielded to the fierce blows of the Tartars.

The passages without were in complete darkness.

Not a glimmer of light was anywhere to be seen.

The Castellan evidently guessed the mode of attack which would be adopted.

The whole castle seemed buried in profound silence.

Seeing this, Mazeppa hurried back to Cassim.

His manner was wild and excited.

"What ails you, my prince?" asked the Tartar chief.

"I fear treachery," said Mazeppa; "I fear lest the Castellan, finding himself again overreached, should bear his daughter away. Let a strict watch, then, be kept on every entrance—every available outlet—from the castle; let the edges of the moat be watched lest anyone should conceal himself there and slip away in the darkness. Go, see to this at once, and meanwhile I will seek throughout the castle."

Cassim immediately proceeded to descend the rope, and made his way as quickly as possible towards the Tartar tents.

Through the passages of the castle poured the Tartar hosts, but through that wing of the place, at least, silence and desolation reigned.

It was the very same thing as at the fortress of Laurinski.

One part had evidently been abandoned for the other.

It was not, however, of the same form, and finding himself compelled to remain where he was or to cross a broad court-yard swept not only by the cannon, but the muskets of the enemy, Mazeppa was at first undecided as to the course he should pursue.

After a moment's thought, however, an idea occurred to him.

By destroying the sides of the courtyard where only a narrow range of outbuildings connected one wing with another, he would be enabled to set fire to the building in which they now were, and reduce it to ashes without endangering the lives of those in the right wing.

This was determined upon at once.

Under cover of the night the Tartars worked in the moat, in the courtyard, and within the building; and by morning there was no connecting link between one wing and another but a solid wall, which it was unnecessary to destroy.

Then all the furniture and fittings were broken up and piled in the centre of the various rooms.

Here they were set light to; and fired thus in twenty places at once, the building soon began to emit flames from every window.

Out from the casements they leaped in the bright light of the morning, looking lurid and spectre-like in the sunbeams.

Down from lofty turrets tottered great beams and huge blocks of masonry.

Everywhere could be seen huge masses of burning wood falling, or hanging ready to fall, into the moat or the courtyard beneath.

Everywhere could be heard the crash of beams—the heavy, crushing sound of vast blocks of stone splintering upon a hard pavement.

Everywhere there ascended to the sky columns of dense smoke and long tongue-like flames.

Cassim approached Mazeppa as he was gazing at the ruins, which still vomited flame and smoke.

"My king," he cried, "I fear the worst."

Mazeppa eyed him in alarm.

"What mean you?" he cried.

"I fear" he said, "that those you seek have escaped."

Mazeppa grasped his arm.

"Tell me at once," he cried, "tell me what it is you fear."

"This morning, about six o'clock, one of our outposts saw four persons creeping away through the morning twilight."

"These you suspect to be"—

"The Castellan, his daughter, and two retainers."

"Great Heaven! can it be possible?"

"I think there can be no doubt," returned Cassim, "from the description which he gave. He said that one among the party seemed reluctant to go, and was compelled to walk—dragged absolutely along the ground. This must have been Theresa."

"But surely he could tell—she must have been the only woman among the party."

"Oh, there was no distinction," returned Cassim, "they were all dressed as men."

Mazeppa thought a moment.

"Which way did they go?"

"Towards Warsaw. He says they went straight towards the high road."

"Well," cried Mazeppa, "then, after all, this will be a war of stratagems. This castle, once razed to the ground, I must go by myself to the capital, and seek by cunning what I cannot obtain by force of arms."

On that day the same stratagem was made use of as had been found of so good effect at the Castle of Laurinski.

The fallen masonry was raised so as to form a barricade, and the cannon planted behind.

Then a tremendous fire was opened upon the castle.

On the morning following a white flag was hoisted upon the gate.

Mazeppa, who was superintending the siege, smiled as he turned to Cassim, who stood near him.

"Ah!" he said, "they show the white feather early. The Castellan is not there."

He hoisted a white ensign.

THE ROBBERS FIND THEY ARE SURROUNDED.

In a few moments the inner gate opened.

An officer appeared.

" I will speak with him," cried Cassim, advancing.

" What is it you desire?" he asked of the Polish officer.

" We desire to capitulate," said he ; " we cannot, nor do we desire, to hold out much longer. Wishing, therefore, to save further loss of life, we are willing to yield the castle and all it contains."

" Good," returned Cassim, " I will so report to the king. But what of the lord of Laurinski and his daughter?"

" They are not with us," answered the officer; " they left here before daybreak."

" Whither went they?"

" I know not."

" That is not true," replied Cassim; " they have gone to Warsaw. However, remain here for a few moments, and I will speak to the king."

The messenger remained standing in the centre of the court-yard, still holding the white flag, while the Tartar chief returned to Mazeppa.

" Well," cried the young prince, " what news of Theresa?"

" She is gone."

" Whither?"

" To Warsaw."

" And what do they desire?"

" They desire to capitulate."

" Upon what terms?"

" He has not stated. I did not ask him. I left that to you."

No. 9.

" Good," said Mazeppa ; " I will speak to him myself."

He advanced.

" Are you aware that you have released those whom alone I wished to take?" cried he. " The lives and the property of those now in the castle are to me worthless; however, I have no desire to provoke unnecessary bloodshed. If therefore the Castellan is willing to march out after first yielding up the whole of the arms and ammunition, I will accept the capitulation."

The officer bowed.

" I will speak to my lord," he said; " I have not the power to accept terms."

He then retired.

The Castellan was in no position to refuse any overtures that the Tartar prince thought proper to make to him.

The castle was in that state of dilapidation that a few more rounds of artillery would have crushed it to atoms.

He accordingly sent to Mazeppa to inform him that he would accept his terms, but would be gratified by a personal interview with the young king.

They met in the courtyard.

The Castellan, who had never before been face to face with the Tartar prince, was struck with his handsome features and noble bearing, and began to doubt whether, after all, he had not been in error in defending the cause of the imperious lord of Laurinski.

" Prince," he said, in a haughty but yet respectful voice, " prince, the fortunes of war are against me. I am before you now, a defeated foe, and it is not for me to dictate terms. Yet, if you will allow me, I will ask one favour."

" What is that ? "

" Your arms have not been directed against me, but against the Castellan of Laurinski ? "

" True."

" He is not here. He has fled; and you can have no interest in bringing ruin upon me. I will deliver up all arms and ammunition, and will allow you to search the castle from top to bottom. All I ask is, that you will spare the place. It will do you no possible good to destroy it. It has been the home of my fathers, and I have hoped to die within its walls."

" If it be not destroyed," returned Mazeppa, " what guarantee have I that this recreant is not concealed in some secret chamber, the door of which would be found not even after the most diligent search ? "

The Castellan drew himself up proudly.

" Prince," he cried, " I can give you a guarantee. I will pledge to you my word of honour that neither the Castellan nor his daughter are within or near the castle. They have gone to a spot far distant from this."

" To Warsaw ? "

" I have pledged my word I would not betray their route, and if you threaten to kill me I will still refuse."

" Good," said Mazeppa; " it shall be as you wish. I will dispense with searching the castle. Your pledged word has been given. I expect to be able to rely on it. Woe be to you and yours, however, if I find you are deceiving me. No man, woman, or child within the castle shall be spared."

" I am to understand, then," said the Castellan, " that you will at once withdraw your forces ? "

" Yes; it shall be so. The conference is at an end."

Upon leaving the castle, Mazeppa made his way at once to the tent where Abder Khan awaited him.

" Father," he said, " the campaign is over."

" Over, my son," exclaimed Abder Khan; " why, nothing has yet been done."

" Nor will anything be done by force of arms. To you I leave the conduct of the army—take them home in safety."

" And you ? "

" I am going to Warsaw."

" By yourself ? "

" No; I will take with me two trusty warriors. I will go in secret, and I will in secret punish this man who, with a vile spirit of revenge, is blighting all my hopes."

The next day the whole Tartar army moved backwards towards the vast Steppes ; while Mazeppa and two warriors, accompanied by Zisco, whose liberation he had demanded of the castellan, departed for Warsaw.

---

## CHAPTER XXXVII.

### THE BARBER OF WARSAW.

IT was market-day in Warsaw.

The attention of the crowd, which was proceeding towards the market-place, was drawn to a placard attached to the entrance of the house of the chief magistrate.

The people, at once putting down their baskets of vegetables and fruits, or the barrels of oil and butter which they bore upon their shoulders, contemplated this document so long that they seemed to be spelling it over three or four times, had there been any reason to suspect these Navarrese of the power of reading.

One staring individual will attract a crowd, so will one gaping crowd be rapidly reinforced by other flocks of curious idlers.

And such was the case with the assemblage in the market-place.

The flux was so great that in a little time the multitude occupied every corner of the square, even reaching up to the window of Padislaus, the barber, who, shaving a customer, found his operations so much impeded by the sudden eclipse,

that he was obliged to suspend them until daylight should again show itself.

Padislaus was a little stout man, of cheerful spirit, as garrulous as barbers in general, and not less intelligent and industrious than his nation in general.

He was of Russian origin, yet his activity was more in accordance with the character of the Poles than of the apathetic Russ.

He drove a thriving trade, to the great jealousy of his competitors, who regularly denounced him to the chief magistrate —once a month—either for sedition, heresy, or sorcery.

Padislaus, leaving his customer half-shaven, made his way through the throng in the vicinity of his house, and without waiting to be asked, began reading aloud the red and black placard, as follows :—

" Faithful Citizens of Warsaw !—Our well-beloved lord and master, Stanislaus, intending to celebrate the anniversary of his accession to the throne, will make his entry into this town by torchlight. The different *employés* of the Government, therefore, are ordered to make proper arrangements in their respective divisions of the city for the proper reception of the royal *cortège*.

    (Signed)      " The Governor,
         " LOUIS PADOVESKI."

Lower down :—

" The carriage of His Majesty and that of his Excellency the Count Palatine, and the officers of the Court, will follow the High-street as far as the Governor's palace, where His Majesty will alight. On the line of procession all windows must be illuminated or ornamented with flowers or the arms of Poland. Of course it is unnecessary to invoke the enthusiasm of the faithful and loyal population of Warsaw. It will readily give expression to its devoted attachment to our well-beloved Sovereign. However, those who disobey this order will be reported at the office of the Governor by me.

     " PAUL LEMINZOFF, Chief Magistrate."

Scarcely had Padisalus finished his reading, when the chief magistrate appeared for a moment on the balcony of his house, and raising his hat, adorned with a large black feather, shouted—

" Long live Stanislaus, our glorious King ! long live Melginieff, his Prime Minister ! "

The multitude echoed a few opposition murmurs, however, which proceeded from a group beneath the balcony.

A burly man, whose black moustaches bespoke him a soldier, but who was in reality the landlord of the Rising Sun, began to talk with an air of authority indicative of a shade of discontent.

" Let us," said he, " by all means receive our new King, the Count, and the suite of the Prime Minister. The Count doesn't mind expense ; his people like good attendance, and will come and regale themselves at the Rising Sun."

" Aye, and they will give orders for splendid gala dresses," added Loveski, the rich tailor, who had just come and mingled with the crowd.

" But," continued the landlord, " of what use are these two regiments they speak of—the Guards and the regiment of the line ? "

" The Guards ! " said Loveski, turning pale.

" Just so," continued the barber, " the very corps that was here last year ; and by the same token, one of the brigadiers lodged at your house, Master Loveski ; I remember him. Paul Strogonoff was his name, and I often met him with your wife under his arm."

" All that he may have told you," said the tailor, evidently annoyed, " is untrue."

" He never told me anything," replied Padislaus, quietly.

" It is, nevertheless, very true what they say," resumed the landlord, raising his voice, " a thousand annoyances result from the march of troops through a great town, to say nothing of our having to support all who are billeted upon us."

" You must admit, however," said the barber, " you must admit that our king must have soldiers for his protection."

" No, he should not," cried an individual with broad shoulders, thick red beard, and a savage eye ; " no," said he, leaping on to a post by way of a rostrum, and addressing the populace from his elevation, "no, it's against the law and our rights."

"He is right," exclaimed the landlord.

Silence spread through the multitude to the stoppage of twenty or thirty little conversations that were going on in different groups.

"What say you?" cried the new orator, to whom the attention of all was directed, "is this not an attack upon our liberties? Ought we to suffer these invasions of armed multitudes, who are half composed of Russians?"

"Long live Captain Stroloffki!" shouted a number of men, who appeared to know the speaker, and who now, mingling with the crowd, augmented the confusion and tumult.

The noise in the street drew the chief magistrate a second time to his balcony, less alarmed at the disturbance than pleased that an apparent revolt gave him an opportunity of displaying his zeal and eloquence; for, to say the truth, the honourable magistrate was very fond of hearing himself speak.

Devoted to the king and the minister, he patiently awaited a superior appointment, of which the count had held out expectations, but which the minister had too much sagacity to bestow upon a fidelity already assured, reserving his favours for doubtful partizans who were yet to be won over.

He no sooner began by saying—

"Faithful citizens of Warsaw," than he was stunned with shouts of "Down with the chief magistrate!"

"Long live the king and his glorious minister!" continued he, trying an appeal that he thought irresistible.

"Down with the count—down with the minister!"

"Just what I was going to say, dear fellow-citizens. Listen to me. My sentiment is 'God save our glorious monarch!'"

"Down with the king, if he assails our liberties."

"Exactly so, dear friends, if you will only hear me. Our liberty for ever."

But again the tumultuous assembly interrupted him.

Everyone apostrophised or reproached him, and the people, excited by the landlord and the tailor, had already torn down the proclamation and trampled it under foot.

But the war, once begun, did not terminate there.

The chief magistrate, placed in the balcony, occupied a strong position, which made him invulnerable to the enemy's army; but unhappily the proximity of the vegetable market furnished the assailants with materials of warfare more injurious and effective than mere words, and they began vigorously to shower a large collection upon the head of the loyal officer.

He looked about for the means of an honourable retreat, when it was suddenly closed against him.

Captain Stroloffki, who had all the agility and look of a sailor, climbed to the balcony by means of the pillars which supported it, and getting behind the chief magistrate at the very moment when that functionary had determined to quit the field of battle, seized and lifted him over the balcony with the view of throwing him into the street.

The mob, who did not expect this *coup de théâtre*, suddenly ceased their noise.

The magistrate took advantage of the silence to call out—

"Hear me, I beg; I am on your side. Citizens of Warsaw, I think with you. Our rights for ever!"

"Long live the chief magistrate!" cried the people with one voice.

"Yes—yes, he will die for our rights," added the captain.

Then, under pretence of exhibiting him to the multitude, he raised him and squeezed him so hard that Leminzoff threw up his arms in the attitude of a man taking a solemn vow.

"Long live our worthy magistrate," cried the people in admiration.

"He will lead us himself to the governor," continued the captain, "he will speak for us. He proposes it himself."

Hearing these words, the people became so enthusiastic that their joy knew no bounds.

The chief magistrate, carried into the street by the captain, was received with redoubled shouts by the delirious multitude.

Before he could open his mouth, he was surrounded and seized by a thousand arms, and carried off in triumph.

A crown of oak-leaves was placed upon his brow, which still bore marks of dirt from the vegetable matter with which he had been previously saluted, and the popular *cortége*, led by the landlord and the tailor, proceeded to march towards the governor's palace across the promenade, already decorated with flowers and foliage, and flags bearing the arms of Poland, in honour of the king's entry.

As for the captain, he had now disappeared; and the barber Padislaus, prudently returned to his shop, saying, in a low voice, to such of his countrymen as interrogated him about the event,—

"Whether the king or the people carry the day is all the same to me. Such as ye and I gain nothing by the victory of either, and are taxed to pay the expenses of a war; so take my advice—be quiet, and dont interfere."

Then Padislaus resumed his razor, and commenced shaving the customers he had left in his shop.

While these events were passing in the centre of the town, a poor boy, about thirteen or fourteen years of age, was wandering through the Nevski Prospect, a narrow winding thoroughfare, named after one of the most splendid streets of St. Petersburg.

His pale and attenuated form bore traces of fever, and his ragged clothes announced the extreme of misery.

A kind and gentle expression pervaded his features, and a ray of intelligence shot ever and anon from a dim but jet-black eye.

He was walking, or rather dragging himself along—faint from hunger.

He had already passed through two or three streets, which, to his astonishment, he found deserted; for the whole population, on hearing the tumult in the market-place, had betaken itself thither—some to look on, some to take part in the disturbance.

The poor child saw a member of the council coming rapidly towards him.

He did not dare solicit charity, but he held out his hand.

The councillor passed on without even seeing him.

A few minutes after, a gentleman appeared, walking slowly, enveloped in a large cloak.

The poor child took off his hat, and timidly saluted him. The stranger stopped, returned the salute, and passed on.

The poor beggar, incapable any longer of bearing up, fell against a door, and heard a woman's voice calling to her child to come to its meal.

"Paul," said she, "your soup awaits you."

He knocked at the door, fancying for a moment that he had been invited; but his knock was useless.

The mother was too much engaged with her own offspring to attend to him.

"Alas!" said he to himself, "I have no mother to call me to a repast."

He rose and wandered towards the great canal, hoping for nothing further from man; for his eyes were raised to Heaven for relief.

At this moment the sun, bursting from behind a cloud, cast its refulgence against a wall.

The boy went to bask in the rays of the great luminary, and while his cold, stiff limbs felt the influence of their genial warmth, and expression of melancholy joy escaped from his discoloured lips.

He smiled to the sun—the only friend that had deigned to smile on him.

Then, as his eyes withdrew from the glare which he began to feel insupportable, he cast them on the ground, and seeing near a *borne* several pieces of apple, he crawled towards them, grasped them with an avidity urged by intense hunger, and was about to eat, when he saw a boy about his own age, as ragged as himself, singing as he advanced.

"You are happy," cried he "since you are so merry."

"By St. Paul, no!" said the new comer, "I sing because I am hungry and have nothing to eat."

Immediately, without saying another word, and prompted by the generosity of his nature, he offered his new companion some of the broken apples he had just picked up, and which had been dropped from some market cart.

The beggar looked at him with astonishment and gratitude. "What," cried he, "have you no other dinner but that?"

"No. I am happy enough to have found even this. Will you share with me?"

Then the two friends began their frugal repast.

Their dining hall was vast and lofty.

It was a street, at that moment solitary, and clean, moreover—thanks to a fountain, the water of which flowed near them and offered them a fresh and limpid drink.

Thus they wanted for nothing.

Opposite was a splendid mansion, over the door of which were inscribed these words :—" Loveski, master tailor."

Their backs rested against the walls of a magnificent hotel and that hotel was the Rising Sun.

At table, an acquaintance soon springs up, so the new comer said at once to his companion,—

"What is your name?"

"Paul. And yours?"

"Michael. And your parents—what are they?"

"I have none."

"Nor I. What was your father?"

"I don't know. I recollect my mother—she must have been a great lady, for she used to be always giving me sugar plums, and dressed so nicely. But one day I awoke on the doorstep of a great building—a monastery. They kept me there I don't know how long, and then the monks sent me away saying,—

"'Seek your livelihood, you idle fellow.' I was hungry, and begged. Then I fell ill, had a fever, and everyone avoided me. Now I am reduced to utter want."

"My mother," said Michael, "was a tall, strong woman, who bore me on her back. I am not a Pole; I am a Gipsy, and come from Spain. One day we were coming from Grenada, down a mountain called Alpeigarras. I do not know how it was, but some men in black seized me suddenly, in spite of my mother's cries and mine. They threw cold water on my head, muttering some barbarous words which I did not understand. My mother cried out, 'He is not a Christian, he never shall be one, nor will I,' and she tried, by wiping my forehead, to efface what she regarded as a stain—a taint—and they killed her."

"Killed her!" cried Paul, frightened.

"Yes, and called her a heretic."

"Heretic," said the child, "what's that?"

"I don't know, but her blood flowed, I saw it. She showed it to me, saying, 'Michael, my son, remember.' Then she became very pale, her lips stiffened, and she ceased to speak. What followed I cannot remember. I only know I met some Gipsies in a wood who took me with them. One day they were attacked by some men when they had wandered into Poland. Each mother fled, bearing away her child. I had no mother, so I remained on the high road. From that time to this I have walked before me, singing and begging."

The two orphans—the two friends—renewed the mutual grasp, and the words, "My brother," escaped their lips.

And in truth there was in their dark complexions, the cast of their features, and their black and expressive eyes, a family likeness, a rather strong evidence that they belonged to the same race or tribe.

"And now," said Paul, "our dinner is over."

"Over," cried Michael, "and I am hungry."

"So am I."

"More so than I was before," continued Michael, "and no hopes of a second course."

"Perhaps," said a soft voice from above.

They looked up.

Just above them a window was open, and a pretty, full-bosomed, rosy-cheeked damsel, not more than twelve, leaned out.

"Here," she cried, "here is some bread and cheese. Be quick with it, or the landlord will see you and be angry."

Never did royal banquet witness guests more jolly or more delighted.

Stimulated by the reinforcement of good things, their appetite, whch had but slumbered, awoke young and splendid.

All their misfortunes were forgotten at once.

They did not, however, forget their young benefactress, but stopped ever and anon to express by a smile or a tender glance their gratitude towards the little servant, who still leaned out of the window.

This pleasing scene was suddenly disturbed by a cry from the girl, which Paul echoed by a second on finding himself violently pulled by the ear by the landlord.

"Ah, ah!" this is the way I'm robbed," cried mine host in a terrible voice, casting towards the girl a threatening look, which was lost, as she had closed the window.

The furious innkeeper, holding Paul's ear with one hand, tried with the other to pick up the remains of the feast, but the little Gipsy, nimbler than he, scrambled for the remaining provisions, and thrust them into a wallet which was not usually so well filled, whispering in the ear of his companion, "To-night, behind the church of Saint Peter."

Then he disappeared like lightning.

---

## CHAPTER XXXVIII.

### THE SHADOW ON THE WALL.

PAUL would gladly have followed his friend, but one of his ears was a hostage in the hands of the fierce landlord.

Besides, an instinctive sentiment of generosity and justice suggested that it would more become him to remain and defend his benefactress.

"Beat me, if you like," he said resolutely to his adversary, for the meal had restored his energy and strength; "beat me if you like, but do not scold the girl."

"Mathilda," cried the innkeeper, "is a little mischievous minx, whom I shall send back to her uncle Padislaus, the barber. I had agreed to take her for nothing, but I see that even at that price she will be dear! The whole of the Polish race are not worth the rope we hang them with, or the wood we buy to burn them."

He is a Russian in heart and in race too, I expect," said Paul, to himself.

"Forgive her," rejoined he, "and I will in all things obey and serve you."

"Done!" cried the landlord, who had suddenly become possessed of an idea—so rare a thing with him, that it disposed him to clemency. "Done—I will forgive you and Mathilda too, and will even give you a rouble."

"A rouble!" said Paul, astonished, and opening his eyes wide, "a real silver rouble?"

He had never possessed such a sum.

"What must I do to earn it?" he added suspiciously. "Surely," he thought, "the landlord would not be so munificent except for a bad purpose."

"Walk up and down the streets until night-time, crying, 'The citizens and their rights for ever!'"

"Nothing else! well that's not very difficult. And shall I have a rouble?"

"Yes."

"And when?"

"Here, this evening I will pay you."

"You swear it?"

"Yes, I swear it," said the innkeeper, opening his fingers and letting go his captive.

Paul no sooner found his ears at liberty, than he ran into the street merrily and disappeared crying,—

"The citizens and their rights for ever!"

Faithful to the instructions which he had received, and anxious like an honest lad to earn the promised reward, Paul paraded the streets, crying out with all his might the prescribed words.

No one said no, as at that time it was not known what turn affairs might take; but two or three boys who were wandering in the streets, as amateurs, ready to join the first drum or noise of any kind, joined him in his exclamations, and the procession increasing at every corner, the young general was soon at the head of a juvenile army, when, on turning into a new street, they fell in with a brigade of about the some number and age, but of a different opinion, their cry being,—

" Down with the rights of the city ! "

War appeared inevitable between the two parties so opposed, when to the surprise of the belligerents, the two generals advanced to embrace each other.

" Is it you, Michael ? "

" You, Paul ! what do you here ? "

" I shout."

" And I also," answered Michael. " I am paid three roubles by the followers of the Count Palatine to cry ' Down with the rights of the city.' "

" And I am to have only one rouble," said Paul.

" The other party is the best," exclaimed the troop, and all, to a boy, went over to Michael. And the two coalesced armies now making only one, it continued its march to the reiterated shout of " Down with the rights of the city."

But suddenly they came upon a body of real halberdiers, with a real sergeant and and real halberts.

It was, the reader will readily surmise, the landlord, who advanced with intrepidity towards them, without being alarmed at the numerical superiority of the enemy.

" Down with your arms," called out the sergeant, " down with your arms."

This was an order the less dishonourable as the opposing force was not in possession of weapons of any kind ; but what caused them some disquiet was that the halberdiers presented arms, to avoid the effects of which manœuvre, the two generals, thinking that they could best beat the real soldiers in racing, cried, " Escape who can ! " and both took to their heels with all possible dispatch.

Unfortunately in their haste they turned into a blind alley —a street without a thoroughfare, in which they were soon captured by the civic guard.

The landlord's victory was complete, and he was moderate in his success, Paul and Michael being detained as prisoners and hostages for the remainder.

The intention of the sergeant had been to place the two chiefs of the insurrection himself in safe custody. But the day was drawing in, and drums and trumpets sounded.

The landlord being obliged therefore to proceed to his position in the line of the escort, deputed two halberdiers to convey the prisoners to a cellar under the Rising Sun, which he specially pointed out, until he had time to see them to a place of security.

As for our two heroes, conquered but not discouraged, they walked along in silence, exchanging now and then looks which said,—

" What are we to do ? what will become of us ? how are we to save ourselves ? "

Paul, to do him justice, thought not of himself at this juncture.

He dreamed only of the means of saving his companion.

But though he wanted neither sagacity, nor wit, nor boldness, the attempt was almost useless ; their captors had not seized them by their clothes, which, seeing the dilapidated state of their vestments, would have afforded little hold.

Paul, however, profiting by a moment when his guard was looking another way, suddenly stooped, and picking up a handful of dirt, threw it into the eyes of the halberdier who walked by the side of Michael, crying out,—

" Away ! save yourself ! Meet me to-night at nine."

Nor did the latter wait to hear it a second time.

This generous act procured a severe beating for poor, weak Paul, after which he was conducted, without chance of escape, into the cellar of the Rising Sun, the key of which was twice turned upon him.

There was no outlet from his dungeon but through a door, which was both bolted and padlocked.

There was no light but what was admitted through a narrow vent-hole, secured by an iron bar.

In short, the place was devoid of all furniture, if we except two old butts, once filled with tolerable wine, which had been sold by the landlord for pure Toquay.

After fruitless endeavours to break open the door, and having in vain cried out for assistance, Paul sat himself down, and, must we confess it ? his courage forsook him.

Our hero began to cry. But what hero is without his weak moments ? And then it must not be forgotten that he had not supped, and his morning breakfast had long since passed from his recollection, thanks to the exercise he had taken and the fatigue produced by the military manœuvres of the day.

He wept then, and, moreover, though not naturally timid, he could not repress the feelings of alarm which overcame him on finding himself in total darkness.

All at once he heard loud cries, and thought his last hour was approaching.

It was occasioned by the cheering of some friends who were becoming intoxicated with the wine of their patron.

Seated around a large table in the finest room in the hotel, they made Mathilda, with whom we are already acquainted, wait upon them.

This girl, only twelve years of age, lovely, obliging, and devoid of all pride, was ordered about and scolded by everybody, and was at this time the assistant of the servants.

" Bring from the kitchen," called out the landlord, in an imperious tone, " the two cold partridges brought down from No. 9. The guests there must have been lovers, for they did not eat."

A triton among the minnows he appeared to his flatterers, and this sally of the landlord was received with great applause.

This was the noise which so frightened Paul, who sprang up, and listened attentively.

A sudden ray of moonlight came through the aperture overlooking the courtyard, and lighted up his cell.

This, however, was momentarily intercepted by the body of some unknown person who softly approached the aperture, remained but an instant, and then, rapidly running away, let fall a roasted partridge at Paul's feet.

Immediately afterwards the soft voice of a young girl was heard from the dining-room.

" I vow there was but one, sir."

" It is very astonishing, then," returned her master. " I put two on the table ; unless these gentlemen "—

He gave a searching glance round the table ; but none of the waiters or attendants of the Rising Sun could reasonably be suspected of an act of such selfishness and indelicacy.

Paul thus was indebted for his supper, as he had been for his breakfast, to the attentions of Mathilda, by whom he was quartered upon the enemy and at their expense.

He would willingly, however, have dispensed with his lodging, and he set his wits to work to find out a method of escape.

The aperture of the vent-hole was in itself very narrow, and the bar of iron rendered it twice as small.

But Paul was so thin that he thought he could, without much difficulty, although he had supped, contrive to pass through this narrow opening.

The great difficulty was to reach it ; but a good dinner, and the love of liberty, doubles one's energy, and the prisoner managed, by unheard-of efforts, to pile the two empty butts one upon the other.

He then attempted his ascent to scale the breach, which he did not accomplish without having hurt and disfigured himself a good deal.

Having got his head between the bar and the wall, he soon introduced the rest of his body, and thus got into the courtyard.

Paul, a beggar and a vagrant, had no ideas of religion or morality, and had only heard the name of the Deity in the daily oaths which were uttered ; but, in spite of himself, he knew not why, an instinct, a motive of gratitude, made him fall upon his knees, though his lips uttered not a word.

Although, then, his heartfelt gratitude showed no visible signs by which it could be recognised, yet there was in his heart a sincere fervent prayer which reached to heaven.

The prisoner had left his cell, but not the hotel.

The courtyard was surrounded by high walls, whose summit he had scarcely any hope of attaining, and still less of being able to descend into the streets on the other side.

Disconsolate and discouraged, Paul had no idea how to extricate himself from his difficulties, and began to give way to despair, and to think that he had changed but one prison for another, where nobody would come to his assistance.

His heart had made him think of Providence—his generosity had provided a friend, and he who in the morning had nothing, found, in one day, two treasures, two consolations—religion and friendship.

Suddenly, on the top of the wall, appeared a shadow.

Then a beam of moonlight displayed to him a brown head, which cautiously appeared, looking down into the courtyard.

It was Michael!

Paul would have cried out, but a motion from his friend warned him to be silent, and a moment after, the Bohemian was on the parapet of the wall, attempting to draw up with him a small, long, and light ladder, which had served to enable him to mount the wall.

Being with difficulty drawn up, it was placed on the other side and let down into the courtyard.

Paul, having placed it properly, got to the top of the wall, where Michael awaited him.

Here, then, were the two friends face to face, striding across the wall.

They embraced, and began to question one another.

" So then, Michael, you have come to rescue me ? " said Paul.

" Yes, forsooth. You gave me your assistance once, and I do the same for you."

" And suppose I had not luckily been in the courtyard ? "

" I would have sought you elsewhere."

" I was in the cellar."

" I should have descended into 'it. I knew you were a prisoner in the inn; that was enough for me, and, no matter how, I should have effected your escape."

" And suppose you had been taken prisoner or beaten ? "

" That was my affair. I have waited since dark outside in the street."

" What where you doing ? "

" Prowling about on the look out."

" For what ? "

" For the means of effecting your escape, which this ladder soon afforded."

" Where did you find it ? "

" Opposite, at the tailor's."

" Did you go there to get it ? "

" No, it was let down from a window, and immediately after I saw descend, wrapped up in a cloak—"

" A thief ? "

" If so, a very juvenile one ; and a soft voice cautioned him to be careful. But I then cried aloud; the window was speedily closed ; and the young man leaped to the ground, and ran away. I then instantly seized the ladder, and here I am."

" Now let us descend, for, though we are well enough here, we can chat more comfortably when we have descended to the other side of the wall."

By their joint efforts, the two friends easily managed to raise the ladder, which was still resting against the wall of the court-yard of the Rising Sun, and they let it down into the street.

Michael insisted on ceding to Paul the honour of descending first, and he accordingly took the lead.

At this moment the moon was obscured by a dark cloud which passed over it—the inn, the walls, and the streets were left in total darkness, and Michael, no longer able to see his friend, said to him in a subdued tone—

" Descend cautiously, for the walls are at least twenty feet high. Have you descended safely ? Speak."

" Yes, here I am."

" I will follow you, then."

This he did in safety.

But only just in time.

Hardly had he placed his foot upon the ground when he beheld several dark figures creeping along the wall towards them.

" Run, Paul," he cried; " run for your life. You know the place of meeting."

At these words Paul, who instantly comprehended that danger was near, started off, and both boys ran away as fast as their legs would carry them by different routes to the same spot.

---

## CHAPTER XXXIX.

### THERESA.

The Church of St. Peter reared its head grim and dark against the sky.

Every one in Warsaw knew it, and Paul therefore made his way with ease towards it.

It was the resort of all the idle people of the town.

The architect had, of course, constructed the broad stone steps for the sake of their beauty.

The beggars and vagabonds seemed to consider that they had been constructed purely for their comfort.

So all day long, when the sun was high, the beggars lay and luxuriated in the bright beams, and in the summer nights slept beneath the portico.

It was nearly winter, now, however, and the cold was beginning to set it, and therefore the steps were completely deserted.

So when Paul arrived he found himself alone.

After taking a few turns up and down, and whistling a tune to keep his courage up, he saw Michael approaching, and welcomed his friend eagerly.

" Let us go under the portico," said the latter in a half-whisper ; " we shall not be observed there."

They went.

Paul was in a state of considerable excitement.

Evidently his friend desired to communicate something.

What could it be ?

They sat down together on the step of the church door.

" You have something to tell me," said Paul ; " I know you have."

Michael laughed.

" Why ? " he asked.

" I guessed from your manner."

" You are right, I have. It is something which may make our fortunes. I must tell you at once, for I have to be at the gate of St. Nicholas by ten, and it is now nearly half-past nine."

As he spoke the clock struck the half hour.

" There," he said, " we have but ten minutes. It will take us a quarter of an hour to reach the gate, and five minutes to look round us."

" Good," said Paul, " I will listen."

" This morning," began Michael, " I started out to beg. I was very hungry, and, as you know, not particular, for I had had nothing since yesterday."

" Like me ! "

" Well, about nine o'clock, I was loitering near the gate of St. Nicholas, when I saw approaching me a gentleman wrapped in a cloak."

" He was very short, and halted a little in his walk."

" I looked down on the ground, and asked for alms."

" He halted without answering me."

" After a moment I looked up in surprise, which soon changed to alarm."

" He was evidently studying me."

" He was very short, with crooked legs and a very big head, with huge mouth from ear to ear."

" He was smiling, but there was something in his smile which alarmed me."

" I was sidling off when he put out a long thin arm and detained me."

" I looked frightened."

" This made him laugh outright."

" ' Don't be afraid of me, my boy,' he said, in a kind voice, ' if you want money I will tell you how to earn it.'

" I tried to smile, but the attempt was useless.

" ' Come my boy,' he said, ' if you wish to earn some

money honestly, say so; if you don't like me because I'm ugly, and you are afraid, why we won't talk any more.'

" Then I thought to myself, why should I not serve this man because he is ugly? and, plucking up courage, I answered—

" ' I'm not afraid, and will do all you wish, please sir.'

" He patted me on the head, saying—

" ' Be at this gate at ten to-night, and I will give you five roubles.'

" I looked at him suspiciously.

" ' What have I to do for it?' I asked.

" ' Merely to follow a carriage and tell me where the people in it alight.'

" ' Why can't you do it yourself?' I said.

" ' Because I should be observed,' he answered, ' but come, my man, I don't stand here to be questioned, but to give directions. Tell me, will you come?'

" ' Yes, sir,' I said.

" ' Very good;' and here is a rouble as an earnest of my good intentions.'

" He took out his purse and was just about to open it when he caught sight of some one on the opposite side of the way, and calling to me, ' Be there, and I will make it six roubles,' darted down a by-street and disappeared. Now if you will go with me to-night, I will keep my appointment and we shall have three roubles a-piece."

Paul laughed.

" Have you then spent the three roubles you have received from the Count Palatine?" he asked.

" No, I never received them."

" What! is he too a breaker of promises?"

" No, I never went to receive them."

" Why not?"

" Because I was prowling about seeking to deliver you. Say now, will you go with me or not?"

The clock struck the quarter to ten.

There was not much time to deliberate.

" Yes," said Paul, " I will go."

And so the two young friends set off towards the great gate.

They arrived there as the clock struck the hour of ten.

Fortune seemed to have resolved that they should have no time for deliberation.

Hardly had they advanced into the shadow of the archway when the stranger stepped forward.

" You are punctual, my young friend," he said; " but who is this who accompanies you?"

" A friend of mine," returned Michael; " you may trust him."

Youthful confidence!

They had known each other but since the morning.

" Good," said the stranger, who was no other than our old friend, Zisko, " now listen while I explain to you the service I require at your hands. Meanwhile here are two roubles."

" Thank you, sir," exclaimed Michael, as he received them delightedly.

" In a few minutes the king's entry will take place," proceeded the stranger, " you can already hear the trumpets in the distance. Behind the king, in one of the carriages, will be a lady and a gentleman. It is my wish to know where these people alight. You and your friend must contrive to follow the procession and watch them."

" That is not difficult," said Michael, " it shall be done."

" Stand back in the shade here then," continued Zisko, " and when I point out to you the carriage, be ready to start off."

For about five minutes the boys waited in anxious expectation.

They were eager for the cortege to appear, not only from the desire that actuated them to earn the money promised, but from the wish to witness the brilliant spectacle.

The city had by this time resumed its quiet aspect.

The revolutionary spirit had subsided under the influence of spirituous liquors.

Russian roubles had procured endless jollification in different parts of the city, and at the Rising Sun and every other tavern inebriated patriots insisted upon the king's entry with a civic guard, while foreign soldiers were inundating the streets.

So, amid the neighing and tramping of horses and the sounding of trumpets, King Stanislaus entered Warsaw.

Two regiments came first—then six carriages—then the King—then six more carriages.

In the third sat two persons—a gentleman and a lady.

"There," cried Zisko eagerly, as he pointed to the equipage, "there are the persons I seek. Be quick—follow them—and meet me here to-morrow morning at nine."

The two boys darted off and were soon lost to Zisko's eyes in the crowd which gradually gathered round the procession.

Those they were pursuing were the Castellan and Theresa.

---

## CHAPTER XL.

### THE STRANGE INN.

PUNCTUAL to their appointment Paul and Michael met the dwarf at the gate of St. Nicholas, as the clock struck ten on the morrow.

" Well," he said eagerly, " and where did they alight."

" At the Hotel de France, kept by a Frenchman, named Lescaut."

" Good, where is the hotel?"

" In the Nevski Prospect, next door to the house of Padislaus the barber."

" Very good—here are your four roubles. Stay, tell me under what name they put up?"

" I cannot tell."

" Where can I meet with you again?"

Michael looked puzzled.

" Have you no home?" asked Zisko.

" No."

" And you," he added turning to Paul.

" No."

The dwarf thought a moment.

" Meet me, then, here to-night," he said, " and I will see what I am to do for you both. Be here at eight."

He then moved away, and the young friends departed in delight.

The sun was now shining brightly upon the steps of the church of St. Peter, and thither, as a place open to all, they repaired, and divided their spoil.

They were engaged in this, when Paul suddenly found himself seized by the ear.

He and his friend started up.

It was Captain Stroloffski.

" Ah, you young rascal," he cried; " so I have caught you at last. It is you who take people's money, and go over to their foes! Ah! ah! my young fellow, I saw you escaping from the inn last night. I suppose that is where you got this money?"

" Sir Knight," cried Paul, "you are mistaken. I am no thief."

" How do I know that?"

" I swear to you I follow no such vile occupation."

" Still, you can give me some information about the house you came from."

" No, indeed, I cannot."

" Well, we will see, you and your friend must come with us."

" Save yourself," cried Paul, as the captain's followers advanced.

Michael at once darted off, and was lost amid the labyrinth of streets.

The captain and his man left town at once.

Horses were awaiting for them without the walls, as also two loaded mules, besides one that carried nothing, which the captain eyed with a grim expression.

The cavalcade started at a trot, continued its way all day, traversed at noon a beautiful river, and some hours after began to ascend the mountains and penetrate into the forests.

When Paul arrived at the Inn of Good Rest, he could not imagine what sort of customers frequented such a spot.

He thought of the hotel of the Rising Sun, where it rained roasted partridges as something magical in comparison, and he almost wished himself back again in the cellar.

The memory of Mathilda, so kind and so pretty, and of his friend Michael, so devoted and so gay, rendered the terrible society in which he was now thrown, still more repulsive.

Not that anything was wanting. The captain's table was well served, the wine was good, and there was abundance of capital spirits ; but what he heard and saw confused his ideas, and troubled his young and inexperienced mind.

The bacchanalian orgies finished most frequently in quarrels.

"You cannot agree, my children," the captain would say, in a paternal tone. "Fight it out, and let it be over."

Knives were drawn, blood flowed, and Paul retired into a corner trembling and crying.

To a poor child, who had never seen nor heard anything of the kind, this horrible tavern was like the antechamber to the infernal regions.

And yet Paul was forbidden to quit it.

That was the captain's order, and he dared not to disobey.

Paul feared the captain far too much even to think of quitting the spot; but one day the weather was so fine, the sun shining so brightly, and no one but himself at the hostelry, that he could not resist the temptation of a walk in order to breathe a little fresh air.

He had been out only a few minutes when he felt himself already refreshed ; a feeling of gladness crept to his heart, and a smile played upon his lips, when suddenly his cheeks became pale and icy.

He was even obliged to seek support from a tree, for he had, on turning a corner in the wood, found himself face to face with the captain.

The captain and his lieutenant, Lubinski, smoked away, spoke of the present posture of their affairs and of an intended expedition.

The former then ordered his men to lead Paul into the dining room, into which many of his comrades had just entered.

In an instant he was stripped naked, laid on his stomach, and Lubinski, taking down a leathern strap which hung against the wall, began to lash the sufferer with a hearty goodwill, which proved the satisfaction he experienced in carrying out out the orders of his captain.

After a considerable amount of chastisement, Paul was carried fainting away, and from that moment he had neither courage nor inclination to quit the inn.

Whenever he went out he was either accompanied by the captain, or by his direction with orders which he implicitly obeyed; fear and the habit of prompt obedience completely extinguished his energies and blunted his natural capacities.

He was sent out to a farm house or to a gentleman's seat in the character of a wandering beggar boy, imploring assistance from the hospitality of the inmates, when, on his return, he was closely questioned as to all he saw, the localities, the numbers of the inmates, masters, and servants.

Paul related everything ; this was all they required.

His happiest days were those on which he performed these journeys, for he spent them away from his den.

Oftentimes he wished to say to those whom he visited,—

"Engage me in your service, I pray you," but the question was, would they have consented ? and then the vengeance of the captain would have been terrible.

One day when he was just about to implore the protection of the proprietor of a mansion, he saw through a window overlooking the park a figure which filled him with affright ; it was the captain on horseback, superbly dressed, who had come to treat with the proprietor for the purchase of the fine estate which was for sale.

After this, even this idea left his mind, and so mysterious altogether were the movements of the captain and his band that he gave up all hope of unravelling the secret.

One of the most curious things was that the inn, although in an isolated position and at some distance from the road, was never shut at night.

Then on the royal road was a dilapidated place, a sort of precipice which was never repaired, but was only covered with leaves, and whenever a postchaise broke down in this detestable place, there appeared on the skirts of the wood, a wood-cutter and his son, who pointed out to the travellers an excellent inn in the neighbourhood, where they could get the best accommodation.

The son even volunteered to act as a guide—this son was Paul, who, much to his dislike, found the friends of the captain act alternately the part of father to him.

All those who were conducted to the inn were wealthy, and after partaking of a magnificent entertainment, they were conducted to a splendid apartment, which Paul was not suffered to enter, but the splendour of which he once saw through the half-closed door.

It contained two beds with rich canopies over them, and gorgeous furniture to match.

It was the only room in the inn that could boast of such magnificence.

One circumstance connected with these chance travellers struck Paul as strange.

They were all early risers, indeed he had never seen them leave the inn, and occasionally so careless were they that they left behind them their conveyances and their horses in the stable, to be sent for, doubtless, on some future occasion.

One day, drinking over his dice, the lieutenant, who hated Paul, ordered him to bring him his pipe.

Paul, on the point of presenting it to him with his usual readiness, received, by way of thanks, a box on the ears.

Forgetting himself for the moment, he dashed the pipe to pieces on the floor and stamped on it.

The lieutenant was particularly fond of his pipe,

"Bravo!" cried the captain.

"Yes, bravo," echoed the lieutenant sarcastically; "look you, my boy, count the fragments of that pipe. You shall have as many lashes from my whip."

He went to the wall where it hung, and, at the same instant, Paul rushed to the table and seized a knife.

The bandits arose in astonishment.

"Don't approach me," said Paul, his voice gaining strength with his rage, "I appeal to the captain—to you all. I have been struck a blow I merited not, and I have heard you say, sir, that a blow demands blood. If you advance one step I'll draw some some of yours, depend on it."

"Bravo!" cried the captain, rubbing his hands with delight.

The lieutenant now approached, flourishing his "cat" over his head, and, encouraged by the bravoes of his companions, struck the boy heavily.

Paul, exasperated, rushed at him and plunged the knife a little below the breast.

The lieutenant fell to the ground, shrieking with rage. The bandits ran to the assistance of their comrade, and then seizing Paul and throwing him down, drew their daggers to dispatch him.

"Hold!" exclaimed the captain; "by all the saints, the combat was a fair one, and the blow right vigorously planted."

"Too vigorously," echoed the lieutenant with a groan.

"Bravo, Paul!" continued the captain, without paying any attention to his fallen lieutenant; "and as for you, my friends, hark ye, harm not a hair of that youngster's head, at your peril. Now that the young tiger has tasted blood, I tell ye he is one of us. Come hither, Paul ; and you, sirs, take the man away and staunch his wounds."

"Be it so," groaned the lieutenant; "but I can tell you that he shall taste the blade of my dagger ere long."

"That is a private affair of your own," rejoined the captain; and while they were bearing Lubinski away, "Paul," he added, "you struck too low; that blow should have been a thought higher."

From that day the captain completely altered his treatment of Paul.

He had despaired of making anything of him, but the event above recorded entirely changed the aspect of affairs, and he now entertained hopes of turning his young apprentice to some useful account.

THE RESCUE.

Selfish motives alone prompted him to act thus, for there was no honourable feeling in the breast of Stroloffski, who, indeed, was the only being in the world for whom that bold bandit entertained the remotest genuine affection.

But, despite his extreme youth, he became conscious of the crimes and vices of his vile companions, and sought to shun them. The tares had not quite choked the grain, and the sound principles which nature had planted in his heart sprung up, despite the corruption around it.

Meanwhile, having become a favourite of the captain, he was treated with more confidence, and although all the secrets of the prison house were not revealed to him, he was suffered to mingle with his companions more socially.

Sometimes, on the arrival of travellers, he was permitted to prepare the mysterious chamber for their reception. This apartment had always excited great curiosity in his mind, especially after seeing, as he imagined on one occasion, some of the splendid furniture with which the room was furnished, stained with blood.

One of the duties he had to perform was to rise betimes and keep watch from the garret of the inn. It often struck him during these vigils as somewhat inexplicable, that he never saw the guests who came over-night leave in the morning, especially if they chanced to possess valuable property. One incident was further remarkable. The landlord of the inn invariably attended his guests at supper, and when that meal was ended and the travellers had retired to their rooms, the captain sat up drinking, and, after the lapse of an hour or two, instead of going to bed, he always went down into the cellar, without, however, bringing up any wine.

In this den of thieves we must for a while leave him, while we return to Mazeppa, whose fortunes became afterwards so terribly linked with those of Paul and Mathilda.

## CHAPTER XLI.

### A FOOL AND HIS MONEY.

WHEN Mazeppa left his army behind him, he proceeded straight towards the capital.

When arrived there, however, he found himself no nearer his object than he was before.

It was Zisko who suggested the probability that the Castellan and his daughter would be found in the king's retinue, and it was with unbounded delight that he heard that the two boys engaged by the dwarf had succeeded in tracing them to the French hotel.

When, however, on the following day it was discovered that Paul had disappeared, they both naturally concluded that he had been carried off by their enemies.

To rescue him, however, was impossible, since Michael, who kept his appointment punctually to the moment, was unable to explain when or where he had before seen the man who had seized his friend.

When, moreover, they applied at the hotel, they found themselves fairly puzzled.

The proprietor declared himself entirely ignorant of any such persons as those named by Mazeppa, and was indignant at their repeated inquiries.

Meanwhile Paul was in a fair way to solve the problem, although the danger he had to endure was terrible.

He had often watched the captain at the head of the stairs leading to the cellars of the inn of Good Rest.

He had seen him open the door with a key hanging by his side and leave the bunch when he descended, but there his discoveries ended,

At length, wearied out with impatience and curiosity, he resolved on following the captain on one of his visits to the mystic cellar.

He was on the point of doing this one day, but his heart failing him at the sound seemingly of some disturbance below, he hurried back to his garret in terrible trepidation.

He never again ventured to repeat the experiment, and the great secret promised to remain a secret as far as he was concerned, for the captain determined on leaving the inn shortly, as its reputation (a ticklish one at all times) began to spread throughout the country rather unpleasantly.

Whilst with his comrades he planned fresh campaigns the lieutenant lay confined to his room.

Although convalescent, he preferred remaining there, simply requesting his companions to supply him with abundance of wine, and promising, like a discreet invalid, to partake of it sparingly.

The juice of the grape sparkled bright and profuse enough in his glass; but with all its genial qualities he that quaffed it looked gloomy and pensive, as though he meditated carrying into effect some long cherished act of vengeance.

In another apartmen one evening, the rest of the bandits were carousing merrily over their wine and a savoury stew, the delicious aroma of which reached Paul temptingly enough, while he, as was his wont, waited on the band.

Suddenly a loud knocking was heard at the gate of the inn.

"Can these be travellers?" exclaimed he, "I hear no wheels."

"Can it be the police?" rejoined his comrades, painfully, bearing in mind the awkward fame of the inn.

"By the saints above," replied the captain, "it behoves us to reconnoitre before we open the gate. Go you, Coloski, cautiously, while Paul pours me out a bumper."

Coloski immediately obeyed the order, and returning shortly, brought with him a little man, with a round, good-natured face, holding in one hand a humble portmanteau, and conducting with the other a smart-looking little girl, who bashfully hung back at the sight of so large an assembly of men.

"Gentlemen," said the stranger, "I am a poor traveller who has met with an accident, and entreat shelter at your hands for myself and my niece here. Why don't you pay your respects to the company, Mathilder?" added he, addressing his niece,

Mathilda curtsied modestly, and Paul shrank behind the captain's chair to avoid recognition.

He was overwhelmed by her sudden apparition.

His remembrance of her was too deeply engraven on his heart to be readily effaced.

Notwithstanding the change that the lapse of a few months had wrought on so young a girl as Mathilda, he recognised her instantly.

His first impulse was to rush to her side and load her with inquiries; but an undefinable dread of danger, coupled with a modesty he could not dispel, checked him, and he remained, as we have said, partly hid behind the captain's chair, and keeping his eye fixed on the fair Mathilda—for, mark you, the pretty little lass was worth the looking at with all the ardour of youth.

As for her, poor thing, she recognised no one, and timidly clung to the side of her uncle.

"Seat yourself, sir," said the captain, "and you, too, miss, by the side of yonder gentleman, who, like yourselves, have done me the honour to patronise my inn, and meditate sleeping here. May I take the liberty of asking," he added, "who it is I have the honour of entertaining?"

"Sir," said the little man, "perchance you have not heard of my fame. Among the knights of the soap and razor I hold a high reputation, and my name is Padislaus, the illustrious barber of Warsaw."

The captain and his comrades bowed respectfully at this grandiloquent announcement, and Padislaus, proud of the effect he imagined he had produced, poured out a cup of wine and continued his harangue.

"Exhausted by acts of injustice which were consequent upon the disturbances which have lately taken place, I have determined on quitting Warsaw forever. I have a relation at Lublin, and having removed my niece from her service at the Rising Sun to accompany me, I am now on my way thither to establish myself in business there with my relation. In order to accomplish this I have disposed of my valuable property in Warsaw, and have brought the proceeds of it in my portmanteau, amounting to two hundred roubles."

Paul, startled at the dangerous turn the conversation had taken, glided suddenly, bottle in hand, behind the barber, and nudging him with it, said, "Rash man, be silent."

"But, my friend, there is no occasion for you to dig that bottle of yours into my side," rejoined Padislaus, addressing himself to Paul, and then, resuming his bouncing order of conversation, he added—

"Yes, gentlemen, there they are, two hundred roubles in gold."

## CHAPTER XLII.

### THE INN OF THE BANDITS.

"And so," said the captain, who, with his comrades, had paid earnest attention to the gossiping story of the barber, "and so, sir, you mean to establish yourself at Lublin with the capital mentioned? Permit me to drink a bumper to your success. Your health, sir, and that of your niece."

"My niece, sir," replied the barber, "does not drink wine; but that matters little, as I can drink for two. Fill your glasses to the brim, gentlemen," continued the little man, gaily. "Here's to your health, landlord, and to all."

The barber then tossed off his tumbler, and, smacking his lips, exclaimed,—

"This is strange, indeed. I, who prided myself on knowing the qualities of every wine, must confess I am puzzled in this instance. Is it from the vineyards of Spain?"

"No," replied the captain; "you are out in your sorcery this time. That wine is from France."

"Indeed," stammered the barber, in evident vexation at the want of judgment he had betrayed; "well, that is strange; I seldom err in any opinion I express."

"Is it so, really?" chimed in the captain and his comrades.

"I assure you," continued the barber, elated with the wine, and speaking like an oracle. "I assure you there is scarcely a single thing that I have foretold which has not come to pass in the end. I predicted that evil would befall my neighbour the tailor when he got married to a pretty wife, and I was right, sure enough. One morning I predicted that the chief magistrate would receive some personal injury, and in the evening they brought him home with a broken arm."

"That's very true, uncle," timidly interrupted the little Mathilda, "but you omit to mention that you saw him in the morning pass your door mounted on a vicious horse."

"What matters that?" rejoined the barber; "are there not multitudes of vicious horses in the world? Is not the one we drove a vicious animal? yet my arm is not broken, and I am, look you," continued the little man, merrily filling his glass; but here the captain interrupted him by exclaiming,—

"By St. James, I will put your skill to the test. Tell me my fortune!"

"With pleasure," responded the barber. "Give me your hand."

"Here you have it."

After examining it very attentively, the prophet of Warsaw exclaimed,—

"Confound it! that French wine of yours has certainly obscured my organs of vision. Either I am wrong in my science, or I read on that hand something so preposterously strange and contradictory, that I barely like revealing it."

" Never mind, let's have it, whatever it be," said the captain.

" It won't frighten you ?" asked the barber.

" Nothing on earth can frighten me," replied the bandit.

" Why, then," continued the barber, in a hesitating tone, " one line in your hands clearly proclaims that you will be burnt to death, and, again, another unequivocally shows that you will be hanged ! However, as one line manifestly contradicts the other, you need not be alarmed for the result. It is obvious you can't die two deaths, and, therefore, my prediction is at fault."

Here the barber laughed outright at his own wit.

But he was the only one who laughed, the captain's comrades knowing full well that one portion of the prophecy was extremely likely to be fulfilled.

The captain was the only one unmoved by this hap-hazard augury of the barber's, and filling a fresh glass asked him if, in his prophetic wisdom, he could not fortel his own destiny.

" As for that," said the philosophic barber, " the contemplation of the future has never disturbed my slumbers. I can tell you now, gentlemen, without the aid of sorcery, what will befall me to-night and to-morrow."

Paul trembled, and the crptain turned pale ; but collecting himself almost immediately begged Padislaus to proceed with his prediction.

" Where," said he, " is it that you read your own destiny for to to-night and to-morrow ?"

" By Jupiter !" answered the philosopher, " I read it, sir landlord, in that physiognomy of yours. I perceive, in the first place, that I have made an excellent supper and have swallowed choice wines pretty freely. In these great facts, however, there is nothing particularly uncomfortable ; but I look to the sequel, sir—yes, it is the sequel that makes me feel monstrous uneasy."

The captain's hot blood was chilled by this remark.

" Yes," continued the barber, " it is the expression of your face that disturbs my equanimity. I can read there as plain as a pikestaff that you are a merry, yet calculating man. You reckon on making me pay heavily for my whistle to-night. But, look you, Mr. Landlord, I tell you candidly beforehand, I am not to be hocussed."

And here again the barber laughed at his own sagacity, whilst the captain, for the first time in his life, turned pale, and the cold sweat absolutely trickled down his brow.

" Ah, sir," added Padislaus, " that face of yours betrays care and fatigue. Doubtless we have kept you up too late to-night, and we should all be better for a little repose. Let us go to bed."

" Well, to be candid with you, sir," said the captain, " I am quite of your opinion ;" and then turning to poor Paul, who stood behind him in agonised suspense, he added, " Paul, go and prepare for this gentleman and his niece the damask chamber, and hasten back to conduct them thither."

Paul took the captain's dark-lantern and went on his errand.

But scarcely had he left the room, before he stopped in uttter despair, hesitating what course to pursue in this sad emergency,

At the risk of his life, he determined, if possible, to save Mathilda from the fate that awaited her.

But how was he to accomplish it ?

To what source could he fly for succour ?

The young girl and her uncle, unconscious of their imminent danger, had no other defender, no other guardian, than a boy.

Alone, too, against a host of bandits, and with only a few fleeting moments to arrange his thoughts and plans.

Gathering up his energies, he ascended the stairs leading to the fatal room.

It was on the first flight, and the door faced a long and narrow passage.

In arranging the chamber for the reception of the guests, he sought, but unsuccessfully, for some clue to the danger with which he felt convinced it was fraught.

In his agitation he upset the light, which, without getting extinguished, rolled on the floor.

On stooping to pick it up, and blundering about partly in the dark, he thought he felt a sort of groove in the planks surrounding the bed.

He applied the lantern to it, and there, sure enough, he beheld a kind of trap-door encircling each of the beds in the room.

Nor was the groove skilfully dove-tailed, for a current of air came whistling through the orifice.

" Here," thought he, " lie, somehow, the hidden secrets."

He felt assured that if Mathilda and her uncle once entered that fatal chamber, they would never leave it alive.

And that which added not a little to his misery, was the reflection that he was the chosen guide to lead them to this terrible destruction.

" Never, never," he mentally exclaimed, as the terrible idea crossed his fevered brain.

He rushed from the room, frantic with these reflections, and passed into the narrow passage with despair.

What was his dismay when, by the glimmering light of the lantern, he discovered, at the further end of the passage, the lieutenant, who, coming from the upper story of the inn with a poignard in his hand, closed the door of the passage, thus cutting off all hopes of retreat.

The lieutenant had seen him enter the passage, and poor Paul had no weapon whatever to defend himself, not even the knife which had proved so useful to him on a former occasion.

He felt his hair stand on end, and in the bitterness of his anguish he bore in mind that his own death would inevitably involve the destruction of Mathilda.

Moreover, he knew right well that he had no quarter to expect at the hands of his savage adversary ; nor, indeed, did it ever occur to him to beseech his pity.

Instinctively he closed the lantern, and instantly all was in utter darkness.

The lieutenant advanced towards him, and Paul, shrinking against the wall, calculated, by the noise occasioned by his footsteps, the proximity of his opponent.

He fancied he almost felt the cold blade of the dagger.

The lieutenant all but touched him, and Paul trembled at the very sound of his voice.

" That little rascal Paul," he muttered, " was here, I am certain ; but he was not alone, I think. There were two— yes, certainly, there were two. I thought I should have only one to dispatch ; but never mind, the more the merrier."

The bold lieutenant, be it said *en passant*, was in that amiable condition in which folks see double.

He could scarcely speak, and lurched like a ship, knocking himself against the sides of the passage.

It was evident that the convalescent had quite forgotten his homily on the virtue of moderation in wine.

At length, stumbling against Paul, he seized him by the shoulder, and his affrightened victim gave himself up for lost.

At this ticklish crisis he heard the dagger drop, which the lieutenant had held loosely in his hand.

Paul picked it up, but not with the intention of using it murderously.

After a brief pause the lieutenant halloed out in a maudlin voice.

" Holloa, there ! is Paul down below ?"

" He is," replied Paul, in a feigned tone.

" Well, then, hark you, comrade, be so good as to send him up to me in my room."

" Yes," answered Paul ; " but you are *not* in your room."

" Egad," added the lieutenant, feeling about in the dark, " in that case, my friend, just show me the way to it, like a good chap, for hang me if these walls here don't seem to me to be perpetually turning round and round, with my room into the bargain."

" See, here is your room," said Paul, shoving the lieutenant into the door hard by, which led to the fatal chamber. The man, stumbling in the dark, rolled up against the bed, and threw himself on it, mumbling,—

"Confound the thing—it is very strange; my bed used to be on the other side of the room, but hang me if everything don't seem to have turned topsy-turvy to-day."

Paul listened attentively till the lieutenant fell asleep.

"Now," thought he, "this is my only chance of saving them."

Having locked the lieutenant in, he went boldly back to the dining hall, where the captain awaited his return impatiently.

"Well, sir?" said the captain, quickly.

"Sir," rejoined Paul, "the room is prepared for the guests, and I am ready to conduct them to it."

"That's all right," exclaimed the barber, "we are quite at your service."

And forthwith he took possession of his portmanteau, and Paul, pale and immovable, betrayed the anxiety he felt.

The captain perceived his consternation and approached him.

Paul thought his last hope had vanished; but instead of the brutal manner in which he was usually accosted, the captain addressed him mildly, and in an undertone,—

"Ah, you see through it at last, then? That is right; but next time you must pluck up more courage. However, for the first attempt it is not so bad."

"We are ready to go, my young friend," said the barber; "good-night, gentlemen; we will settle the account to-morrow, landlord."

"To-morrow," rejoined the captain, gravely, "all accounts will be settled. Your room is ready—good night. For my own part I must sit up yet awhile to attend upon these gentlemen over their wine."

He shook hands with his guests and then said to Paul,—

"Show them their room and go to bed—I will attend to the rest."

Paul guided them up to the steps, but was ascending so fast that the barber called out to him not to be in such a hurry.

"What's the matter?" cried the captain, opening the door of the dining-room.

On hearing his voice, Paul paused and answered, explaining the cause of the barber's exclamation.

"Is that all?" rejoined the captain, once more closing the door.

Paul breathed once more on hearing the door shut; but on reaching the room in which he had deposited the drunken lieutenant he could not help pausing to take breath.

"Is this the room?" asked the barber.

"Oh, no," said Paul, endeavouring to hide his emotion and ascending the second flight of steps.

The barber and his niece were somewhat startled by the strange conduct of the guide.

At length they reached the garret were Paul slept.

He begged them to enter, and, after shutting the door, he checked the barber, who was about to address him.

"Silence," said he, "silence, or you are a lost man."

On hearing this the barber's gaiety instantly forsook him.

"Lost—lost!" he cried, nor could he utter a word beyond these distracting monosyllables.

"Mathilda," exclaimed Paul, "do you not recollect me?"

She gazed at him earnestly.

"The poor little beggar you once saved."

"Oh, yes, I do now."

"Well, then, remember that I am grateful. Listen."

He then made them acquainted with the kind of inn they were visiting—what was the captain's calling, and their chances of escape.

"They are by this time all gone to bed," said he, "and will sleep for an hour or so. The captain will then, in all likelihood, descend into the cellar. Then will be the time for us to quit this horrible dwelling. How we are to accomplish this I must confess I don't exactly see at present; but be quiet here while I keep watch."

---

## CHAPTER XLIII.

### SUSPENSE.

OUR readers must not think that we have abandoned altogether our hero Mazeppa; but it is necessary for awhile to follow the fortunes of Paul in order to show in what way he became acquainted with the Castellan and his daughter.

Leaving the barber and his niece more dead than alive, and descending a few steps, Paul lay in a recumbent position, eagerly listening to ascertain the movements below.

Some considerable time elapsed before he heard the bandits betake themselves severally to their rooms.

He then descended to the ground-floor and listened again.

Presently he heard a door inside the dining-hall opened.

Entering the room stealthily he saw the captain going down into the cave, and leaving the door of it open. Paul double-barred it, locking the captain in.

Having secured the bunch of keys that hung to the door he hurried back to the garret where he had left his friends.

"Now," said he, "we have not a moment to lose—follow me. Doubtless among these keys we shall find one that will open the gate leading to the wood. Failing that, it is all over with us."

"Saving," said Mathilda, "to commit ourselves to heaven."

As for the barber he was speechless.

"What shall we do," cried the young girl, "about our cart and mule?"

"You must think no more of such things," rejoined Paul; "it will be as much as we can do to save ourselves. We shall have to wander about the wood all night, and perhaps in the morning we may find some refuge and protection."

"Ah, you are our protector," exclaimed Mathilda, throwing her arms round Paul's neck.

"This is not the time," added he, "for thanksgiving. As yet I have done nothing for you. Pray hasten and follow me."

"Oh, yes," replied Mathilda, "let us hurry away. Our time is short indeed, and you, uncle, lie there heedless of our impending fate."

Padislaus would willingly have acted promptly upon this timely summons, but that was out of his power.

He hung down his head and closed his eyes.

Urged by fear he would gladly have aroused himself; but his legs refused their office, and heavy sleep overcame him.

At length, after struggling for awhile against its influence and exhausted with the effort, he fell back upon the bundles of straw and was instantly—to the horror and surprise of his companions—fast asleep.

All their efforts were in vain to wake him from this strange slumber.

He blubbered forth a few incomprehensible words—that was all.

"Ah!" said Paul, "it is that wine that has done it—that wine of French vintage, as it was called. In order to run no risk, to render their victim powerless, they have, no doubt, drugged it."

"I see it—I see it now," exclaimed the frightened Mathilda; "what will become of us?"

"Even if we tried," said Paul, "it would be impossible for both our united strengths to lift that heavy weight of your uncle. All now left for me to do is to secure your safety—you, my dear benefactress. Haste—haste, then, and follow me. Already have we lost too much of our precious time."

"No," emphatically rejoined the maiden, "whatever may happen I will never desert my uncle."

"As for myself," added Paul, "whatever peril befalls us I will never desert you—we will die together."

And thereupon he seated himself by her side on the straw, and Mathilda, crossing her arms over her breast, began muttering a prayer to herself.

"It is well," murmured she; "child of the forsaken, thou wilt die—a better destiny than to live alone—uncared for in this world."

At this crisis a great uproar was heard in the house.

Down in the cellar a desperate struggle had commenced between the captain and the lieutenant. The latter, although in a state of insobriety, was aroused from his lethargy by the descent of his bed; and although he barely knew where he was going, he had an impression that he was being murdered.

Immediately on alighting he leaped from his bed and flew at the throat of his supposed assailant, who, anticipating no resistance whatever, was thrown by his adversary, and in the fall the light got extinguished. The two combatants rolled on the floor, and as their physical strength was pretty equal the tussle for mastery was fierce in the extreme, the more so that Paul had robbed the lieutenant of his poignard and the captain's pistol had fallen from his side in the commencement of the conflict.

The terrible uproar below awoke the bandits above.

"Help, help!" exclaimed Coloski, "the alguazils have no doubt got into the house, and are attacking the captain. Burst open the door, my fine fellows."

Some arrived with pick-axes; and others, with implements ready at hand, vigorously went to work, and the noise they thus created was that which reached the two captives in the garret, for as for the third, he was incapable of hearing anything.

"We have no hope left," said Paul, leaning over the staircase, "all the brigands are up, rioting about the house, and if they come in this direction we can have no escape."

He gazed at Mathilda vacantly, and the poor girl, overcome with fear, exclaimed, appealing to Paul, "Oh, save me! save me!" and then looking at her uncle, she added, "Fool that I am to dream of it—I see it is impossible."

"No, no," cried Paul, struck suddenly with a happy thought.

The garret in which they were ensconced had but one window, looking upon the forest. Paul pushed open the shutter, and by the rays of the sun Mathilda saw the tops of trees waving in the wind.

"You perceive," said her young companion, "we have but one source of escape."

"I see," said the girl, approaching the window, "thank heaven the height is immense, and if they persecute us here, we have the alternative of throwing ourselves into the abyss below."

"No, no," replied Paul, "there is no occasion for that, but we may escape by descending that same abyss."

"And what is to become of my uncle?" asked the girl.

"I will undertake to save him also," was the reply.

"But how?"

"See," said he, pointing to the rope and pulley, with which the bandits were in the habit of hoisting the hay and straw into the garret, "if," added he, "you are not afraid to make the attempt, and will trust yourself to me"—

"I will—I will," boldly interrupted the girl.

Immediately on hearing this courageous remark, he passed a slip-knot round her person, and commenced lowering her gently, previously cautioning her to shut her eyes, and on her safe arrival on *terra firma* to intimate to him the fact by jerking the rope.

Presently she disappeared in the darkness, and then, after awhile, the weight was released, and he pulled up the rope easily.

Now was it the barber's turn to undergo the same operation.

He was awakened with difficulty; but, without intimating to him the perilous journey he had to perform, Paul launched him in the same way he had adopted with the niece, holding with difficulty the awkward weight he had now to manage.

In due time he felt a heavy bump, assuring him of the safe descent of his charge, and the rope, released by Mathilda, once more ascended.

Paul securely fastened one end of it to a beam in the garret, and boldly ventured out, and slid down it.

"Are you there?" he asked, in a low voice.

"Yes, brave young man," said Padislaus, who spoke much more distinctly than Paul had reason to expect.

The fact was, the fresh air and the shaking had greatly revived him.

"I can never," said he, "forget the substantial services you have rendered me, my young friend."

"Silence," answered Paul, checking the exuberance of his gratitude, and reminding him that although they were out of the inn, they were still within reach of their enemies.

The day was now about to dawn, and their wisest course would be to penetrate as deep as they could, during the darkness, into the heart of the forest.

The barber readily acquiesced in all these prudent projects, and it was evident that with the return of his reasoning faculties he was again paralyzed with fear.

The fearful altercation in the house added not a little to the apprehension of the fugitives.

Without the slightest knowledge of the locality, they entered the dense forest, and walked for a full hour straight before them.

At the expiration of that time, the barber declared he could proceed no further.

His legs gave way under him, and again he was overpowered by sleep.

"What! again?" exclaimed Paul, in despair.

The barber made no answer, but prostrating himself on the moss and closing his eyes, fell into a disturbed sleep.

Paul in vain attempted to arouse him from this untimely fit of lethargy, and while he was so occupied, Mathilda exclaimed, clasping Paul by the hand—

"Listen! listen! do you not hear that noise? It must be those dreadful people in pursuit of us."

Paul listened attentively, and heard the clanging of horses' hoofs.

"Yes," he added, "it is they, no doubt."

"And galloping this way, too," exclaimed the terrified girl.

Let us now return to the Inn of Good Rest, where, after great labour, the banditti had succeeded in breaking open the door of the cellar.

The band had precipitated themselves towards the spot whence the noise emanated, and, by the light of torches, a horrible spectacle was presented to them.

It was the captain and his lieutenant, bloody and disfigured, who, worn out by the struggle which had taken place, had both reeled on the ground, without loosening their hold.

Instantly the light of the torches was reflected by the sombre and dark walls of the cellar, a cry of surprise arose, and the combatants paused.

"Is it you?" said the captain, furiously, "you, Lubinski, who have raised your hand against me?"

"Me, captain," returned the lieutenant, "you who have allowed yourself to strangle or assassinate me! For whom did you take me?"

"For one of our guests," said the captain, good-naturedly, "but it was your fault."

"No—it was yours."

"Why were you not in your own bed?"

"Truly," said the lieutenant, "it is singular."

"Why were you sleeping in the grand chamber?"

Lubinski could recollect nothing, and, of course, could explain nothing.

"And the barber and his niece?" said the captain.

The whole body rushed to the Red Chamber.

Empty!

They searched the other rooms.

Empty!

"What means this?" said the captain.

"I knew," said Lubinski, gravely, "that that accursed barber was a heretic and a sorcerer."

"Nonsense," said the captain.

"Don't you recollect the face he made when he said, 'To-morrow we will settle'? He spoke truth; he has gone without paying."

"Gone—and how?"

"How can we tell? unless through the air on a broomstick."

Lubinski believed what he said.

"It is he," he cried, "who has bewitched the house. It is he who has made us fight one against the other. Heaven defend us!" and he crossed himself.

The captain was confounded.

Recollecting the ironical tone of the barber, they began to believe him a wizard.

"And Paul," he cried, suddenly recollecting himself, "it was he who took him to the Red Chamber. Where is he?"

They hastened to the chamber of Paul. It was shut. They knocked, then burst open the door to find it empty.

"What of that?" said Lubinski, "the wizard has carried him off too."

After an hour spent in fruitless poking into every hole in the house, they began to think that Lubinski was not far wrong, and prepared to return to their beds.

They had hardly come to this determination when a loud knocking was heard at the principal entrance of the inn, and at the same time the neighing of horses with the sound of many voices.

"What is this?" exclaimed one of the band.

People of his profession had lately been so seldom troubled that it was little to be wondered at that the good captain was surprised.

"Some other piece of the Moor's witchcraft," said Lubinski.

"Impossible," returned the captain.

Then poking his head out of the window he cried—

"Who goes there?"

"The Queen's Regiment."

"You are welcome, cavaliers. You travel betimes."

"Yes; and as we proceed we clear the highway of rogues, commencing with yourself, master landlord."

"I am known," said the captain. "Go below, Lubinski; pack up the luggage, and be ready for a start by the little door. Let the rest do as they can."

He then endeavoured to gain time with the young officer.

"I think, good cavalier, you are mistaken. You will, I am sure, agree with me after accepting my hospitality."

"It is too expensive," replied the officer. "In the first place we have a few questions to ask concerning the barber, Padislaus. Where is he?"

"You see," muttered one of the men, "always that accursed fellow."

"I think you are right," muttered the captain. Then, he added aloud, in a taunting voice—

"I was not aware that the worthy barber was a friend of yours."

"Enough, open and surrender."

"Yes; open," added a brigadier, "for though our commander, officer of the Queen's Regiment, is not in the habit of thief-taking, yet, if you insult him, death to every one."

"The house is surrounded," whispered the lieutenant, coming up; "we have no choice; we must surrender."

"No," said the captain, wildly; and then he added, "Ten thousand excuses, officer of the Queen's Regiment, for keeping you waiting. You request an answer. You have it."

He fired with the word.

Irritated by this bold move, the officer, pointing to the bandits, cried,—

"Fire, and no quarter."

A party immediately dismounted and climbed over the wall of the small court.

The assault then commenced, and the Inn of Good Rest, well defended, was attacked on every side.

"Hold out, my men," cried the captain, "hold out. These beggarly soldiers are cowards after all."

"But they fight well," suggested the lieutenant, grimly.

The captain laughed.

"Don't be afraid, Lubinski," he cried, as he sent a well-directed shot among the troopers, dismounting one of them. "Don't be afraid; the place is too strong for them to take. Fire away, my fine fellows, you can't send bullets through stone walls."

The captain was right.

The Inn of Good Rest could not be taken by assault.

But there was a more terrible agent yet to be employed— FIRE!

## CHAPTER XLIV.

### THE FLAMES.

PAUL and his fair companion had distinctly heard the sound of horses.

They were on the skirt of a forest, in a dell.

They could have concealed themselves in the foliage; but they would not have, perhaps, found Padislaus again, and they could not abandon him.

Mathilda and Paul leaned one against the other, both trembling with fear.

Fear, too, prevented them from observing that the troop was composed of two cavaliers only; but the moon bursting suddenly from behind a cloud, enabled them to distinguish them perfectly as they came up.

They had evidently journeyed far and fast, for they now walked their horses.

One rode ahead, while the other, more aged, followed at a respectful distance.

The first was evidently the master.

He was a handsome young man of melancholy but gracious aspect, wearing a costume somewhat at variance with that of the day.

It was Mazeppa.

A splendid sabre, suspended by a gold chain, hung at his side.

His horse was a magnificent Tartar steed which he patted gently as it champed the bit, and would have started off, saying,—

"No—no, Kalid! no, my good companion, let us rest. We are not far from our destination.

"Fear nothing," said Mathilda, in a low tone, "he is not a Pole."

Paul instantly hastened forward and threw himself on his knees before the horse, which reared on high.

"I understand," said the Tartar prince to his horse, in his own language, "you like not Polish beggars."

Then addressing Paul, he added, coldly,—

"It is very late to beg. If your companions be concealed in the wood, tell them that in the morning I have gold for those who ask it. At this hour I have but iron."

As he spoke he placed his hand on his sword, while the servant took aim with a musket.

"Stay—stay," cried Mathilda, in the Tartar tongue, "we are Russians, not Poles. We are hiding from our enemies."

Mazeppa gazed at the beautiful young creature with wonder and amazement.

"Tell me," he said, "what has happened to you?"

In a few words she told him all.

"Good, my lad," he said, as he turned to Paul, "continue, and you will be an honest man."

Paul trembled with delight.

"Ah!" said he, "if everyone had spoken to me thus. But when you are gone what is to become of the unfortunate beggar?"

"You shall be a beggar no longer. It is only fools who beg. Here," he said, as he wrote some words on a tablet, "here is my address. Come and find me and you shall learn how to be an honest man. And here, also, is gold—it will enable you to perform your journey."

He stopped his thanks.

"Come, my little one," he added to Mathilda, "we must take you and your uncle out of this place. Here—place yourself before me; and Hassan," he continued to his follower, "do you take her uncle."

When the little girl was seated before him on his horse, and the barber before Hassan, he turned again to Paul,—

"We cannot bear you also away; but you can soon follow. Remember, at Lublin I shall expect you. Adieu."

Mazeppa, then loosening the reins of his horse, disappeared in an instant, followed by his servant.

On their way they fell in with the Queen's Regiment, and easily persuaded the officer to go to the attack of the Inn of Good Rest.

While the combat was taking place, of the end of which we

are ignorant, Paul was giving himself up to thoughts of ecstasy and delight, mingled with a faint feeling of regret as he thought of the fair girl who had just left him.

He pondered over his new friend, so elegant, so distinguished, who had said, " good, my lad," and those words acted upon him as an incentive to a virtuous course of life, very dissimilar to his recent career.

Michael had been but a companion, a friend, but the stranger had been to him, as it were, a superior being—a divinity. He could barely persuade himself that all was not a dream, and as he almost unconsciously pressed the tablet to his heart he cherished the thought, so new to him, that there was one in the world interested in his future destiny. Suddenly the fact crossed his brain that he could not read. Of what service was the tablet to him in this predicament? He consoled himself, however, by the reflection that he could get it read for him on the following day, by some wayfarer.

At length, overcome by the fatigues of the day, he chose a secluded nook in the forest, and firmly clasping the treasured tablet in his hand, he fell fast asleep on the grass, thinking of the unknown, lulled by the gentle waving of the foliage and the refreshing perfumes of a summer's night.

The morning air. was heavy and suffocating, indicative of a day of more intense heat even than the preceding. The clouds were charged with electricity, rendering respiration difficult. Paul, labouring under the influence of these oppressive sensations, awake suddenly with a start.

It was broad day. But what was his amazement on awaking to find himself in the presence of that arch-demon, the brigand chief, who held him tight by the throat.

The captain was in a very sorry plight, covered with blood, blackened by powder, and his clothes in tatters. He held in his hand the tablet and the purse he had torn from Paul whilst he slept, and looking at them contentedly, and with a ferocious laugh,—

" Ah! ah!" said he, " you thought to escape me. You thought me dead, perchance. You have commenced betimes, my fine fellow, to betray those who succour you, and to denounce them as spies, like an aguazil."

" No," exclaimed Paul, trembling.

" Yes, your yonder soldiers, that you sent us, very nearly realised the prediction of your accomplice, that cursed heretic and sorcerer, the barber, who shall yet pay the penalty."

" Sir captain, I am ignorant of what you are speaking."

" Well, well, there's no use in prevaricating; *we will settle our accounts now*, as the barber observed. Sent by you and guided by the instructions you doubtless gave them, they found the way to the Inn of Good Rest, and as I declined surrendering, they set it on fire. Yes, the royal soldiers set it on fire. That rascal Padislaus predicted that I should be burnt to death, and you two set your heads together to realise the augury."

" Listen," said Paul.

" Did they listen?" said the captain; " did they not fire upon us as we struggled to escape the flames? May hell exterminate them along with those who suffered themselves to be entrapped like foxes gone to earth. These royal soldiers calculating on securing me with the rest; but I gave them the slip. I expect I am the only one who did, out of the lot, in the midst of the heavy firing. And mind you, I shall not yet be hanged, but live, master Paul, to perform the hangman's office upon you."

" I am not guilty, indeed I am not, I swear it to you," cried the terrified Paul. " Listen."

" Do you take me for a magistrate, or a counsel learned in the law?" rejoined the captain coldly. " Think you that I am going to listen to your lies? No, no, I have fully resolved that you and that Satanic barber who was with you, and especially your incendiary friend, shall die the death I have designed for them, and I mean to finish you to begin with!"

Holding Paul with one hand, he tore up some pliant osiers with the other, to make a rope with. Having collected some half-dozen also of the finest, he composedly amused himself by fastening them together, previously taking the precaution to throw Paul on the ground, and to sit upon him, so as to prevent all chance of escape.

So situated, the poor captive ran a fair risk of suffocation from the enormous weight he had to bear. The captain, paying no attention to his groans, and evidently gratified at this novel mode of torture, continued his labour of love quite contentedly, whistling a jocund air.

" Have mercy on me, have mercy on me, I do implore you!" bitterly exclaimed Paul, in suffocating tones.

" Have mercy, quotha?" responded the monster. " By my mother, yes, yes, I'll have mercy on you. It is my firm resolve to confer on you an immense favour. I purpose giving you a very exalted position indeed, my pretty captive starling. But, hark you! I like to be generous. You shall have your choice on which of yonder oaks you will swing."

Paul made no reply to this brutal railery, seeing it was all hopeless trying to mollify the heart of this insatiate tiger.

" Look you, Paul," continued the captain, after having completed his rope, " do you see, on the margin of that road in the distance, that magnificent oak towering to the skies? That tree, possessing all the requisite advantages, will serve to shade your delicate person from the scorching sun. What say you?"

Paul made no answer.

" Just at a convenient distance from the ground there is a branch too, that will serve magnificently to bear your weight, and seems indeed to have been created expressly for the purpose; and besides, should your friend of the tablet chance to pass this way, he will enjoy the happiness of seeing you in a very comfortable position, and of learning also how Spoloffski avenges a wrong. Yes, that will do very nicely indeed, and with Heaven's assistance—"

Paul understood that he was about to die, and he gave his last thoughts to the unknown.

Here the captain was interrupted by the report of a gun in the forest.

Although the sound was distant, it was more than probable that he who fired the gun would pass in the immediate vicinity of the spot above described.

The captain accordingly jumped instinctively to reconnoitre.

Not being far from the tree which the captain had so picturesquely pourtrayed, Paul, liberated of his burden, started off and sprang up its branches like a cat, and in an incredible short space of time found himself perched on a branch, some twenty feet from the ground.

Paul had recourse to this attempt at escape, feeling convinced that the captain, in consequence of his corpulence, could not follow him. He was not wrong in his calculations, for the bandit, furious with rage, halted at the root of the tree, whilst the fugitive, breathless, but in comparative safety, continued his ascent.

" Come down, you young scoundrel," shrieked the baffled bandit, drawing a long pistol from his side, the last weapon he had left; " come down and I will pardon you, and if you refuse I will shoot you to a certainty."

Paul was perfectly conscious of the dangers of his novel position, but, dreadful as they were, they were not so terrible as those he had just escaped. As to trusting to the clemency of the captain, that was the last thing he dreamt of, and so he determined to try if, by stratagem, he could possibly save his life.

The captain, meanwhile, kept dodging round the trunk of the tree to get a fair aim at his target, whilst Paul, carefully watching the movements of his fearful adversary, concealed himself as well as he could behind the branches.

At length the captain, seizing a favourable opportunity, fired, and a shriek of horror immediately succeeded the report of the pistol. Paul fell headlong, and Spoloffski gave one furious shout of savage triumph—as the hyena howls with delight when it has secured its prey.

But the captain had not secured his prey. The ball had simply shattered the lofty branch on which Paul was placed, and down they came together; but happily in their descent the branch and its weight were arrested by the huge limbs of the oak, which stretched out between the captain and the object of his aim. Paul responded, in a spirit of prophetic composure, to the triumphant exclamation that had escaped the bandit.

"Spoloffski," said he, "you have been without pity for a helpless child, but rest assured that child will live to become a man, and, in his turn, will evince no mercy towards you. Remain as long as you please below, but the time will come when my cries from this asylum will attract some traveller to the spot, and then justice will have its course. You are an assassin, a bandit, an arrant coward, for you have assailed a defenceless child, who has defeated you."

"Ah! war! war!" rejoined the captain, with a roar of laughter which echoed through the forest, "he challenges me to the combat, and I am not loth to accept it. The cost of the campaign shall be defrayed by the enemy, for have I not in my possession this smart purse, crammed with doubloons, and this elegant tablet, with one solitary name thereon inscribed? —the name, doubtless, of one who offers you protection and wealth, for I know him to be one of the wealthiest men in this part of the world. I rejoice that he has dared to offer you an asylum, for that very offer has sealed his death warrant, though he be a king."

At this idea Paul uttered a shriek of despair.

"And," continued the captain, "hope not to frustrate my plans of revenge; your hour is come. You have chosen that tree as a shelter; you refused to be hung, the refuge you have chosen shall be your funeral pyre."

Paul could not at first conceive what the bandit meant; but he was, alas! very soon let into the mystery.

"Ah! you proclaim war, do you? You shall have it to your heart's content," continued the captain, collecting round the tree all the dried wood and foliage with which the forest abounded. "war! war! you wished it to be satisfied," and he laughed with his infernal laugh, "it will soon be lit."

While Paul watched with uneasy and alarmed thoughts these preparations, the brigand proceeded, and having collected a large heap he quietly took from his pocket a flint and struck it sharply over the pile, smiling contentedly, and resuming his merry song.

The mass shortly got ignited, and gradually the dense smoke ascended in spiral columns.

For some time the green branches arrested the progress of the flames; but the fiend by their side fed them diligently, and a strong wind that unhappily rose at that critical moment but too successfully aided the efforts of the demon.

The tree became first covered with a black, viscous sweat, the froth oozed forth soon, to disappear, then the branches gave forth a crackling sound, some breaking and giving food to the flames. To heighten the scene of horror, dark clouds began to dim the light of day.

He thought the smoke alone would suffocate his victim. Presently Paul was completely hidden from his enemy by the thick smoke that surrounded him.

Not a sound, saving an occasional scream of dread and agony, and the crackling of the burning timber, disturbed the silence of the awful scene.

The merciless Spoloffski still fed the flames incessantly. At last, tired of his task, and having taken it for granted that Paul lay smothered above, or even if he attempted to descend he would be burnt alive, he left him to his fate, rejoicing at the success of his horrible project.

Moreover, it was not improbable that the glaring beacon that occasionally burst forth, lighting up the dismal forest, would attract travellers, and lead to his discovery. He therefore thought it prudent to retire, and casting one more anxious look at the infernal pyramid he had erected, he soon disappeared in the tangled forest.

Paul, meanwhile, as the devouring flames gradually approached him, climbed higher and higher to avoid them. The tree was an immense one, its topmost branches towering to the skies; but still, as upwards he went, the destructive element gained fast upon him.

The feathered denizens of the adjacent trees sought safety in flight; but alas! he could not follow them.

Perched at the greatest height he could possibly attain, he tremblingly contemplated the fearful death he now saw no chance of averting. He had seen the captain disappear, but he had left his work too well accomplished to extend any hope of escape by descent.

At one time, as a *dernier ressort*, he thought of climbing to the extremity of one of the broadest branches, and dropping himself clear of the frightful furnace beneath him; but then again he remembered the tremendous height he had to fall. To complete the hopelessness of his position, the oak was too far apart from any other tree to permit of his leaping from one to the other.

Thus debarred of all possible chance of escape, the poor little fellow's heart failed him outright, and he burst into tears. From whom now could he seek solace and soothing? He was alone in the world! alone! and yet one ray of hope cheered his sinking heart.

Mathilda, when surrounded by danger and imminent death, had appealed for succour to the God of her fathers. Why should he not do the same? And thereupon, whilst still the ruthless flames ascended, he cast his eyes to heaven, and in the full bitterness of his broken spirit prayed aloud.

"Oh! my God! oh! my God!" he exclaimed, "to die so young, just when the joys of life were bursting upon me! when this very night such sweet dreams lulled my sleep. Oh, suffer me to live, that by the virtuous future, I may blot out the crimes of the past. All is ended! I die!"

And still the flames ascended.

"Have I not, oh Heaven! been bereft of all earthly bliss— a vagabond wanderer, with the street for my country, and the pavement for my home, without the love and tenderness of a mother, seeking my bread in sorrow and taking it by stern necessity from the hands of the robber? If I have erred in society so contaminating, oh, suffer me yet to live that I may wash away the stain. Have pity on me, oh, my God!"

And still the flames ascended.

"Oh, if I could but escape the terrific fate that awaits me— could but fly from the flames so fast surrounding me, and the merciless smoke suffocating me by degrees—if I could but escape these appalling terrors, the rest of my days should be devoted to thy service. I would employ them in no selfish pursuits, but for the benefit of my fellow-creatures. This do I pledge myself to fulfil faithfully. I would do for them what thou hast done for me. Listen then, my only protector, to these my earnest supplications, and suffer me yet to live. Oh, protect me in this hour of peril! Oh, save me! save me from this terrible fate."

For a moment he despaired.

The flames still ascended.

---

## CHAPTER XLV.

### DELIVERANCE.

STILL the flames ascended!

Higher still ascended the fervent prayer of the perishing child.

Heaven heard his prayer, and in its mercy answered it, for a heavy storm, which had long been threatening, suddenly burst over the tree in which he had taken refuge, and torrents of rain fell, extinguishing the fire which had almost reached its victim.

In the exuberance of his joy, with his eyes uplifted to the source of timely aid, he cried—

"Heaven has heard me, and wills that I shall be an honest man."

The tempest continued to rage for a full hour, and right gratefully did Paul welcome the torrents of rain which rescued him from his impending fate.

The blazing branches were successively extinguished, and presently a pool of water was formed at the base of the oak, where but now was a huge furnace.

Paul commenced his descent when he perceived the flames had ceased to blaze, but the descent was by no means an easy matter.

The copious fall of rain had rendered the branches slippery, and others, by the action of the fire, had become brittle, and would break even under the slight weight of Paul.

THE CAPTAIN FOLLOWING PAUL.

When he had got about half-way down, and was congratulating himself on his safe arrival on *terra firma*, he heard, amid the howling of the tempest, the trampling footsteps of a man advancing towards the spot.

His progress was impeded by the mud, and he helped himself onwards by leaning on a double-barrelled carbine which he held in his hand.

Worn with fatigue, he halted immediately beneath the oak in which Paul was still a captive.

Presently, taking off his cap, to wipe away the rain and the perspiration which poured down his brow, he gave utterance to a horrible imprecation. The voice, which Paul knew too well, was that of Lubinski, the bandit lieutenant.

The wretched captive, who was dreaming of life and liberty, tried to conceal himself behind the little foliage the tree had left.

"Ah!" said he, "Heaven has not heard me yet, and I am still doomed to die."

The brigand remained motionless, leaning against the tree, as if in the act of listening.

Paul could not at first comprehend the object of this deep silence and profound attention, which, however, saved him, as it prevented the bandit looking upwards; but presently, in the distance, he perceived a carriage, dragged by four stout mules, approaching them down the road.

The postilion had much tough work to get through, for the road was rendered extremely heavy by the storm.

As the carriage neared the spot, Paul hesitated whether it would be good policy to cry aloud for help.

He abstained from doing so, knowing that it would betray his whereabouts, and the lieutenant would most assuredly give him the benefit of one, if not both of the barrels of the ugly carbine, and then, in all probability, escape unscathed into the heart of the forest.

He was disturbed in these reflections by a noise that made him tremble.

Lubinski, who was by no means a man given to thinking on such occasions, prepared for action.

When the carriage, which was a costly one, and laden heavily with luggage, was within a few paces of the bandit, he saw at a glance that there were but three persons in it—an old man and two young girls.

It being evident that the postilion, a stout young fellow, was the only one likely to offer any obstinate resistance, Lubinski shot him dead on the spot, and, levelling his second barrel at the carriage, which now faced the tree, he called to the old man—

"Your purse, and the ladies' jewellery."

The door of the carriage was opened, and out came a grey-headed gentleman, with a stern cast of features, and placing himself before the girls, by way of rampart, drew his sword.

"Down with that bit of iron!" cried the bandit.

"Never!" rejoined the gentleman.

"Resistance is perfectly useless; your purse, and down with your arms, or I will shoot you."

"Fire away!" cried the old man, "I will never surrender to a rascally bandit like you."

"Ye shall have it, sir, seeing you wish it," replied Lubinski, levelling his carbine slowly.

No. 11.

"Oh! mercy!" cried the girls, who evidently were mistress and maid.

"The children are right," said the bandit, slowly, "why, old man, you are not worth the powder in this barrel. I don't exact at your hands homilies and morality—all I want is the gold and silver you have about you. Make haste, for I am in a hurry."

By way of rejoinder to these remarks, the old gentleman made a thrust with his sabre at the bandit.

"Come," said Lubinski, "we must finish this."

And leaning against the tree, he took a deliberate aim, and was on the point of pulling the trigger, when Paul dropped himself heavily on the uplifted arm of the bandit, and thus turned away the shot in a contrary direction.

Though astounded at first at this wholly unexpected attack from above, he speedily recovered himself, and seizing his new opponent, cast him on the ground roughly, exclaiming, in utter amazement at the sight of Paul—

"'Tis he, indeed—this time, at all events, he shall not escape my vengeance."

And thereupon, with one foot on the trembling body of his feeble adversary, he was about to break his head with the butt end of his carbine, when a hand, vigorous in its old age, sent a sword up to the hilt into the body of the bandit.

Lubinski had got his *quietus*, and with one howl of rage and agony, he rolled over—a corpse.

"Ah! ah! that word was of no use to either of us, but the wild beast is slain," said the old gentleman. "I have hunted them before now, but never such a dangerous one. But what's the matter with you, my child? She has fainted, poor thing. Zenitha," he added to the maid, "bring her to her senses, while I go to the assistance of our young defender yonder, the poor little tattered beggar, who has in him more courage than strength."

Then the gouty old gentleman hobbled up towards Paul, who, though bruised, was not much hurt, and in rising, offered his arm to his defender.

"Why, I was coming to your assistance, my little fellow, and you come again to mine. Who are you?"

"Paul."

"Your business?"

"I have none."

"Who are your parents?"

"I have none."

"Where do you come from?"

"The top of that tree."

"Do you dwell there?"

"I have since this morning."

The old gentleman looked at the oak, the trunk and branches of which were charred by the fire, and said smilingly—

"Your dwelling is in a sadly dilapidated condition, and I offer you, if you will accept it, a somewhat better one at my house in Lublin."

Joy and gratitude sparkled in Paul's eyes, and so choked was he, that he could utter no sound, and could only press his new master's hand to his lips.

Meanwhile they had reached the carriage, and the young lady having recovered from her fainting-fit, leaped from the carriage, and threw herself on her father's neck.

The Castellan of Laurinski, for it was he, was unused to such exhibitions, but in the excitement of that moment Theresa forgot all his past unkindness.

Paul stood by the door, calmly contemplating a scene of tenderness so perfectly novel to him.

He had never beheld such exquisite loveliness as that on which he now gazed.

Mathilda, who had hitherto been his paragon, sunk down to a very ordinary person indeed.

One, to his thinking, was of earth, the other was heavenly.

And when Theresa fixed her radiant eyes upon him, sparkling with kindly feeling and gratitude, and thanked him for his opportune assistance, and complimented him on the courage he had displayed in their cause, he felt a sensation he had never before experienced, and could not possibly define.

"We will take him with us," said the Castellan; "hence-forth he shall be one of our household—he shall be my page. But in the interim," continued the old man, looking at the postilion, who lay grim and prostrate on the turf, "I wonder if our new page can do anything with the horses."

"Most assuredly," exclaimed Paul, closing the door of the carriage, and jumping on one of the mules, which he encouraged with voice and gesture.

Getting them into a gallop, he speedily cleared the forest, and on the following day, happier than the king himself, with a proud air, a glad heart, and a doublet in rags, he entered the city of Lublin.

"Where shall I drive you?" he asked of his new master.

"To the viceroy's palace," cried the Castellan.

The ragged boy then turned his horses heads towards the palace.

In his delight and pride he never once observed the constant and curious glances which were cast at the strange postilion, but looked straight before him.

Arrived at the palace, he drew up at the grand entrance.

The Castellan, without waiting for him to open the door, alighted.

"Take the mules and the carriage round to the stables," said he, as he helped his daughter and her maid out; "give them something to eat and drink, and be ready to meet me here again at eight to-night. Meanwhile, here is a purse: procure yourself some better clothes."

The ragged postilion touched his ragged cap, and obeyed orders.

The men in the viceroy's stables laughed at him, but of this he did not take much notice.

His heart was swelling with joy, and as soon as his animals were disposed of he sallied forth with one of the men, who volunteered, upon seeing that the young fellow had money, to show him where to obtain his clothes.

These were not long in being procured, and the ragged Paul —the beggar boy of Warsaw—having indulged in hair cutting and washing at a barber's, sallied forth into the streets of Lublin unrecognisable in his suit of new attire.

Unrecognisable by some, we may add.

He was not unrecognisable, however, by one who had long been watching him,

Ever since he had entered the streets of Lublin, eyes had been upon him.

Eyes which never for one moment lost sight of him.

When he issued from the barber's shop, they saw him, and a man stepped hastily to his side.

Paul started.

"Have you forgotten me?" inquired the stranger.

"No, indeed."

It was true.

The new comer was Mazeppa.

"No!—yet you have been in Lublin hours and have not sought me?"

"I have had as yet no time. I have been engaged in my master's business."

Mazeppa smiled.

"Your master," he said; "do you know who your master is?"

"All I know is, that when I had been robbed of all you gave me, and nearly murdered into the bargain, he came to my assistance."

"Do you know no more than that?"

"No more."

"Then I will tell you who he is. He is my deadliest foe."

Paul turned pale.

The adventure might not after all turn out so pleasantly as he had expected.

"Your enemy?" said Paul. "I could not know that. He succoured me and in return I assisted him out of a dilemma, as his postilion was dead."

Mazeppa thought a moment.

"Paul," he said, "I told you you would be an honest man, so I think I can trust you now. Theresa, the lady who is with that gentleman, loves me—I have long been seeking her, but her father likes me not: do you understand?"

Paul thought of Mathilda.

"Yes," he said, "I understand."

"Well then," continued Mazeppa, "take this letter and give it to your mistress. Do you not remember following their carriage one night at the bidding of a dwarf?"

"Ah! yes, I remember."

"That dwarf was my servant. But come, we must not be talking too long. We shall be seen and discovered. Remember, deliver that letter safely, and honour and rewards shall be yours."

He then gave him his address and walked rapidly away.

Paul stood for a moment as one petrified.

He hardly liked his mission.

It seemed like practising deceit upon his master.

"Yet still," he murmured, as he turned his steps towards the palace, "they love one another, and Mazeppa was my first benefactor."

---

## CHAPTER XLVI.

### THE RED CORRIDOR.

IF Paul had imagined that the delivery of a letter from Mazeppa to Theresa would be an easy matter he was grievously mistaken.

He saw nothing of the Castellan, or of his daughter, or of the servant, until late in the evening.

At the hour appointed he brought out the horses, put them to the carriage, and brought it round to the door of the palace.

The old gentleman came out, led his daughter down, then the maid also entered, and he followed.

Paul had no chance of being near Theresa.

"Where am I to drive to?"

"To No. 10, in the street of the Four Chimneys."

Paul was bewildered.

"I am not acquainted with this city, sir," he said; "where is this street?"

Another boy would have been afraid to confess his ignorance. The Castellan smiled.

"Drive to the end of this street," he said, "and ask the first passenger you meet."

Paul bowed, closed the carriage door, leaped on his horse, and soon the horses, led by their light postilion, were dashing down the broad street.

At the corner he stopped.

There was only one man in sight, and he hailed him.

"If you please, sir," cried Paul, loudly, "which is the way to the street of the Four Chimneys?"

The man approached close to the door and looked in, without answering.

Paul repeated his request.

The man turned round, so that his back was to those within.

"It is the second street on the left, in that turning opposite," he said.

Paul saw his face as he spoke, and recognised it at once.

It was that of Mazeppa.

Fearing that there might be an unpleasant discovery, he put spurs to his horse, and was soon dashing again along the road.

At the house they stopped.

Paul could not have mistaken it.

It was impossible to do so, for over the door swung a heavy lamp, with the number 10 painted on it in red letters.

The Red House was a strange looking place.

It was built entirely of wood, and those who had been engaged in its erection seemed to have been allowed to exercise their own fancies in regard to every portion of it.

As there was without no window like another, so within two rooms could not be found with any degree of similitude.

Here was a window with an arched top—here a square porthole—here a tall and narrow oriel—here a barred casement.

On one side of the house was a tall turret—on the other it sloped, like the roof of the palace of the Tuileries.

Within you might easily have lost yourself.

Here was a broad stone passage conducting you to a huge courtyard, which was more like the cloisters of a cathedral than anything else.

Here you ascended a broad staircase leading you to a handsome corridor.

Here again you crept up a narrow winding series of steps, like a ladder, and found yourself in a close passage, which was dark and gloomy and sepulchral.

Here was a spacious banquetting chamber, and there a little room where deadly crimes seemed to lurk in the shadows.

When the great door swung back upon its hinges, and Paul peered into the vast hall, a chill crept through him.

In spite of the brilliant light which inundated the place, there seemed to be something inexpressibly gloomy in it, and he almost started when the Castellan said to him—

"Take the horses round to the stable, Paul, and then come up into my room. One of my servants will show you the way."

The old man made a sign to one of the men, who immediately followed Paul into the street.

"Come on, my young friend," he said, laughing, as he gazed at the diminutive postilion; "come with me and I will show you the way."

Paul led his horses round to the stables willingly and rapidly.

His first alarm gone, he felt a curiosity to explore the queer loooking old house.

In ten minutes he had settled everything, and was led up the broad staircase to the room where the Castellan and his daughter were sitting.

The Castellan eyed him curiously.

"What is your name?"

"Paul."

"Paul what?"

"I don't know, sir."

The old man smiled.

"True," he said, "so you told me before. And what is your age?"

"Fourteen, I think, sir."

"Good: now my reason for calling you down here to-night is this: I wish you at once to take your footing in my house. You saved my life and the honour of my daughter, no doubt, and I have promised to recompense you. There are two posts you can fill: you can either continue to drive my horses, or you can be my daughter's page. It is for you to choose."

Paul's heart bounded.

The ready answer leaped to his lips, but even he, boy as he was, had the discretion to restrain them.

He paused.

"Well," said the old man, which is it to be? Come, tell me."

"I will be your daughter's page, sir," returned Paul.

The Castellan laughed loudly.

"And why do you choose that?" he asked, good humouredly.

Since he had been rid of Mazeppa his temper had wonderfully changed.

Paul blushed deeply.

"Please, sir, I don't know," he said, in a trembling tone.

Theresa came to the rescue.

"Don't confuse him," she cried, "I dare say he will be a good boy, and I am quite willing to accept his services."

"Well, well, said her father, "so it shall be then. There is one advantage in him, I will say—you are not likely to fall in love with him, as you did with Mazeppa; his youth protects me from that."

Paul started.

Was Mazeppa, then, a page?

Was that elegant cavalier—that richly-dressed gentleman, a discarded page?

The Castellan did not fortunately observe his temporary emotion.

"Well, my boy, since you have so chosen," he said, "you shall be Lady Theresa's page. You will have an easy time of it, I am thinking; yet you must attend to all her biddings, and remember one thing especially—be honest and you will be trusted; be dishonest once, and you will forfeit all confidence."

Paul did not answer.

His was, at that moment, a heavy heart.

He thought of the letter which was concealed within his bosom.

Was it honest to conceal that?

Was it honest to deliver it to his new mistress without the knowledge of her father?

The Castellan attributed his thoughtful demeanour to his happiness.

"Go now, my boy," he said; "early in the morning be ready in the red corridor. There your mistress will expect to find you awaiting her commands."

Paul stood irresolute.

He felt lost in this strange great house, and when the Castellan bade him go, the only question in his mind was "whither?"

His master saw and understood his bewilderment.

"I see, Paul," he said, "you do not know where to go."

He struck a bell, which gave out a dreary gong-like sound.

A young girl appeared.

Paul turned deadly pale.

It was Mathilda.

This time his emotion did not escape the Castellan.

"Do you know one another?" he said.

"Yes," returned Mathilda, "I know him. He saved my life, and the life, too, of my uncle."

The Castellan smiled upon him benevolently.

"You are quite an universal deliverer," he cried. "Well, your young friend here, will doubtless—although newly arrived here—be able to direct you. Good night."

"Good night, Paul," added Theresa, sweetly, and the boy, after bowing dumb acknowledgements, left the room.

"And now, Theresa," said her father, "let me explain to you, ere you retire to rest, my wishes as regards yourself."

The girl made no reply. It was the old story, she feared.

"To-morrow, as you are aware," he continued, "the Count Floreski is to visit us here."

"I am aware of it," she said, coldly.

"Long since," he proceeded, "you must have given up that mad dream about Mazeppa. That fierce and desperate impostor has long since, doubtless, returned to his native wilds, and united himself to some native beauty. Now, our fortunes being ruined, it behoves either you or me to retrieve them. I have found it to be impossible—the task then remains for you."

Theresa turned pale again, and glanced at her father deprecatingly.

"You seem to think," she said, "that I was born to be merely the regenerator of our house. What do I care for wealth if I have not the love of one whose affections I esteem?"

Her father interrupted her.

"Precisely so," he said, "precisely so. You do not care for wealth—how could you care for it with one whom you disliked? But the Count Floreski is a nobleman—he is one whom you could esteem—he is one I am convinced whom you would soon learn to love."

"Love!" cried Theresa, "no—I could never love another."

Her father was straining for a great point.

He was willing, apparently, to conciliate her in every way.

"Well, well," he answered, in a kind and gentle voice, "since Fortune hath decreed that your affections are to be centred on that wild youth, Mazeppa, it may be difficult, indeed, to alter your feelings. But let us say esteem—since you cannot love him—let us say at least you may esteem him."

Theresa sighed deeply.

"When am I compelled to see him?" she asked.

"He hopes to see you to-morrow."

"But only in a first interview? He does not hope for any final answer?"

"Oh! no, he only desires to see you—to be allowed to become intimate with you."

"I am willing to receive him," said Theresa, "but it must be merely as a friend at first. After having been so short a time since bereaved of my first love—after having passed through so terrible an ordeal of war and bloodshed, I cannot bring myself to think of another husband."

The Castellan was annoyed inwardly, but was too prudent outwardly to evince his vexation.

"Very well, my dear daughter," he said, "be it so. To-morrow Count Floreski will be here. I will see him first, and I will tell him that at present, at least, he must abstain from pressing his suit."

Meanwhile Paul had been conducted by Mathilda into a spacious room, where, among the other servants, he was regaled with a fine supper.

But he could not eat.

The letter concealed in his breast was like a dead weight.

How could he deliver it?

Should he trust to Mathilda?

"Where does your mistress sleep?" he asked of Mathilda.

"In the state room in the red corridor. But why do you ask?"

Paul smiled.

"I wish to speak with her. When does she retire?"

"At eleven."

"It is now half-past ten; I must lose no time."

Mathilda laughed.

"Are you in love with my lady?" laughed Mathilda.

The boy blushed.

"No, you can hardly think that, Mathilda; but come, will you aid me? This time I must lay claim to your gratitude."

"How can I aid you?"

"By leading me to the red corridor, and pointing out to me the chamber of Lady Theresa."

"I will do so."

"And meanwhile will you tell me how you came hither?"

Mathilda laughed.

"Through my uncle Padislaus, the barber of Warsaw."

"And he—how did he know of this establishment?" asked Paul.

"Through the young man who met us in the forest."

Paul started.

It was then through Mazeppa that she also had obtained a position in the house of the Castellan.

Had she, then, a communication from the Tartar prince?

"Mathilda," he said, "you are afraid to trust me."

The young girl opened her large eyes wide.

Astonishment and amazement also were depicted in her gaze,

"What do you mean, Paul?" she said; "you are talking to me in riddles."

"No," he said, "I will explain. You are here because the young stranger—Mazeppa, the Tartar—desired you to come. Is it not so?"

Mathilda blushed.

"Yes," she answered, "it is so."

Her boy lover—for such in truth he was—took her hand.

"You should not keep secrets from me," he said; "I, also, am here at his bidding. We must help one another."

Mathilda looked up into his eyes.

"I will," she said. "Come, and I will show you the way."

The other servants were too much occupied in their boisterous merriment to notice the two children, as they called them, and so they passed out of the room unperceived, and made their way upstairs.

---

## CHAPTER XLVII.

### BEHIND THE IMAGE OT THE VIRGIN.

ON reaching the red corridor they found themselves enveloped in such dense obscurity that the feeble lamp which Mathilda carried only served to render the place more gloomy.

"This seems a pleasant house altogether," said Paul, laughing.

Mathilda laughed too.

"Yes," she cried, "it is gloomy, but if we succeed in achieving what Mazeppa desires, we shall not be here long. See, there is my lady's room."

Paul approached the door, and then looked around him.

Where could he conceal himself?

Opposite the door was a statue of the Virgin, in a deep niche.

A bright idea struck him.

Here he could hide until she retired, and as she entered her room could give her the letter.

He pointed it out to Mathilda.

"Here," he said, "I will conceal myself. But tell me, has Mazeppa given you any instructions?"

"No—none."

"Why, then, has he placed you here?"

"I know not. I suppose that he desired to make sure of one person in the household, if you failed him."

Paul laughed.

"You are a little philosopher," he said; "but hark, some one is coming. We are discovered. What is to be done?"

"We must use your expedient," returned Mathilda, in a whisper. "Quick—let us not be found here together; they will certainly suspect us."

To suggest the expedient was easy—to perform the task was another thing.

There was scarcely more room behind the statue than was necessary for one of them; but necessity is the mother of invention, and before the new-comers had arrived they had contrived to squeeze themselves into the narrow space.

Those who came, however, were not those they expected.

They were two servants, who were talking eagerly as they approached.

They entered Theresa's chamber, leaving the door ajar.

"I am undone," said Paul, "my plan has failed. If these girls are in her room they will give the alarm."

"I think they are only there in order to prepare her bed. But listen—what is it they are saying?"

Paul and his youthful beauty listened eagerly.

"The Count is coming to-morrow," said one of the servants; "he is such a handsome fellow."

"Is he, indeed?" returned the other, who was no other than Zenitha.

"Have you not seen him?"

"No—indeed."

"Oh! then you will be delighted. He is such a nice man."

"You seem to know him well?"

"Oh! I do—he is so kind, and has made me such handsome presents."

Zenitha was silent.

This girl was evidently in the pay of the Count.

It was necessary to be on her guard in respect to everything.

"Have you noticed that girl?" asked Theodora.

"What girl?" asked Zenitha.

"Mathilda—the little girl introduced by Padislaus, the barber.

"Yes—I have observed her. Why do you ask me?"

"Because I think she is a spy."

"Not the only one," thought Zenitha.

She added aloud—

"Indeed; what makes you think so?"

"Have you not noticed how she watches every one and drinks in every word that is spoken?"

"No, I have not observed her, but really if I had I should have taken little notice, for she is so young that I doubt the possibility of her being a spy."

Theodora had now apparently completed her work.

"Good night, Zenitha." she said; "I will now leave you, and tell our mistress that her room is ready."

The girl then came forth and hurried away down the passage.

In a few minutes Theresa appeared.

She was not alone—her father was with her.

"Good night, my dear," he said, "rise early, for at eleven the Count Floreski will be here."

She entered her chamber, merely murmuring "Good night," and the Castellan departed.

"Now," said Mathilda, "I will slip away—the last door on the left is your room—within it is your lamp. The servant now with her is her confidential servant, therefore you have nothing to fear. Good night."

"Good night!" returned Paul, and then—must we tell tales of him?—yes, we must—he stooped down and kissed the ruby lips of the little maiden.

Mathilda laughed—a low, musical laugh—and ran away lightly.

Paul approached the door.

It was still slightly ajar.

All was still within.

He peered in.

Zenitha was engaged in undressing her mistress, who, now in beautiful *deshabille*, sat in a chair by the bedside.

Paul knocked.

The girl started.

"Who can that be?" cried Theresa.

"Be not alarmed," said Zenitha, "it can be no one but one of the servants. I will go to the door and see."

For a moment Paul hesitated.

Should he remain?

Should he trust this girl, or should he rather fly away, and put the meeting off until to-morrow?

While he hesitated Zenitha opened the door.

Theresa had now entered her bed.

Her maid started back aghast when she saw Paul.

"What do you want?" she cried.

"I have a letter for your mistress," he said, "from a friend."

Theresa heard him.

"Let him enter," she said, "some one will go past and see him at my door."

He entered.

The room, by the lamp, was inundated by a muffled light; but he could see her—whom he had thought beautiful as a goddess—half sitting, with her head resting on her hand, and her bright tresses falling over her white shoulders, and coiling over her rounded arm.

"Close the door carefully, Zenitha," cried her mistress.

Then she beckoned Paul to approach and deliver his letter.

He did so, and then at her bidding sat down.

A cry of delight escaped Theresa's lips as she read the missive, and when she had concluded she exclaimed aloud,—

"Oh! Zenitha, I am so happy! This letter is from Mazeppa."

"From the Prince himself?"

Paul started.

The word "prince" puzzled him.

"Was he whom the Castellan had called a page a prince?"

"Yes," said Theresa, "and what is still better, my new page here, and that little girl of whom you were speaking, are both sent hither by him."

She turned to Paul.

"You are a brave boy," she said. "Tell me, how did you contrive to come to my room? I did not hear you approach."

Paul smiled.

"No, my lady," he said. "I have been concealed a long time behind the statue of the Virgin which stands before your door."

"When do you see Mazeppa again?" she asked, after a moment.

"I can see him to-morrow night."

"Good; to-morrow morning I will give you a letter for him, till then, good night. Some one may be on the watch."

She extended him her hand, which he kissed respectfully, then Zenitha opened the door and he glided away along the red corridor towards his own room.

Reaching this unmolested and unperceived, he entered, closed the door behind him, and going to his casement, gazed out.

His window looked out upon a huge courtyard, round which rose tall and black buildings.

Here and there a dim light flickered in a bedchamber; but elsewhere everything was in darkness.

All except watchers had apparently retired to rest.

One thing, however, Paul observed and took a note of.

Theresa's bedroom being on a line with his own, he could see the window.

From this window streamed a flood of light, as if the lamp had been placed close to the glass.

Presently, on the opposite side of the courtyard a similar phenomenon presented itself.

In this instance, however, Paul could see what was being done.

A form which he seemed to recognise as that of the Tartar Prince.

A lamp was placed in this window, and the dark figure seemed to be making signs.

It was evidently a lover's telegraph, and afterwards he discovered that it was.

Paul watched until all was dark, and retired to bed.

There was no doubt that he was on the high road to fortune if some sudden discovery was not made to foil his plans.

## CHAPTER XLVIII.

### AN OLD FOE WITH A NEW FACE.

On the following morning Count Floreski presented himself at the house, and was led by the Castellan into the presence of Theresa.

He was a young man, apparently about thirty years of age, and not by any means one whom a young girl whose heart was disengaged would have been likely to reject.

He was handsome, well built, and had an easy, graceful manner with him, which spoke of a habitual intercourse with good society.

The Castellan having introduced the two young people, left them together.

"Your father has already explained to you, Lady Theresa," began the Count, "the object of my present visit."

"He has spoken to me of you," returned Theresa, coldly.

"I have heard much, my lady," continued the young Count, "much of your beauty and your accomplishments. Believe me I am astonished at the realisation of my dreams."

Theresa smiled.

"You are complimentary, Count, she answered, "but I fear your dreams, if they have spoken to you of me for a wife, will not be realised. My heart is and has long been another's."

"Your father said something to me of a certain Tartar page, who eventually turned out to be the heir apparent to the throne of Tartary. Quite a romance it was, I will allow; but you will never see him again, and it would be folly to waste your whole life upon a vision."

"You can give good advice, Count," said Theresa, "because the advice suits your own purpose; but let me assure you that Mazeppa is not lost to me. Some day or another I shall be his bride."

The Count frowned.

"The barbarian has dazzled you by the prospect of sharing his throne," he cried; "but rest assured, your queenly dignity would be of but short duration."

"Why so?"

"Even now the armies of Poland are gathering; the commanders far and near have received orders to hold themselves in readiness. Many months will not have passed away before the wild hordes will be scattered, and the young Tartar king destroyed with his men."

For a moment Theresa's heart sank within her.

Then she remembered the inaccessible nature of Mazeppa's dominions, the vastness of his armament, the bravery of his men.

She smiled.

"You are talking of destroying him," she said; "his power is greater than that of the King of Poland. He would not fear his army; but seriously, Count, did you come hither to talk politics to me?"

The Count was annoyed at her evident spirit of jest.

"No," said he, placed in an awkward position by her manner; "no, I came—authorised by your father—to make you an offer of my hand and heart. I fear I have been misled."

His voice trembled, and his manner altogether sufficiently proved that he was hurt by her behaviour.

The idea at once struck her—was she justified in thus annoying him? Was it his fault that he was there?

Was he to be blamed for desiring to marry her?

She would have been less vain than most women could she for one moment have thought this.

She smiled upon him, and said,—

"Count Floreski, allow me to say one thing. I love Mazeppa; I have already told you this. I have explained all the circumstances. Until, therefore, he releases me from my compact, or abandons me, I cannot consent to be another's. If you are content to wait, I am willing to give you hope. You must understand, if you reason at all, in what a difficult position I am placed."

Count Floreski bowed.

"Lady Theresa," he said, "I forgive you, and must ask you to forgive me for my harsh words. I have learned to love you from the descriptions I have received of you. A few weeks' intercourse with you daily I perceive would make me your slave. I am quite certain that you will never again see this person upon whom your affection is placed, and I am quite willing, therefore, to wait if you will but name a time."

Theresa thought a moment.

"Yes," she said, "I will name a time. If in one year Mazeppa does not come to claim me then I will be yours."

The Count knew nothing of the Castellan's schemes.

He was unaware of the utter ruin which threatened the family, and still less was he aware of the fact that he was looked upon as the means of warding off this ruin.

He rose to take his leave.

"For this hope, Lady Theresa," he said, "I thank you. Upon the strength of it I will venture to continue my visits. I am young, I am wealthy; my family is one of the first families in Poland. I can offer you a home worthy of any woman in the country, and a heart which, once yours, will be faithful to you."

Soon after this interview—so little satisfactory to one or the other—Paul received from Theresa the letter which he was to deliver to Mazeppa.

When evening shades fell over the city he started.

Mazeppa's address was in his pocket, but had it not been he would have found it easily the house.

He knew it as the third house from that occupied by the Castellan.

At the door the dwarf met him.

He laughed loudly.

"Ah!" he said, "I should scarcely have known you. Your rags are looped up with gold to such an extent that I should never have recognised them. However, never mind any jests, my master is within, and will be right glad to see you."

So saying, he led the way into the house.

He need scarcely have apologised for his joke.

Ridicule would have sat very ill upon him.

Attired as he was in a bright livery, his distorted limbs were shown off to their full extent, and as he waddled up the broad passage he looked supremely absurd.

Mazeppa received Paul with eagerness.

He took the note without speaking, and read it through.

When he had finished, and gazed fondly at the superscription, he said—

"My boy you have done well; continue as you are doing now, and depend upon me for honours and wealth."

"I will, my prince."

The boy made an obeisance as he spoke.

Mazeppa started.

"How know you my rank?" he said.

"From the Lady Theresa."

The Prince smiled.

"She is not prudent," he said, "but she supposed she could trust you. Have you seen your young friend there—the girl whom I met with you in the forest?"

"Yes."

"You see I took double means of providing communication between myself and Lady Theresa."

As he spoke he took from his pocket a purse and gave it to Paul.

"Take this," he said; "I will give you a letter to your lady. Deliver it and fear nothing."

He sat down at a table and indited a long and loving epistle to Theresa.

This he delivered to Paul, praised him again for his courage and address, and dismissed him.

It was quite dark when he issued forth into the street, and the streets looked gloomy enough, illumined as they were by the dull oil lamps swung across them.

He had not far to go; and then he was in no danger of missing his way, otherwise he would have found it a matter of no ordinary difficulty to thread the intricate thoroughfares.

He had not passed many yards from the house of Mazeppa when he became conscious that some one was following him.

He stopped.

To have his footsteps dogged by some one in a strange town was no pleasant matter.

A murder could, in a dark street such as that he was now in, have been effected without any trouble.

The citizens were used to outcries in the streets.

They would have only rushed to their windows and looked out.

By the time they were ready to render assistance, the crime would have been consummated.

Paul looked around him, and his hand naturally sought his dagger.

For some minutes he could see nothing.

Neither could he hear a sound.

Presently, however, a figure emerged from the shadows.

Paul knew him not; but he appeared to know him well.

"Ah! ah! my young hearty," cried the stranger, "your roasting seems to have done you good."

Paul knew the voice.

It was that of Captain Stroloffski.

But how changed was the man!

His face was begrimed with dirt, his hair was rough and uncombed, and his clothes hung in rags about him.

"What want you with me?" cried Paul friendly.

The captain laughed.

"Well, that is a question which I haven't asked myself," cried he; "come nearer the light and let's have a look at you."

Paul moved not.

"Don't lay a finger on me," he cried, "I have a dagger, and you have taught me how to use it."

"Well, well, don't be angry. I see you are well dressed, while you cannot fail to observe how changed things are with me. I want some money—in that big house yonder there must be abundance."

"What then? It is not mine."

The captain laughed again coarsely.

"No; but it can become yours."

"How?"

"If you take it."

"You want me to turn thief."

"Have you become squeamish suddenly?"

"I never was a thief."

"I think you have served a pretty long apprenticeship."

"A forced one; no, no. I am no thief, Captain Stroloffski, and so let me pass."

The captain drew his sword.

He had exchanged his fine dress for rags, but he would not trust himself without his bright blade.

"Now, look here, young fellow," he cried, "the law is hunting me down. I fear an enemy in every shadow. I am safe nowhere. I want money to enable me to leave the country. In yonder house there is, as I have said, abundance; of this abundance I must have some. Do you understand me?"

"I understand," he said.

He was trembling now, for his position was becoming alarming.

What was he to do?

To refuse any longer would be to enrage his adversary.

Uselessly, too; for how could he pretend, with his slight dagger, to confront a strong man armed with a heavy sword?

The only way of escape which appeared to present itself was to promise obedience to the thief's demands, and thus pacify him for the time being.

"Captain," he said, "you are a great villain."

Stroloffski chuckled.

"That is nothing new," he cried.

"And you are a coward."

"By St. Peter, no."

"You are."

"Why?"

"Because you take advantage of me simply because I am a boy."

"Not so; were you a man it would be all the same; but come, let us not parley any longer. When will you get me this money?"

Whatever time he might name might be occupied by another engagement, and then in the passion of disappointment the captain might betray him.

A happy idea struck him.

Mazeppa's purse.

He took it out.

"There," he said, "that is for a beginning."

The captain eyed it wistfully, and, turning it over, opened it.

"Gold," he cried; "gold, by St. Peter! This will last me a day or two. When shall I see you again?"

The captain was in a good temper now, and Paul therefore ventured to speak more plainly.

"Captain," he said, "if I were to make an appointment with you I could not keep it, because my master or my mistress might detain me."

"What then?"

"You must take your chance of seeing me. Good-night."

Before the captain was aware of his intention, he had darted away and was at the door of the Castellan.

He was admitted fortunately at the first summons, so that Stroloffski was unable to catch him up.

He crept into the kitchen, had his supper, and retired to rest at the usual time.

He did not retire to rest, however.

He waited until Lady Theresa went to her room, and then delivering his letter, related his adventure with the captain.

Theresa could suggest no means of avoiding him; however, she volunteered to supply Paul with money in case the robber chief became dangerous in his importunities.

Greatly relieved in his mind, Paul retired to his room.

Scarcely, however, had he lain down to rest, when a low chuckling laugh aroused him, and starting up he saw the dark face of the captain at the window.

---

## CHAPTER XLIX.

### THE ROBBERY.

THE first idea of Paul when he saw the dark face of the captain at the window, was that it was a dream.

But this notion was quickly dispelled.

The low chuckling laugh, which had roused him at first, was again distinguishable, and then with a violent push, the bandit opened the window and sprang into the room.

He laughed as his eyes fell upon Paul's astonished face,

"You did'nt expect me here," he said.

"No, indeed," said Paul, trying to muster up courage to speak firmly; "and now you are here, I cannot think how you came."

The captain chuckled.

Then, pointing to the window, he said,—

"You have not looked round you much since you have been here, or you would have noticed that your chamber forms with the next house, the angle of the court, so that the window of your neighbour adjoins yours. Thus, I had only to lean out of one room and enter the other."

Paul shuddered.

The captain was used to such feats, and thought nothing of the danger.

The boy, however, remembered that the slightest false step would hurl the adventurer some sixty feet below.

" And now you are here," said Paul, " what do you want ? "

" Well, that is a curious question to address to me," returned the captain. " I have come here for money or money's worth. I am not particular which, so that I can carry it away with me."

Paul thought a moment.

He was trembling in every limb.

What was he to do ?

If he had refused to comply with the request of the captain instant death no doubt awaited him ; if, on the other hand, he consented to aid the captain in his pilfering expedition it was almost a certainty that he would be discovered, and as dismissal would of course follow this discovery, all chance of aiding his benefactor, Mazeppa, would be taken from him.

One thing was certain.

He must temporise.

He approached the door.

" Stay," cried the captain, fancying that he was meditating an escape, " stay, what are you about there ? "

Paul sidled still closer to the door.

" I must go, and reconnoitre," he said.

The captain, however, suspected his intention.

" Stay, my friend," he cried, " if there is any reconnoitering required, we will reconnoitre together."

" Come, then," said Paul, despairingly, " you must be as still as the grave. I have many enemies here who will be glad to discover anything detrimental to my character."

He then noiselessly opened the door.

All was still.

The captain drew the boy back into the room.

" Well," he said, " fortune favours us ; to what part of the house are we to go ? "

" I don't know," said Paul, doggedly.

The captain drew his dagger.

" Now look you here, young fellow," he said, " I have not come into this house to be made a fool of. You know already what sort of person I am ; I shan't stand any nonsense, so if you don't explain quickly how we are to commence operations I shall slip this dagger through you, and take my own chance in the search."

Paul plainly perceived that all further resistance was useless. To endeavour to rouse the house, would be to call down immediate death upon himself, for there was no doubt that the captain would exact from him the extreme penalty before making his own escape.

" I am not well acquainted with the position of the rooms in this house," he said, " but I will do my best to lead you to the chamber where the Castellan himself sleeps. There, most probably, you will find valuable property, or the keys of the chest, where it is deposited."

They now opened the door, and crept along the red corridor, approached the grand staircase.

The Castellan slept in a chamber on a floor below that in which was situated the apartment of his daughter.

Paul leaned over the heavy balustrade and listened.

All was quiet below.

" Come," he said to the captain, " let us descend now. Yet stay, even now I shall refuse to proceed and shall take my chance of provoking your anger, if you do not make me one solemn promise."

" What is that ? "

" That if we are discovered, and you find yourself irretrievably in the power of your enemies, you will explain to the Castellan my share in the matter."

The captain smiled grimly.

" I give you the promise," he said, " but I don't see that it will be much use to you. Be quick now, or we shall rouse the whole place by our talking."

They descended cautiously.

Paul felt as if on the point of committing a murder. His heart quaked, and as he went down the old staircase he trembled so violently that he had to cling to the balustrades for support.

They at length reached the broad passage, into which opened the door of the Castellan's chamber.

This door was partly opened.

Through it into the passage came a muffled light.

They glanced in.

The old man was sleeping soundly.

By his bedside was a small table, on which stood a lamp, whose feeble rays but ill dispelled the darkness.

" Go in," whispered the bandit to the trembling boy, " go in and fetch that lamp."

Paul hesitated.

" Are you not going to search this room first ? " he asked.

The captain stooped down and spoke in Paul's ear,—

" No, no, my eyes have caught sight of something better. Do as I bid you, and quickly, too, or it will be the worse for you."

Paul had no choice.

Slipping off his shoes he crept stealthily into the chamber, taking no heed of the injunction which the captain had whispered to him as he left his side.

The injunction was,—

" Take my dagger, and if the old man wakes up, kill him."

The boy's feet made no sound.

The lamp was taken, yet the Castellan stirred not.

When Paul was once more safely in the corridor, the captain took the lamp from his hand, and led the way into an adjoining room, which was, in fact, the Castellan's plate room, and the door of which the careless steward had left open.

Paul gazed around him with bewildered eyes, as the captain, with his habitual chuckle, turned the key in the lock, and closed them in from observation.

The captain, taking from his pocket an instrument of peculiar formation, proceeded to gather up the smaller pieces of plate and crush them into shapeless masses.

When he had collected sufficient for his purpose, he tore down part of the heavy hangings which had obscured the window, in which he wrapped the stolen property.

Paul was curious to know how he intended to escape.

" And now what are you going to do ? " he asked.

The captain smiled.

" You must let me out by the front door," he said, " I could not pass safely over that tremendous height with such a load as this."

" He is determined to destroy me," said Paul to himself. However, nothing was to be done but to submit.

" Come," he said, " and come quickly. You cannot hope to wander about the house like this all night with impunity."

So saying he opened the door, and the captain with his load followed.

Separating the corridor in which the plate room and the Castellan's bed-chamber were situated from the rest of the house, was a door which completely shut out all sounds from below. The dismay, therefore, of Paul and his companion may be imagined, when, upon opening this door, they discovered that the servants had not yet retired to rest.

This fact was too evident from the loud laughter and singing which was heard proceeding from the large hall below.

At the moment that Paul swung open the heavy gate, one of the male retainers was singing lustily the following song :—

| Think of me when the moonbeams stray | Think of me ! when o'er the rose Morning's softest breath is stealing, |
| O'er the dewy evening flowers ; | When the bee is gathering sweets, |
| Think of me, when night's sweet bird | And the lark's full notes are pealing. |
| Is warbling in the distant bowers. | Think of me—I love thee still ! |
| Think, love, when the violet sighs, | Think, then—for I ever will ! |
| And the wandering beetle flies | Think—full oft' I've thought on thee, |
| (From his mid-day's secret haunt) | Fairest ! think, oh, think on me ! |
| Onward with a drowsy chant. | |

There was nothing in the song itself to alarm anyone engaged in an ordinary occupation. But to Paul and his vile companion it conveyed a most direct warning.

The distinctness with which they were able to define the words of the song, proved that the door of the great hall below was open, so that the servants would certainly be able to see them as they passed to reach the front door.

The revelry in which they were engaged might perhaps drown the sound of light footsteps; but it was scarcely prudent to trust to such a chance. The captain, himself, had he known how to let himself into the street, would have run the risk.

It was not so with Paul.

He well knew that the great entrance gate could not be closed without a loud noise, and when, therefore, the captain was clear off with his booty, he would be found there, and, though perhaps not for the moment suspected, would be charged with the robbery as soon as discovered.

He closed the door at the head of the staircase, therefore, and said firmly,—

" Captain, I will not venture down, you must go out as you came in, through the window."

## CHAPTER L.

### TREACHERY.

THE captain laughed good-humouredly at the suggestion of his young guide.

" I think," he said, " you are right, that is the alternative; but it will be a difficult matter to carry with me all this plate. You must hand it to me piece by piece as soon as I am fairly in the other house. Come, ascend before me, I like to see

where you are going, for I have not much faith in you, as you are aware."

Paul ascended first as directed, and in a few minutes they were once more in his bedchamber.

Once more the captain undid his parcel, and piled the pieces of battered plate upon the table near the window. Then with the rope with which he had tied up his booty, he fastened a running knot round Paul's arm.

" What is this for ? " cried the boy.

The usual mocking laugh was his reply.

" You'll see," returned the captain.

He then got upon the window sill and crept cautiously in at the window of the other house.

For a moment the fearful hope entered Paul's mind that he would fall into the terrible abyss beneath him. But as quickly was it banished.

The captain had secured himself against all chances of treachery.

If by accident or otherwise he were to fall into the court-yard beneath, the boy must either be dragged down with him, or his arm must be torn from its socket.

As soon as the bandit was safely within the apartment from which he had originally emerged, he said to Paul,—

" Come, now, hand me the things over quickly, there has been too much delay already."

For a moment Paul hesitated.

The captain saw his doubts, and drawing a pistol from his pocket, said,—

" I'll tell you what it is, Master Paul. Considering that at our last meeting we didn't part the best of friends, you have not behaved badly up to the present moment, but if I see any attempt to elude me, mark you, I'll blow your brains out."

In a few moments the captain was once more in possession of the stolen property.

"Now," said Paul, "let me go."

The captain laughed loudly.

He seemed to be in no fear of being discovered by anyone in the house into which he had escaped.

"No, my bird," he said, "you don't escape so easily. You have got out of my clutches twice, after having given information to the authorities about me, and I am one of those men who never forget an injury."

With these words he commenced dragging towards him the unhappy boy, who had no means whatever of resisting him.

He plainly perceived the murderous intention of the bandit. Beneath him was a fall of sixty or eighty feet.

What was to be done?

A sudden thought flashed through him like an inspiration.

Suddenly swaying himself on one side, he seized one of the heavy doors of the large French window and swung it to with all the strength he could muster.

The cord was jammed in—his course was arrested—the more the bandit pulled the more tightly was the window closed.

The baffled robber, uttering a loud curse at his disappointment, drew himself up again to the window and tried to push it open.

But the delay had already enabled Paul to release his arm from the loop.

Again the captain with all his strength pressed against the sash.

Fool that he was, not to be contented with his booty, and leave the work of vengeance alone.

There was a cry, a heavy fall, and the bandit was dangling in mid-air.

What was the impulse of Paul?

This man had but a moment before attempted his life; but it was a natural instinct which made him instantly meditate upon the means of saving his fellow creature.

He was rescued from his dilemma in a manner which he might have anticipated. The rope, which was strong enough to drag the arm of the boy nearly from its socket, was not sufficient to sustain the weight of a heavy man like the captain.

His fall from the window had already broken some of the strands, and ere he had been hanging a minute the remainder of the rope gave way, and he was dashed down, down into the fearful abyss beneath.

There was no cry.

The only sound was the heavy thud of the body as it fell into the courtyard beneath.

There had been no appeal for help.

The fall from the window against the wall had stunned the captain so completely that he had no power to speak or comprehend his danger. Had he been able to he would certainly have risked the chance of discovery, and have shouted for help.

The boy listened for a moment in breathless silence.

All was still.

There was nothing now to show the destruction of a human being, but the mangled mass on the ground, which other eyes than his would discover.

He closed the window.

His first feeling of terror gone he had time to think collectedly, and to thank Heaven for his escape.

He knew well that upon him depended more than his own fortunes, and that had the bandit succeeded in compassing his destruction the flight of Lady Theresa with Mazeppa would have been indefinitely postponed.

For their sakes, therefore, as well as his own, he had every reason to be grateful.

Suddenly a new idea suggested itself.

Might not Theresa escape in the same manner as the bandit had hoped to escape?

The only way to discover the possibility of flight was to enter the house and explore it.

. . . . ous as was the attempt he resolved at once to make it,

and then if he discovered that flight was possible, he could return at once and inform Theresa.

No sooner had the idea formed itself in his mind than he proceeded to put it into execution.

To an active boy, like Paul, who had been used to scrambling about all his life, the feat which he had to accomplish was not a difficult one.

But it was evident to him that if Theresa was to adopt the same mode of exit, some other means must he adopted than those which were sufficient for him and the bandit.

It would be impossible for her to venture upon such a passage without a plank or a bridge of some sort.

Once within the house it was quite evident to him that it was quite uninhabited.

There was a hollow sound about the passages and the rooms, and as he proceeded downwards, there was a damp, earthy smell, as if it had been uninhabited for a long period.

He descended to the hall.

All was silent.

He tried the bolts of the great door. They were unfastened. The bandit had left everything ready for flight. Except a single bolt, nothing was between Paul's friends and liberty, could they be brought into that hall.

With a heart elated beyond measure, Paul was about to retrace his steps to inform Theresa of his discovery, when he remembered something which served considerably to damp his hopes.

In the morning, of course—a morning, by the way, which was now fast approaching—the robbery of the plate would be discovered, and not only might his means of egress be seen and for ever closed against him, but the vicinity of the stolen articles to the window might point him out as the thief.

In order, therefore, to prevent a too searching inquiry into the robbery, it would be necessary, not only to hide the plate but also to conceal the remains of the bandit.

A boy who had been unused to scenes of blood would have shrunk from such an enterprise. But Paul had served a rough apprenticeship, and was afraid of nothing.

After a little time spent in searching, he discovered the door leading to the courtyard, which was half open, as if the bandit had gone out to reconnoitre before he made his attempt at the window.

He passed out.

A light rain was descending, but this rain was the only thing stirring.

Paul approached the bandit, and seizing the mangled body by the legs, dragged it with difficulty to the head of the stairs leading to the cellars: down these he allowed it to fall. Then he closed the door carefully and bolted it.

He troubled himself not about the blood in the yard. That the rain would clear by the morning.

In a few minutes after he had reascended the stairs, hidden the plate in a huge cupboard, the door of which he locked, and threw away the key. Then he entered his own room, once more entered his own bed, and was soon sleeping profoundly.

---

## CHAPTER LI.

### WAITING FOR THE END.

THE hard experiences of an unfortunate life had taught Paul prudence.

Most boys under similar circumstances would have been elated by their success, and would have rushed instantly to inform Theresa that her escape was at length practicable.

But Paul remembered that even were they once in the old house it would be unsafe to venture into the street. They knew not where to go. They had no idea which was Mazeppa's house, because even though they had seen him at the window there was nothing to show to which residence it belonged.

Besides, he was well aware that Zenitha had, for some reason or another, been replaced by a strange maid, and it would scarcely be safe to venture into her room.

On the following morning, as soon as Theresa called him to

her side, he made a sign that he desired to speak with her in private.

She took him on one side.

"What is it, Paul?" she said.

"I have found the means of escape," he answered.

"In what manner?"

"I cannot explain now. What maid attends you to-night?"

"Zenitha."

"Why was she not with you last night?"

"She was ill."

"Good! Hold yourself in readiness," continued Paul; "do not undress, but rather don your travelling costume, for this night you shall be free."

He could say no more, for at this moment the Castellan entered, and Paul hastened from the room.

His first visit was to Mathilda.

He was not skilled enough in the art of deception to conceal from any one the emotion which agitated him.

Mathilda at once perceived it.

"What is the matter, Paul? You seem strangely agitated."

Though others were in the room, Paul could scarcely restrain his feelings. He grasped her wrist.

"Come," he said, "follow me, I have much to tell you."

He then quitted the room, and in a few moments was joined in the corridor by Mathilda.

"To-night," he said, eagerly. "Mazeppa will enter this house and carry off the Lady Theresa."

Mathilda stared at him in bewilderment.

"Does he come by stealth," she said, "or does he intend to force his way into the house?"

"He comes secretly," answered Paul, "and in secret he will depart. I go with him, and in the land where he is king I shall rise to be one of his greatest chieftains. This he has promised me."

Tears started to the young girl's eyes.

"I am sorry you are going to leave us, Paul," she said.

In countries where marriages are entered into so extremely early, love, too, has an early dawning.

Paul felt his heart influenced by this young girl in a manner in which it had never been influenced before.

He was determined to abandon all idea of following Mazeppa, and sharing in the glory which had been promised to him, rather than quit Mathilda. So we must call the feelings he expressed for her, love—love as pure, as strong as Mazeppa felt for Theresa.

"You must come with me, Mathilda," he said.

Mathilda started.

He had given utterance to her own thoughts.

The young girl had little to bind her to her native land. The only person whom she knew to be related to her, was the barber Padislaus, and from his tyranny and folly she would be glad to escape. In all her reflections, therefore, upon the meditated flight of Mazeppa and Theresa, the idea had suggested itself, "Would that I could go also."

Paul misjudged her emotion.

"I will give up all the honours which the king has promised me," he said, "rather than leave you, and yet you do not wish to come with me."

"Yes, yes, Paul," she cried, "I will come, and yet I fear the prince will not desire so many followers."

"Leave that to me," said Paul in a delighted voice, as he pressed the young girl to his heart, and imprinted the first kiss upon her lips. "Be at my chamber at eleven to-night, and knock three times. Let us not meet again to-day for fear the slightest suspicion should be aroused.

They then parted.

At five o'clock Paul left the old house, and bent his way towards the street where he had upon the last occasion met Mazeppa.

The prince was punctual to a moment: from Paul's delighted face he guessed that something advantageous to his cause had happened.

"Well, my young champion," he cried, "what has occurred? you seem as happy as a few days ago you were miserable. Is it on my account, or your own?"

"Both," replied Paul, and he then proceeded to narrate the events of the preceding night.

The Tartar prince listened in delight and in wonder too at the boy's extraordinary sagacity and courage.

When Paul had concluded his narrative, Mazeppa shook him by the hand.

"You are no longer a boy," he said, "you are a man. When I reach my kingdom, you shall be my chosen companion and friend; the highest honour in Tartary shall be yours."

The boy's cheeks flushed with delight, as Mazeppa renewed his promises.

What a difference had a few weeks made in his position! Yesterday, the starving beggar boy, fed with a few broken victuals by Mathilda in the streets of Warsaw.

To-day, the favoured friend of a great prince.

"At what hour to-night," said Mazeppa, "am I to be ready?"

"If you bring a carriage to the door," said Paul, "at half-past eleven I will let you in at the gate of the empty house."

"What is the carriage for?" said Mazeppa.

"To bear away the lady Theresa," returned Paul.

Mazeppa smiled.

"Up to this point," said he, "your sagacity has been equal to your courage, but here you have failed. No carriage can leave the city of Lublin, at night, without undergoing a rigorous examination. This certainly might result in nothing, but I should not care to run the risk."

"What, then, is to be done," said Paul, "we cannot escape from the house in the daytime."

"No, but instead of entering a carriage and leaving the city immediately, we must bring her round to this house, and keep quiet until the morning, when we can leave the city without suspicion.

"Do not engage any postilions," said Paul, "I have driven the Castellan's carriage, and can drive yours. We need thus let no one into our secret."

Paul hesitated a moment, as if he had been about to add something, but had changed his mind.

"What is it now?" said Mazeppa, "have you anything to ask me?"

The boy flushed with crimson as he said,—

"Yes, my prince," he said, "I have something to ask you. It is of vital importance to me, for unless it is in your power to grant it I must remain behind in Poland."

"And what is this great favour?" repeated the prince.

"You remember Mathilda," said Paul, "the girl whom you met with me and her uncle in the wood?"

"I do. Have you fallen in love with her then, Paul? Is that your story?"

"I don't know," said Paul, ruefully, "but I cannot leave her behind."

The prince laughed. "Well, well," he said, "we must take her with us if she is willing to come. Farewell! Now I will go and make the necessary preparations; at half-past eleven precisely I will be at the door of the empty house."

They then parted, and it would have been, indeed, difficult to say at that moment which was the more elated of the two.

The evening drew on apace. At six the Count Floreski presented himself, and seemed disposed to make a long stay of it.

Theresa, although annoyed by his coming, and anxious as to the result of the night's adventure, betrayed no emotion. She had so often been foiled in her attempts at escape that her very fear enabled her to school her countenance and her voice. She was more than usually polite to the count, who exerted himself in every way to make himself agreeable, and her father was evidently delighted by the manner in which she received his courtesies.

The young count himself was somewhat astounded by a kindness which he did not expect; but neither he nor the Castellan could, of course, suspect for one moment the cause of her alteration in manner.

It was ten o'clock before Floreski departed.

When he did so the Castellan sitting down by his daughter said,—

" It has given me great pleasure, my dear child, to behold your kindness to my friend, Floreski. I could see that the poor fellow, whom you used rather roughly the other day, was quite enraptured with the change."

Theresa smiled faintly.

" I am sorry," she said, " if the count has augured from my manner that I am willing to accept him as a husband, for I feel after all that I can never marry him."

" Why so ? "

" He is not the kind of man that I could bring myself to love."

" I fear you say that of every one," said her father.

" Not so, my father," said Theresa, " I would rather marry that old General Lukrowsky, whom we met the other day at the ball."

The Castellan thought a moment.

Then he proceeded,—

" Well, well, my child, my object is, as you know, to retrieve the fortunes of our house. If you like the General Lukrowsky better than the count, I have not the slightest objection to your marrying him, for he is a rich man, and all that I could desire in a son-in-law."

After a little more conversation of the same kind, Theresa said good night to her father, and retired towards her room.

In the red corridor she met Paul.

" Go not to your own room," he said, " come to mine. I will go and apprise your maid."

Lady Theresa willingly obeyed her young friend, who in a few minutes returned with Zenitha.

At eleven arrived Mathilda, the last of the conspirators: the door was then locked, and Paul, opening the window, crept into the other house.

---

## CHAPTER LII.

### REUNITED.

THE feelings of Theresa and her companions, as they waited in Paul's bedroom for his return with Mazeppa, may more readily be imagined than described.

Theresa sat down near the window, and remained silent.

Zenitha stood near her—while Mathilda sat at her feet.

One could see from the sparkling of Theresa's eyes—the heaving of her breast—the nervous starts which she gave ever and anon, how intensely she was agitated.

Zenitha leaned over her, and took her trembling hand.

" Courage, dear mistress," she said, " courage—escape is near."

" Escape has often been near," she murmured, " and yet how often has it deceived us."

" True; but this time our friends have laid their plans well."

At this moment a movement in the house startled them.

" What is that ? " cried Theresa.

Footsteps were heard creeping along the passage.

The girls crept to the door and listened.

The footsteps came nearer.

" Which is the entrance ? " said a gruff voice.

It was that of the Castellan.

Theresa trembled.

" My father here," she murmured; " what can he be seeking ? "

" I trust he is not seeking you," whispered Zenitha, " but hark ! he is speaking again, let us listen."

" It is behind the image of the Virgin, near the Lady Theresa's chamber," returned a servant.

" And how do you enter ? "

" By touching a spring—I will show my lord."

" They are seeking the secret passage," whispered Theresa.

Zenitha nodded assent.

" Be careful," said the Castellan, in a subdued voice, " do not wake my daughter. She must know nothing of this."

At this moment there was a sound in the adjoining house.

The girls started up.

" They are coming," said Theresa.

Meanwhile, Paul, on entering the deserted mansion, made his way in all haste to the basement.

He had not long to wait.

In a few moments a tap at the gate announced the arrival of Mazeppa.

He instantly admitted him.

" My faithful young friend," cried the Prince, with emotion, " you are punctual to your time."

" Yes, my prince," returned Paul, " I have even waited."

" And now," cried the eager lover, " let us hasten. I long to see again the one I have so long mourned. In cases like this delay is always dangerous."

" And rashness more so," cried Paul, as he led the way.

Without noticing the maxim of the young philosopher, Mazeppa hastened up the stairs with Zisko, and the two soon found themselves in the chamber adjoining Paul's.

" Theresa," murmured a well-known voice.

The young girl sprang to the window.

" Mazeppa," she cried, " I am here."

Zisko, pushing his king back, leaped nimbly across the dangerous gulf.

Then he raised Theresa to the sill of the window, and held her forward until Mazeppa could receive her in his arms.

Then, after one fond embrace of his mistress, the Prince received Zenitha in a like manner, and after her Mathilda.

" Now close the window," said Mazeppa to Zisko, " and let no clue to our manner of escape exist."

The dwarf smiled grimly.

" Not so," he said, " I wish to enter here again. When we arrive home I will explain."

In a few moments more the fugitives were in the street.

The shops were all closed, and scarcely any one was abroad.

A few watchmen eyed them suspiciously as they moved along; but they were not molested, and reached the house of Mazeppa in safety.

" Mine—mine at last ! " cried the prince, as he folded his mistress again and again to his heart.

Theresa smiled.

" Say not so, dear Mazeppa," she said; " how often have we thought so before. Wait until we are far beyond the reach of our enemies—wait until you are my husband. Then, indeed, we may assume that we shall never be separated, but not till then. We have been subjected to so many misfortunes that I begin to disbelieve Hope itself."

At this moment Zisko entered the room where the Prince and his mistress were seated alone, taking their last farewell before separating for a short night's repose.

" My prince," he said, " I desire one] word with you apart."

Mazeppa arose.

" Excuse me one moment, dearest," he said.

Then he accompanied Zisko into an adjoining chamber.

The dwarf's eyes were glistening with joy.

" You seem pleased, Zisko."

" I am, and I have good reason to be."

" At what ! "

" The time has come for revenge, and I am about to take it."

" Revenge ! this is no time for revenge, Zisko, but rather for escape."

The dwarf shook his head.

" My prince," he said, " you have pledged me your word that you would permit me to take my revenge, and you will not retreat from your word."

" No," returned Mazeppa, gloomily, " but I fear the worst."

" Why ? "

" Our escape is even now uncertain, and some rash attempt on your part may throw everything back, and destroy the result of all my patient labour. At least if you are so bent upon revenge, defer it for a time."

The dwarf smiled grimly.

" To delay is to postpone for ever," he said, " to-morrow morning the Castellan will discover the flight of his daughter, and all means of approach to him will be cut off. No—no— this night I will enter the house and destroy him."

THERESA IN HER FATHER'S CHAMBER.

Mazeppa eyed him sternly.

"Zisko," he said, "there must be no murder done. Had I approved of assassination, the Castellan, ere now, might have been dead; but I do not, and cannot allow it."

"No murder will be done by me," returned the dwarf. "I will enter his chamber and force him to fight me. Fortune must then declare for him who is most brave and most active."

"Will you not defer it?" again urged the prince.

"I cannot."

"In that case you must follow us. I cannot risk my happiness and the happiness of Theresa for the sake of affording you an opportunity of destroying her father. I have promised not to thwart you in your revenge; but as it is useless in my eyes, and dangerous also, I do not desire to run the risk of being compromised. Ten miles from Lublin we will await you."

"At Elsdorf."

"Yes, at Elsdorf, and instead of going in a carriage we will quit this city on horseback."

"But Theresa will be recognised, and, at any rate, it will be regarded as strange for a lady to be travelling on horseback along the high road."

Mazeppa smiled.

"I shall provide against all that," he said, "Theresa will dress in men's clothes, and will pass for one of my followers."

"I will go now, then," returned the dwarf; "perhaps ere morning I may rejoin you."

"Pray do not," answered Mazeppa. "As you are resolved to carry out this scheme of revenge, the risk must be on your own head. The deed once consummated there will be a hue and cry throughout the city, and your person, which is not of an ordinary style, you will allow, will be described minutely. You would be certain to be recognised and your arrest would involve the arrest of all. I am grateful for your services—I shall never cease to be grateful; but I cannot consent to compromise my own happiness and that of Theresa for the sake of useless revenge. Once more I entreat you to abandon your scheme, and let the loss of his daughter be the punishment of the Castellan."

"No—no, I cannot," returned Zisko.

"Then you must meet me at Elsdorf."

"How long will you wait?"

"Two days."

"It is unnecessary; if I am not with you by to-morrow evening some evil has befallen me. Most probably I shall be there as soon as you."

He extended his hand.

"Adieu, my prince," he said, "adieu—we may never meet again."

Mazeppa shook his hand.

"Adieu," he said; "you seek danger needlessly."

The dwarf then silently quitted the room, and Mazeppa rejoined Theresa.

## CHAPTER LIII.

### THE DWARF'S REVENGE.

THERESA listened with some alarm to Mazeppa's account of Zisko's project.

"The dwarf is unscrupulous," she cried, "he knows no limits to revenge—he will murder my father in cold blood."

"No, dearest," said the prince, "there is no fear of that. Had I doubted his intentions for a moment I would have retained him forcibly as a prisoner. But I have no doubt of the truth of his promise."

"And this promise?"

"Is to give the Castellan his sword, and let the contest be an even one."

"My father is brave, and a good swordsman, and will kill Zisko," she said.

Then another thought entered her mind.

Tears started to her eyes.

"What ails you, dearest," asked her lover, as he pressed her soft and yielding form to his breast, in all the fervour of unrestrained affection.

"If my father succeeds in destroying Zisko," she said, "he will institute a search throughout the house, and finding that I have fled he will give immediate notice to the police, and we shall be unable to leave the city."

"Fear not, dear one," returned Mazeppa; "but there is one thing which I must ask you to consent to for the sake of safety."

"What is that?"

"You must dress in man's clothes," returned her lover, "and Zenitha also."

Theresa blushed and smiled.

"You are going to use the same means as my father did when we fled from Spolovski; but how are we to obtain dresses to fit us?"

"In the morning, in your room, you will find your suits ready. Now, love, I must part from you and lead you to your chamber, for to-morrow early we must be on the road, and we shall have a long journey before us."

He took the lamp, led her to the door of the chamber, where Zenitha already awaited her, and after one more fond embrace retired to his own room.

Meanwhile Zisko proceeded eagerly towards the house of the Castellan, or rather the deserted house which adjoined it.

He had left the door unfastened, and he found no difficulty, therefore, in entering and making his way into Paul's chamber.

Paul had given him a description of the mansion, which enabled him to find the Castellan's room without difficulty.

Creeping down the stairs therefore as the bandit had done before him, he made his way into the room in which Stanislaus lay sleeping.

Entering here he locked the door, and drawing his long sword from his scabbard, approached the bed.

With the hilt of his sword he struck the Castellan rudely on the shoulder.

"Awake!" he cried.

The Castellan, being a soldier, awoke immediately.

He recognised Zisko, and springing out of bed grasped his trusty blade.

"Have you come here to murder me?" he cried, as he placed himself in an attitude of defence; "if so, you have made a mistake."

The dwarf gazed at him with a look of bitter scorn.

"If I had wished to murder you," he said, "I could have done so when you lay asleep. It was a blow, however, from the hilt of my sword which roused you."

"Why, then, are you here?"

"To demand justice."

"In what way."

"You have a sword—I have one also, fortune must decide between us."

The Castellan's lip curled in disdain.

"Do you think I will fight with one who has been my slave?" he cried; "let me pass. I will call my servants and have you expelled the house.

Zisko drew back towards the door, and drew from his belt a pistol.

"Stir not one step, attempt not to escape," he cried, "or I will fire."

The Castellan saw that escape was impossible.

Low born as he was the dwarf must have his will.

"Come on, then," he cried, in a voice of fury, and dashed violently at his opponent.

The clash of steel resounded through the small chamber.

Yet it was heard by none.

The Castellan knew this.

His room was isolated.

The chambers in which his servants slept were above and below.

And so they fought on, and none knew of their conflict.

The contest was unequal.

The Castellan was tall and powerful.

The dwarf was short and strong, but he was awkward in his movements, though active. Zisko drew the first blood.

Plunging forward in his passion to attack his foe, he slipped, and falling on his adversary's sword he was transfixed.

Zisko drew it out, and then with a fiendish laugh plunged it into his neck.

The Castellan fell with a heavy fall.

"Cursed slave," he groaned.

The dwarf knelt by his side.

"Theresa and Mazeppa are now encircled in each other's arms!" he cried; "they are happy while you are dying. Remember how you caused me to be scourged—remember the caldron of boiling lead into which you would have plunged me. I will reward you for both!"

So saying, he drew his poignard and plunged it into the eyes of the Castellan, saying as he did so—

"This is for the scourging—this is for the boiling lead."

With a shriek of agony the Castellan yielded up his spirit, and the dwarf's revenge was complete.

Leaving the body where it was, with the dagger still sticking in the right, he, Zisko, opened the door, and glanced out.

Here an unlooked for incident occurred.

One of the servants, feeling restless, and hearing strange noises in the house, dressed himself, and taking a sword and lamp proceeded to examine the passages.

He searched the mansion from bottom to top, and found not only Theresa's room empty but Paul's also.

Not understanding anything about Theresa's amour with Mazeppa, he could not account for her disappearance, but fancying that it could not be right to leave Paul's window open, he closed it.

Just as Zisko, emerging from the Castellan's room, was making his way towards the stairs, he encountered this servant, proceeding with bare feet and naked sword.

For a moment they glanced at one another in silence.

Then the servant asked,—

"Who are you, sir, and what is your business here?"

The dwarf endeavoured to pass him.

"I am in haste," he said, "let me pass directly."

"You must first give me reason for your going and coming," returned the servant.

"I am seeking the Lady Theresa," returned Zisko.

"Are you, then, one of the household?"

"Yes."

"Ah! now I know you are a lying knave," cried the man, and seizing a rope which ran up one of the pillars, he pulled it and it rang a loud bell.

Zisko sprang forward with his drawn sword, and the servant stood on the defensive.

"Let me pass," cried the dwarf, "or it will be the worse for you."

The man, however, made a furious thrust at him, and a short contest was the result.

The dwarf, however, heard approaching the footsteps of servants, who were hurrying to the rescue, and knowing that to be discovered by them would be instant death, he plunged forward and threw the servant over his head.

Then he dashed up the stairs and made for Paul's chamber.

At his heels, however, was the servant he had thrown, and a yelling crew of domestics after him.

As he reached the door of Paul's room, he found that the door was locked and the key gone.

"What was to be done?

Suddenly, as despair was about to take possession of his heart, he remembered the Statue of the Virgin, of which he had heard Paul speak, and towards which the Castellan had that evening directed his steps, though with what object was never known.

No sooner did the thought occur to him than he put it into execution.

He rushed to the statue—touched the spring, and in another instant he had disappeared behind it.

He was now in total darkness.

He felt, however, that he was at the summit of a flight of spiral stairs.

Down these he crept—gradually, slowly—until he reached the ninth step.

At the tenth he trod on space.

Down—down into a deep abyss he fell.

Down—down, until the splash of waters below announced that he had reached the bottom—dead and mangled and crushed.

This was the secret of the Statue of the Virgin.

---

## CHAPTER LIV.

### CONCLUSION.

As the early rays of the sun illumined Lublin and the country round it, Theresa and her maid made their appearance in the room where Mazeppa awaited them.

Zenitha, being tall and rather slender, looked very well in her man's clothes.

Theresa, who was stouter, and whose limbs were full and rounded, betrayed her sex to a greater extent; but when, at length, they mounted their horses at the door, they appeared like a party of gentlemen riding out with their two pages, for Mathilda was attired in the same costume as Paul.

As they passed the mansion of the Castellan all was quiet.

Evidently his death had not been discovered, or the secret of Theresa's flight was buried in oblivion.

They pushed on towards Elsdorf.

There they saw no signs of Zisko.

Unwilling to depart too soon, Mazeppa, even at the risk of discovery, remained for three days.

Then, being assured that something had happened, he once more set out.

Messengers dispatched by him some time beforehand had requested Abder Khan and Cassim to meet him in the forest near Laurinski, and when at length their tired steeds arrived at the spot whence he had started on his perilous ride a number of Tartar horsemen met them.

Among them were Abder Khan, Cassim, Abdallah, and Zuliska.

After the others had greeted the young prince and his bride warmly, Zuliska approached.

"My prince," she said, in a soft tone, so that she was heard by him alone, "I can congratulate you the more readily because I am now a wife."

"Indeed! Whose?"

"Abdallah's."

As soon as they reached the Tartar encampment, Mazeppa and his young queen were united amid the acclamations of all.

"I am afraid, Mazeppa," said Theresa, as they sat in their tent on the evening of their wedding day, "I am afraid my love is scarcely enough to recompense you for all the dangers and the trials you have endured."

Mazeppa pressed her passionately to his heart.

"I would go through it all again," cried he, "if it were to bring me again this happy moment."

Two years after, Paul was united to Mathilda, and here amid the splendour of the young Prince's court, they soon forgot the troubles which they had experienced when they were children.

Of Michael they heard afterward as high in the service of the king of Poland.

\* \* \* \* \*

The adventures of Mazeppa would always have possessed a charm for the lovers of the romantic or the marvellous had they never been made a theme for the beautiful poetry of Byron.

At the present time our youthful readers have evinced more than usual interest in the theme, and as a kind of epilogue to our story we may mention a few facts in reference to the various narratives of which it has formed the staple.

The history of Mazeppa is related by Voltaire in his history of Charles XII., and by Lesur in his "Histoire des Kosacques."

According to this, Mazeppa was born in the Palatinate of Podolia, and, being of good family, was made page to Jean Cassimir, King of Poland, at whose court he acquired some knowledge of the belles lettres, but having been discovered in an intrigue with the wife of a Polish nobleman, he was scourged, and then tied on a wild horse from the Ukraine, which carried him into the desert.

Here, when he was almost perishing with fatigue and hunger, some peasants came to his assistance, and he recovered.

He enrolled himself among the Cossacks, soon distinguished himself by his bravery and superior talents, and became Hettman of the Cossacks and Prince of the Ukraine.

At the battle of Pultowa, Mazeppa, who had taken part with Charles XII., was present with a troop of Cossacks, and after that fatal defeat, he retired with the king to Bender, where he died at the age of eighty; but whether he poisoned himself or died of sorrow is doubtful.

Lord Byron makes Mazeppa the narrator of his own adventures; he is supposed to relate them to Charles XII. during the defeat above alluded to, as will be seen by the following few lines with which the poem opens:—

'Twas after dread Pultowa's day,
　When fortune left the royal Swede,
Around a slaughtered army lay,
　No more to combat and to bleed.
The power and glory of the war,
　Faithless as their vain votaries, men
Had passed to the triumphant czar,
　And Moscow's walls were safe again,
Until a day more dark and drear,
And a more memorable year
Should give to slaughter and to shame
　A mightier host and a haughtier name;
A greater wreck, a deeper fall,
A shock to one—a thunderbolt to all.

Lord Byron confines his poem almost to the first remarkable incident in the life of Mazeppa.

In the drama, justice is done to his after achievements, and such variations and episodes introduced as were requisite for making an interesting and popular spectacle.

Upon this drama we have founded our tale, and we have preferred to do so because the greater portion of it is borne out by Eastern chronicles.

Lord Byron gives the same account as we do of the discovery of Mazeppa by a female Tartar, who rescues him from his situation, and in recovering him paves the way for his future fortunes.

We quote this both for the sake of its beauty and the moral it conveys:—

A slender girl, long-hair'd and tall,
Sat watching by the cottage wall;
The sparkle of her eye I caught,
E'en with the first return of thought;
For, ever and anon, she threw
　A prying, pitying, glance to me,
　With her black eyes so wild and free:
I gaz'd and gaz'd until I knew
　No vision it could be—
But that I lived and was released
From adding to the vulture's feast.
And when the Cossack maid beheld
My heavy eyes at length unseal'd,
She smiled—and I essay'd to speak,
　But fail'd, and she approach'd and made
　With lip and finger signs, that said,

I must not strive as yet to break
The silence, till my strength should be
Enough to leave my accent free;
And then her hand on mine she laid,
And smooth'd the pillow for my head,
And stole along on tip-toe tread,
    And gently op'd the door, and spake
In whispers—ne'er was voice so sweet!
Even music followed her light feet!—
    But those she called were not awake,
And she went forth; but, cre she pass'd,
Another look on me she cast,
    Another sign she made, to say,
That I had naught to fear, that all
Were near at my command or call,
    And she would not delay
Her due return—while she was gone,
Methought I felt too much alone.

She came with mother and with sire—
What need of more!—I will not tire
With long recital of the rest,
Since I became the Cossack's guest:
They found me senseless on the plain—
They bore me to the nearest hut—
They brought me into life again—
Me—one day o'er their realm to reign!
    Thus, the vain fool, who strove to glut
His rage, refining on my pain,
    Sent me forth to the wilderness,
Bound, naked, bleeding, and alone,
To pass the desert to a throne.
What mortal his own doom may guess?
Let none despond, let none despair.

AND now, having exhausted our theme, we respectfully, and not without regret, bid the reader who has followed the course of this narrative a kind adieu.

Between the Author and those whose eyes have followed the tracings of his pen there must necessarily spring up a strong intimacy, and when the last words came to be written the toil of the work on which the tale-teller has been engaged is forgotten, and he only remembers that he is passing from the gaze of those whose interest he has awakened and whose sympathies he has enlisted for a length of time. It is, therefore, regretfully that we stop our pen and " draw close the curtain."

Our aim has been to show that the true end of romance is to convey instruction in a pleasing form.

The characters we have created are those we meet in the walk through life at every turning, and by holding the mirror up to nature, by praising virtue and showing vice her ghastly image, we claim to be the disseminating medium of a wholesome moral influence. Never mind how sensational our incidents. They are not outside the pale of nature.

Experience has taught us that truth is much stranger than fiction, and that the human brain cannot conceive more startling imagery than the human hand can mould.

We live in an age when wonders spring up with startling rapidity, and we appeal to the reader to say if the daily chronicles of the journalist do not surpass in intensity of sensation incident the creations of the romancist.

We are not the apologists of romance; we conceive that the novelist requires no defender: for those who attack him are beneath his and our notice.

In this spirit we have written the romance of MAZEPPA, and we have filled it with the dazzling hues of the wildly beautiful country in which its scenes are laid. We have made our characters speak and move like the men and women of real life, and we appeal to our readers whether we have succeeded in beguiling a few hours which would otherwise have hung tediously and passed wearily.

If we have done this, and at the same time conveyed in the garb of romance some of the facts of history, we have succeeded in our aim, and can joyously wish our friends

ADIEU.

www.ingramcontent.com/pod-product-compliance
Lightning Source LLC
Chambersburg PA
CBHW081211170626
46811CB00010B/3245